HAM MARTIN, *Class of '17*

HAM MARTIN, *Class of '17*

by EDWARD STREETER

1817

HARPER & ROW, PUBLISHERS

NEW YORK, EVANSTON, AND LONDON

FIRST EDITION

LIBRARY OF CONGRESS CATALOG CARD NUMBER: 67-13698

HAM MARTIN, *Class of '17*

I

THE PORTER TOOK HIS SUITCASE AND waited for him to climb, somewhat stiffly, aboard the parlor car.

"What seat, sir?"

"Fifteen."

"You goin' through to New York?"

"All the way."

He sank into his chair and turned it so that it faced the window. Opening his evening paper he held it so that it hid his face from anyone passing through the car in either direction. He had traveled far to rejoin his classmates. Now he was through rejoining and had no intention of talking to one of them all the way to New York.

This did not mean that, after three days, his classmates had become anathema to him. It was merely because he was not only tired—dog tired—but also emotionally depressed. Why not? In a way he was saying good-by to this familiar city and to a half century of Harvard. Cambridge would be there, of course, whenever he chose to return, but last night, following the 50th Reunion dinner, the Class of '17 had ceased to be, in spite of all the oratory to the contrary. Like a cloud in a blue sky, which is suddenly torn apart by invisible winds, it had disappeared when its members and their wives took off into the night for their various destinations, more intent on finding their parked cars than in saying good-by to those whom they had come so far to see.

He noted with embarrassment that he was still wearing his shiny reunion nameplate. Removing it quickly, he looked about to see if anyone had observed him. The passengers were all buried in their newspapers or had closed their eyes in an attempt to fall asleep before the train began to lurch westward over the ancient road-bed. He glanced once more at the red-bordered nameplate before hiding it in his pocket.

1917

H. ALLEN MARTIN

50th Reunion

It seemed incredible. A half century! His creative life suddenly a memory rather than a hope. Time was the world's greatest practical joker. At one moment it pretended to be infinite, without beginning or end. An awesome concept. And then it suddenly became distressingly finite, only one wasn't aware of the change until some particular chapter ended with the decisiveness of a slammed door.

Objects on the station platform began to move slowly backward. Then the platform itself disappeared, to be replaced by a succession of small factories and ancient warehouses. He shut his eyes to blot out their ugliness. He had four and a half hours to relax and return to normalcy. He needed them. It was why he had instinctively chosen to return to New York by train rather than to fly.

As the car passed over the switches in a series of gentle bumps, he became conscious of the fact that he had a slight hangover. Three days of Scotch and water were hard on any constitution, but particularly on one which would soon pass its seventy-third milestone. The trouble was that after you had said hello to a man whom you had not seen for twenty-five years or more and had never known well in the first place, there was not much left to do but have a drink with him.

It was surprising how many of his classmates he had not known. He couldn't even recall ever having heard some of their names before. He was also disturbed by the number of his old friends who had not turned up. In the course of half a century the cards became reshuffled. The bon vivants thinned out. The more serious-minded came to the top. So many of these fellows whom he had just left were specialists, a number of them world famous: like Jack Boaz, the botanist, who had flown back to the Reunion from the Far East and would return in a few days to his beloved jungles (who the hell was Jack Boaz anyway?); and Bill Bartow, the geologist, still doing special jobs for oil and mining interests in God-forsaken places. That funny-looking, thin chap, whose name he had already forgotten, had been an astrophysicist. He had confided to Martin over a drink that his particular field was the invisible stars.

They all looked so fit, so full of wiry vigor. Most of them had been lean. There hadn't been half a dozen paunches in the lot. Were the fat fellows all underground or sitting at home hopelessly attempting to contemplate their navels? He passed an appraising hand over his vest. Not too bad, but not too good either.

What an unrealistic concept a fiftieth reunion was; a group of men whose only common bond was four years spent at Harvard a half century before. Yet the bond was so strong that it drew them back like a magnet from all parts of the world. Now they were dispersing again to pick up the threads of their normal lives. In a few hours the Merchants Limited would eject him into the ceaseless roar of New York. The warm, even though somewhat artificial, camaraderie would be over. He rather dreaded that moment. When he arrived at the house on 72nd Street Patrick would spring from behind the wheel of the Cadillac to open the car door and then follow him up the white stone steps, carrying his suitcase. As he entered the vestibule the heavy iron-grilled entrance door would swing slowly open, disclosing old Udding, looking like a gaunt funeral director in his morning coat and sharply creased striped trousers. Udding would not smile. He had never smiled, while on duty, for twenty years. The muscles of his thin face would merely contract into a butler's traditional expression of welcome. As the door clicked heavily shut behind him the sound would seem to echo through the empty house, shutting out the world and leaving him unbearably alone.

He recrossed his knees impatiently as the train pulled into Back Bay station. He was becoming mawkish. He only got that way when he was exhausted. Those two weeks before the Reunion, which he had spent flying about the country trying to consummate a merger which kept coming apart at the seams, had taken more out of him than he realized. His head ached and he felt a dull pain in the region where his heart should be. Dr. Partridge had warned him sternly about his heart the last time he had been checked up. Damned old alarmist.

Opening his briefcase he pawed through its jumbled contents until he located a bottle of aspirin; not perhaps what Partridge would have prescribed for a pain around the heart, but at least it was medicine. He pushed a button for the porter and asked for a Scotch and water. He had more faith in that than he did in the aspirin.

He closed his eyes again. After a while the pain subsided into mild discomfort. He must see Partridge the first chance he had. Oh, to hell with it! Far better to be carried off the battlefield on one's shield. Then the depression came galloping back at full charge. In his usual methodical way he squared off to fight it.

Of all the people he knew he had the least cause for feeling depressed. He had made more money than he had ever dreamed of possessing. He was on so many boards that his name took up half a page in the Directory of Directors. He owned a big house in New York, and another behind the dunes of Rock Harbor that was often mistaken for a hotel. He belonged to every important club from Antigua's Mill Reef to Boston's Somerset, and to cap it all he felt reasonably sure that he was generally liked and respected.

Last night at the final Class dinner he had been one of the speakers. It had probably been a good speech. He had worked hard enough over it; but the applause which had followed it contained more than approval. It was also an expression of friendship and esteem; a recognition of his accomplishments.

He knew all these things yet his black mood lay like an

undigested meal, deep within him. There was something missing; something unfinished, something basically wrong with the picture. Where had things started to go off the track?

Like a homing pigeon his mind flew back to the little college town where he had been born and where he had lived until he went to Harvard. The seed of the answer had been planted there. In those days Messina, Indiana, had been an ugly collection of bad Victorian architecture bisected by Main Street. On Saturday afternoons and evenings the iron hitching rails in front of the stores were crowded with the wagons and buggies of farmers. While the women shopped, the blue-jeaned men squatted on sinewy hams in the shade of the two-story brick buildings, exchanging news or views or merely leaning against a doorjamb, listening with weather-lined, expressionless faces.

At the north end of the town, just before Main Street escaped from its red brick confines into the freedom of the open country, stood Messina College. Its buildings were set well back from the street on a spacious campus shaded by ancient elms and oaks. The college had never quite grown up to its campus. The size of the trees, rising from close-cut lawns, made the old brick structures look shabby and insignificant.

In one of these ancient buildings, whose high, round-topped windows looked out over the gently rolling Indiana farmland, Professor Oswald Martin presided over the English Department. It would be more accurate, perhaps, to say that he *was* the English Department. The horizons of his world were shelves of books and his mission there was to arouse, in the unresponsive souls of an endless succession of farmers' sons, some appreciation of the beauty and the inspiration which lay between their worn covers. He gained his happiness and replenished his enthusiasm from his few successes. His failures he took for granted.

Each morning as he left for his classroom, his wife, Fanny, accompanied him to the front door of their old house on Maple Street. This was his checkpoint. Before he disappeared into the world of scholarship and restlessly shuffling feet she made sure that he had the right books in his faded green cloth bag and that his curly gray hair, forever in need of cutting, was at least temporarily in order; that he had on his overshoes and muffler when the cold winds of winter rattled the bare branches of the trees; or that his seersucker suit was reasonably free of spots when the heat shimmered upward like colorless smoke from the pavement of Maple Street.

Young Horace Martin's earliest recollections were projected against a background of books. He was the fortunate product of two people whose interests were identical. His mother did her kitchen chores with an open book on the sink shelf. From time to time she would stop in the midst of waxing the floor or scouring a pot and read a few paragraphs, propping herself on her elbows. When she moved on to another part of the house her book went with her.

In later years Horace's memory of her was always sharper than that of his father, perhaps because the latter was considerably older. The recollection of her slight figure, covered by a faded blue housedress and an apron, her chestnut hair parted in the middle and drawn back tightly into a bun at the nape of her neck, forming a natural frame for the fine, bony structure of her face and her brown, understanding eyes had never faded. He couldn't imagine her hair tortured into the artificial mounds and sworls which the other faculty wives spent so much time in achieving.

Each evening, from his first beginnings of understanding, she read aloud to him while he was having his supper on a little sewing table in the kitchen. He would always remember her most vividly sitting beside the green-shaded lamp, constantly recapturing a lock of hair which was forever escaping from its restraining pins and tucking it impatiently back into place while she read.

Book after book passed before his awakening consciousness. He was always allowed to choose the ones he wanted. She never forced anything on him, either directly or indirectly, never read beyond his interest. She reread certain favorites half a dozen times if he asked her to, until they both knew them almost by heart. She must have been dreadfully bored at times, but if she was she failed to show it. Books which were friends of his were also friends of hers.

"What will we read next, Allen?" He had been christened Horace Allen Martin, but she hated his first name as much as he did and conspired with him by ignoring it. Eventually it disappeared from the scene except for his father.

"The Five Little Peppers."

"But we've just finished it, sweet."

"Read it again," he demanded. And she did.

Thus it was that books became as natural a part of his life as breathing or applesauce. They were not injections, intended to stimulate his mind, but open doors through which he could move from reality to make-believe and back as easily as one moved from one room to another.

The Martins were always poor. Professors at Messina were supposed to soar through the blue unhampered by the materialism of more earthbound mortals. Their house on Maple Street had been built during the gingerbread period of American architecture. It was small, in need of paint, and a

few of the scallops on its eaves had succumbed to the batter-
ing of summer heat and winter ice. Within its spotless interior a narrow hall ran from the front door to the kitchen,
half blocked by the steep stairway. To the left of the entrance what had once been the living room had been converted into Professor Martin's book-lined study. In front of
its end window stood the Professor's desk, a behemoth of a
piece covered with an untidy jumble of books and papers.
With the exception of his desk chair and a huge, beaten-up
old armchair there was no other furniture for the good reason
that there was no room for anything else except an occasional
pile of books on the floor beneath the shelves. The dining
room, on the other side of the hall, had been converted into
a living room and before Allen was born they had used a
windfall, which the Professor had earned by translating, to
add a small dining alcove to the kitchen. From the kitchen
one passed into the back yard through a shed which was a
catchall for the things that one hated to throw away because
they might someday be useful. It was a gold mine to Allen,
who spent hours retrieving discards and planning fantastic
uses for them.

His father didn't pay much attention to his son during
those early years. He was gentle with him, patting him on
the head when they met and asking how things were going,
but obviously thinking of something else while he did so.
"Little boys belong to their mother, Fanny," he used to say.
"You have something to give Horace right now that he needs
and that no man can give. Later he will turn to men and
that's where I will come in."

He became conscious of Millie Gardner during his tenth
year. Up to that time he had thought of girls as an undesira-

ble species to be avoided whenever possible. Millie was not one to accept anonymity, however. She caught up with him one day when he was walking home from school. "Your name's Allen Martin," she said. "Your father works in the College."

He stared at her silently and continued to walk.

"My father owns the hardware store," she said.

"I know it," he replied. "So what?" Dropping his books on the sidewalk he vaulted over a low rail fence they happened to be passing. "One hand," he said and vaulted back.

She dropped her books and rushed at the fence, her jaw set, ending up straddling it. She giggled. "Pfui," he commented, picking up the end of the strap that bound his books.

"I'm having a birthday party Saturday," she said. "Want to come?"

"No," he said. "I'm doing something."

"You're not. We're going to have ice cream and a cake with candles."

His face brightened. He picked up a stone. "Bet I can hit that tree."

"Bet you can't. If you miss you got to come to my party."

The stone missed the tree by a foot. "You're coming," she cried, clapping her hands. "There'll be prizes. I'll see you get a good one. Four o'clock." She picked up her books. "There's Jane and Polly." She dashed across the street, her skinny legs flailing out behind her. At the opposite curb she paused and looked back. "Don't forget," she called.

He never went, but a barrier had been broken.

Everything happened at once. The circus was coming to town and Uncle Charlie, who lived in New York, was going to stop off on his way to Chicago.

To Allen the circus was the culmination of a year's work.

The last time it had pitched its tents in Messina his mother had given him the money to buy a ticket, but she had explained to him that they were poor and he must try to help by earning money for things like circuses or snacks. He was not quite sure what she meant by "poor." Such an idea had never occurred to him, but if his mother had said so they must be and he immediately began to concentrate on the problem of making money.

It was a new idea with all kinds of possibilities and it excited him. He had no trouble getting jobs. He delivered the *Star* for Mr. Carstairs, the news store man, when the regular boy didn't show up, which he failed to do with accommodating frequency. He raked leaves, shoveled snow, and one proud day he distributed leaflets in front of Bradford's Department Store announcing a sale of white goods, whatever *they* were. His rewards were not great. In 1906 there were no minimum wage laws, but in the tin cough-drop box on his bureau lay $4.72.

For days before Uncle Charlie's arrival his mother spent her time scrubbing and scouring the little house, beating rugs, polishing her wedding silver, washing windows, and hanging freshly laundered white curtains in every room. "Is Uncle Charlie awful clean?" asked Allen, watching her fit fresh paper on the pantry shelves.

"Uncle Charlie lives in a huge big house in New York," she said, pausing to push back the strand of hair, "where everything is always in order. His house is filled with beautiful things."

"Uncle Charlie must be busy keeping so many things tidy."

"Oh, he doesn't do it himself, Allen. Uncle Charlie has servants. Lots of them. He's very rich."

"How much is rich?"

"I don't know, Allen. I guess it all depends on what you

want. Your father and I are rich. We don't have much money, but we have the things we like best in life. Riches can be inside you."

Allen watched her in silence for several minutes while he tried to straighten out this puzzling statement.

"When you told me I'd have to earn money if I wanted to go to the circus you said you and Dad were poor."

"I meant that we didn't have much money to spend. Riches aren't always money, Allen. They are not always dollars and cents that you can count. They can be other things like the ability to paint a beautiful picture or to write a book or to compose great music. They can be just appreciating and enjoying things that are done by others. The last are the kind of riches your dad and I have, I guess."

"I like money riches," he said, sliding down from the kitchen table where he had been perched. "I like to count 'em. Know what? I've made $4.72. It's upstairs in my bureau drawer."

She crouched and put her hands on his shoulders. "Allen, *you're* rich. Where in the world did you get all that money?"

"Oh, doing jobs," he said, squirming. Having his mother at eye level made him uncomfortable.

"But how did you *do* it, Allen? I'm so proud of you!"

"Oh, I got jobs after school. It wasn't hard. It just took a long time."

"I'll bet you're going to use it to go to the circus."

"Sure. An' I'm goin' to all the side shows an' I'm goin' to buy things to feed the elephants an' lemonade an' a banner for my room an' . . ."

"But, Allen, you won't have any money left."

"Oh, I'll make some more. It's not hard. It's kind of fun. I got to go now. I got to do something." Anything to get away, but as he walked aimlessly down the street to the place where the circus was going to be located he felt proud. Apparently he had done something much greater than he had realized. He could tell by the way his mother had looked at him. Making money must be a very fine thing to do.

Uncle Charlie arrived in a whirlwind of commotion which always seemed to accompany him wherever he went. The hackman carried in his bags. Allen's father and mother both embraced him at the same time and Uncle Charlie bellowed. He was a huge man who wore a vest winter and summer, with a heavy gold chain looped across its bulging front, but his outstanding characteristic was his voice which he seemed incapable of modulating. Even his simplest remarks seemed to be addressed to a vast invisible audience. He terrified Allen, who shrank into the shadows under the front stairs.

"Where's that boy of yours? He's the one I came to see," boomed Uncle Charlie. "Where are you hiding, boy? Behind a pile of books?"

"He was here a minute ago, Allen," his mother called. Forced out of the protective darkness under the stairs, Allen approached Uncle Charlie cautiously.

"Hiding from the big bear, eh?" Uncle Charlie clapped him across the shoulder with such affectionate vigor that Allen almost lost his balance. "My goodness, boy, the last time I saw you you were playing with blocks. Now you're halfway to being a man."

The Professor interrupted. "Now, Charles, you'll want to freshen up. Horace will show you where your room is. We have dinner in the middle of the day out here. We'll eat in half an hour. I have a two-o'clock class. I'm afraid I can't offer you much in the way of liquid refreshment."

"Don't give it a thought, Os. I knew you and Fanny didn't

drink much, but I thought you ought to have something in the house, so I brought Fanny a couple of bottles as a hostess present."

Allen took the smaller of the two bags and preceded his uncle up the stairs to the immaculate guest room.

"That bag's pretty heavy for you, boy."

"Oh, no, sir."

"Don't call me sir. Call me Uncle Charlie. By the way, where's the W.C.?"

"The what, sir—Uncle Charlie?"

"Gracious, you do lead a sheltered life. The bathroom."

"Oh. At the end of the hall."

"Of course. I'd forgotten. It's been so long since I was here last. By the way, what's your name, anyway? Your father calls you Horace and your mother calls you Allen."

"Horace Allen Martin. Mom doesn't like Horace."

"Neither do I. Horace Allen Martin. H.A.M. I'm going to call you Ham. Come into my room, Ham, and talk to me while I get into a clean shirt."

Allen followed him into the guest room with misgivings. "Sit down on that chair, Ham. There's not much choice. It's the only one in the room. I'm just going to unpack this little bag. The big one is for the West. I'm going out to look at some mines. Did you ever see a mine?"

"No, sir—I mean, Uncle Charlie."

"I'll take you with me someday when you get a little older. By the way, how old are you now? I never can remember birthdays and things like that."

"I was eleven last January 22nd. I'm halfway to twelve."

"What are you going to do when you finish school?"

"I don't know. Go to work I guess."

"What do you *want* to do? That's the point."

"I don't know. Something to do with books, likely. Dad

teaches people about them. He and Mom want me to be a writer."

"A WHAT?" Uncle Charlie's bellow was incredulous.

"They want me to write books. Mom says it's more fun to write books than to teach people about them."

"Good gracious, Ham, nobody makes any money writing books. What are you going to live on?"

"Oh, I don't know. I'll get a job. I got a lot of jobs right now."

"What kind of jobs, Ham?"

"Oh, any old jobs. I got $4.72 I made doing jobs."

Uncle Charlie reached across the bed and patted him on the shoulder. "That's the boy. You'll be rich someday. Now I've got to wash or we'll be late for dinner and that would never do, would it? Do you read much?"

"Yes. Mother used to read to me a lot. She still does, but now I read a lot myself, too. Want to see my books? They're upstairs in my room."

"I certainly do, Ham, but after dinner, after dinner."

That evening Fanny excused herself early and the two men sat in Professor Martin's study for a long time discussing old memories over one of Fanny's hostess presents.

"It's a funny thing, Os, how two brothers could be so entirely different. Here you are, struggling to pound some appreciation of the English language into the heads of a lot of oafs and all for a washwoman's salary and yet you've got a wonderful wife, a smart kid, and seem to be perfectly happy. And here am I with all the money a man can use, a widower with no family and restless as hell—"

Professor Martin smoked his pipe in silence for some time.

"We're each doing what we want to do, Charles," he said finally. "Your life would drive me crazy in a month and I don't think you could stand mine for a week. Yet, as you say, I'm perfectly contented and I don't believe you are really unhappy; a bit lonely perhaps, but not unhappy."

"I suppose you're right, Os. I'd like to have a wonderful, gentle soul like Fanny pattering around the house, though."

"You'd drive her insane."

"And a nice, bright kid like Ham."

"Like who?"

"Ham, your son. I just christened him that because it's what his initials spell. That boy's got intelligence, Os, and drive. Don't moor him in a backwater. Given the right kind of training he could go places. I can pick winners, even when they're eleven years old, and that little boy has what it takes."

"I agree with you, Charles, but that lad is just as different from you as I am. He has the creative instinct. I didn't, unfortunately. I'm just a dried-up old scholar, Horace is going to be a book man. You wait and see. I've been watching his compositions. His teacher shows them to me once in a while. For an eleven-year-old boy some of them are remarkable. He gets at the heart of things, even now. I'd like to see him teach a bit to begin with and write on the side. I think he has it in him. Our grandfather did."

"Grandfather! My God, Os, he was a hack writer for some Minneapolis newspaper and nobody ever read what he wrote. Anyone can write. The trick is to get somebody to read it. Give Ham his head, Os. If he wants to write he'll write, but if he doesn't really want to— Well, I've seen a lot of good lives messed up over this sort of thing. Oh, by the way, to change the subject, did you know that Aunt Delia had a stroke the other day? She . . ."

Allen was restless that night and each time he turned over he could hear Uncle Charlie's voice booming like a bass viol in a distant orchestra. Then the study door opened and the two brothers mounted the creaking stairs. Allen slept.

He returned from the circus completely broke. School was out. There really wasn't much to do in a town like Messina except to fool around with the gang. He missed the activity, the compulsion, of the precircus days when he had a goal.

Nature abhors a vacuum and Mr. Carstairs became nature's unwitting agent. As Allen was passing his news store Mr. Carstairs beckoned to him. "What are you doing now, boy?" he asked, removing his battered pipe and wiping his mustache with the back of his hand.

"Nothing," said Allen. "Could you use me, Mr. Carstairs?"

"That no-good paper boy just told me he was quittin'. Want the job?"

"How much do you pay?"

"My God, boy. You're gettin' hity-tity. You ought to be glad to get the job."

"How much did you pay the other boy?"

"Oh, come now. He was older. He had experience."

"But you said he was no good."

"I ain't goin' to argue, boy. I'll give a dollar a week. Take it or leave it."

"Did you pay the other boy by the week?"

"Just like I'm proposin' to pay you."

"I want to go by the day. Twenty-five cents and if I don't show up I don't get paid."

"That's too much, boy. Eat up all my profit."

"Then twenty cents a day an' my father gets his paper free."

"I can't figger as close as that, but I got to have them papers delivered. I think I'm stuck, but we'll try it, startin' tomorrow mornin'."

Several days later, returning home along Maple Street, Allen saw old Mrs. Quackenbush mowing her lawn. An idea began to form. "Good morning, Mrs. Quackenbush," he said.

She stopped pushing the mower and peered at him near-sightedly. "Ain't you Professor Martin's boy?"

"Yes, ma'am."

She shook her head in amazement. "You've certainly shot up."

"I'm strong too," he said, coming to the point immediately. "You wouldn't want to hire me to cut that lawn for you, would you?"

She looked at him dubiously. "I'm too old for this sort of thing, but then again maybe you're too young. How much do you charge?"

"A quarter an hour." He swallowed hard. "But if I do it in less than four hours the job's worth a dollar."

She looked at the lawn appraisingly. "That includes picking up papers and trash?"

"Of course."

"All right," she said. "I shouldn't spend the money, but I guess I can't take it with me. Come around next Tuesday." She picked up the handles of the mower and began to push.

"Excuse me, ma'am," said Allen, taking it from her. "I'm going to finish this. I don't want any pay. I just want to show you how good I am."

She relinquished the machine and wiped her hands on her apron. "You're a smart boy," she said. "Someday you'll be a rich one."

Ever since Uncle Charlie's visit Professor Martin had been paying more attention to his son. It was as if he realized that the predicted time had come to remove him from the protective aura of his mother and teach him the facts of life from a male point of view. He didn't propose to go fishing with his son or to take him on long walks. His own life didn't include such things. Instead he introduced him to the books which lined the walls of his study. The door was never closed now. If he saw Allen passing he would call to him. "Come in, Horace, I've something to show you.

"Everybody likes stories of adventure, Horace. Here's a book about an adventure that really happened. I think you'd like it. This fellow Dana was rather a puny sort and in order to make a man of himself he joined up as a common seaman on a square-rigger. As the title shows, he lived that life for two years. He tells you what happened. Take it. Let me know what you think of it. And here's a short one called *Dr. Jekyll and Mr. Hyde*. It was written by another sick man. His name was Robert Louis Stevenson. There was a man who could really write.

"Take them along, and remember, every book in this room is yours. There are some exciting fellows sitting up there waiting for you. There's Conrad. He was a Pole, but he wrote in English that has seldom been matched. Gad, how many of these fellows wrote under a handicap of one kind or another—Parkman, Scott—

"Then there's Hardy; way up there on the top shelf. And Thackeray and Dickens and Dumas. Oh, Horace, I envy you. I envy you almost as much as I envy them. I would have given up my whole career as a teacher to have written just one of their books."

There was something in the tone of his voice which caused Allen to look at him curiously. The expression of his handsome bearded face retained its usual quizzical calm, but for an instant Allen had been able to see his father for the first time as a human being.

His arrangement with Mrs. Quackenbush began to have repercussions. Mrs. Pottle, who lived on the next block and suffered from peripatetic arthritis, sent for him.

"My dear, I wouldn't tell anybody about this but you," Mrs. Quackenbush had said to her friend. "He's the most thorough little worker I ever had and he cuts that big lawn of mine for a dollar. One dollar, Minnie! Imagine. Picks up every twig and scrap. Don't tell a soul or they'll steal him. But I knew the fix you were in getting help an' with your arthritis an' everything."

"It's gone into my legs today," said Mrs. Pottle complacently. "Yesterday it was in my right shoulder. I never can tell till I get up in the morning where I'm going to hurt. Send him 'round. I got nobody at the minute and he'll certainly be better than nobody."

Allen cut grass for Mrs. Quackenbush and Mrs. Pottle through the hot summer. In the fall he raked and burned their leaves and cleaned out their flower beds. In the winter he kept their walks clean and occasionally sawed up firewood for them.

Others heard about him and would lean casually on one of his employers' picket fences while he was working, trying to persuade him to do similar work for them. His paper route and his two jobs, however, already took up more time than he could afford. Spurred on by his father's suggestions he was reading now with an ever-increasing eagerness, curled up in the big chair in the Professor's study. His former fear of his father had disappeared. He was proud of the confidence which this austere and grizzled man had so unexpectedly expressed in him and he wanted desperately to please him. He wrote a poem and a short story, the latter sounding remarkably like *Dr. Jekyll and Mr. Hyde.* The poem was terrible, but, to his amazement, they were both accepted by the school paper, whose editor was fed up with writing everything himself. He was embarrassed by the unrestrained pleasure of his father and mother. So it was as easy as that!

Millie had never quite forgiven him for not coming to her birthday party and, to his great relief, had snubbed him on every possible occasion. When his story appeared in the *Potpourri,* however, she condescended to speak to him and would have walked home with him if he had not been agile. Shortly after his poem was published, she asked him to dinner before a school dance, two weeks in advance. She caught her lions early.

He didn't want to go. He didn't dance well. It would be more accurate to say he didn't dance at all. His mother insisted, however, and so, feeling like a fool in his first blue suit with long trousers, he presented himself sheepishly at Millie's door.

The meal was a nightmare. Every time he raised his eyes from his plate either Millie's father or mother would be staring at him as if he were some new kind of bug. After a while he didn't raise them. The ordeal over, he and Millie walked silently to the school. "You dance the first dance with me," she announced as they entered the auditorium, "because I asked you for dinner."

"I don't know much how to dance," he said desperately.

"Of course you do. Everybody knows how to dance. Come outside. I'll show you."

She led him to a room off the auditorium in which somebody had placed a few potted palms and folding chairs. It was dimly lit by several Japanese lanterns. The music had started. "Hold me like this," she said, placing his arm around her waist. "Gracious, don't you even know how to hold a girl?"

He tried to pull away, but her left hand on his shoulder held him fast. "Now just follow me and do what I do."

He stumbled after her, trying to avoid contact with her lithe little body. "Dance closer," she said, jerking him toward her.

He had never been so close to a girl before. Her face was only a few inches from his. She was laughing at him. Instead of getting mad he found himself rather liking it. He hoped, however, that none of his friends would see him.

The music stopped. "You're going to be a good dancer," she said. "You just need practice. Look, I haven't anybody for the next dance. Why don't we just stay in here and I'll teach you some more. Want to sit down and talk to me?"

There was nothing he wanted to do less, but he was trapped.

"I've got a trade last for you," she said.

"A what?"

"A trade last. Don't you know *anything*? Somebody says something nice about you. You think up something nice somebody said about me. Then I tell you and you tell me. See?"

He remained silent studying his hands. "All right," she said finally. "Jane Simonds thinks you're the nicest boy in the class. She has your poem pasted inside the cover of her desk."

"Jane Simonds?" he said, being unable to think of any better comment.

"I hate her," Millie said. "She's silly. I cut out your story. I have it home in my memory book."

Fatty Perkins looked in the door. Fatty was the town spark. "What you two doing? Toozing?" The music started. "Want to dance, Millie?"

"I'm taken," she said, glancing at Allen.

"No, no," Allen protested. "You go ahead and dance with Fatty. I don't feel good."

She tossed her head. "All right," she said. "See you later."

He went out and stood unhappily in the back of the stag line for a few minutes. Then he went home.

His mother was reading. "Why, Allen, it's only half past nine. Did you have fun?"

"Oh, sure."

"Whom did you dance with? Tell me."

"Oh, everybody."

"Want a glass of milk?"

"No. I guess I'll go to bed."

She looked after his retreating figure with smiling eyes and picked up her book. That night it took Allen an unusually long time to fall asleep.

All through the winter and spring of 1907 he worked for Mrs. Quackenbush and Mrs. Pottle and read prodigiously. He was a regular contributor now to the *Potpourri*. He never wrote any more poems, but he and his father had long talks about his stories. "He's the best pupil I ever had," he told Fanny. "He knows how to take advice."

There was no question that Allen wanted above all things to please his father. A word of praise from the Professor set him up for the day and when he failed he had the feeling that he had somehow let his father down.

As the grass began to grow long and the remnants of last autumn's fallen leaves began to be blown out of their hiding places by the fresh southeast breezes, Allen was obliged to turn down more and more jobs. He had grown like a weed during the past year and his thin little body had filled out. Although he was only fourteen he looked older than his years and his face was beginning to show traces of his father's aquiline features.

He was no longer a little boy to be hired with a patronizing smile, but a young adolescent quite capable of doing any ordinary job, and on his own terms.

Mrs. Henry Jackson, who was unable to do more than hobble to the grocery store, wanted him to cut her grass and keep her two flower beds weeded. Similar requests came from Old Colonel Carter, Miss Susan Brophy, and half a dozen others. It broke his heart to say no, but he couldn't take on anything more and still have time for his homework and reading in his father's library.

One morning he had an idea. Immediately after school he went to see Mr. Carstairs. "Hello, boy," said Mr. Carstairs. "I was just goin' across the street to talk to some friends. What's on your mind?"

Mr. Carstairs spent more and more of his time "across the street." He had a large hand bell which his customers were supposed to take outside and ring on such occasions, but during the past year its clangor frequently didn't penetrate to Mr. Carstairs' cozy corner in Hambros Bar, so after a while the retail trade passed him by in favor of the up-and-coming new stationery store three blocks down.

Allen didn't quite know how to begin. "I've got so many jobs offered me I can't take 'em all—"

"Well, well," interrupted Mr. Carstairs. "Ain't that fine—just fine? You always was a smart lad. Well, I guess there won't be no customers comin' along for a space so I'll run across the street an' see a friend." He sarted for the door.

"But I've got something I want to talk to you about."

Mr. Carstairs paused on the threshold. "All right, boy, only make it quick. I'm awful busy."

"I can't take on any more jobs," said Allen. "So I'm going to get four or five fellows and we'll form a sort of company. I want to kind of make your store our headquarters. When people want us to do something they can call here and leave a message. Then I'll go round and see 'em. The company'll give you five cents a message."

"S'pose I ain't here?"

"We'll put a pad of paper on the counter an' I'll make a sign saying to write messages on the pad. Then I'll come round every once in a while an' see if there's anything on the pad."

"Sounds like a lot of trouble," grumbled Mr. Carstairs. "Pads an' signs an' what not, but go ahead. We'll give it a try. Might bring people in."

Allen asked four of his friends to attend a meeting in his bedroom at four o'clock the following Thursday. It was a hand-picked group: Tom Alison, Peter Brodski, Sam Trench, and Mike O'Hara; all of them hard-working, conscientious boys, but none of them very bright.

He described to them the two jobs he already held, including his financial arrangements. "Now, here's my plan. This town is full of people with sore backs an' sore arms an' sore this an' that, an' they all want jobs done. They're lookin' for somebody to do 'em, but unless we sort of get together in a kind of company they won't know about us. My idea is to get a notice printed something like this." He opened his bureau drawer and pulled out a dog-eared sheet of paper.

THE UNITED JOB CORPORATION, INC.
Grass cutting, weeding, woodcutting, snow shoveling,
or any other odd job you can think of, done quickly,
neatly, and *inexpensive*.

He looked about for approval. Everyone seemed to be struck dumb by the magnitude of the idea. "How do we get paid?" asked Peter Brodski finally.

"*You* get 25 cents an hour, but we raise our price to 35 cents an hour. I'm president. I got charge of gettin' new business an' keepin' things goin'. For that I get 5 cents an hour from each of you. The other 5 cents goes to the company. Peter Brodski's going to be treasurer."

"What's the company goin' to do with the money?" asked Sam Trench suspiciously.

"Expenses. The notices are going to cost something unless Sam can get his father to do them on that machine of his."

"How are people goin' to get hold of us? S'pose old Ma Whitaker wants her walk shoveled. What's she goin' t'do; yell out the window?" He looked around smugly.

"She's goin' to drop in at Carstairs' news store. The notice is goin' to say 'Headquarters, Carstairs' News Store. Please leave message.' Mr. Carstairs is goin' to take messages for a nickel apiece. I'll be there right after school an' if anybody wants us I'll go see 'em an' then round up you kids to do the work."

"Ain't you ever goin' to do any work yourself?"

"Sure I am."

"When you do, I s'pose you get 30 cents an hour?"

"No. I get the same as you all an' 10 cents goes to the company instead of 5."

That seemed to satisfy everybody. "S'pose we get more work than we can do. What then?"

"We have a meeting and elect new members. Only new members have to pay a dime to the company to get in."

The venture succeeded beyond all expectation. Before snow began to fall Allen's crew increased to eight and he was receiving over 50 cents a day as president. His standards were high. Anyone who didn't do their job well was thrown out and there was always a list of applicants to choose from.

Each afternoon he went directly from school to Mr. Carstairs' store where he did his homework while waiting for callers. Occasionally he waited on customers while Mr. Carstairs was relaxing across the street. As the latter discovered that Allen was dependable he tended to relax more and more until occasionally Allen found that the only way he could leave was to lock up the store, cross the street, and slip the key in Mr. Carstairs' pocket.

One Saturday morning Mr. Carstairs sat down at his battered roll-top desk, turned in his swivel chair, and looked over the shelves and counters. "They's somethin' goin' on round here," he said. "Things look different somehow."

Allen felt his face growing red. "I hope you don't mind, Mr. Carstairs, but once in a while when I've got a few minutes I straighten out one of the shelves so it'll be easier for me to find things."

Mr. Carstairs stared at him with bleary eyes. He pulled a cuspidor from under his desk with his feet, spat in it, and returned it to its place by reversed foot power. He only did this in moments of emotional crisis. "Well, I'll be damned," he said finally. "Why do you do all that work for nothin'?

Allen shuffled uncomfortably. "I don't know. I guess I like to see things in rows."

Mr. Carstairs stood up and made a closer inspection of the shelves and counter, running his fingers through his thin hair. "Gosh," he said, reseating himself. "I couldn't lay my hands on nothing as you got 'em skewed around, but it certainly *looks* more shipshape." He studied Allen closely for several minutes. "Look here, boy. You're a smart kid. I'm gettin' older. Need a little letup now and then. How'd you like to carry on just like you're doin' for, let's say, two dollars a week?"

"I'd like it," said Allen. "Just like I'm doin'. Nothin' more."

"Good. I'll just be across the street. Ring the bell an' I'll run right over. You're on the payroll. Now I think I'll slide out for a few minutes."

At supper that night Allen told his father and mother about his new job. To his surprise they seemed more disturbed than pleased.

"You're working too hard, Allen," his mother said. "You never play. You've got a whole gang of boys working for you like Snow White's dwarfs. You're up at six delivering papers. Now you've taken on a new job. It isn't right, Allen."

"But, Mother, I *like* it. It's *fun*. And once you told me I ought to help out by earning money."

"What did you tell him, Fanny?" asked the Professor sharply. She looked embarrassed. "Oh, Os, I just told him years ago that if he wanted to go to the circus or buy candy and that sort of thing he should earn the money. I wanted him to learn the value of a dollar. I didn't mean he was to go into *business*."

"Tell me all about what you've been doing, Horace. I've been so busy I'm afraid I haven't paid as much attention as I should."

Allen told him the whole story with mounting pride. After dinner the Professor invited him into his study, where he sat in his high-backed desk chair, fingertips pressed together.

"Horace, my boy"—he had never called him "my boy" before—"you're too young to know what you want to do when you grow up, but not too young to think about it once in a while.

"Since the time you learned to read you have always had your nose in a book. Books are very real to you. They are a part of your life. Isn't that so?"

"Yes, sir." Allen wondered where all this was leading.

"It runs in the blood, my boy. Books are my world and to a great extent they are your mother's also. We were both brought up in an atmosphere that took books for granted. My father was a great newspaper editor. His father (that would be your great-grandfather) was an English professor at Johns Hopkins, a man of immense learning. And so it goes all the way back.

"Your mother's family was much the same. Her father could have been a first-class poet, but he allowed himself to drift into hack work in order to make both ends meet. You never knew either of your grandfathers because your mother and I married late. Too bad."

It was the first time Allen had ever thought of himself as having two grandfathers. The idea confused him. All he could think of were the pictures of the two bearded men on the Smith Brothers cough-drop boxes.

Professor Martin picked up a paper cutter and examined it as if he had never seen it before. "When I was an under-graduate at Messina, Horace, I wanted to be a writer. I dreamed of writing a great novel someday. I worked hard in college and when they offered me a tutorial job in the English Department while I was working for my M.A. and later my Ph.D. I accepted it gladly. It would keep body and soul together while I was writing and completing my grad-uate work.

"I tried hard, Horace." There was a slight note of pleading in his voice which made Allen uncomfortable. "Before I had obtained my Ph.D., however, I knew that I was a scholar rather than a writer.

"There is a tremendous difference between a scholar and a writer, Horace. Scholars are expected to produce books and they do, but they are written for other scholars, not for the general public." The Professor was talking to himself now.

"The scholar is a kind of archaeologist in his given subject. He has his particular 'dig.' He turns up a lot of artifacts, arranges them neatly, then describes them to his contemporaries in a book. His god is precision, exactness, and his greatest fear is overstatement. As a result most of his books are as dry as mummy dust.

"A writer, Horace, is a different breed of cat—and listen carefully to this . . ." Allen shook off the feeling of drowsiness which was creeping over him and sat straighter in the big armchair. His father evoked a feeling of awe in him when he couldn't quite understand what he was talking about.

"A writer is an interpreter of life. One of the great differences between a writer and a scholar is that, instead of drawing everything with a hard, sharp line, a writer deliberately throws his scenes slightly out of focus the way a great photographer will soften the edges of a face in a camera portrait."

Professor Martin threw down the paper cutter so impatiently that Allen wondered if he had done something to annoy him. "But why am I talking like this to you? I guess it's because the moment I begin to talk I slide into a lecture. I wanted to talk about *you* and your *future*, Horace, and perhaps get you dreaming in the right direction. Dreams are more important to our futures than we sometimes realize.

"Your mother and I have been watching your work in school, and, as far as we can tell, you are headed down the same path that both of our families have followed for generations.

"You will either be a scholar or a writer. That may be wishful thinking, but it's what we see now. We both hope you will turn to writing because we feel that you have the imagination and sensitivity so essential to a creative writer. Take the story that you told us tonight. It took imagination to conceive the idea of a group of boys forming a service company and to put poor old Carstairs' store in order." Allen breathed easier. Instead of being displeased, his father apparently approved of everything.

Professor Martin studied the tips of his fingers for several moments. "Some day, when you have children of your own, Horace, you will learn that every parent has ambitions for his offspring. Your mother and I have ambitions for you. Perhaps they are particularly strong in your case because you are an only child. We want you to become a writer—not a mediocre writer, but a *great* one. Now, writing is a peculiar art. You can't *teach* anyone to write. That may be heresy coming from a teacher, but I believe it to be true. The only way to learn to write is to *write*.

"You can't start too early. Although you may not realize it you have already started. Keep eternally at it. Next fall you will be entering high school. The opportunities for writing there will be greater than they have been to date. There is no reason why you shouldn't be editor of the school paper if you really go after it. It will consume time and energy, but the end is worth it."

Allen stiffened. He began to see the direction which this conversation was taking. "At the present moment your service company, as you call it, and all the other things you are doing eat deeply into your available time and energy.

They have been good experiences, but now they have served their purpose. You should move into the field where I hope you are going to spend the rest of your life and concentrate there."

"You mean quit all my jobs?"

The Professor nodded. "That's the wisest thing, Horace. Quit them in order to take on a bigger one."

"But, Dad, all those kids are kind of depending on me. So are Mrs. Quackenbush and Mrs. Pottle and Mr. Carstairs an'—oh, gee, there's a bunch of them. I do a lot of homework and reading at the store. Honest, Dad—" He *must* make his father see the point.

The Professor shook his head. "There is no such thing as the indispensable man, Horace."

"But, Dad, I can't just let all these people down kerbang. It wouldn't be honorable." (He had played his trump card. It was his father's favorite word.) "I have to find someone to take all these jobs. Then I have to show him how to run them. High school doesn't start till fall. Couldn't I just go on like I'm going till I find somebody to take my place? Maybe I'll need more than one. You'd want me to be honorable, wouldn't you, Dad?"

His father looked up at him from under his thick white eyebrows with his quizzical, classroom expression. "Of course I want you to be honorable, Horace—always. Take your time and by next fall you'll be ready to start on your real work."

As the train came to a cushioned halt, H. Allen Martin of the Class of '17 returned to the present. The familiar white walls of the Rhode Island State-house looked down from the hilltop on to the grimy station. Providence. He readjusted his seatback and, as he heard the fluttery voices of new passengers entering the car, he shut his eyes once more.

How many years had rolled by since that memorable talk with his father! It must have been in 1909. He had wanted so to please those good simple people and it wasn't as if their ambitions for him had run completely counter to his own. As the Professor had said, he had been brought up with books. They *were* part of his life. The idea that some day his name might be on the title page of one had excited him even though it sounded ridiculous.

During the remainder of the spring and the summer he had reorganized his affairs. Tom Alison took the paper route, Peter Brodski became president of the United Job Corporation, Inc., and Sam Trench agreed to help out at Mr. Carstairs' store after school hours.

He had not realized what a reputation he had made until high school opened and he was elected president of his freshman class. Allen hadn't seen much of Millie Gardner in the past two years. He had been too occupied with bigger things. Now, no longer to be denied, she came forward with a rush.

It started at the high school dance which incoming freshman classes gave two weeks after school started. Millie had asked him to call for her. He would never forget her as she opened the door for him that evening. The pigtails were gone and her lovely copper-colored hair was pinned up like a grown woman's. She had on some kind of pink evening dress which showed enough of her maturing body to cause him acute embarrassment.

"Do you like me?" she asked, spreading her arms wide.

"Gee," he said. "You certainly are all dolled up."

They walked silently toward the high school, suddenly shy.

"I'm so *proud* of you, Allen," she said finally, taking his arm and pressing it against her. "Being made president of the class! You're wonderful. I got a lot of votes for you."

"Thanks," he said, slightly irritated.

She sensed this and pressed his arm so close that he became conscious of the softness of her breast. He tried to pull away, but she held him tightly. "I hear you're going out for the paper," she said. "Oh, Allen, I'm *so* proud of you."

He could think of no answer to this. "Are you proud of me?" she asked.

"Of course," he said. Why were girls always fishing?

"Oh, I'm so glad. I think we're kind of special, you and I. Would you like to be special?"

"Sure," he said. He was far from sure what she was talking about, but he sensed danger. Invisible ropes were beginning to bind him and he didn't know how to avoid them.

They were approaching the school through the shadows of a double row of elms. Much to his relief a group of boys and girls were coming up behind them. "You're dancing the first dance with me," she said; then, giving his arm a final squeeze, she turned to Ben Oakes, who had moved up beside her. He had never liked Ben Oakes.

All through the years that followed the memory of that evening remained undimmed. He had started the first dance with her, but before they had gone round the room someone had cut in and he had returned unhappily to the stag line. He watched another boy cut in on her and then another. He tried cutting in himself, but it only made him more unhappy when she was torn from him in a few feet by some pimply kid. Nobody cared about dance cards any more.

When she danced with him she nestled her cheek against his shoulder and didn't seem to have anything to say. With everybody else she threw back her head, looked into her partner's eyes, and immediately began laughing and chattering. Obviously he was a tongue-tied fool who bored her stiff.

Without question she was the prettiest girl in the room; the most vivacious; the most popular. He wondered why he had never noticed these qualities before—before it was too late. She had said, "Would you like to be special?" and all he had said was "Sure." Now she was gone.

She danced past him with a big lump of a boy called Tubby Carlton. Shoving his way through the stag line he brushed Tubby aside savagely and took her in his arms.

"Want to eat supper with me?" he asked gruffly.

"Oh, Allen, I can't. I just told Tubby I'd have supper with him. There's a bunch of us going to sit together. You come too. *Please*. It will be fun. Then maybe afterwards we can sit out for a dance. Look, the doors are opening now. Let's grab Tubby and we'll find a good place."

Tubby was right behind them. Millie waited for him, took his arm and laughed at something he said. Allen let them go on, picked a handful of sandwiches from the supper table and walked out a side door onto the tennis courts, miserable and unnoticed.

The stars were brilliant. He leaned against a net post and looked up at them, slowly munching a sandwich. When they were all gone it was obvious that he couldn't stand there all night gawking at the stars. Inside the building just a few yards away they were all huddled in a corner, laughing and making fools of themselves. He hated the pack of them—including Millie.

Suddenly she was beside him. "Allen Martin, what in the world are you doing? I've been looking for you everywhere. We had a sit-out date. Don't you remember?" Her hand was on his arm. It was the same hand that had been on Tubby's arm a few minutes before. He shook it off roughly. "I got a headache," he said.

Her hand smoothed back his hair. "I'm sorry. Let's find a place where we can sit down a few minutes. Maybe it will go away." She led him across the courts to the wooden stand on which the referee sat during special matches. In the shadows on one side was an old bench on which the players threw their sweaters and towels.

They sat down and Millie moved closer to him until he became aware of an unaccustomed fragrance. He suddenly felt as if a warm current was passing between them. He had never experienced anything like this before and it scared him even while it filled him with a strange excitement. He knew something was about to happen. He anticipated it eagerly yet at the same time wanted to run away. Suddenly Millie's arms were around his neck and she was kissing him. He had kissed girls before, but it was only a peck on the cheek; a forfeit in some silly game. This was something quite different. He could feel her soft lips against his and the increased pressure of her arms.

He reached out clumsily, but she suddenly moved away from him and stood up. "We only have half an hour left. *Please* cut in. And don't forget you're taking me home."

She dodged behind the referee's stand and disappeared momentarily among the clump of trees that bordered the courts. Then he caught the glint of her dress as she passed a lighted window and moved swiftly around the corner of the schoolhouse.

Allen walked slowly across the courts, filled with such exalted self-confidence that, given the slightest provocation, he would joyfully have knocked down half the freshman class.

The music had started. Emily Battle, the homeliest girl in the class, was standing, alone and unwanted, just inside the auditorium door. "Come," he said. "Let's dance."

On the way home Millie found his hand in the darkness, held it for a few minutes, then suddenly dropped it. He considered how they would say good night when they reached her front door. This time he would not be so clumsy. He would hold her in his arms the way they did in the movies. They would stand that way for a long, long time and she would kiss him the way she had at the tennis courts.

These dreams became so real that he was nervous as they mounted the steps of Millie's front porch. She had her key in her hand and opened the door noiselessly, leaving it slightly ajar. Turning back to Allen she placed her hands on his shoulders. "Never forget we're special," she said. He tensed himself for the big finale.

"Thanks for a lovely evening," she said. Then she was gone and the front door clicked behind her.

He stumbled down the steps utterly bewildered. He hadn't even said good night.

He woke up the following morning filled with confusion and dismay. He had always regarded girls as nuisances, a race apart, to be avoided whenever possible. He had looked on them as a species rather than as individuals. Now one of them had suddenly and unaccountably detached herself from the species and become a person—one who seemed to feel that she had a special key to his private life. What had she meant by this "special" stuff? Did she think she was going to lead him around on a leash? Well, she wasn't. He'd seen that kind of thing happen to older boys and it made him ill.

Millie was not so easy to avoid. She always seemed to be popping up in unexpected places. If he went to get a drink at the water cooler she was apt to come wandering by. At the noon recess, if he went around the corner of the building to look for someone, she would be sitting under a tree reading. Their meetings were brief. He could never think of anything to say that didn't sound stupid. She did all the talking. She never mentioned the tennis court evening. For that he was grateful and at the same time puzzled and annoyed. She talked entirely about what he was doing. She persuaded him to go out for the football team although the season had already started. To his astonishment he made the squad, where he sat on the sidelines and shivered through the fall. She also made him go out for the school paper and when his first piece was accepted she acted as if it had been the Gettysburg Address.

"Oh, Allen," she had said, "I'm so proud of you."

"Shucks," he said. "That wasn't anything. I just sat down an' wrote it off one day when I didn't have anything to do."

"You did not," she said. "That was a wonderful story. You're going to be a famous writer someday and you'll write books and stories an' plays an' everybody'll be talking about you."

"Oh, rats," he said. "That was just a silly old story. I've got to go."

"Let's walk home together after school."

"I can't. I've got to see some fellows."

She gave her head a characteristic toss and walked away. He felt vaguely upset. Girls were funny. You never could tell *what* they were going to do.

He didn't seem to run into her as much after that and when he did she was always with a group of girls. Twice he saw her walking home with Tubby. This infuriated him, but if she was the kind of girl who saw anything in a big dummy like that he was well rid of her.

That summer Millie went to visit her aunt who had a cottage on the shore of Lake Michigan. Allen got a job in Bean's lumber yard and pretended he had forgotten her.

He was lonely, restless, and hurt without knowing why. The arrows of puppy love were entering virgin flesh.

That fall he became a first-string substitute on the football team and experienced the heady thrill of hearing his name attached to the end of a cheer when he made his one and only touchdown. He also became a junior editor of the school paper which pleased his father so much that he presented Allen with an autographed copy of Owen Wister's *The Virginian,* after which he proceeded to get slightly fuzzy on sherry. He was also taken into a fraternity.

He hadn't seen much of Millie that fall. He didn't avoid her purposely, but she never seemed to be where he was. On the day he received his fraternity pin, however, she was standing beside the entrance door. She fell in beside him. "I've been waiting for you," she announced.

It was so unexpected that he couldn't think of a reply. They walked together to the street. Normally she would have turned to the right in the direction of her house. He turned to the left.

"So long," he mumbled.

To his dismay she turned with him. "I want to talk to you, Allen," she said. "I've *got* to talk to you. Let's go down to the Grove where we can be by ourselves." The Grove was Messina's traditional picnic area.

"It'll be full of people," he said.

"Not at this hour. We'll have it all to ourselves."

"I promised Joe Carter I'd do something with him."

"You didn't promise Joe Carter anything of the kind. You're going to the Grove with me. Please, Allen. I have to talk to you or I'll bust."

"Gosh," he said. "It's crazy."

"What, to bust?"

"No, to go to the Grove this time in the afternoon."

"I don't care. I can't stand in the middle of the street and talk to you. Come on. Let's go."

He felt trapped and at the same time was conscious of a mounting sense of excitement. The Grove was deserted. A small brook ran across one corner. Millie's plans were definite. She proceeded directly to the brook and seated herself under a huge oak tree. "Sit here," she commanded, patting the ground beside her. "There's plenty of room for both of us to lean back against the tree."

It was one of those rare November afternoons when the combination of cool, thin air and brilliant sunlight makes people conscious that they are alive and grateful because of it. They sat watching the rippling play of the afternoon sun on the tiny stream. The next move was up to her. She placed her hand on his where it rested beside her on the grass.

"Allen, I've been awfully unhappy."

"What about?"

"About you, stupid. We were so very close and then something happened. I don't know what it was, but all of a sudden we weren't special any more."

"Tubby was," he said grumpily.

"I hate him."

He looked at her with surprise. Nobody could possibly understand girls. "You didn't have to see him all the time if you hated him."

"I did it to make you mad because you didn't seem to like me any more. Oh, Allen, you knew I liked you all the time. You're so wonderful. You practically made the football team, you're on the paper, and now you're in the best frat in school. Have you got your pin yet?"

He nodded.

"Can I see it?"

He took the little box out of his pocket, opened it and handed the pin to her. "It's beautiful, Allen. Can I hold it?"

She turned it over and over, then replaced it in the box.

He started to put the box in his pocket, then hesitated. Slowly he drew it out again and reopened it. She never took her eyes from his face. He removed the pin, unclasped it and, leaning toward her, attempted to pin it to her dress just below her shoulder.

"Ouch," she said. Her fingers met his, removed the pin and fastened it to her dress. "Allen," she whispered, moving closer to him. "Do you *really* want me to have this?"

He nodded. The next minute he had his arms around her and was kissing her. Gosh, how did he ever get into a thing like this? Suppose somebody should see them. She'd probably slap his face in a minute. Serve him right. A nice girl like Millie. To his amazement her arm was around his neck and she was drawing him closer. He could feel her soft, yielding young body against his. He wasn't used to soft, yielding young bodies. It gave him a panicky feeling.

Suddenly she released him, pulled away, and sat up very straight against the tree. It was becoming such a familiar gesture that he was prepared for it. Her hands flew to her disheveled hair touching the pin in their ascent. "Oh, Allen, you must think I'm awful. I've never done that with *anybody* before; honest I haven't. Just you, Allen. And I'm not sorry. I'm glad. I'm happy." She wriggled closer until their shoulders touched, but still kept her back pressed firmly against the tree. "Do you know why I'm so happy, Allen? It's because now we're special forever—forever and ever. Are you happy?"

"Yes," he said, then, feeling this was rather inadequate, he attempted to put his arm around her shoulder. He lost his nerve at the last moment and began to pick at the tree bark above her head. So now he had a regular girl, but that "forever and ever" business bothered him. It seemed like a long time. Somehow it sounded like a gate closing and, although he was too young to be fully aware of it, he hated to be fenced in and always would.

"Come," she said. "It's getting late. Mother will be wondering what's become of me." They rose. She reached behind her and put his arm around her waist as they walked to the entrance of the Grove. He was embarrassed, but didn't try to pull away.

Those last two years at high school were busy and heady. Everything seemed to come his way. He made the football team, was re-elected president of his class in his senior year, and became editor in chief of the paper. Through it all ran the memory of Millie. Ever since the day he had given her his frat pin she had changed completely. She was selfless, seemingly only interested in what he did; a sort of one-girl cheering section. She was never possessive, never intruded, but she was always there when needed and he found himself needing her frequently.

The old Professor spent more and more time now talking to him about books and their authors.

"Read Conrad, Horace. There's a man who had a true ear for words. He handled them the way a great painter handles colors. There was only one right word for him—one word that would instill life into the scene he was trying to create and he wasn't satisfied until he found it.

"He took infinite pains. That's the secret of great writing —infinite pains. Macaulay wrote only a few words a day, but he worked over them. Other writers do four or five drafts of their books before they are satisfied. Perhaps a real author is never satisfied. They spend their lives trying to achieve perfection but never reach it.

"But I am boring you, Horace. The things that I am talking about you can only learn with maturity. You have to live life in order to write about it. Don't forget that no one can pour water out of an empty pitcher. The immediate thing is that next year you will be entering Messina College as a freshman. Scatter your courses over the whole field of human knowledge. To write about people you must know all you can of how they lived; what made and still makes them tick. You must know about their stupidities as well as their accomplishments.

"When you graduate I feel quite confident that I can get you an appointment as an English instructor while you are studying for your M.A. If you are going to write, a Ph.D. is not necessary. After that you may want to get a minor job with one of the big New York publishing houses like Harper or Scribner's. That would put you in touch with the world of books and you could write in your spare time. Or you may want to work for a newspaper. Newspaper training may be the best for you. You have to write under pressure and you are forced to look at life from street level instead of from an ivory tower.

"There have been many newspapermen in both your mother's family and mine. Your grandfather Martin wanted me to go into business, but I didn't have the flair for it. All my leanings were toward scholarship, but I guess the creative urge is in my blood. That's why we have pinned our hopes on you since you were a little boy."

He glanced at Allen who sat drowsy-eyed in the big chair, trying hard to listen while he was lulled into sleep by the even tones of his father's voice saying over again what he had said so many times before.

"But come, son, you're half asleep. I always talk too much when I get started. You're not out of high school yet. We

have years to talk about these matters. You go first and I'll
turn out the lights."

He was elected valedictorian of the graduating class, an
honor which gave him indigestion during most of the spring
term. Uncle Charlie came all the way from New York to hear
him, which scared him even more. The address went off
well because Allen was bound that it should even if it killed
him. He recited it so many times in front of the mirror in
his bedroom that he could just as readily have begun at the
end and talked back to the beginning. His father wanted
to help him, but he refused to let him even read it. This
was going to be *his* show for better or for worse.

He was only too conscious of the fact that his father and
mother would be there, proud and anxious; that Millie
would be there, and that Uncle Charlie, supercritical because
he had come such a long way, would be glaring at him with
his bulging brown eyes.

Eventually the ordeal was over and his classmates crowded
forward to congratulate him. He saw his father and mother
standing at the edge of the group. Jumping down he pushed
his way through to them. For the first time in his life he
read deep emotion in his father's handsome face. As he
put his hand on Allen's shoulder it shook slightly. "My
boy, that was splendid. There was thought behind that
address—thought and feeling. You really *said* something
and that makes it different from any valedictory *I've* ever
heard."

To his amazement his mother seemed to be on the verge
of tears. She took his hands, leaned forward, and kissed him
silently. Uncle Charlie's bellow rose above the confusion

of voices in the auditorium. "Ham," he roared, "William Jennings Bryan couldn't have done better. They *listened* to you, boy. I watched 'em. You had 'em sitting up in their seats. That was a lalapalooza, boy."

Where was Millie? He had spotted her in the fourth row just before he rose to his feet, praying that his knees might stop shaking. Their eyes had met and she had winked at him. That wink had done the trick. Now she was nowhere to be seen. Millie was always doing unexpected things. He was uneasy. She was the last person he had supposed might be disappointed. Uncle Charlie was shouting again.

"Come on. Let's get this circus on the road. I need a drink and you and Fanny do too, Os. I don't even think a little dollop would do Ham any harm. How about it, boy?"

"Charles, *please!*" said his mother. It was the first time she had spoken. They moved toward the entrance doors.

"You go ahead," he said. "I have to speak to someone. I'll catch up with you or meet you at the house."

"He's got a girl," roared Uncle Charlie. "He's got a sweetie and she ran out on him." Several nearby students giggled.

His face crimson, Allen squeezed between seats and escaped through a side exit. Millie was waiting for him outside the rear door of the school building. Disregarding the stragglers, she threw her arms round his neck and kissed him.

"Oh, Allen, you were *wonderful*. You were so good you almost scared me. I kept thinking how can a ninny like me hope to hold anyone with brains like that. I'm even scared yet, Allen. We're still special though, aren't we?"

"Of course we are," he said with a trace of impatience in his voice. Apparently girls had to be assured about things like this every five minutes.

"Oh, now I'm happy again; happy and proud of you. You

have to go now. I know it. Your family will be waiting for you. Allen, let's see a lot of each other during the next few weeks. I'm going to my aunt's the middle of July and I won't be back until after Labor Day. She wanted me to come up right away, but I managed to put it off because of you."

"Sure thing," he said, conscious of curious eyes looking at them. "I got to go now. My uncle's here." Before she could become emotional again he dashed around the corner of the building and disappeared. Part of him wanted to escape; part of him wanted to go back. It was confusing.

That evening Uncle Charlie and his father closeted themselves in the study. Allen and his mother talked together in the kitchen. What they said had faded from his memory, but he never forgot the tenderness and pride in her voice. He had always felt close to her, but it was the closeness of a little boy who seeks snug harbor. On this evening their relationship matured. He saw her for the first time as a person—gentle, intelligent, self-effacing; a person who lived for only two people.

"Gracious," she said, breaking off suddenly. "It's almost eleven o'clock. What *are* those two men talking about? You must go to bed, Allen. This has been a big day for you. You're exhausted. I can see it in your eyes. I think I'll go too. They may jabber away for hours. We'll just leave the light on in the hall."

At the top of the stairs she paused, put her hands on his shoulders, and kissed him lightly on the forehead. "Good night, Allen. You're a good boy. You've never disappointed me. Never will."

As he slid into bed that night he resolved that he never would. He sensed the fact that he was entering a new world and for the second time that day he was scared. He opened his eyes and turned on the light. The faded wallpaper was still there. His bureau stood where it had always stood. On the opposite wall was a steel engraving of the Acropolis which his father had hung there years before. Reassured he snapped off the light and fell asleep.

II

He was late for breakfast the fol-
lowing morning. His father and mother and Uncle Charlie
had almost finished.

"Well, if it isn't Demosthenes," roared Uncle Charlie,
wiping a bit of scrambled egg from the fringe of his mustache. "The late Mr. Demosthenes."

"Allen deserves to be late for once," said his mother.

"He certainly does," agreed Professor Martin. "That was a
fine job you did yesterday, Horace."

"Horace, Allen, Ham! He's like a character in a Russian
novel. I don't see how the kid knows *who* he is."

The two men suddenly became silent. His mother placed a

heaping plate of scrambled eggs before Allen and resumed her seat. He ate rapidly, uneasily, aware that they were all watching him. Something was brewing. For once he knew that he had done nothing wrong. They had obviously been talking about him, however, when he came into the room and that usually meant that something was going to happen that he would not like.

His father broke the silence. "Horace, when you have finished your breakfast your Uncle Charles and I would like to see you in my study."

"Nonsense," cried Uncle Charlie. "Why do we have to make such a to-do about it. All this secret-chamber stuff. Let's talk right here. Fanny has a right to be in on it. She's his mother, isn't she?"

"Very well," said Professor Martin with ruffled dignity. "Your uncle is a generous man, Horace. He's been watching you grow up and he believes that you have talent. He discussed all this with me last night—"

"Fiddlesticks," interrupted Uncle Charlie. "This isn't a public address. Let *me* tell Ham. We've been talking about your future, boy, and while I've got nothing against Messina College I've felt for a long time that you should go to a bigger place where you can stretch your brains a bit and learn what's happening in the world. I went to Harvard and that's where I want you to go."

Allen stared at him. "You mean I wouldn't go to Messina at all?"

"Of course that's what I mean. You can't go to *two* places. I'm a widower, as you know. I've plenty of money and nobody to spend it on. What's the use of having money if you've nobody to spend it on but yourself? So I've asked your pa and ma as a special favor if they would let me put you through Harvard. It was a tough sale. They don't like to see you go so far away, but by God I won. While you were pounding your ear upstairs your father collapsed—threw in the sponge."

"Only because Harvard can give you a broader education than Messina," interrupted Professor Martin. The defeated note in his voice was an indication of what this admission cost him. "You will be studying under some of the best men in the country. There are giants on the Harvard faculty. I fear that I cannot say that of Messina—but don't mistake me, you can get a splendid education here if you really want it," he added hastily. "One only has to be receptive to learning."

"This is going to take some doing," interrupted Uncle Charlie impatiently. "There are some minor nuisances like entrance examinations to be passed. I saw the Dean before I came out and signed all the papers and that sort of rigmarole." Professor Martin looked surprised, but said nothing. Fanny was dabbing her eyes with her napkin; one of her best linen napkins—brought out for Uncle Charlie.

"But those damned exams have to be passed. They come up in two weeks. I've made arrangements to have you tutor with the Widow Nolan from now till exam time. Anything you don't pass you can take again in the fall and you can work all summer at the Harvard Summer School. It's not a bad place. I'll run up every once in a while and we'll go on a bat."

Again they were all staring at Allen, waiting for him to speak. He had nothing to say. It was all too big for him; too strange. It had been thrust at him too quickly. Messina represented security. All the things that Uncle Charlie talked about involved the unknown. He wanted to escape to his room and cry, but even that privilege was denied him.

His mother sensed his floundering thoughts. She reached over and put a reassuring hand on his and his feeling of panic abated. He looked into her steady gray eyes, seeking advice. They said "Go." Hadn't he promised himself that he would never disappoint her? Without taking his eyes from hers he said, "It sounds wonderful. Thank you, Uncle Charlie."

Uncle Charlie slapped him on the shoulder. "Thata boy, Ham. That was a hard decision and you made it fast. We leave for Boston on the 7:45 tonight."

The Professor and his wife looked startled. "But, Charles," Fanny said, "that's too soon. He hasn't the right clothes for a place like Cambridge. I have to buy him all sorts of things."

"Nonsense." Uncle Charlie tugged impatiently at his mustache. "That's typical of a woman to think about clothes at a time like this. The lad only has two weeks to stuff himself full of knowledge before he faces those exams. I'll take him around to J. August's when we get to Cambridge and buy him what he needs. They know more about those things than anyone in Messina. I've got the railroad tickets in my pocket."

"You seem to have taken it pretty much for granted, Charles, that we would fall in with your plans."

"Come on, Os. Don't be so touchy. Had to make a quick decision. No time for a slow one. If you'd said no last night all I had to do was to cancel the goddam train reservation (excuse me, Fanny), and wire Harvard."

"Don't think we don't appreciate what you're doing, Charles," Fanny said quickly. "It's the most wonderful chance Allen ever had, only—well, it's all happened so suddenly."

"I don't know that I would have agreed to it as readily as I did," said Professor Martin, "if Harvard did not have such an outstanding group of men in its English Department; I'm afraid Messina couldn't quite live up to their standards."

And so it was decided.

Immediately after breakfast Allen hurried over to Millie's house. He caught her just as she was coming down the front steps.

"Allen, what's the trouble? You look as if something had been chasing you."

"Which way are you going?"

"Down to Siegle's to do a couple of errands."

"I'll walk down with you. I have to talk to you—quick."

He told her the story, looking straight ahead, avoiding her eyes. When he had finished they walked in silence. "Oh, Allen," she said finally. Her voice was almost a whisper. "Four years! You'll never come back."

"What do you mean I'll never come back?"

She shook her head.

"Do you think I shouldn't go?"

She stopped and turned to face him. "Allen, don't *say* such a thing. Of *course* you should go. It's the most wonderful chance you've ever had. You're going to be a great writer, Allen, and Harvard's the place to begin. When you told me, though, it was so—oh, I don't know—so much like an explosion—that it sort of knocked me off my feet. It's because I—because I'll miss you terribly. You'll write to me—won't you?"

"Of course I will."

"When did you say you were leaving?"

"On the 7:45 tonight. I've never slept on a train before. Will you come down to the station to see me off?"

She shook her head. "No. I don't like seeing people off. They never have anything to say to each other."

He looked puzzled. "Well, can I come and say good-by to you this afternoon?"

Again she shook her head. "No. We've really said everything now. I couldn't bear going all over it again. You know

I believe in you and you know I'll be thinking of you all the time. I'm going to say good-by to you now—right outside of Siegle's, and this is it."

To his embarrassment she leaned forward and kissed him, then she turned, passed through the swinging doors of the store, and disappeared.

He walked home through a black cloud of depression.

Holworthy Hall
Harvard University
Cambridge, Mass.
June 14, 1913

Dear Millie,

I haven't had a chance to write you before because I've been up to my neck cramming for these exams. Every morning I go over to the Widow Nolan's only he's not a widow at all. He's an old man, with a big walrus mustache, and he has spots on his vest and his office or schoolroom or whatever you call it is over a store on Massachusetts Avenue. The Harvard Yard is right across the street. He has every subject boiled down to what he calls syllabuses. Each syllabus is pasted to a big block of wood so as his students won't swipe them. Behind his desk is a coal fire which keeps going all year round no matter how hot it is which means it's pretty awful right now. He also has a Boston terrier which is so fat it can't walk much. It just lies in front of the fire all day and snores. Sometimes I feel like doing that too.

The Widow says I shouldn't have too much trouble with my exams. He thinks Messina High must be pretty good. I hope he's right. I think I can handle math and physics. They seem to come easy. English ought to be a cinch when you think of all the trouble Dad took to pound it into me. Latin and French I know I'll have to take again in the fall. I just don't understand those two languages. Never will.

Well, back to work. Best to your father and mother.

Allen

He passed his math and his physics exams and, to his great surprise, his Latin. He flunked French and also, of all things, English.

He never did remember that summer very clearly. Uncle Charlie came up twice from New York and they took long walks together, once going out to Walden Pond which he found rather disappointing. The rest was a jumble of hot classrooms, written papers, reading, reading, reading, and struggling to remember what he had read, long lists of words that must be memorized; hot, lonely evenings; confused meals at the Harvard Union surrounded by strange faces, faces which chatted with a glib familiarity which he couldn't achieve. At night the arc light on the street beyond his window shone through the gently moving leaves of a huge elm and formed changing light patterns on the ceiling.

Holworthy Hall, where he had been assigned a room, was old. He had no idea how old, but someone had told him of the famous men who had lived within its rose-brick walls. He thought of them, lying in bed in the very corner which he now occupied, watching the first gray light of morning filter through the small-paned windows, walking down the two worn steps outside the entrance door into the unchanging elm-shaded Yard.

They were shadowy beings which had passed this way and vanished. What was *he* doing here? He was no shadow, famous or otherwise. He thought of his little room in Messina, of the familiar smell of his home, of the gang and the crazy things they had done together. Those were the nights he suffered. A boy's homesickness can involve real suffering.

He flung himself at his work with redoubled energy after one of these spells of depression and, partly because of this, he passed his exams at the end of the summer.

Uncle Charlie wrote him a congratulatory letter enclosing

a round-trip ticket to Messina, instructions as to when he should return to Cambridge and what he should do when he got there, and a check for an amount ten times greater than he had ever possessed before.

As the train approached Messina he was conscious of a mounting excitement. He peered through the window at the fresh, early-morning landscape, watching for the first familiar object. There it was: a white farmhouse and a cluster of red barns standing in a grove of trees. He had driven there once with his father in a hired buggy. The purpose of the visit had long since been forgotten. He had sat in the buggy while his father transacted his business inside, the reins held firmly in one hand in spite of the fact that the horse was asleep. The other hand was busy supplying his insatiable appetite with crisp red apples. He could still recall their taste.

And there was Knobly Hill with the two great trees on the crest like a chieftain's feathers. He could just see them from the window of his bedroom at home and if you looked at them through the faulty pane in just the right way they became four trees.

The train was on the long downgrade now, coasting into Messina. He could feel the brakes beginning to slow it down. There was Pickets Pond where sleigh rides ended up and became skating parties. Over the rise were the big silos of Burke's farm. The landmarks came so fast that they merged into one familiar scene and as the train rounded the bend and he saw the oasis of Messina surrounded by rolling farm country he knew that he was home again.

He was suddenly shy and nervous, like a hospitalized

patient returning to the daily life of the normal world. Several traveling salesmen got off the train ahead of him, the mailsacks and a few packages were thrown from the baggage car onto a waiting handtruck, the conductor signaled to the engineer and swung himself aboard as the train moved slowly forward. Allen was alone on the platform.

Mr. Brophy, the station agent, came around the corner to get the handtruck. He squinted at Allen curiously for several seconds.

"Hello," he said finally. "Didn't recognize you in them fancy clothes. Been away, ain't you?"

Allen acknowledged that he had.

"Funeral or som'thin'?"

"No. I've been at Cambridge studying for exams."

"Cambridge? Where's that?"

"Right outside of Boston. You know—Harvard."

"Harvard!" exclaimed Mr. Brophy incredulously. "You aimin' to go *there?*"

Allen nodded.

"What do you want to go to a rah-rah-boy place like that for? What's the matter with Messina? Good enough for your dad, wasn't it?"

Allen felt trapped. Whatever he said was going to be wrong and Mr. Brophy would make it wronger in the re-telling. "I *was* going to Messina," he said after a moment's hesitation, "then Dad wanted me to go to Harvard."

Mr. Brophy removed his shapeless cap and scratched his head as if trying to massage this extraordinary statement into his brain.

"Well, I'll be damned," he said. "Yes, sir, no less. After the careful way he brought you up. Well, I guess it's none of my business. You got a bag? I just bought me one of those Ford machines to help me get the mail up to the post office and suchlike. If you'll wait a minute I'll ride you round to your house. I'll bet it'll give your mother a start to see you come back home ridin' in a thing like that."

It did indeed. Fanny had heard the train whistle and was sitting on the porch waiting for him. When the Model T Ford stopped in front of the house, so suddenly that its occupants were almost thrown against the windshield, she rose quickly. Like a telegram, such an unusual visit could only mean trouble. Then she recognized Allen and rushed down the steps. Her arms were around him and he found himself looking uncomfortably over her shoulder at Mr. Brophy, who was twirling his cap uncertainly.

"I best be gettin' along," he said to no one in particular, "before that goddam contraption of mine shakes itself to pieces."

His father was at the college, so Allen did not see him until he came home for lunch. "Well, my boy, you've done a good job I hear. Your uncle keeps me posted. How in the world did you happen to flunk English?"

"They asked me to compare or criticize books I hadn't read."

Professor Martin shook his head sadly. "That may be my fault, Horace, I led you off the beaten paths. What did they have you reading this summer?"

"Oh, Scott and Thackeray and Hardy. The old standbys. Then I had to take a course in contemporary novels—you know, *Graustark*, London's *Call of the Wild*, and that new writer, Willa Cather."

Professor Martin snorted. "Why do they want to fill your mind with that rubbish? When I was about your age—"

"Oswald, please. Your lunch will be cold if you begin running on about what you did when you were a boy. I'm sure you were wonderful, but so is my soufflé."

That afternoon he went to see Millie. She had just returned from Michigan, tanned and freckled by the summer
sun. He thought she had put on a little weight. In her
shadowed front hall she threw her arms around his neck in
the old way murmuring, "Allen, Allen." Then she released
him and held him at arm's length, searching his eyes with
hers. "I'm a little scared of you, Allen. You've been so many
places that I don't know anything about. You've met
so many people that will always be strangers to me. You
can't be the same Allen. You *must* have changed—but
how?"

Emotional scenes upset him. "Nonsense," he said. "Why
should I change?"

Tears came into her eyes. She buried her face on his coat.
"Oh, but you have," she said in a muffled voice. "I can feel
it and you've only been in the house a few minutes."

She straightened suddenly, pulled his handkerchief from
the breast pocket of his coat, and wiped her eyes.

"What a ninny I am. Forgive me, Allen. I was just so glad
to see you. Let's take a walk."

They walked along the hot elm-shaded streets with apparent aimlessness, but when they reached the entrance to
the Grove they turned in as if by prearrangement. It was all
as it had been on that day so long, long ago. They paused by
the brook.

"It all seems the same," she said. "It all is, I suppose. Yet
something's happened that makes old things different."

"How do you mean?"

"Oh, it's so hard to explain. You see I'm pretty stupid really
only it doesn't show when we're both in Messina and fooling
around with the old crowd. Everyone's equally stupid, if you
know what I mean. But you're never coming back to Messina, Allen. There's nothing for you here. You're different.

I'm afraid if we found ourselves together in a bigger world it would show."

He reached toward her clumsily, but she avoided him. "No, Allen, dear." She had never called him that before. "I want time to think. I'm going to get a job this winter. I'd go crazy doing nothing. Before I look around though I'm going out to Minneapolis for a couple of weeks to visit a girl I saw a lot of this summer."

"But I'll be gone before you get back," he said.

"I know it. It will give *you* time to think too. It's good exercise if you don't overdo it."

He had always taken Millie for granted. Now the import of what she was saying suddenly dawned on him. He was losing her. "I love you, Millie," he said. Now she was in his arms.

"And I love you, Allen, and you know it and you've always known it. That's the trouble. It doesn't mean we'd live happily ever after." She kissed him long and passionately, then pushed him gently away. "Come," she said. "We must go home. I promised Mom I would go with her to call on Aunt Lizzie this afternoon. She's all crippled up with something."

He left her at the end of her front walk. "Good-by, Allen dear." She glanced up and down the street, gave his cheek a hummingbird's peck, and ran up the walk toward the house. At the top of the veranda steps she turned and waved. "Don't forget to think," she said. Then she was gone.

Uncle Charlie had rented rooms for him in Randolph Hall, a students' dormitory on Mt. Auburn Street in the heart of what was generally known in those days as the "Gold Coast." Uncle Charlie had written him enclosing duplicate keys and apologizing for not having located him in Dunster where he had lived during his first three years in college.

I couldn't find a one-bedroom suite in Dunster. If you were coming from an Eastern prep school you would know plenty of boys and could have picked out a roommate. You come as a stranger, however, and it's much better for you to live alone until you can get your bearings. Don't be in too much of a hurry to make friends. Take things easy. The sheep and the goats will sort themselves out pretty quickly and you don't want to find yourself penned up with the goats.

I hope you are going to be comfortable. I've asked a friend of mine in Cambridge to buy the necessary furniture. You know: tables, chairs, linen, rugs, lamps, that sort of thing. Most of it will be secondhand so I am not as generous as you think.

You will need other things. I want you to let me know what they cost. Then I'll send you a check. You'll also need money for pocket cash, clothes, and God knows what all. I'm going to give you an allowance—$150 a month. My fear is not that you'll spend it unwisely but, brought up as you have been, you won't spend it at all. Remember you can't make an omelette —and all that sort of thing. Move around. Get to know people. They can be terribly important to you later. But this is some-- thing I'll talk to you about when I see you.

In the meanwhile work hard, play hard, keep your eyes open and your nose clean. I'll be up in a couple of weeks and we'll get quietly ossified.

Faithfully yours,
Uncle Charlie

As he opened the door with his own key and entered his new home he could scarcely believe he was in the right place. He had visualized himself as living in some sort of cubicle. This was no cubicle, but a kind of house—a house on one floor. He had never seen an apartment before and could only think in terms of houses. It had a living room with a real fireplace, a bedroom, and a white-tiled bathroom. There were several letters on the mantelpiece addressed to him. One was from Uncle Charlie, and one from his mother. Then it was true. This extraordinary place was his.

He opened his uncle's letter first. It contained a check and a brief note.

> Here is the first installment. Open an account with the Cambridge Trust Co. I don't know why they accept no-good accounts, but they do. Never draw out more than you have in the bank. That may be okay in England but it is frowned upon in this country.

He sat down in an ancient Morris chair and stared at the check. He couldn't remember ever having seen a check of this size before.

Then he read the letter from his mother. It must have been mailed before he left Messina in order to greet him on his arrival. He read and reread it, hoping to gain confidence from the affection that flowed from the familiar handwriting. The effect was quite the opposite, however. The letter merely emphasized the fact that he was alone—alone in a huge, complex organization, where everyone but him seemed to know what they were doing. Sinking back in the Morris chair he stared at the empty fireplace.

It was almost dark when he finished unpacking. No matter how slowly he moved or how often he rearranged his few possessions, the time came when he must face blankness. Where in the world was he going to eat? He decided to go out and buy a paper. This would give him a chance to look around a bit. Having selected a lunch counter on Massachusetts Avenue, he returned to his rooms and started to glance through the Boston *Globe*.

There was a knock on the door. What did a freshman do when someone knocked on his door? He had heard a great deal about hazing at Messina. Wise boys didn't go out on hazing night. If this was It, a casual "Come in" might sound fresh. The best thing to do was to open the door and face them.

Two men were standing in the hallway. He braced himself for the worst. One was a big fellow, not particularly good-looking, but with a jovial, kindly expression that belied his errand. His companion was a tall, thin young man, with a bony face somehow reminiscent of a well-bred horse. He was immaculately dressed and his hair, parted just off center, was combed back and plastered tightly against his skull.

"Are you Allen Martin?" asked the big man.

"Yes," said Allen, swallowing a "sir."

"My name's Sam Potter," said the stranger, extending a huge hand, "and this is my roommate, Swinky Grew." Allen shook hands gingerly, expecting to be yanked from the doorway into the hall. "Your uncle and my father roomed together at school. Your uncle wrote Dad and said you were coming in with the Class of '17 and would I look you up."

"Won't you come in?" said Allen. It sounded like some old lady in Messina, but it was the best he could do at the moment.

"No, thanks. We were just on our way over to Memorial to get something to eat. We thought if you had nothing better to do you might like to come with us."

"It's depressing," said Grew, "like eating in Grant's Tomb."

"Depressing or not, we have to eat."

"Sounds good to me." Allen tried to keep his voice from being overeager.

They walked up Linden Street toward the Harvard Yard. "That's Gas House," said Grew, indicating a brick Colonial building on the left. Allen glanced at it in bewilderment. Don't show your ignorance. Bluff. "Yes, I know," he said casually. Then his brain began to operate. Gas House was a *club*—Uncle Charlie's club! "My uncle was a member."

They looked at him with new interest. "Was he now?" said Grew. "I suppose that's where you'll be heading?" Keep still. Say nothing. Then they'll think you know something you can't tell. They crossed Massachusetts Avenue and entered the Yard.

"Where did you go to school?" It was a question Allen would learn to dread during the next few weeks.

"Messina High," he said.

There was a silence broken only by the sound of their footsteps on the hard surface of the path.

"Is that in the United States or Italy?" asked Grew finally.

"United States. Right in the middle of them." He had always taken Messina for granted; certainly he had never thought of it apologetically. Now he suddenly realized that to these two boys it sounded ridiculous; something to joke about like Podunk.

The clock in the tower of Memorial Hall struck seven. Three boys met them at an intersection of the path. They all seemed to know one another. Potter introduced Allen offhandedly. The group walked together toward Memorial kidding and laughing. They all had a casual, sardonic approach to everything which was almost studied and which reduced Allen to silent self-consciousness. What he wanted most in the world was to take a train back to Messina.

That night he met Roger Baker: tall, snub-nosed, with clear, confident brown eyes. He was very much one of the prep school crowd, but it didn't seem to envelop him like a cloak as it did so many of the others. Roger didn't think Messina was an odd-ball place in which to live, but seemed genuinely interested in the life of a small, Midwestern town. Allen found himself talking more and more freely to this young freshman who seemed equally at home on either side of the fence.

They walked back together after dinner. "Come on up to my place for a little while," suggested Roger. "It's in Dunster. Hell of a mess at the moment, but we might be able to dig up a couple of bottles of beer."

Dunster Hall looked like a palace to Allen. Roger's big living room was a mess as he had warned, dominated by a baby grand piano. He produced two bottles of beer from a small icebox in one of the closets and swept two armchairs free of magazines and books.

"You look like a football player," remarked Roger. "Did you play at high school?"

"Yes. My last two years."

"Whereabouts?"

"Halfback."

Roger looked him over appraisingly as if he were a horse. "Had a hunch you did. Why aren't you out for freshman football? They started three days ago, but it's not too late."

There it was again. Everyone seeming to know just what was going on except himself. "I didn't know about it. Anyway, I don't think I'm good enough."

"Leave that to Bob Sweeney. He's the coach. Can you be at the field at 2:30 tomorrow afternoon?"

"Sure. If you think it's worthwhile."

"I'll tell you what I'll do. You seem kind of strange around this place. Meet me here at half past one. I'll take you down and get you outfitted before things begin to pop. So much

for that. Tell me more about yourself." What other sports
did Allen like? What he was going to major in and what was
he going to do with his life aiter he graduated? Allen told
him about his father and mother; how they wanted him to
be a writer and how he planned to major in English with
that rather nebulous end in view.

Roger nodded approvingly. "Good," he said. "At least you
more or less know where you're going which is far more
than I do. The only thing I give a damn about is music and
the only thing I'd really like to be is a professional pianist,
but if you mention those things to Dad he goes off his trolley.
I don't know why it is but the more successful a fellow's
father is the more hopeless it is for his son to do what he
wants. If he won't go into his old man's business he's carefully protected from doing anything else."

"Is your father as successful as all that?"

"My old man! I'll say he is. Wait a second. I'll take you
through the family art gallery." He went into a bedroom and
returned with several photographs in silver frames. "Here's
Dad, lurking behind his mustachios. Looks as if he ate babies
for breakfast in that picture, doesn't he? That's probably the
way he wanted to look. Actually he's a little fellow. He tries
to make up for it by looking fierce. And this is Ma. I'll bet
she spent three days at the hairdresser's before that one was
taken. And this is Barbara. She's my young sister. At the
moment she was trying to look like Maud Adams or somebody. Rather a sentimental girl. A bit on the silly side. She
thinks she's a misunderstood intellectual. She's got brains
on the brain. Dad says brains are a very dangerous trait in
a woman. And these are the barracks we live in in Rock
Harbor during the summer." It was a photograph of an
enormous house, its lower floor encircled by a deep veranda.

Allen lay awake that night checking over his first day in a

new world; a world filled with people who were strange to him. They hid their emotions behind a curtain of flippancy and attempted to approach all subjects obliquely. Everyone appeared to have known everyone else from childhood. Money was a commodity which seemed to be taken for granted. Their manner of speaking, their dress, their approach to everyday happenings, were so alike that they might have been cast from the same mold.

Except for Roger's sister. There was something about her lovely, oval face that set her apart from the others. He spent at least five minutes pondering this phenomenon before he fell asleep.

To his surprise he didn't get thrown off the football squad on sight. Day after day he went to the field, aching and weary, only to hurl himself once more against tackling dummies and on top of rolling footballs. Gradually his flesh hardened so that the impact with the ground was no longer torture. His breath no longer came in short, stabbing gasps. The expenditure of energy became a sensuous joy. In later years as his body took on weight, his muscles softened and he spent much of his time fighting fatigue, he would recall these days with a trace of sadness and would find it difficult to recognize the Ham Martin of 1913.

He sat on the players' bench all fall, wrapped in a fleece-lined canvas coat, waiting in vain for the sign that would send him into action. It came during the last few minutes of the Yale game when he was put in just long enough to win his numerals.

To his surprise the coach beckoned to him as he was leaving the locker room after the game. "Look here, Martin.

Don't get discouraged because you've spent the fall sitting
on your ass. You're fast and you've got the makings of a
football player. You just need more beef. Work in the gym
this winter, play squash, anything, and then in the spring
go out for freshman crew or something like that until they
throw you the hell off. Exercise a lot, sleep a lot and good
luck."

Roger Baker was waiting for him outside the locker room.
"What in the world have you been doing? I'm nearly frozen.
I feel like getting drunk. Let's get hold of a few reprobates
and go in to the Lenox."

The idea of going someplace for the sole purpose of getting drunk was a new concept to Ham. In Messina to be
drunk was a disgrace and if "nice people" inadvertently took
"one too many" it was never mentioned publicly. Yet here
was Roger Baker, whom he admired, suggesting mass intoxi-
cation. He must be joking; exaggerating to be funny. The
thing to do was to fall in with Roger's mood; see what happened. "Sure," he said. "Get boiled as owls."

Roger slapped him on the back. "Thata boy," he said. "I
haven't had a drink since the night you came up to my flat
just after you arrived. I'll collect a few lowlifes and meet
you in front of the *Lampoon* building at eight. We'll pick
up a cab outside Dan's place."

It had never occurred to him that undergraduates would
hire a cab to go all the way into Boston when the trip could
be made by the trolley car for five cents. This was probably
why they called Mt. Auburn Street the Gold Coast. It was
probably what Uncle Charlie had done when he was here.
He might even have had such things in mind when he gave
him such a generous allowance. Best to swim with the tide.

Roger was with Carl Tinsdale, Swinky Grew, and a round-
faced lad with very red cheeks who spent a large part of

his time laughing. "This is Ben Parsons," said Roger. "He's a moron."

"That's why he looks so healthy," said Swinky Grew.

At the Lenox they all seemed to know their way around. "We'll stop at the bar," said Tinsdale. "I've reserved a table in the corner afterwards. The whole squad's going to be in here tonight shedding its physical fitness."

Ham was about to order a beer, then decided to wait and see what the others took. To his surprise they all ordered Scotch and soda. He did the same, and after the first drink it began to taste better and before he had finished the second all men were his friends. He was no longer the shy stranger from Messina, but Ham the beloved enlivener of parties.

He told stories, he kidded people whom he had never seen before. Eventually he found himself at a table where he tried to sing a song, but was booed down. For a brief period he felt ill. What a terrible thing it would be if he suddenly threw up. Drops of cold sweat began to appear on his forehead. Swinky Grew looked at him curiously.

"You look awful," he commented. "Are you going to park your cookies?"

Ham nodded miserably. "Come on outside and get a lungful of fresh air," said Swinky sympathetically. "This place is so full of smoke it would put a fireman under."

They walked up and down in front of the hotel. The sharp November air revived him and as he listened to Swinky's nonstop chatter it occurred to him that it was Swinky who was tight and that he was sober as a judge. "Come," he said, grasping Swinky's upper arm firmly. "You got to sit down somewhere an' cool off."

The evening became a jumble of disconnected impressions: deafening noise; tables covered with glasses and cigarette ashes; figures pushing restlessly between them; "Bar's closing in twenty minutes"; "Three apiece for everybody"; rows of highballs on a soaked tablecloth; someone standing on a chair trying to make a speech and the confused realization, as he fell off, that it was he; the musty smell of a cab; some kind of an altercation in Dan's lunchroom; and blankness.

His first sensation the following morning was one of pain so generalized that it took him some time to locate it. It concentrated in his head, which seemed to be splitting open. He tried to dive back into oblivion, but the pain was too great. His stomach felt as if a pair of millstones were grinding some kind of sour mash slowly inside him. His ears buzzed. The light hurt his eyes.

He groaned and buried his face in the pillow, partly to shut out the morning sun and partly to help him think back to the cause of this hideous situation. Yesterday afternoon he had played for a few brief moments in the freshman game against Yale. That was an anchoring point. He must cling to it. What happened afterward?

Roger Baker! That was it. Roger Baker, the big heiney, had met him after the game and suggested a party. They had ridden into town in a cab with several others. After that everything blurred into a haze of smoke and noise. He must go over and find Roger Baker. *He* would know what happened, or would he? What a way to start his freshman year. What would his father and mother think if they knew? What would Millie think? It was the first time he had thought of Millie in a long while.

Engulfed with remorse he forced himself out of bed, shaved, and took a cold shower. It made him feel a shade better but it was a faint shade. No one was stirring in Dunster Hall as he climbed the marble stairs to Roger Baker's suite. He found the latter curled up in bed, a sheet over his face. "Go away," he said as Ham entered. The sheet was pulled away and Roger gave him a hostile squint. "Go away," he repeated. "I thought you were dead. Or are you?" He ducked under the sheet again. After a few moments he pulled it away impatiently, swung his legs out of the bed and stared. "God, what a sight. A fine friend you turned out to be. Naïve little lad from Messina: nuts. Go find some elevating reading while I sway around in a shower. You eaten? Good. As soon as I get some clothes on we'll go out and try to force down some breakfast."

"Now we're going to walk," announced Roger, after they had wolfed a huge meal at Dan's lunchroom. "Walk till we wear our legs down to stumps. Let's go up the path along the river by the infirmary."

At the end of an hour Ham sat down on the grass, exhausted. "Holy cow, I'm a sick man. What do you think we're in training for anyway?"

"Nothing," said Roger, throwing himself down beside him. "I'm trying to get the blood flowing through your stagnant arteries. Let's talk about something more cheerful than circulation. For instance, what are you going to do with yourself for the rest of the year besides getting drunk?"

"Well, that's one thing I'm not going to do. I'm ashamed of myself about last night and it's not going to happen again."

"Nonsense." Roger lay on his back and stretched himself luxuriously. "Utter nonsense. Last night you went on a richly deserved binge. I wouldn't want to do it every night. Probably because I'm delicate. But binges have their place. Every once in a while a fellow's got to explode. The best way is to go on a binge. That's called the rhythm of life."

"Does everybody do that?"

"Listen, my country friend, I'm just as new here as you are except, perhaps, I went to prep school and learned a bit more about the birds and the bees than you did in Messina. You've had your nose either in a book or in the mud of Soldiers Field ever since you came here in September. You don't know your Harvard yet. It's a big place. All sorts of people, leading all sorts of lives. In the dorms on the other side of Memorial you're apt to find the boys who paid a high price to come to Harvard; no higher than us, dollar-wise, but a lot higher in terms of sacrifice. They're here to get their money's worth. The best place to get to know them is in classes or in the library. They're good Joes. Four years from now they'll walk off with the honors, but on the *other* side of the Yard they're known as the 'greasy grinds.'

"That happens to be the side you and I know—the Gold Coast. It's the center of intellectual distractions, just as the other side is the center of intellectual concentration. It's where the clubs are located and outfits like the *Crimson* and the *Lampoon* and the Pudding. It's where most of the under-graduate leadership comes from as well as the athletes, not because the guys who live there are any better. It's because they're not straining for honors. They belong to the 'Gentleman's C' group."

Ham watched a single shell row by against the current. "Perhaps I belong on the other side of Memorial."

"Nonsense. You want to write someday. Well, if you're going to be any good at that trade you have to live in the heart of things where you can watch what's going on. Writers need eyes more than honors. You've got to know them all, though; the greasy grinds, the athletes, the drunks, and the christers. I'm sure of that, but the rest of this writing business is a bit hazy to me. How the hell does one become a writer anyway?"

"I don't know. That's something I hope to find out here. Dad used to say that a writer becomes a writer by writing.

That's too simple though. I'm going to try for the *Crimson* and the *Advocate*. I don't even know how you try for them, but as soon as I can see straight again I'm going to snoop around and find out. I'm majoring in English. That ought to put me in touch with at least a few members of the faculty who would be willing to answer questions. I've got to feel it out I guess. Everything seems more complicated now that I'm here than it did back home."

Roger lit a cigarette, took a puff, and flicked it away. "Ugh, what a taste! Tell me about Messina. You've told me a little, I know, but what are your father and mother like? And this Uncle Charlie you mentioned. He sounded like a good egg."

He listened, chewing on a blade of grass, while Ham poured out the story of his home life and how Uncle Charlie had changed everything at the last minute by sending him to Harvard.

"What does Uncle Charlie think about this writing idea?"

"I don't know. He's never really gone into it."

Roger rolled over on his back and clasped his hands behind his head. "I don't want to discourage you," he said finally, "but I have a hunch he's going to be just as enthusiastic as my old man is about my becoming a pianist. As a matter of fact I have never run into any writers, but somehow you're not my idea of what they're like. You strike me more as what the after-dinner speakers call 'a man of action.' In addition, you've got a great way with people. Everyone on the squad liked you. And last night, although you probably don't remember it, you were a wow. I know what your father and mother want, but what do *you* want? Do you really want to be a writer?"

"I think I do. I've never really questioned it since my mother used to read to me before I learned to read myself.

I've been brought up with books. They're all we talked about at home. Father used to spend hours discussing books and authors and the English language in general when I was so young I only half understood what he was driving at. If ever anyone was trained in the background of a profession I've been—if you call writing a profession. It's in my blood I guess. Most of my family seem to have had inky fingers. I think it would kill Dad and Mother if I didn't carry on with the old torch."

"How I envy you," said Joe. "You know where you want to go and your family have always wanted it that way. If I only had the courage to stand up to my old man. Well, to hell with it. Let's start tottering home. I'm hungry again and it's after one o'clock. At least you've talked me out of a hangover."

Spring had thrown a mantle of delicate green over the trees in the Yard, a mantle of such gossamer texture that it could only be perceived at a distance and, like so many beautiful things, it tended to disappear if one approached it too closely. A divine restlessness flowed through the veins of students and faculty alike, urging them toward undefined and occasionally improbable horizons. The important projects of yesterday lost their significance and became old men's dreams in competition with a world renewing its youth. In spite of the warning sound of final exams, grumbling like early thunder just over the hills, it was a time for indolence and contemplation of the long free days ahead.

Ham and Roger sat on the window seat in the latter's living room watching the blue smoke from their cigarettes drift lazily through the half-opened window.

"What are you going to do this summer?" asked Roger.

"I don't know. Haven't thought much about it. Go back to Messina I guess. It's a terrible thing to say, I suppose, but I sort of dread it."

"What are your father and mother going to say when they see you smoking those things?"

"I've thought about *that* plenty. I don't want the old folks to have a stroke. I've fooled around with the idea of taking up a pipe. Dad smokes a pipe, but he connects cigarettes with lost souls."

Roger nodded. "I know. My old man's the same way. You can kill yourself on cigars. As long as they're expensive you're a sound fellow, but he'd never trust a man who smoked cigarettes. What in the world are you going to do in Messina?"

"Nothing. That's the trouble. Hot as the devil and nothing to do."

"Look here. How would you like to come down and stay with me in Rock Harbor? At least you can keep cool. God knows there's not much to do, but there are a few good-looking girls around. How about it?"

"I'd rather do it than anything I can think of, but I couldn't disappoint Dad and Mother. They're looking forward to having me with them."

"Okay. What about compromising? Come with me when college closes and stay till the first of August. Your family will be sick of you even if you hang around from the first of August until college opens."

Ham looked troubled. "It sounds swell," he said, "but the idea scares me to death—I mean Rock Harbor and all that sort of thing. I know you'd pull me through somehow or other and not let me make an ass of myself. Let me write to Dad. He might say yes."

"Good. Then it's settled. I don't know why I didn't think of it before."

The tables in the Hotel Touraine dining room were lit by shaded electric candles. Uncle Charlie was making one of his periodic dashes to Boston to keep in touch with Ham; up on the one o'clock from New York, back on the midnight. He seemed to have a bottomless well of vitality stored within him. Nothing tired him; no pressures seemed capable of dulling his enthusiasm. Now, after two martinis, they were attacking a thick steak. A bottle of wine stood in the cooler beside the table. Ham had just told of his invitation to visit Roger Baker.

"My boy, that's the best news I've heard in a long time," Uncle Charlie roared, wiping his mustache with gusto. "Splendid! Just what the doctor ordered! Minton Baker is one of the rich and influential men in New York." Ham's heart sank. "But that isn't the most important thing by any means. You'll meet all kinds of younger people who are going to do something in this world—just as you are. If you're going to be a *doer,* Ham, you must run with the doers. When does he want you?"

Ham told him. Uncle Charlie twirled the stem of his wine-glass reflectively. "There're two things we have to consider. One is clothes. Clothes are something you don't have to think about as long as you wear the right ones at the right time. People only notice men's clothes if they're wrong. Now, places such as you're going to have their own clothes customs. Silly damn things. No reason why you should know 'em but there they are. Could you get away for a day in the middle of the week and come to New York? I'd like to take you to Brooks Brothers and get you fitted out."

Ham said he probably could but . . . Uncle Charlie held up a restraining hand.

"No, no. This is just as much a part of your education as books and classes. Now, there's another thing we've got to think about. These young fellers that you are going to be hanging around with are pretty much outdoor kids. They learned games before they lost their diapers. What sports are you any good at besides football, which won't be of much use to you in Rock Harbor?"

"I've played quite a bit of basketball and I used to run the half mile, though I have never won anything and—let's see—I've played vacant-lot baseball since I was a kid and I used to hunt jack rabbits occasionally. I'm afraid that's about all."

"Good God!" roared Uncle Charlie agitatedly, gulping half a glass of wine. "Can you swim?"

"Oh, yes, sir. I didn't think of that as a sport."

"It's a good means of self-preservation though. Can you play tennis?"

"Not really. I've been thinking of taking it up around here this spring if they throw me off rowing."

"Splendid. Get hold of a pro, if there is one. Take some lessons. If there's no pro here, see if you can join some little tennis club in Cambridge. Ever played golf?"

"No, sir."

Uncle Charlie scratched his balding head. "Well, at least you know how to use your hands and feet pretty well. I'll tell you what we'll do. I belong to a pretty good country club around here. Don't know why. Never go there. Might as well get some use out of it. I'll write the pro tomorrow and tell him you're coming out to learn how to hold a stick. Give you some kind of a card. I'll tell him to make up a bag of clubs. You can pick it up there and he can fit you with some shoes and all that sort of junk. I'll write you all the details.

We'll make a country club athlete out of you if it kills us both."

"But Uncle Charlie . . ."

"No, no. Don't argue. I tell you this is part of your education."

"What I was going to say was I'd feel like a phony if I learned all those things and tried to make people think I'd done them all my life. I'm just a boy from Messina, son of an English professor in a little fresh-water college most people never heard of. I'm proud of it. Can't I just be myself?"

"Of course, of course, of course. Good God, if you tried to be anybody else you'd make a mess of it. Never try to be anybody but yourself. At times you'll find it's hard enough to be that. As you move around the world, though, you're going to meet all kinds of people. They'll have different habits than yours. You know, different idiotic ways of enjoying themselves. If you want to mingle with 'em you must do as they do. Don't expect 'em to do as you do. The 'give' is always up to you. Don't ask me why. I don't know.

"Rock Harbor is full of top-grade citizens. Most of 'em have been top-grade so long they don't have to advertise their bank accounts. They're conservatives, that's what they are; pleasant, quiet conservatives.

"Good crowd, Ham, good crowd. Glad you're going, but you've simply got to do things their way or they won't understand. Begin to see what I mean?"

Ham nodded. "Yes," he said. "I'm afraid I do and I wish I hadn't told Roger I'd go."

Roger's father had given him a Mercer. In later years Ham would remember it as one of the neatest little sport cars

ever produced in this country. Low slung, with two bucket
seats, its passengers practically sitting on the floor of the
car with the steering wheel resting almost straight up and
down in the driver's lap. It was topless. When it rained it
rained and that was that. And it had power; not the elastic
purring type of the high-speed motors that were to follow
later, but a deep thrusting power that imparted a sense of
strength and exhilaration to those who controlled it. Why
were good things like the Mercer always pushed aside by
newcomers which had neither their charm nor their efficiency?

It was a clear, warm day in June when they drove out
of the Harvard Square Garage and headed for Rock Harbor.
The baggage rack and the space between it and the gas
tank were piled high with strapped-down suitcases and
golf clubs.

There were no thruways in 1914, merely a chain of local
roads twisting and interlacing in pretzel-like confusion,
some good, most of them indifferent, and a few where they
had to bump along the ruts in second gear.

The sun was hot, the sky blue, and Ham was happy, but
it was a happiness against a background of uneasiness, the
happiness of a small boy who has played hooky to go to a
baseball game. His father and mother had been unquestion-
ably disappointed at the idea of not seeing their son until
August, but they had been unable to stand up against Uncle
Charlie's exuberant letter. They accepted the fact that Ham
should move out into the outside world rather than spend
his entire summer in Messina. They knew that Uncle Charlie
was right but it saddened them.

"Tell me more about Rock Harbor."

"Oh, it's just a small country village which has pretty well
lost its identity since the summer crowd took it over and

remodeled the old houses. We live a mile or two out, behind the dunes on Long Beach. Dad likes space, inside and out-side. He's not the type that thinks it's quaint to bang his brains out on low doors and sloping ceilings. There's not much to do there. Sailing's pretty good. I play the piano a lot."

"Is your house big?"

"That all depends on who you happen to be. Dad calls it a simple seashore place. From my point of view it's as simple as Madison Square Garden. You can judge for yourself." Ham began to wish that he'd gone directly back to Messina when college closed.

"Who'll be there?" he asked nervously.

"Just my sister Barbara and Dad and Mother. In a place with so many spare bedrooms there are bound to be a few strays passing through all the time. Sort of an overstuffed flophouse. Mother loves strays. Dad hates 'em. Barbara doesn't give a damn. That's what you call a balanced family. You'll see it in a minute or two. We're coming into the town now."

They rounded a corner and there it was, the white steeple of a church emerging from the green elmtops, its narrow main street lined on one side with automobiles. Sun-tanned men and women moved slowly along the brick sidewalks.

"We'll turn off here. This way's a bit longer, but the street down below is so jammed it would take a snake to get through."

White Colonial houses with small vivid flower gardens hiding behind picket fences, finally giving way to a rolling, bush-covered moor extending to a wall of grassy sand dunes, triangles of blue sea showing between their sloping shoulders.

Roger turned oceanward. On a rise of land behind the dunes looking seaward over their shaggy tops stood a two-

story white house so long that Ham thought at first that it
was a hotel.

"That's it," said Roger. "Our snug little nest on the dunes
where one leads a life of utter simplicity with the help of
about fifteen serfs."

They crunched to a gravelly halt at the foot of broad
steps leading up to a deep veranda. A man in black trousers
and a white coat came quickly down the steps.

"Glad to see you, Mr. Roger. Trust you had a pleasant
trip. Your father and mother hoped you might arrive in
time for lunch." He was removing baggage from the back
of the car as he talked.

"How are you, Harry? Can you put Mr. Martin in the
room next to mine? This is my friend, Ham Martin, by the
way."

"How do you do, sir," said Harry, continuing to unstrap.
Ham was about to shake hands, but decided to play safe.

"How do you do," he said, nodding awkwardly.

The front door opened and a thin little man with a scrawny
neck and a huge mustache appeared.

"My, my, my," said the little man, running his finger
around the sharp edges of his wing collar, "you must have
been held up by something. Your mother—you know—she
gets nervous."

"Dad, you always seem to forget that Boston is a long
way from Rock Harbor except for birds."

"Quite so, quite so. Only your mother— Paper. Did you
bring a paper?"

"No, sir. We didn't. Sorry."

"Good heavens. What's the matter with you young fellows?
Aren't you interested in *anything* but motors and girls, girls,
girls? By the way, who's this young man? Clearly he's going
to stay here. Why don't you introduce him?"

"Sorry, Pater. You haven't given me a chance. This is Allen Martin, commonly known as Ham. I wrote you about him."

"Quite. Quite. Glad to see you, Martin. Don't stand around that—that thing. Come in. Meet the rest of the family. Hurry. Your mother—" He turned on his heel and entered the house followed by Ham and Roger.

Ham had never seen a house like this. The enormously broad hallway ran from front to rear. Through the windows at the opposite end he could see the ocean sparkling under the afternoon sun.

"All right, all right," cried Mr. Baker, hopping slightly with impatience. "Don't stand staring at the ocean. It'll be there when you come back. Mrs. Baker's waiting. I'll lead the way."

Ham followed him through two large rooms which seemed to serve no particular purpose other than to contain furniture. "Watch yourself," warned Mr. Baker, hopping suddenly down three broad steps. "Dark in here. Plaguey veranda."

Ham found himself in a third enormous room which he thought at first was also unoccupied. Then, as his eyes became accustomed to the gloom, he saw a large woman reclining on a sofa in a dimly lighted corner, a book on her lap. A young girl who had been sitting at a piano rose as they entered and stood near the head of the sofa. They might have been posing for a mother and daughter daguerreotype.

"Edith, this is Mr.—Mr.—"

"Martin," said the large woman on the sofa.

"Quite. Quite. And this is our daughter, Barbara."

Mrs. Baker extended a cluster of limp fingers in Ham's direction. "We're delighted to have you with us, Mr. Martin. Roger has told us about you in his letters, and as Mr. Baker has indicated, this is our daughter, Barbara."

Ham allowed the fingers to fall after what he deemed to be a polite interval and turned to the girl. It was impossible to see her face clearly in the deep shadows of the room. He was conscious only of the fact that she was tall and dark haired, and that she had a firm handshake and beautiful eyes which seemed to be searching his face curiously.

"They've just taken away the tea things, but you might like some after that horrible ride. When we drive here from New York each spring it puts me to bed for two days—absolutely exhausted—if you know what I mean."

They both declined tea. Mrs. Baker seemed relieved. "Is this your first visit to Rock Harbor, Mr. Martin? I can't call you Mr. Martin, can I? What do you like to be called?"

"My name is Allen but all my friends call me Ham, and it *is* my first visit."

"I hope you're not going to be too bored. I think our young people have a good time but Rock Harbor's a very simple place. Now, if you're used to Newport. I warn you."

Roger interrupted. "Mother, Ham's an outlander. He comes from Messina."

"Oh, really. How colorful. You must tell me about it. Well, you boys will probably want to freshen up before dinner. We expected you for lunch, by the way. You young people are so undependable. We don't dress for dinner down here, Sam; just white flannels and a blue coat. We'll make up for the tea by giving you a glass of sherry or something before dinner, won't we, Minton?"

"Quite, quite. Ho, ho," said Mr. Baker in the startled tone of one whose thoughts had been gathering wool in distant places.

He saw her more clearly in the bright sunlight the following morning as they walked around the grounds inspecting the gardens and stables. She was tall—almost as tall as he was. She looked like Roger with her short nose and brown eyes, but there was an animation in her face that his did not have. It seemed to play across her features like sunshine across meadow grass. It was a face which constantly expressed a keen interest in life: the way she held her mouth slightly open when listening to someone; her habit of squinting her eyes when she talked; the little attention lines that gathered on her forehead when trying to understand.

"Do you want to walk on the beach? There's miles of it and the tide's low right now."

He did.

"Then put on some old trousers that you can roll up. We walk barefoot and sometimes you get a little wet. Meet you here in ten minutes. Bring a pair of sneakers to get you there."

He would never forget her as she reappeared. A little straw hat turned up in back and down in front was raked over one eye. Strands of her dark-brown hair had already been broken loose by the southwest breeze. A yellow sweater, a short khaki skirt, and a pair of battered sneakers completed her costume. "We're off," she said, starting briskly down a sandy lane without bothering to see if he was following.

They walked for a mile or more up the damp, firm sand. It was hard to talk against the competing sounds of the wind and surf. Finally she turned in through the loose, dry sand of the upper beach. Rounding the corner of a hummock they found themselves in a big dune-surrounded sand pocket. The wind was suddenly cut off and the sound of the breaking waves muted. They were alone in the semistillness of a sun-soaked bowl.

"Let's sit down with our backs against this old log," she said. "I couldn't hear what you were saying out there. It's worse than New York."

As he sat down beside her he panicked. They were so alone that they might have been in a moon crater. What did he have to say to this radiant creature from an unknown world? Think of something, say anything. He stared mutely at the sand between his bare feet.

"Roger tells me that you're going to write," she said. "I've never met a writer before! How do you go about it?" (That was the first question they all asked. It was embarrassing in view of the fact that he didn't know himself.) "Most of my friends get jobs when they graduate—usually through friends of their fathers. I'm sure you won't get a job as a writer through friends of your father. What *do* you do?"

"I haven't the slightest idea," he admitted.

She looked at him curiously. "How do you even know you can write?"

"I don't. But how can anyone know they can write until they try?"

"Haven't you ever tried?"

"Oh, sure. I guess I've been trying all my life without realizing it."

"Ever had anything published?"

"Just in school magazines—that sort of thing. The Harvard *Advocate* took a couple of my stories last year."

"I'd like to read them. It must be wonderful to see something in print that you've dreamed up out of nothing." She hesitated uncertainly. "I envy you so. You must have the urge to write or you wouldn't have been doing it, as you say, all your life! Don't let it go cold. Just keep blowing on it until it bursts into flame. Then you'll be able to lead whatever kind of life you choose instead of having it molded for you by outsiders."

"Has your life been molded?"

"I'll say it has. You can't escape it if you live in this kind of environment."

"What's wrong with this environment? It looks pretty good to me."

"Oh, Ham, you don't know. You haven't lived in it all your life. I'm not talking about just Rock Harbor in the summer. I'm griping about my year-round world. I hate it because it's a money-based world—a world in which financial success is the yardstick by which people are measured. I walk down a road that's fenced in on both sides by unwritten rules and taboos. Above all things, in a world like mine, you mustn't climb the fences. If people started to do that they could bring back disturbing ideas and that is something to be avoided like poison ivy. The result is everyone ends up doing and saying the same things over and over again. The emphasis is not so much on doing the right thing as it is on not doing or saying the *wrong* thing. Eventually it becomes a kind of tribal ritual. As a ritualist I guess I'm a washout."

"Not a washout exactly. A rebel. But what are you rebelling about? What kind of world would you *like* to live in?"

"Well, for one thing I'd like to live in a world where people aren't afraid of being individuals; a world where everyone says what he thinks; where ideas are at a premium even if they knock the established order into a cocked hat. A world where people dare to venture into strange areas and where stuffed shirts are exiled."

He raised himself on one elbow and looked at her curiously. "That all sounds so bitter. I just don't get it. You talk about a money-based environment as if it was something evil. What's wrong with money? I'll bet you'd be miserable if you didn't have any. And you seem to think that all businessmen are a lot of dummies and only intellectuals have any sense. That's just plain not so. I'll bet you'll find just as many idea men among the business crowd as you will among the intellectuals and just as many stuffs among the intellectuals as you will among the businessmen."

"Oh, I don't know, Ham. It's hard to explain to you because you're free. If you become a professional writer it will be your business to look at everything as if you were seeing it for the first time and to live every day as if it were your first day on earth. With me everything seems to have been decided generations ago. Nothing has two sides. It's there and that's that. I'm supposed to accept it, lock, stock and barrel. Tea dances, coming-out parties, dinner parties, bridge parties, house parties—parties, parties, parties! It's a cross between a rat race and an auction block and I'm sick of it."

She stretched out on the warm sand and rested her head on the log. "Good Lord," she said, "I've done nothing but rant about myself. How about you doing some of the talking? First of all you're going to be a writer."

"God help me if I'm not."

"What do you mean by that?"

"Because it would almost kill Father and Mother if I weren't. They've trained me for some kind of writing career ever since I learned to read. You talk about your world having been prearranged. Well, mine has been, too, I guess."

"But you don't seem to object."

"No. I suppose my father and mother did a better job of indoctrination than yours."

As he lost himself in his early background the words began to flow more freely. Eventually he came to the end and looked at her sheepishly. "Why in the world did you let me spend a beautiful morning on all that nonsense?"

"Because I wanted to hear it and it wasn't nonsense." She glanced at her wrist watch. "Gracious, look at the time. We must be going home or we'll be late for lunch. It always exhausts Mother for the whole afternoon if anyone is late for lunch."

He lay in his lower berth and listened to the sound of the wheels clacking over the rails, now slower, as they approached a curve or a town, now faster as they gained momentum on a downgrade. It was hard to believe that time, which last June had seemed to stretch into infinity, had slipped through his fingers, robbing the past weeks of their reality by eliminating his sense of their passage.

July had become a memory focused on a girl, a new type of girl who felt and talked differently than any he had ever met. Of course he was not in love. How could someone who didn't have a penny, or any idea where he was going to find one when he finished college, afford to love a girl brought up in the midst of affluence which he could never reproduce? No, he must be careful not to fall in love, but memories cost nothing.

He was unhappy and restless. It was as if a gay, sunny day had suddenly grown overcast. He was going back to Messina, to his home, his family. He loved his father and mother of course, but they had also become unreal. He seemed to be suspended between two dream worlds. The only reality was the clicking of the wheels beneath his berth.

He rolled over on his side and buried his face in the space between the two Pullman pillows. Barbara, Barbara, Barbara, sounded the wheels. Why did he have to fall in love with such a girl? But he wasn't in love and didn't intend to be. Why couldn't he have stuck to someone like Millie? Millie! What in the world was he going to do about her? He couldn't remember when he had written to her last. They didn't seem to have anything to say any more—anything in common. My Lord, women made life complicated.

The porter was shaking him gently. "We'll be in Messina in half an hour."

They were at the station to meet him; his father and mother, standing in front of a new Model T Ford, eagerly looking over the few sleepy-eyed passengers who were getting off. His mother saw him first. "There he is! Allen! Allen!" She ran toward him and threw her arms around his neck so violently that she almost knocked his suitcase out of his hand. "Oh, darling. I am *so* glad to see you."

Professor Martin was right behind her, his hand extended. "Horace, my boy, welcome home. Good heavens, we thought we were never going to see you again."

"Oh, Allen, you've changed so. You've become bigger and broader and—oh, I don't know—older somehow. But come. We've a big surprise for you. We've bought a car. Isn't it a beauty? Oswald, Allen can't see it if you stand right in front of it. But you must be starved. I've got a tremendous breakfast all ready for you. Everything you used to like. Get in. I have to crank it. Your father doesn't like to. He says he's afraid the crank handle will get caught in his beard if it backfires or whatever it does every so often."

Ham pushed her gently aside. "You get in, Mother. This is my job."

"But do you know how, Allen? It's very dangerous if you don't know just how to do it."

"I know how, Mother. I took a course in it at college."

She never stopped chattering on their way home from the station; news of his friends, of the college, changes in the town. Then as they approached the house she suddenly seemed to run out of news and was silent for a moment. "I hate to tell you, Allen," she said finally, "but Millie's gone away. She's gone to visit her aunt in Michigan, the way she always has in the summer, only this time she's going to stay later than usual. She won't be back

until long after you've returned to Harvard for that early
football practice or whatever it is. Your Uncle Charlie
wrote and said it was very important, so I suppose you
have to go, but it seems a shame for you two not to see
each other."

He knew that she was watching him and he mumbled
his disappointment. Inwardly he found himself torn between conflicting emotions. One was relief. He was released from a problem that he had not known how to
handle. Now it had handled itself by ceasing to exist. At
the same time he was conscious of a wave of depression.
Millie had done this deliberately—knowingly. The curtain
had come down on something fresh and tender; something
imbued with a springlike quality which he knew instinctively he would never experience again.

Was he crazy? Did he want both Millie and Barbara?
Millie belonged to an existence that had become part of
the past. The interests which had held them together
were dissolving. He felt confused, frustrated, relieved, and
unhappy. The world of Horace Allen Martin was growing
complex.

They were so anxious for him to enjoy his visit, so
fearful lest he be bored, that it amounted to an admission
on their part that there was almost nothing for him to
do in Messina. His old friends were all working. He would
meet them in the evening for a glass of beer at Logan's
Bar and he went to several parties. Everyone was glad
to see him, but he didn't have much to talk about, nor
did they. Their interest was in local happenings. They
knew nothing about his life away from Messina. In a vague
way they seemed to resent it. He hated to leave a group
knowing that he would be discussed and branded, by
some at least, as stuck-up.

After a while he wearied of the effort and either took long walks or stayed home and read, wondering, as he turned the pages, what Barbara might be doing at that particular moment.

His father was working on a book and hardly knew what was going on, but his mother saw all too clearly and realized the implications.

"Allen dear, wouldn't you like to ask a few of your friends over some evening? We could give them a little buffet supper and we could borrow a Gramophone so you could dance afterward."

He smiled at her troubled face and patted her hand. "Don't worry about me, Mother. I'm perfectly happy doing nothing. I want to store up every bit of energy I can before I go back."

"Why don't you talk more to your father?" she said. "I'm worried about him. He's aged in the last year—the way people often do—all of a sudden. That book he's writing seems to be taking a lot out of him. Every free moment during the college year he comes rushing home and shuts himself up in his study and all this summer he's been chained to his desk. Break in on him once in a while, Allen, and try to pull him out of himself. He thinks the sun rises and sets in you, dear, but he's so absorbed in that book that half the time I don't think he even knows you're here."

"Of course I will, Mother. I haven't dared to go near him because I didn't think he wanted to be interrupted. I'll go right now if you feel it's all right."

"Oh please do. He's been working all day and he must be exhausted."

A few minutes later Allen knocked timidly on the door of his father's study. There was no response. He opened the door quietly and peered in. The old man was sitting in his familiar high-backed chair, his head slumped forward on his chest, his beard spread out like a napkin over his vest.

Allen had a moment of panic as he looked at the silent figure. Then to his relief the hairs of the mustache were stirred by a deep snore ending in a snort. The eyes opened sleepily.

"Sorry to disturb you, sir, I was looking for something to read."

"Who's that? That you, Horace? Come in, my boy. Come in. Glad of an excuse to relax for a few moments. I was thinking. Often shut my eyes when I'm thinking. Old habit. Sit down. I've been so busy that I haven't had time for a good chat with you since you got home."

Ham sank into the old leather chair on the opposite side of the desk and watched his father fill a battered pipe.

"Mother tells me you're writing a book."

"Yes, Horace. It's my last one perhaps. At any rate I'm pouring in all the flotsam and jetsam of a long life."

"What is it about—or should I ask?"

"Of course you should, my boy. There's no secret about it. No secret at all. The University of Chicago Press wants it. They're going to publish it. We have no formal title picked out yet but I guess you might call it 'The Development and Decline of the Novel.' "

"It sounds interesting."

Professor Martin waved a deprecatory hand. "Just another scholarly book," he said, "that will never be read by anyone except a few other scholars. Even they won't *really* read it. They'll just skim it to make sure it doesn't contain any new ideas they might use."

He swung around in his chair and looked out at the sun

setting through the orderly row of maples along the curb.
"Scholars talking to scholars," he said, half to himself.
"Manufacturers of mummy dust." He turned back to Ham,
charged, from some mystic source, with a new vitality.

"That's why I've tried to train you all these years to
be a popular writer," he almost shouted, "a writer whose
works the commercial publishers will be eager to bring
out because they know the public will *buy* them; a writer
who knows the thrill of seeing his work reviewed in the
Book Section of the Sunday *New York Times*." He lowered his voice suddenly. "Those are the moments that
writers of scholarly books will never know."

"Father, how does one become a popular writer, as you
call it?"

Professor Martin looked at his son with a hurt expression
in his eyes. "By writing, Horace. I've told you that for
years."

"Yes, but it doesn't answer the question. It's too vague,
too idealistic. Writers have to eat and put a roof over their
heads while they're writing, besides which they have to
accumulate some experience. They can't pour water out
of an empty pitcher, as you yourself have told me."

Professor Martin looked frustrated. He was not used
to being forced to answer practical questions of this kind.
All his life he had lived in a comfortable rut, running
between his home and his classroom. At each end he was
protected from reality by a rampart of books and the
watchful ministrations of a loving wife. He thought he
lived in the world; unaware of the gentle conspiracy
which kept him out of it.

"Quite," he said. "Quite so. When you graduate from
Harvard I could easily get you an instructorship at Messina. This would bring you in a little money. Not much,

to be sure, but enough to keep you if you live at home. Your tutorial duties would not be onerous and you would have lots of time to 'fill your pitcher,' as you call it."

He beamed at Ham, pleased with himself for having solved a difficult problem so easily.

"But, Dad, I'd be moving into the very situation that you're objecting to in your own work. I'd be filling my pitcher at the well of scholarship instead of at the well of reality."

He wanted to kick himself as soon as he had said it. He had hurt his father. Professor Martin could say things like that, but *he* could not. The expression on his father's face told him that his instinct was sound.

"I don't know how to answer that, Horace. I've always said to you that, if you've the ability to write, nothing can stop you from being a writer except lack of ambition or diligence.

"Experience is something else. I like to think that a cross section of Messina College contains the same elements of real life as a cross section of Harvard or Oxford. Perhaps that is because if I didn't feel that way, my life's work would have been to some degree wasted. Perhaps Harvard might give you a more broadening experience. Perhaps, as you indicate, you should avoid scholarship entirely and work on a newspaper, let us say, for a couple of years. We have a pretty good little paper right here in Messina as you should know, you used to help distribute it. You could live at home and sometimes I might even be able to help you with your writing."

His voice was almost pleading. Ham was aware that he was the unwitting cause of a deep emotional disturbance within this man whom he had worshiped all his life as the fountainhead of wisdom and the possessor of a strength beyond that of ordinary men. He couldn't bear to watch the transition that was taking place across the desk or the thought that he was responsible for it. He wanted to leave, but knew that he couldn't until he had brought the conversation to some rational conclusion.

"Well, Dad, we don't have to decide everything today. I have three more years to think—and advise with you," he added quickly. Professor Martin looked pleased. "And in the meantime I'm not wasting my time just playing football." He told his father of his efforts to make the editorial boards of the *Crimson* and the *Advocate*.

Professor Martin began to rub his hands together; a sure sign of pleasure. "Splendid. Splendid," he cried. "You're following the first rule of writing. Putting words on paper. What I've always advised. Send me some of your work whether it's published or not. I might be able to make an occasional suggestion. I've picked up considerable experience myself in this little backwater seat of learning."

Ham was on his feet. He wanted to terminate this conversation on an upbeat. "I'll do that, Dad, and I appreciate your advice. This talk has helped me a lot."

Professor Martin had come round his desk and was showing Ham out as if he was a visitor. "Any time, my boy. Any time at all. I don't want to intrude too much. You must learn to stand on your own feet, you know. But the door is always open."

III

HAM RETURNED TO CAMBRIDGE KNOWING
that a chapter in his life was over. Messina, the house on
Maple Street, his father and mother were all there, but it
was as if a great crack had appeared in the earth separating
him from them. He could see them, hear them, but he could
no longer reach them. Henceforth he was on his own. Whatever decisions must be made would be his. The idea dismayed and at the same time exhilarated him.

As he looked back on it now, he was about to enter one of
the most successful and satisfying years of his life. He made
the varsity squad, which aroused him to such a pitch of
derring-do that he permitted a Holy Cross halfback to break

97

two of his ribs, after which he spent the remainder of the season shivering under a blanket on the sidelines. He was accepted by the editorial boards of the *Crimson* and the *Advocate.* And then one night there was a knock on his door and Joe Thatcher, star end on the football team, entered accompanied by two men whom he did not know.

Joe was not one to beat around the bush. "We want you to come to Gas," he said.

Ham hesitated. He wanted Gas more than any other club because it had been Uncle Charlie's. On the other hand, Uncle Charlie was undoubtedly the reason these men were here. He would have liked to make a club on his own instead of riding in on Uncle Charlie's coattails.

There was a brief silence. Thatcher and his companions exchanged glances. "You'll probably be asked to join other clubs," said Thatcher. "Perhaps you already have been, but we're asking you early just as we're asking your friend Roger Baker—because if you and Baker want to come we want you to put your heads together and suggest a few of your 1917 friends that you think would make a congenial group."

"I warn you we probably won't take any of them," said one of the two men who had thus far remained silent.

Ham tried to keep the tension out of his voice. "Have you asked Roger Baker?"

"No. We're going to talk to him when we leave you."

"And don't bother to telephone him we're coming," said the third man.

Ham pushed around a paper cutter on the table. "Don't think I'm unappreciative. I never was more flattered or more pleased and all that sort of thing, but would you wash your hands of me if I said I wanted to think about this for a few hours. Would it be all right if I let you know the first thing tomorrow morning?"

Thatcher grinned. "Sure. I know. I'll tell Baker to get hold of you as soon as we're through softening him up."

They hadn't been gone ten minutes before the phone rang. "Ham, old boy, old boy, old boy." It was Uncle Charlie at the top of his bellow.

"Good evening, Uncle Charlie."

"I'm at the Gas. Thatcher been around?"

"He just left."

"Then you're good as in. What'd you say to him?"

"I told him I'd let him know tomorrow morning."

"You *what*?" Ham could almost feel the diaphragm of the receiver bend inward under the impact of Uncle Charlie's roar. "What's matter with you? Crazy?"

"No, Uncle Charlie. I want Gas, but they've gone to ask Roger Baker if he'll come along." He explained Thatcher's proposal. "I thought I ought to talk to Roger before I said yes."

"If he doesn't take it I'll ring his father's neck. The old bastard was so stupid he never even got *into* Harvard. Prob'le reason he made so much dough. Can't make dough like that if you got too many brains. When you going to talk to that fathead Baker?"

"He's going to call me when Thatcher leaves."

"Okay. You call me here. Club. Understand? An' you talk sense or I'll cut you off without a penny."

"All right, Uncle Charlie. Don't worry."

"What d'you mean 'don't worry'? You're the one t'do the worryin'." He heard the phone slam into its hook and relaxed to wait for Roger.

On the following morning he awoke with a sense of well-being so strong that it took him several minutes to trace the source. As things came into focus he realized what the last two months had brought him. Roger was going along.

He had told Uncle Charlie. Nothing left to do but call Thatcher. All in all he was not doing badly for a boy from Messina.

Keep your balance; don't go overboard. There will be some dirty break waiting for you up ahead, sure as shooting. He took a shower, dressed with studied casualness, and went down to Jimmy's Hole-in-the-Wall for breakfast. It was midafternoon when he returned to his room. His mail had been laid on the floor outside his door. Among the bills and notices was a letter addressed in Millie's childlike scrawl.

He turned on the light beside his Morris chair and stared curiously at the envelope. Did it contain something that was about to disturb the placid waters of his life? Frowning slightly he ripped it open.

Dear Allen,

This letter is just to set things straight. When you left Messina, almost a year and a half ago, I loved you. I like to think you loved me just a little bit and that, way back in a corner of our childish brains, we thought that someday we might get married. [Oh, oh! Here it comes.]

What I don't believe either of us realized was that when you went to Harvard you moved into a different world—a world where I could not follow you. It worried me terribly at first and then I realized, Allen dear, that I really didn't want to follow you.

I am a Messina girl, quite happy living the life of a stupid Indiana town. I would be desperately unhappy trying to live on a bigger stage.

With you, Allen dear, it is quite different. You are going to write. Through your writing you are going to become famous. The outside world will claim you and you will fit into it whereas I would be just a miserable hanger-on.

You know all this. I am not telling you anything new, but I wanted to put it down on paper so there could be no misunderstanding and we could be friends. Last summer I ran away until I was sure you had gone. I am tired of playing cops and robbers with you. We are too old for such nonsense.

And so, Allen dear, the strings are untied, if there ever were any. We are both free—as free as we were that day when I asked you to come to my birthday party—and you didn't.

I won't say "good bye." Let's never say that. And I won't say "sincerely" because I reserve the right to set aside a tiny corner of my heart which will always belong to you.

Your Messina friend,
Millie

P.S. no. 1. Please, please, *please* don't answer this letter. I have said everything there is to say. An answer would be a flat tire and besides you are a writer and I really don't want an example of your Famous Last Words.

P.S. no. 2. We have given one another various little things in the past. For pity sake don't let's start sending them back to each other now. I *want* what you gave me. I hope you feel the same about what I gave you.

P.S. no. 3. I have absolute confidence in you—always have had —always will. Don't let anything sidetrack you. My proudest moments in the future will be when I am reading the books that you write.

He read the letter twice, replaced it in its envelope, and laid it on the table. She sure had stirred things up all right. And in some subtle way she had made him feel that it was he who had spoiled the broth. What broth? Why did women always have to be so dramatic? Why couldn't they let things just peter out? Well, at least he didn't have to answer. That had been rather understanding of her.

He wished that everyone wouldn't keep pounding so constantly on the subject of his being a writer. Damn it all, he'd said he was going to be. They acted as if they didn't believe him and kept dangling the carrot of fame in front of his nose to spur him on.

He found himself pacing nervously up and down the room. Eventually he stopped before the table and placed Millie's letter in the back of the drawer. Another tie with his old life cut. He had a restless desire to walk. It was almost dark. The lights from the street lamps were softened by a curtain of drizzling rain. He left Randolph and turned aimlessly up Mt. Auburn Street.

July, 1915. The tempo of the European war grew fiercer each month as the stream of men and matériel, endlessly flowing to the western front, steadily expanded. The casualty lists became so enormous that they lost their meaning. One could react to an explosion in a Jersey munitions factory which killed a hundred men, but an attack which pushed the enemy back a half mile at the cost of ten thousand lives was so incredible that human emotions failed to respond.

In their sand bowl among the dunes Barbara and Ham ate their sandwiches and drank iced tea out of thermos-bottle tops, their backs supported by the warm sands of a dune in which they had hollowed out little niches. Later they wriggled down to more level ground and stretched out side by side on beach towels, watching the clouds emerge over the crest of the dune and move slowly inland.

"They come, and they come, and they come, on and on," she said. "One behind the other—without end. That is what is happening in Belgium and France today. It's horrible, ghastly, but do you know—and I wouldn't dare say this to anyone but you—instead of being frozen into a sort of permanent despair, I feel suddenly alive—excited. I hate to admit it but it's almost a strange kind of elation. Oh, I know it's all wrong, but it's the *truth*. And do you know what I think the reason is? A war as savage and as big as this blasts everyone out of his rut. To the man not yet in the service war means that, in one way or another, he will soon be released from his boring job in some delicatessen store, or furnace room, or accounting office. He won't have to sit and look at his dull wife all evening. Maybe she feels the same way. He doesn't think of the filth and the hardship and the inane cruelty that lie ahead of him. At the moment the war is a release from intolerable boredom. I suppose if it were not for this sort of reaction it would be impossible to start wars. The nabobs could declare them, but the little people would just laugh and go on working."

This was a new girl talking; a girl of whom he was just a bit afraid. "But *you* don't have to go to furnace rooms and accounting offices. Why should you feel so elated?"

She turned over, rested her cheek on her tanned arms, and looked at him in surprise. "That's the stupidest remark I ever heard—after all I've told you about myself. You know I'm bored; not with you—you must know that too. I'm bored to the screaming point with a life devoted to a nonstop, deliberate wasting of time with the 'Right People.' "

"I sometimes wonder why your family give me houseroom," he said, burying a piece of clamshell in the sand with his finger. "I'm not a 'Right Person.' "

"Well, you're a little different. First of all you're a friend of Roger's and then you joined one of the right clubs and you have a rich uncle. On top of all that you haven't asked me to marry you and for God's sake don't spoil this beautiful afternoon by doing it now just to be polite."

At that moment he knew, somewhat to his dismay, that it was just what he wanted to do and he also realized how hopelessly remote she was. He had no background of the kind that meant anything in this sort of group; no money, and worst of all, perhaps, was his declared intention of earning his living by some form of writing. The last would be enough to put him out of the running. Writers, artists, and actors were conversation pieces in Barbara's world. He had already discovered that. Their books were read and discussed lightly, their pictures were purchased for huge prices, people flocked to see their plays. To allow any of them to enter its inner sanctums, however, was another matter. There were exceptions, of course, but they were few.

"Have you gone to sleep?" she asked.

"No, I was thinking."

"Just a shade of difference sometimes." She resumed her position on her back and put on a pair of dark glasses. "I wish I was *graduating* from Smith instead of finishing my freshman year. I'd head for a nursing school so quick you couldn't see me for dust. I want to get into this show and I want to get into it over in France. It wouldn't surprise me if our country eventually becomes involved and I want to be over there when that happens."

They walked back along the beach, the late-afternoon sun shining in their eyes. She slipped her left hand into his with a quick, shy motion. "Thank God for you," she said. "You're not stuffy and when you get out of Harvard you're going to do something on your own—something different."

He stopped and tried to take her in his arms, but she sidestepped and hurried on. "Come on," she said. "I want to get home for tea. Father'll be there and he'll have all the news."

"If I were a 'Right Person' I'd ask you to marry me," he said.

"If you were a 'Right Person' I'd say no."

June, 1917, was on him before he realized it. Life had been a race, for the class of 1917, as to whether it would graduate before the United States became involved in the war. For Ham the day-to-day demands upon his time had gradually pushed aside all outside happenings and eventually had eliminated time itself.

During those crowded days of a Cambridge spring, Congress declared a state of war on Germany. It was none too soon. The Allies were fighting desperately, their ranks were growing thin and their supplies scarcer. In the month of April alone 881,000 tons of Allied shipping had been sunk. The French offensives in the Aisne and Champagne had failed. The British offensive in Flanders had won but little ground at the cost of enormous casualties and Russia was about to suffer a defeat which would lead to a separate peace. It all seemed remote as the elms of the Harvard Yard took on their first cloak of yellow green and Graduation Day suddenly appeared just around the corner.

Ham's mother came east to see him get his diploma. Professor Martin was not up to the trip. Uncle Charlie was there, seated beside his sister-in-law. Ham could see them from where he sat with his black-gowned classmates. Fanny looked older, more fragile. Perhaps it was because he was seeing her with the eyes of one who was no longer in day-to-day contact. Uncle Charlie's face was redder than usual. He regarded the ceremonies with the fishy stare of one whose sole interest was in their termination and he was obviously not paying the slightest attention to what was being said.

Ham heard the mellifluous voice of President Lowell, but the words that he was speaking conveyed no meaning to him either. The only important thing was that this day marked the end of another chapter. Life seemed to be a series of chapters. There was the happy, carefree opener which had ended when he entered high school. This would always be his favorite. The second closed when he climbed aboard the train bound for the Harvard Summer School. Now the academic gates were about to swing open and he would find himself standing once more in unknown country.

The chapter which lay ahead was different from the others. In spite of his feeling during the past few years that he stood alone, he realized now that he had been living in a guided world, one in which definite goals were prescribed for him, each to be achieved at stated times; a world of bells, announcements, and rules.

In the new world which he was entering there were also rules, but they were not printed and pinned up on a board. You had to discover them by trial and error and then you were at liberty to obey them or not as you chose. It was well to remember, however, that if you chose to disregard them you were dropped quietly over the wall into an uncharted country in which you made your own paths. You made them in whatever direction appealed to you and no one cared where they led except in the rare cases where they came out in some Shangri-La. In such an event you were immediately hauled back over the wall, feasted and anointed while everyone tried to give the impression that he had contributed in one way or another to your success.

Perhaps that was what was meant by freedom.

Eventually the gates opened. His mother returned to Messina on the first available train in order to care for the ailing Professor, who was much more real to her than her successful son who seemed to move so easily through surroundings which left her utterly confused. Ham sat with Uncle Charlie on the brick-enclosed patio behind the club, sipping a mint julep.

"First of all," Uncle Charlie was saying, "you have nothing to write about. You're going to compete with the pros and you'll find it a damn sight tougher than it was on the *Advocate* or the *Crimson*. You think you're God's most finished product. In the eyes of the world you aren't dry behind the ears."

Ham flushed, but said nothing. "In the second place," continued Uncle Charlie, "we're at war. It's not a question of writing. It's a question of fighting. Now, my theory is, if you've got to go through hell, do it in the most comfortable way. That means becoming an officer and that means going to Officers' Training Camp at Plattsburg."

"But, Uncle Charlie—"

"Don't interrupt. I know a lot of these military blokes and I've been checking around a bit. You can get in the group starting August first. As a matter of fact I've made all the arrangements. It's fixed. Done. Bango! You'll get complete instructions during the next week or so. Let's have another of these damned things. They don't know how to make 'em here, but at least they're wet."

The patio was suddenly invaded by undergraduates. Uncle Charlie made a noise like a seal coming up for air. "No privacy anywhere," he exclaimed with loud disgust. "Let's go upstairs to the library. I feel like talking. Nobody ever uses the libary unless they want a quiet place to pass out."

Ham followed him up the red-carpeted stairs. "Now let's see. Where were we?" bellowed Uncle Charlie, lighting a fresh cigar. "Oh, yes, the war. You've got about five weeks before you leave for Plattsburg. You'll want to go out to see your family. Then you'd better come back to New York so I can get you outfitted. It's going to take a little time. Everybody wants their equipment yesterday. You'll live with me of course. Give me a chance to show you around a bit."

Ham noted the glitter of anticipation in Uncle Charlie's eyes. He realized that his war might start ahead of schedule.

The white-coated steward brought in fresh juleps. Uncle

Charlie took a long drink and placed his glass on the window sill. "They never get them frosty enough," he complained.

In those distant days on the east side of the Plaza Hotel there was an open-air restaurant where one could dine during spring and summer evenings looking out over the fountain and the last of the functional hansom cabs as they moved slowly up and down Fifth Avenue.

It was a pleasant corner of the world, uncongested and relaxed. As the twilight faded into the darkness the widely separated tables on the recessed porch became islands of light. Barbara and Ham sat near the outside parapet. He had never seen her look more beautiful. As he listened to her deep, throaty voice and watched the play of the candlelight on her face, he realized how essential this girl had become to him. When she was with him everything seemed simple and possible. His surroundings took on color and vitality just as the monotonous gray-green tones of a seaside marsh spring alive as the sun escapes from the shield of a passing cloud.

The tragedy was that although they seemed to have been moving steadily closer during the past three years the movement was an illusion. She still lived in a different world and was as unattainable today as she had been the first time he met her. This is the way things would always be.

She was a romanticist and he realized that the idea of marrying a poor young writer might have appealed to her, largely because, having always been surrounded with money, she had no concept of the part it played in her life. He would never put her in a position where she was forced to find out when it was too late. What was more, he didn't propose to be a vassal of old Mr. Baker or of Uncle Charlie or, for that matter, of anyone else. He was going to work out this problem himself which meant without Barbara—for the time being at least—which in turn meant when it was too late.

He suddenly became tongue-tied. The words which had poured forth so eagerly a few moments before now sounded forced and clumsy. She noted the change, looked at him questioningly, and his obvious embarrassment became contagious.

"I can't bear the thought of your going," she said for the tenth time. "If I ever graduate from nursing school perhaps I can get over myself." They watched the traffic on Fifth Avenue until the silence became unbearable.

Suddenly she reached across the table and stroked the back of his hand. "Ham dear, why don't you ask me to marry you? It would be so much more chivalrous of you than to leave the job to me. Please, Ham. Ask me to marry you."

He looked at her, astonished. "I can't," he said. "Don't you see, I can't."

"But why? We love each other. I'm sure of that and I thought when two people loved each other they were married and lived happily ever after."

"I can't," he repeated almost roughly. "In spite of the fun we've had together I don't belong in your setting and you wouldn't belong in mine."

She threw back her head and laughed. "How noble! Do I have to tell you all over again, Sir Galahad, that what you call 'my setting' is just exactly the setting that I don't want? And just why wouldn't I belong in yours? Just what *is* yours, by the way? I love you. We love each other. That's all that counts.

"Let's get away from this stupid talk about settings. I want to live my life with you, surrounded, I hope, by intelligent, creative people who have ideas about more interesting subjects than making money.

"The only thing that bothered me at first—and I'll admit it, darling—was that I might be using you as an escape hatch. You had everything I wanted: charm—yes, dear, charm—intelligence, modesty, but above all the creative urge.

"You could lead me into the world I want. It would have been so easy to *think* I loved you—so very, very easy. That was the one thing I had to be sure of for *your* sake. There was no room for mistakes based on wishful thinking.

"One morning I woke up and I was sure. I will never forget the sheer delight of that moment. I reached out to hug you; to share my happiness with you, but you were not there. After that all I had to worry about was whether you loved me enough to marry me."

"You *knew* that or else you were very dense," he said. "I've loved you since the morning you took me for our first walk on the beach. You *must* have known it.

"I love you, darling. It's as simple as that. But what right have I to marry you—or anyone else? I'd be dead broke if it weren't for Uncle Charlie. He's given me a wonderful start, but when this damn war is over I'm on my own and what have I got to offer? Writing? I don't even know where to begin. Besides all this, anything can happen in a war. Quite a prospect. I can just see your father's face if we walked up to him hand in hand and asked for his blessing."

"He'd probably have apoplexy, but don't let's forget, Ham, that we're talking about *our* lives and no one else's."

"That's what worries me," he said. "It's *our* lives I'm thinking about. Wealth isn't what's bothering me. I'm just concerned with plain living-money. I grew up in a family which had very little of it and yet it was a happy atmosphere. But we lived in a simple little town. *No* one was rich. There were no dinner parties, no social life of the kind you are used to. Each family was a self-contained unit. We seldom came together except at public shindigs which didn't cost anything, or at church.

"What I'm trying to say is that wealth is relative. In Messina we had enough. You couldn't stand a town like that, though, any more than Mother could take New York."

She opened her mouth to interrupt, but he held up his hand. "I know what you want, but the sort of atmosphere we're both talking about can only be found in the big cities and there the contrast between rich and poor is much sharper than in towns like Messina."

"Ham, I don't think you have the slightest idea how I feel about . . ."

"Perhaps not, but perhaps I know more about the facts of life than you do. Let's think where we'd be forced to live. You couldn't swallow the phony intellectualism of Greenwich Village. Neither could I. All right. Let's move uptown. Now we have a choice between expensive apartments and tenements. You don't want to live in a tenement any more than I do, but it's academic because at the moment I couldn't even afford that.

"Let's face it. You're in love with a subsidized pauper and I'm damned if I'm going to marry you or anyone else on such a basis."

"Well, if I'm going to get turned down you've given me some small comfort."

"What is that?"

"That little phrase 'or anyone else.' "

"Listen, dear, I want you more than I've ever wanted anyone, but I don't think you'd respect me if I married you knowing that your father or Uncle Charlie was going to support us. 'Hoping' might be a better word than 'knowing.' "

"But what are we going to *do*?" she asked miserably.

"Work," he said. "While the war is on I'm going to make notes and try to do a few things on the spot. Then, if I ever get back, I'm going to try to get a job on some magazine or newspaper—just to keep me in soup and hot dogs—and write, write, write on the side. I might have a go at a war book. I have an idea I'd like to try out. If it succeeded—but what's the use in planning so far ahead?"

"Oh, Ham, it all sounds wonderful if it were not so hopelessly distant. I'll be your literary agent—for free. We'll rent one of those charming little doll houses on East End Avenue looking out over Carl Schurz Park."

"With what?"

"With the royalties from your book. There is a whole row of those little red houses between 86th and 87th streets. You'll have a room on the top floor where you'll write all morning while I shop for bargains in the food stores. In the afternoons there are all kinds of exciting things to do for free. I'll learn to cook so that we can ask writers and artists and that sort of people for a beer and macaroni supper and we can sit on the floor and talk our heads off. I'll learn to sew too and make my own clothes. I'll make yours if you want me to. Wouldn't you like me to make you a nice suit, dear? And I'll take a course in stenography—"

"Right now let's take one of those hansom cabs and go for a ride in the park," he said. "I'm so full of happiness that I haven't room for any more food, or time for any more common sense."

"Pay the check," she said, "and hurry."

On the following evening he dined with Uncle Charlie. As they sat together before dinner in the warm, subdued light of the library the war would have seemed remote had it not been for the red-faced man opposite who seldom seemed able to put it out of his mind.

"We're going to be in this show much deeper and much

longer than anyone realizes." Uncle Charlie's hand shook as he poured himself a second martini from the glass stirring-pitcher on the table beside his chair. "The Allies have been bled white. As a matter of self-interest as well as sentiment we can't let 'em down.

"We're going to be in deeper eventually than any of 'em. You wait and see. We have the money, the manufacturing ability, the manpower, and we're too far away to have our factories blown up. We have to get in this thing all the way up to our backsides. We're the only ones who can finish it."

Uncle Charlie's mustache was beginning to bristle as it always did when he became belligerent. It occurred to Ham that the men who were the most enthusiastic about war were those who had passed the age of participation.

"Now you go out to Messina and see your ma and pa, but don't let them hold you too long. You and I have business to do and then you better figure on paying a little attention to Barbara. She's panting for it. Take it from me. Look here. Why don't you marry her, boy? Right now. That's a sound idea. Everyone is goin' to start crowdin' to the altar rail any minute now. Beat 'em to it before the supply of padres runs out. How about it?"

"I'm not going to marry until I'm earning enough to support my wife."

Uncle Charlie groaned. "Don't be an ass, Ham. You don't have to accept anything from that old dodo Baker. I'm your uncle. I'm family. Families are supposed to take care of one another and you're not going to need taking care of for long or I miss my guess. Marry her, boy, before she marries some pipsqueak on the rebound."

Ham shook his head. "I'm sorry," he said, "but I couldn't do it. I've been trained to be a writer and that's what I am going to do, or try to do, at any rate. That's a dandy time to take on a wife."

"Any time is a good time to take on a wife," said Uncle Charlie, "but I'm not going to argue with you. Go to Messina and think, and if you can't work things out, the patter of bullets on your tin hat may eventually stimulate your common sense. Come on, let's go in and eat. We're having a porterhouse and it's no good if it's not rare."

He didn't spend much time in Messina. Most of his old cronies were married and had jobs or they had left the old town in search of greener pastures—or they were in training camps. When he did run into someone he knew, he found that there was little to talk about. They were preoccupied with the impact of the war on their personal lives. They did not understand the things that he had been doing and apparently they cared less.

He spent more and more time in his room, his feet on the window sill, staring through the bare branches of the maple tree just outside. They symbolized the passage of time. When he first came to this room he could look down at these branches. Now, when the wind blew, he could hear them scraping against the shingles of the roof.

The past had been good. What of the future? Uncle Charlie had said to him on the night they had dined together before he left for Messina, "You're seeing the end of an era, boy, Humpty Dumpty and all that sort of thing. The old comfortable way of life is being smashed and they will never be able to put the goddam pieces together again. Too much capital being burned up unproductively. In addition to that, men are being changed. War teaches men to be aggressive. When they come back they're not going to accept their old humble niches. The opportunities for making money will be greater, but so will the competition. The bright boys are going to run things. And it won't make much difference whether they went to Groton or Muskegee High. It is going to be tough on the rich lads without brains who've always ridden in on their fathers' shoulders."

Well, to hell with the future—they couldn't take away the past. Stuck in a picture frame was a yellowing card. He rose and took it out. "The United Job Corporation, Inc." How those kids had worked for him. Why didn't everyone get other people to work for them? "Grass cutting, weeding, woodcutting, snow shoveling, or any other odd job you can think of, done quickly, neatly, and *inexpensive.*"

He wondered what had become of Mr. Carstairs. A new modern office building occupied the block in which his untidy stationery store had been located. The ground floor was tenanted by an A & P, a Rexall drugstore, and a beauty parlor advertising "Moderne Coiffures." People like Mr. Carstairs—kindly, bumbling people—had disappeared in the rubble of the old demolished buildings.

Hanging from the mirror above his bureau was a collection of dance cards. On one of them he knew Millie's name appeared for every dance. He had gone to see Millie the day after he came home. She had married the son of that cadaverous-looking man who owned the department store and now lived in a white clapboard house on Broom Street. Millie herself was as comfortable looking as her house although extremely, almost immodestly, pregnant. Her eyes still danced and she laughed just as easily except that now there was a surety in her laugh that he hadn't remembered and it no longer included him. She was too obviously contented.

She made him tell her about Harvard and Plattsburg. Then she brought him up to date on his old friends in Messina. Suddenly there was nothing more to say without wandering into areas which neither of them wished to enter.

When he left she accompanied him to the front door. As she was about to open it she threw her arms around his neck impulsively and kissed him.

"Good-by, Allen. I hope to see you again before you go

back. If I don't you know I wish you everything good—always." As he walked down the street it occurred to him that she had never asked him about his postwar plans.

But what were they? Uncle Charlie had predicted that postwar opportunities would be greater, but so would competition. The plums would go to the geniuses. There would be no leftovers for the mediocre. He was not even sure of achieving mediocrity. To marry a girl with Barbara's background one needed money. He was about to start down one of the most uncertain paths in the world. It simply did not add up. He was unable to sit still and found himself pacing up and down within the narrow confines of the room. This was sheer dramatics. The next thing he knew he would be trying to tear his hair. He forced himself to sit down on his only chair.

What the hell. In a short while he would be walking up the gangplank of some troop transport. After that everything —anything could happen. How ridiculous to worry about a future that might not be there. His role was to enjoy the present; to get back to New York and spend these last few days with Barbara. He pulled a crumpled timetable from his pocket.

The sudden silence of the rails brought H. Allen Martin, principal speaker at his Fiftieth Reunion, back to the world of the living, although he was not quite sure for several seconds in just what part of it he had landed. As his mind slowly came into focus he recognized New London. On his right was the same ugly, shabby station which had looked just as dilapidated the first day he saw it as a freshman fifty-four years ago. On his left was the Thames River filled as it had always been with small craft of every description. Forty years ago, on the night before the start of a Bermuda race, he had slept aboard a trim Alden schooner, anchored behind that time-blackened warehouse. Nothing changed around here except human beings. What would he give for the energy that was his in those days; to exchange this stretched feeling of weariness for those surplus reservoirs of vitality which demanded release through action.

He pressed the button on the seat arm and allowed the chair to tilt back another notch. God, he was tired! His head still ached and he still felt that same dull pain in his chest.

He had always expressed the hope that eventually he would die of a heart attack. Yet, in spite of that Spartan desire, he had hurried to Dr. Partridge like a scared rabbit on the several occasions when he had felt discomfort in that part of his body. The human being had not yet evolved into a completely logical animal.

He closed his eyes again, thus preventing himself from seeing any old friends who might be passing through the car on the way to the diner. The 16-millimeter film had begun to unroll again before the train left the station.

The war had become for him a series of sharply etched vignettes; some poignant, some trivial, some sordid; Barbara visiting him in Plattsburg and Camp Dix, looking primly beautiful in her nurse's uniform like a James Montgomery Flagg poster; standing the dawn watch on the bridge of a transport; riding with someone along a muddy road through a French woods, with the ever-rumbling explosion of heavy guns ahead. They passed a house set back from the road among the trees. When they stopped to ask for water two charming American women led them into a huge bedroom where, mud-caked, unshaven and exhausted, they threw themselves on immaculate beds and fell asleep almost instantly. Several hours later they were awakened, given a hot meal that they would never forget, and sent on their way. Where were these two extraordinary women now? Why had they been living in that shell-pocked woods? He would never know.

He was a liaison officer with the infantry, stretched out beneath the sketchy cover of a roadbank in front of a patch of woods waiting for the American barrage to move forward. Through the smoke screen which had been laid down at dawn appeared the figure of a lone German soldier. He was running toward them uttering no sound. Someone fired. The man fell sideways and backward into the thin bushes where he rolled silently from side to side, one arm flailing the bushes rhythmically like a professional wrestler protesting an unfair hold. Then he was still. Through the smoky air came a dozen more Germans their hands upraised, shouting "Kamerad." The still body on the ground had been one of them. He had almost made it, but he had run too fast. Then came the sickening realization that it was he, Ham Martin, who had fired that shot.

He was approaching the front lines on an overcast night in a motorcycle sidecar. The low clouds were lit by the wavering light of gun flashes and the sudden intense incandescence of searching flares, exposing the barren no man's land of fear and death.

He remembered and recognized the tired, anxious faces of the women and old men (all the young men had been killed in the war) in the little village of Koenigsdorf near Coblentz where the battery wintered after the Armistice; the restless stamping of horses on a picket line; the soothing touch of linen sheets during a three-day leave in Paris; a refugee Belgian girl in a little town near Bordeaux whose memory had haunted him for weeks. Occasionally they walked together through the countryside, silent because she spoke neither French nor English, but happy nonetheless. Four French poilus eagerly cutting up a dead artillery horse by the side of the road in anticipation of a steak dinner; silver planes, like a flock of geese at sunrise; cobblestones worn shiny by the feet of centuries; "goldfish"; fatigue; exhilaration; boredom.

During the winter that he spent in Germany after the Armistice he wrote a number of sketches and two short stories, all of which he sent to Barbara. She had sold two or three of the sketches and then the *Atlantic Monthly* bought the second story. It was about the Belgian girl. He called it "C'est la Guerre, Belgique." To his surprise it had received sufficient acclaim to have been included in an anthology of war stories. Barbara wrote excitedly that she was receiving letters from editors and publishers wanting to see more work by this talented young writer. Perhaps his father's advice was sound. The way to be a writer was to write.

Barbara and his mother and Uncle Charlie had been at the pier to meet him when he returned from France; Barbara in her nurse's uniform, Uncle Charlie ruddier than ever, and his mother frail and nervous in an obviously new suit and hat.

Uncle Charlie took them to Delmonico's for lunch. Fanny was uneasy. No one had told her much about Barbara, but she instinctively dreaded this meeting with the girl who was apparently going to be her daughter-in-law. She had already decided that Barbara was just the type she had pictured: beautiful, sophisticated and confident. Everything about her was in harmony with the elegance of the room in which they sat. She belonged there, Fanny didn't. It all made Messina seem shabby and insignificant. Was this also happening to her handsome son?

Uncle Charlie ordered champagne. She had never tasted champagne and the idea of drinking in the middle of the day shocked her. When a headwaiter eventually uncorked the bottle and started to fill her glass she covered it quickly with her hand.

"Nonsense," bellowed Uncle Charlie. "This is a celebration. Hero's return and all that sort of thing. Why, you could give that stuff to a baby. Captain, fill Mrs. Martin's glass." Fanny, dismayed by the fact that Uncle Charlie's booming voice had caused several people at adjacent tables to glance toward them, removed her hand and allowed the headwaiter to fill her glass without further protest.

Uncle Charlie raised his. "Here's to Oswald!" he roared. Fanny lifted hers with fingers that shook slightly. Half closing her eyes she took several quick gulps, set her glass down and held her napkin over her mouth. "Gracious," she gasped. "Those bubbles." Her half-empty glass was refilled. She didn't try to prevent it. Color was returning to her face and confidence to her spirit.

"I know you don't like it," said Uncle Charlie, putting his hand on her arm, "but you must have some to drink a toast to Ulysses. Just sip it. I know you're not used to it."

So that was it. To these people she was just a simple, untutored product of the Indiana farmlands, someone to be treated with condescending gentleness. Her back stiffened. She'd show them.

Taking a preliminary drink from her glass, she lifted it as Uncle Charlie had done. "Now *I* want to propose a toast," she said, "to the best son a mother ever had and a brave soldier. One who never flinched—" Her voice rose.

The people at the surrounding tables paused to listen. "A man who—" she glanced around desperately. "Oh, we're so glad to have you back."

Tipping her glass she drank until she was seized with a coughing fit. Uncle Charlie reached over and patted her back with a force that reflected his irritation at being denied the chance to make the toast to Ham which he had prepared so carefully.

Ham waited until her coughing had subsided. "I'm not going to propose a toast," he said, "my heart is too full to express what I'd like to say. I merely drink to you all."

There was a pause. Barbara leaned toward Fanny. "Tell me about Ham when he was a little boy. He just clams up when I try to find out."

"Well, let's see." Fanny took several thoughtful sips of champagne. "You know, one could grow to like this. It's very pleasant. Did you ever hear about the company Allen formed when he was in school?"

"Oh, Mother, please."

"Tush," she said. "That's what my grandmother was always saying. Tush. Now, what was I talking about when I was interrupted?"

"You were going to tell a story about Ham."

"Who? Oh, yes, Allen. Of course. These names get me all mixed up. His father always insists on calling him Horace. I call him Allen. Those are his names, of course. Both of us are right. Now you call him Ham. Sounds like a pig.

"I'll never forget the argument we had about naming our only child. My mother wanted him called Stanley because that was her maiden name. She was a strong woman, my mother. Very intelligent. Just been made head of the Peoria Public Library when she married. Purely coincidence. I was brought up in Peoria. Guess that's where we all inherited our love of books." She put her hand over her mouth. "Excuse me," she said picking up her water glass. "It's those bubbles."

"Sip it slowly," advised Uncle Charlie soothingly.

She chattered on, scarcely touching her food. Finally her voice trailed off and her eyelids began to droop sleepily.

Barbara interrupted. "Ham, you haven't said a thing. Tell us about that Belgian girl in your *Atlantic Monthly* story. She sounded too real to have been made up."

Ham plunged in with both feet. Anything to shield his mother. Why did Uncle Charlie feel that no occasion was complete unless he turned it into a brawl? Uncle Charlie ordered brandy. Barbara shook her head.

"I guess it's just you and me, sir," Ham said.

"I have a date with your mother," said Barbara unexpectedly. "We're going back to her hotel to have a nice cozy talk. Why don't you men run along? I know you have important things to do. Pick us up at the Biltmore around five. That will give us a chance to chat awhile before your mother goes to the train."

Sunk deeply into a leather chair at the Knickerbocker Club Uncle Charlie lit a cigar. "My sister-in-law got it up her nose a bit," he said, tossing the match in the direction of an ashtray. "Never saw her do that before." He looked pleased.

"I'll bet you never will again," said Ham. "I doubt if she even touches tomato juice for the rest of her life. Poor Mother. She'd never been in an environment like that. It confused her and scared her."

Uncle Charlie blew out a cloud of smoke impatiently. "What's the matter with people?" he snorted. "Why do they want to hide themselves in a place like Messina? A good smart nun knows more about life than Fanny."

"She's happy," said Ham. "Knowing about the world doesn't make people happy. I'd say it was sometimes the reverse."

Uncle Charlie was unwilling to be drawn into a philosophical discussion. He stared intently at the ceiling obviously turning something over in his mind. "What are you going to do with yourself from here in?" he asked finally.

"I knew you were going to bring that up, Uncle Charlie, and I'm ashamed to tell you I don't know. I've always thought of writers in the simplest terms—you know—people that wrote. Now I suddenly realize that they must eat as well. I have brains enough to know that I can't support myself in the beginning just by writing. I must have a job and write on the side.

"The question is what kind of job. If I'm going to write, the job should have something to do with the ink business. I've thought a lot about getting a reporter's job on a morning paper in some medium-sized city like Cleveland or Springfield. That forces you to write with a deadline right in front of your nose."

Uncle Charlie looked bored. "Listen, Ham. Do you know what a cub reporter gets in a town like Springfield? Not more than $40 a week, if that. How are you going to live on $40 a week?

"As for doing something in what you call 'the ink business,' I couldn't disagree with you more. What you need is to experience *life*. You don't want to be an observer watching the wheels go round. You want to have a hand in making them turn. Ivory towers are for later in life. Right now you want to be down in the market place where you can find out how simple it is to make money once you learn how!"

"But I don't want to make a lot of money, Uncle Charlie. I want to write. Not just trash. Something worthwhile. Something good."

Uncle Charlie shrugged his shoulders. "That will *ensure* you of not making money. The written word defies all economic laws. The better it is the less you receive for it.

"You seem to have forgotten Barbara. You're engaged to be married to her, boy. You talk as if you only had yourself to think about. You'd better begin thinking double or you'll lose her. She's not one to stand around waiting for you to write your nonselling masterpiece.

"Now I've been thinking this over, and I've come up with a plan. It's simple and it gives you room to turn around. Get a job in the Bond Department of the Guaranty Trust Company. Stay there for a year. They're goin' to run a kind of a training course for young cubs like you, just back from the wars. You'll learn something about securities and how to read corporate figures and all that sort of stuff. They may even let you break your heart trying to sell bonds. You'll meet a fine bunch of young fellas; the lads that'll be running this town twenty-five years from now. And what'll please you most of all, you're not goin' to get rich doing it. They'd make fellas like you pay toll if they dared.

"At the end of the year, if you survive, I'll give you a job in my firm. There you get closer to the machinery. The Guaranty will teach you *how* to use the tools. When you come to me you'll actually *use* 'em. That's the blueprint. How does it strike you?"

Ham, aware of the fact that Uncle Charlie was watching him closely, had no idea what to say. All his life he had been brought up to believe that he was eventually going to make his living in what his father called "the field of letters." In spite of Uncle Charlie's talk about the need for experience, he had a suspicion that an artful attempt was being made to sweep his long-planned career under the rug.

He didn't think of himself when he considered the effect on his future of such a drastic change of course. He thought of Messina; of his father and mother and how disappointed they would be. He even thought of Millie. She used to be so proud of his small successes.

And he thought of Barbara, who was depending on him to take her out of what she called the "stuffed shirt environment" that she thought she loathed. Girls were so impractical, so romantically blind. Poverty to her was just a word. It probably meant a chintzy little apartment in the East Seventies just off Park Avenue, where she could play happily in a gleaming white kitchen ignoring the fact that at the moment she had no idea how to light an oven.

He couldn't and wouldn't disillusion her. He simply couldn't marry until he had a job which paid him enough to support her decently, in which event writing must become his avocation, temporarily at least.

But where in the world was he going to get such a job except through Uncle Charlie? He was a well-educated young man with absolutely nothing to offer. Some of his friends with writing aspirations were considering becoming copywriters in advertising firms where they would compose jingles on soaps and soups. The idea made him sick. He knew Uncle Charlie was right about newspapers, and besides such work would take him away from New York and Barbara. He had been over the ground again and again and had always come back empty-handed.

For the first time he was being offered a job that more or less solved all his problems. Uncle Charlie had said that it wouldn't pay much at first, but if he worked hard— He could write on weekends, and the financial world was full of legal holidays. This would at least partly satisfy his father and mother. He was sure Barbara would go along. For quite different reasons a move such as this might even help to thaw out her parents.

"How do you know I could get a job at the Guaranty?"

"I talked to the president. Good egg. Said to send you in so they could throw the book at you and see if you had any brains."

Ham stared at the fireplace where two logs were burning feebly. This thing had gone further than he supposed. Now the president of the Guaranty was in it. He wished Uncle Charlie would let him fight his own little war instead of bringing up all the big guns. There wasn't much he could do. You didn't start your career by telling the president of the Guaranty to go jump in the lake.

"I'll take it, Uncle Charlie," he said. "You've been wonderful to me. You've given me an education that I could never have afforded otherwise. You've spoiled me with generosity. Now you're offering me a business opportunity that I would never have had without your help. From here in I don't want to be a financial burden on you. I'll live on what I make and if I don't make enough to live decently that will be my fault."

Uncle Charlie stared at Ham as if trying to comprehend the meaning of what he had just said.

"Ham, sometimes you talk like a prig. You remind me of that Rollo fella. Whatever you do don't let yourself turn into a prig. Are you trying to say that you're going to take a cubicle in some goddam Y.M.C.A. and wash your own underdrawers like Nellie the beautiful cloak model?"

Ham flushed. "I guess that's about it, sir."

"Well, you're not going to do anything of the kind. I've got a place with so many spare bedrooms that I've never had time to count 'em. You're coming to live with me where I can keep an eye on you an' you can keep me company. So that's settled. All I have to do now is to break the news to that musty brother of mine and your darling mother. By the way, it's time to go down to the Biltmore and pour her on the train."

Ham dined with Barbara that night at a little Italian restaurant on 49th Street west of Fifth Avenue. He had dreaded telling her about his talk with Uncle Charlie lest she think he was renouncing all his old plans; closing doors upon which she had depended for escape.

As he told her he emphasized his plan to write on weekends and warned her that it would mean a dull life for his wife. Again and again he reminded her that he was only taking this job in order to earn enough money to support her decently while he got his feet wet as a professional writer. If he succeeded he could quietly drop the banking job. If he failed at least they would not be on the beach.

She listened to him at first with eyes full of anxiety; eyes which seemed to be probing for the real truth behind all this logic. Then the tiny muscles of her face gradually relaxed.

"Oh, Ham, I couldn't agree with you more. It is the only sound thing to do. I don't know whether you or your Uncle Charlie dreamed up the idea, but it's wonderful. Promise me one thing, though. Don't let's ever forget that this is a double-purpose plan. I'm not going to let you forget. I'm going to hound you until your fingers are splayed from hitting typewriter keys.

"And while we're getting started, Ham, we don't have to see a lot of stupid people, *do* we? There's no reason why, because you're working in the Guaranty, we have to *marry* the place. We can see people who are *doing* things—"

"Bankers are doing things," he interrupted defensively.

"Of course, but I meant creative things—you know. I want to be with people who talk and don't just make noises. Oh, darling, I can't wait. We'll have a tiny apartment on one of the side streets [here it came just as he had envisioned it] where the sun pours in all day. It will be painted white with lots of bookcases and a few really good prints and we'll make it all gay and chintzy. I know just the kind I want. I was poking around today.

"The kitchen will be small but dreamy. Pure white with red-checkered curtains and red geraniums. It will be equipped with every known kind of gadget. I'll buy cookbooks and turn out foreign dishes for your dinner that will either make you swoon or sick. Then, in either event, I'll play the piano all evening while you pour out great thoughts."

"Where do the interesting people come in?"

"Oh, they'll be there."

Two days later she called him excitedly on the phone. "Ham, I told Mother and Father last night about your plan to go with the Guaranty for a year and then move over with Uncle Charlie. They are so happy about it. They're like two different people. I'm afraid they've been worrying about us. You know how they are—so darn conventional. They'd never been forced to come to grips with a live author before and I guess it upset the old dears.

"Mother asked me at breakfast this morning if I thought you and Uncle Charlie would like to come for dinner next week. I told her you were the most popular young man in town, but there was nothing like trying."

"Did you tell them I was going to write on the side?"

"No, I didn't, Ham. They seemed so happy. What was the use in upsetting them?"

IV

Ham became an employee of the Guaranty Trust Company on the following Monday. As he looked back on it now, forty-eight years later, it was one of the low days of his life. He had visualized himself as starting off with an interview with the president because of Uncle Charlie. Several days before, however, Uncle Charlie had received a terse note from the president's office requesting that he instruct his nephew to report to Mr. Babb in the Personnel Department. Mr. Babb turned out to be a red-faced, corpulent little man who was out of sympathy with training programs.

"Good God," he said. "The brass upstairs seems to think

this is a rehabilitation center for discharged officers. They're pouring in on us so fast we can't find enough desks and chairs for them, to say nothing of jobs. The only encouraging thing about it is that at the end of the year most of them will think they know all there is to know and go somewheres else. Ho hum. Let's see now. Sales is all jammed up. You got a pretty good college record." To Ham's amazement he pulled out a card covered with figures and began studying it. "Yes. That's a pretty fair showing. I'm going to put you in Statistics. You're lucky. You don't have to go out when it rains or get turned down by people who don't want to buy bonds. Here, give this to Mr. Plunkett in Statistics." He scribbled something on a card, handed it to Ham, and turned to answer his phone which had been ringing for several minutes. Ham hesitated a moment, then, deciding that the interview was over, left without the slightest idea where Statistics was.

As he told Uncle Charlie at dinner that night, "The whole place was so big, so hurried, so discouragingly impersonal." Uncle Charlie nodded, smiling slightly. "I know," he said. "I know all about it. Only tomorrow it won't seem quite so big and the day after it will be a little smaller and at the end of a week you'll begin complaining about being over-crowded. Right now study the people around you, who they are, what they do, how well they're doin' it—grab every scrap of information you can pick up about them. Store it away like a squirrel. After a while you'll discover that most of 'em are more confused and frustrated than you are. It's their own fault, but they don't know it and most of 'em couldn't help it if they did.

"The thing that's goin' to surprise you most is how easy it is to succeed during the first part of your business life. You'll go through your competition like a hot knife through butter and then, just when you're beginning to think you're the cat's meow, you'll hit a stone wall so hard it'll jar your teeth. Why's that?"

Ham didn't regard this as a question and kept quiet.

"During the first part you'll be dealing with fellas who either lack your brains or your drive or have no ambition or whatever you want to call it. Some of 'em are just plain lazy. Some'll go through life thinking of their work in terms of a job instead of a career. Some are so shy they have a nervous breakdown at the sound of their own voice. Some are so brash they can't get along with anybody. Some can't take responsibility without getting the heebie-jeebies. Others just plain don't want it.

"Those are the boys you'll find if you're not scared to look an' unless you're one of 'em you'll walk right through the whole crowd. The pathetic thing to me is they don't even try to trip you up as you go past."

Uncle Charlie took a long sip of wine. "Damn good lecture I seem to be giving."

"It sounds good from where I sit, Uncle Charlie. How about the place where I hit the stone wall?"

"To some degree the timing depends on how good you are, but in the long run money is the determining factor. While the prizes are still small there are plenty to go round and nobody bothers too much, but when the prizes get big they get scarcer. Then you suddenly discover that to keep moving ahead you have to have new qualities in addition to your old ones."

"What kind?"

"You have to work harder, for one thing. You got to be hungry for responsibility. An' perhaps the most important thing of all—you got to start bringing in business. Real business. The kind that sticks to the ribs—the kind that sticks to the till might be more accurate. You're out of the clerk class and if you don't want to fall between two stones you got to produce. Producing is something that's born in a fellow, Ham. I've had fellows in my office who couldn't close a deal to save their lives—bright fellows—but they were just too well brought up to give the final push, the coup de grâce."

Uncle Charlie shoved the bottle across the table to Ham. "Fill your glass. You won't get wine like that every day." They were silent for a few moments. "I had a note from old Mrs. Baker this morning," said Uncle Charlie finally. "She wants us both to dine with her next Tuesday. God, what a bore! It's all right for you. You'll have Barbara, but I'll have to listen to her ladyship while she tells me the family connections of everybody in town and if there are any spare moments old cold-bowel will try to pump me about the stock market. If I knew what the market was going to do I certainly wouldn't tell *him*—or anybody else, for that matter."

"Speaking of making money, Uncle Charlie, how did Mr. Baker make his?"

"Quickest and surest way. Married it. With a going business all ready to take over. Nobody in his wife's family had enough brains to come in out of the rain. They just handed him the business with a cheer and went back to their polo ponies. He built it into a three-ring show. I've seen some hard-boiled old pirates, but he was the champion. Never think it to look at him. Even in those days the company had plants scattered all over the country. He never wanted to see one of 'em. Never has. Just sat in his office down in Wall Street an' looked at figures. He told me once if he ever went around one of his plants he'd never be able to look at it objectively again—whatever that means. I guess he feels that he can operate better if he can forget that human beings work there."

The Baker dinner turned out just about the way Uncle Charlie had predicted, but there was no doubt that the wind had swung to a more favorable quarter for Ham.

"I think it's so nice that you're going with the Guaranty," said Mrs. Baker, drawing Ham aside after dinner. "The Guaranty's very chic—I keep my little account there and they have some of the nicest young men in town—people whose fathers and mothers we know intimately, if you know what I mean. And then it's so nice about your joining your uncle's investment business after a year or so when you've learned all about the banking business. I always feel that unless you are the head of a corporation like Mr. Baker it's much more chic to be a partner in a financial firm like your uncle's —and I should think it might also be more profitable."

It was the natural time for him to tell her that he had not abandoned his plans for writing; that he was merely trying to make some money to support himself until he could become established in his chosen field. But he didn't.

Uncle Charlie and Mr. Baker were arguing about something in the opposite corner of the room. Barbara was strumming idly on the piano.

"I only hope I don't let my uncle down," he said.

She patted his arm reassuringly. "You won't," she said soothingly. "You're a smart boy."

He had expected to be bored in the statistical department; the very name suggested dullness. To his surprise he found himself excited and stimulated. He took evening courses in accounting and in corporate finance and instead of falling asleep like most of his classmates he was always hungry for more.

He wasn't consciously "on the make." He wasn't trying to impress anyone. The simple truth was that he instinctively dramatized figures. They were not dull. Read properly they told romantic human stories of success and failure. As one learned to interpret them better they usually showed the reason why. Here was a family-owned company which turned out one product only—a product superior to anything else on the market, but its management became bored and took to the bottle while inferior competition nibbled away at the company's edges. Here was another whose only asset was age. Its products had become outdated. A ruthless shake-up in management had caused it to leap forward like an animal released from confinement. One could read the stories of fine old companies run by the remote control of second generations, no longer spurred by necessity, or those of young companies with enormous potentials which in the hands of impatiently ambitious men were expanding faster than their capital warranted. The variety was endless.

Ham grew to read figures as a musician reads a score. They told the fang and claw story of industrial America, its fierce energy, the growth of the strong and the disappearance of the weak, until only the strong survived.

He said little about these things to Barbara, but she recognized the new eagerness that reflected itself in everything he did and she guessed its source.

"Ham, you're so absorbed in that old bank that I don't believe you've done a bit of writing or even thought about it since you walked through those sacred doors."

He felt a wave of irritation. Women had so little understanding of a man's problems. In addition to which they did not seem capable of keeping in mind what had already been discussed and decided upon.

"Don't you remember, dear," he said with forced patience, "that we agreed I couldn't support a sick cat by what I might hope to make from writing until I established myself as a writer—and that's a bit paradoxical for me. So," he was watching her eyes, "the obvious thing was to get a job, work up to a livable salary as quickly as possible and then start the life of genius on the side."

Her eyes looked doubtful. His flippancy was a cover-up. "You're worried," he said.

"It's all so fuzzy, Ham. You'll start writing when you're making enough for us to live on. How much is enough? And while we're arriving at that vague point we'll be traveling in the same old rut that I had hoped so desperately we might escape."

"Listen, Barbara. You always talk as if you were panting to go down and live in some Greenwich Village attic. These Villagers aren't your kind of people and they're not mine. You'd be bored. So would they."

"I want *intelligent* people," she interrupted. "People who talk about something besides their friends and what they're going to do next summer and who's going to marry whom and why—and who's invited to the Poopadoop party. I want people who are doing things—preferably important, but at least things; people who are interested in what's going on around them, books, music, politics—anything."

"All right. You want to go around with intelligent people. Well, why can't you? What's stopping you? Why does the fact that I work in a bank instead of writing novels have anything to do with it? If *we* are intelligent we'll naturally gravitate toward intelligent people. If we're dumb we'll gravitate in the direction of dumb bunnies."

She looked at him, still doubtful. "I suppose you're right, Ham. You usually are. Perhaps I'm not very clear about just what I *do* want. Perhaps I just know what I *don't*."

Ham was baffled and worried. It was quite obvious that he and Barbara were not rolling in the same groove. To him, what he proposed to do after they were married was the only logical—the only possible—solution to the situation. Barbara appeared to have her doubts. Was it because she did not quite trust him? Did her instincts tell her that once he was swimming in the deeper waters of the financial seas he would never want to leave them for the insecurity of a creative life? Could she be right? It was a thought which, quite honestly, had never occurred to him. As he turned it over in his mind he began to wonder, but dispelled the idea quickly. All the years of training were not going to be thrown away at the beginning of the race. Nor was he going to disappoint the people who, for various reasons, expected him to follow the path to which this training led.

He asked Roger Baker to meet him at the Harvard Club. In those days it was a less crowded, slower-paced organization than it was to become as its membership increased. Red carpets covered the tiled floor of the dining room, and the tables were set far enough apart to enable one to have a private conversation; an easygoing, quiet place, where one could meet a friend and escape for a bit from the noisy bustle of the city.

Seated under the head of a caribou which hung from the paneled wall like an eavesdropper, he told Roger of his recent conversation with Barbara and of his misgivings.

When he had finished Roger began to make crosses on the tablecloth with his fork and did not speak for several minutes.

"The trouble with Barbara is," he said finally, "that the poor kid doesn't really know what she does want. You've guessed right. She has a good brain, so they send her to that damn-fool boarding school where they teach her how to come downstairs in front of a group of people without falling on her face, and how to enter a drawing room without catching her foot on the leg of a chair. Having mastered these arts, her education as a lady is completed. They call them finishing schools. That's a wonderful name.

"So she comes home and Ma takes her in hand and begins grooming her for the auction block. Of course she rebelled, but rebellion is hard to put over for a girl in Barbara's position. The old purse strings and all that sort of thing.

"Then she saw you riding over the hill in shining armor with your pen couched. Barbara is intellectually bright, but like most of us she has her blind spots. She has always been surrounded by money and she takes it for granted. It has never occurred to her to wonder where it comes from.

"My advice to you is not to give an inch. If you deserted Uncle Charlie now, the family would throw you out as if you were some old bum who had wandered into their house by mistake. Everything will work itself out."

"I don't know, Roger. You make it sound simple but something tells me it's not that easy. Forget it. You've got your own problems."

Roger looked up as if this was a thought that had just been going through his mind. "I'm far worse off than you. There is only one thing I want to do, as I've told you many times. I want to be the best pianist in the world. Perhaps I don't have the ability, but at least I want to try. Here's the old man with all the gold of the Incas, but not one thrippenny of help will I get from him if I choose to be a musician. His idea is that gentlemen who have artistic talents only use them for parlor entertainment. A gentleman, in Father's book, makes money, not with his own hands of course, but by getting other people to work for him. In some mysterious way a gentleman is always head of a company, whatever the company may be."

Roger's hand trembled a bit as he lit a fresh cigarette. "So here I am, denied the use of the only asset I have and forced by the old man to go into business and make money. What in God's name does he want me to make more money for? He is going to have trouble getting rid of what he has already. I'm not going to be any good at business. I have never liked it; but I have been brought up with too many silver spoons in my mouth to start my musical career in some saloon. I'm caught, Ham, caught in the old spider's web. There are moments when I hate my own father and there are moments when I almost hate you because you have a chance to go in almost any direction you want. If you really want to write, Uncle Charlie will eventually see you through. I have a hunch that you are going to like business though. I have a hunch it's your dish and if that's so he'll see you through with a whoop. You're free as air, my boy, and as for that little sister of mine, she's going to be so happy to get out from under the family's wing that she'll approve of anything you do."

Ham looked at his watch. "I have to go," he said. "They give us only an hour for lunch and we've gone way past that. I guess you're right about Barbara, and I wish I could help you with your own problems. If there is ever any way that I can, let me know." They went through the revolving doors onto 44th Street.

H. Allen Martin and Barbara Baker were married on October 1, 1919, in St. James' Episcopal Church on Madison Avenue, a spectacle of tremendous proportions followed by a corresponding mêlée at the Colony Club. The bride and groom had lost their plea for a tiny wedding in Rock Harbor after which the family and any summer residents who were staying down late could relax at Dune House. Mrs. Baker snorted at the suggestion and wouldn't even discuss it. Her only daughter was going to be married properly; no wild ideas until they left on their honeymoon. After that her authority ceased. Her chin jutted forward slightly when she said it.

It had taken two long-distance telephone calls from Uncle Charlie to persuade the Professor and Fanny to come on for the wedding. The horizons of Professor Martin's world were contracting. They had never been broad, but they now encompassed little but his study and his classroom. To Fanny, New York was a vortex of confusion to be avoided at all cost. It was only because Uncle Charlie insisted that they stay with him and promised to protect them from the encroachments of the city that they had consented to come.

Barbara phoned Ham late one night shortly before the wedding. "Darling, you'll never guess what happened. Dad asked me to come into his study after dinner tonight and told me what he was giving me for a wedding present. You'll never guess. He's setting up some kind of trust fund for me with half a million dollars. Isn't that quite a lot of money, dear?

"I don't see why you can't start writing immediately. And, oh, Ham, you must come over and see the other things that are piling in. We've got enough glassware to set up a saloon. I don't know what we're going to put in the glasses now we're going to have this prohibition thing. And there are stacks of beautiful plates and enough silver trays to serve the royal family—"

When she had eventually talked herself out and hung up, Ham turned off his bedside light and lay for a long time staring into the darkness. So the old man was going to see that his daughter lived up to the prescribed standards. In a way it was a vote of lack of confidence in him. The more he thought about it the more upset he became. Since he had become engaged to Barbara he had been increasingly aware of what was involved in marrying into a rich family. He must achieve material success or be a kept man. Old man Baker's wedding present confirmed this. He would accept the challenge which this gift symbolized, the challenge of the great house behind the dunes and the marble and Caen-stone mausoleum on 72nd Street. Someday he would dwarf both of them if he killed himself doing it.

A wave of confidence surged through him. He suddenly knew that he had the ability and the realization gave him a fierce joy such as the old Viking leaders must have felt as they stood in the bows of their high-prowed boats and headed westward through the tumbling rollers of the North Sea.

Six weeks later they faced one another across their new dining-room table in what was considered, at least by Barbara, a small apartment on East 82nd Street between Park and Lexington. It contained a good-sized living room, a dining room, a large master bedroom, a guest room, two baths, a kitchen, pantry, maid's room and bath. Barbara purred over it with delight. To her it was a doll's house and she wore herself out buying just the right rugs, furniture, and chintz until eventually Ham returning from work each night could scarcely believe that this was his home.

"And, darling, do you realize that Mother's wedding check not only paid for the whole thing, but there was a good chunk left? You should be proud of me as a buyer."

There it was again. This wasn't his home. It was Barbara's. He tried to be enthusiastic, but he wasn't convincing.

The sun streamed over the debris-strewn roofs of the neighboring buildings, pushed between the new chintz curtains, and sent silver flashes from the gleaming tea set on the new mahogany sideboard. Maggie, as new as everything else in the place, even though not so shining, brought in orange juice, poached eggs, bacon and coffee.

"Oh, Ham, it's all too dreamy. I feel that I'm going to wake up and find myself in that great barn of a dining room on 72nd Street."

He glanced at her over the top of his morning paper. "Sorry, dear. I'm afraid I wasn't listening."

"Forget it. You go right on reading your stupid old paper. I think a man should be left in peace to read his paper at breakfast. It's part of his business to know boring things."

There was silence for a few moments. "I have to talk to you, dear. I hate to interrupt, but when I think of things I have to tell you and breakfast is the only chance I get all day. First of all, now that we're all settled in I think we should have a housewarming."

"Good," he said, lowering his paper impatiently. "This will be the first opportunity you've had to invite those interesting people you're always talking about. Who are you going to have?"

She smiled sheepishly. "You're a pig and you know it. We haven't had *time* to develop our long-haired geniuses yet. I thought we might ask some of our *friends,* then; just as a starter, we might invite that nice Ben Bowman who works for some publishing house. I've forgotten the name of it, but I guess I can find out. Then there's Harry Adee. I don't think you know him. He's going to be a novelist, but while he's getting started he's working in some advertising agency. Oh, yes, and we might try to get hold of that young man that we met on our wedding trip who is studying to be a pianist. His name is Benjoffski or something. I have it in my address book. Don't you think that might lead to something?"

"To anything, from selective mayhem to mass murder."

She threw a piece of toast at him. It missed and fell to the floor unheeded. "Go ahead and read your stupid paper. You're of no use to me or anyone else except the *New York Times.*"

Silence. "I'm going to join the Junior League," she said.

"What's that? It sounds like trouble for somebody."

"No. On the contrary, it does nothing but good, but I'm not sure just what kind of good. All I know at the moment is that when you die they say down near the bottom of your obit 'she also belonged to the Junior League.' Stelly Wharton is up to her beautiful hips in it. I'm lunching with her today."

He rose, folded his newspaper, tilted her chin with his forefinger and gave her the businessman's farewell. She reached up and threw her arms around his neck. "None of that peck and run stuff," she said. "This is the way *we* say good-by."

The telephone rang in the living room. He went to answer it. When he returned to the dining room a few minutes later she was busy with her daily check list. "Come here." She dipped a corner of her napkin into her water glass. "You're a mess of lipstick. Who in the world have you been talking to on that phone?"

"Your brother."

"What did he want?"

"To play squash Sunday morning."

"Did you tell him we were going to church every Sunday?"

"No, I said I'd play squash."

"Do you think your muscles are more important than your spiritual life?"

"Yes."

"I'll go alone. Kiss me again, muscles, and wipe the lipstick off yourself."

January, 1920. Once more Ham was seated in Uncle Charlie's library. "But, Uncle Charlie, I've only been with the Guaranty for six months. I don't feel I know enough yet to go to Martin and Kuhn."

Uncle Charlie made a noise like an impatient polo pony. "Nonsense. You can learn just as much with us as you can with the Guaranty. You're not being asked to come in as a senior partner, my boy; just as a junior clerk. You seem to have fallen in love with the statistical department. All right, I'll put you into ours for a change. You'll find it a lot more active than where you are now. As a matter of fact, it doesn't make any difference where you start. Before you're finished you're going to be familiar with every department in our shop."

Uncle Charlie cut the end off a fresh cigar and lit it with ceremonious care. "Pity you don't go for these things," he said, releasing a cloud of blue smoke toward the ceiling.

"They're better for you than those damn cigarettes. Let's see. Where were we—if anywhere? Oh, yes, Martin and Kuhn. Well, that's settled then. Tell the boys at the Guaranty you're pulling out. Not that they'll give much of a damn."

The Guaranty might not give a damn, but what about Barbara? He felt like a swimmer crossing a river who finds himself being pulled downstream by an increasingly strong current. He could still get across it if he tried, but did he really want to try? Uncle Charlie's offer stirred up an unexpected excitement, raising questions that he had thought long settled. For the first time he sensed that, faced with the choice between an ivory tower and the market place, his instincts led him to the latter. It gave him a Benedict Arnold feeling.

His experience with the world beyond the confines of Messina had convinced him of several things.

First of all, as Uncle Charlie had already taught him, money was not hard to make if one approached the task from the proper angle. It was a commodity in which men dealt just as they dealt in cotton or wheat; a commodity which you had to understand, but once familiar with its intricacies it could be made to work for you day and night.

He had also grasped the fact that to succeed in the manner of Uncle Charlie it was necessary to be your own boss. Those who sold their services for a wage might achieve distinction and high honors, but they would never soar into the economic blue like those whose flight depended solely on the strength of their own wings.

He was also convinced that the acquisition of money was not an end, but a means to an end. The key to this beautiful, paneled library was not in the hands of scholars, but rather in the hands of those who could afford the deep-pile rugs, the red leather armchairs, its books, its crackling fire, and the service which maintained it all. His father-in-law's places in New York and Rock Harbor were the products of money converted into beauty—as the Bakers conceived it.

People said that money didn't necessarily bring happiness, but wasn't that, in part at least, a defensive phrase, coined by those who didn't have it? Happiness was a state of mind which should be far easier to achieve in a palace than in a hovel in spite of what the poets said to the contrary.

And finally, money, like a turbine, was a power generator. People scraped and bowed to Barbara's father, but if he didn't have money, if the power was not there, he would be just a silly little man. The noiseless, obsequious service which caused this apartment house to run so smoothly merely symbolized money being transformed into a sanctuary where one might escape from the rough edges of the world. Money was an abrasive which polished the rough surface of life, permitting one to move through it with a minimum of friction.

"I don't know why you're so good to me, Uncle Charlie. All I can say is I'm grateful and I'll try not to let you down."

"Nonsense," snorted Uncle Charlie. "Of course you won't let me down. You have a tendency to talk in a series of clichés. Avoid 'em. If there's one thing I can do it's to pick men. I picked you early. You haven't disappointed me yet. Nor will you. Talk to the Guaranty. Then let me know when you'll be moving in."

Ham walked home slowly that night torn between elation and depression. He might not be letting Uncle Charlie down, but was he letting *himself* down? Why must he always make things so complicated? Nothing had changed. He was merely continuing on a course already plotted. But even while he rationalized he knew that the course had been altered.

She was in bed, reading. He sat down on the edge of the bed and told her of his talk with Uncle Charlie, but his attempt to be casual did not ring true. She caught the suppressed excitement in his voice and interpreted it correctly.

"It sounds fine," she said coolly. "Uncle Charlie is certainly putting you over the jumps. We can talk more about it tomorrow. I'm so sleepy I couldn't stay awake another minute if he made you president of United States Steel."

She reached up and turned off her reading lamp. "Good night, tycoon," she murmured, burying her head in the pillows.

He lay awake for a long time, his eyes closed, his head filled with jumbled, uneasy thoughts. He knew that Barbara was awake. What in the world had he done to create this sudden tension? Most people would have thought he was getting along rather well. The more he thought about it the more irritated he became until irritation was transmuted into a dull anger. This was no prelude to a sound night's sleep. He went to the bathroom and took a sleeping pill.

Now, forty-seven years later, as he looked back on the months that followed, they seemed so recent, their edges so clear in his memory. That was a sign of old age, wasn't it? The distant past came into focus while yesterday began to blur.

The day after he departed from the Guaranty, leaving not the smallest ripple behind him, Uncle Charlie had asked him to come down to Wall Street for lunch. "Meet me at my office about twelve. Show you round the money factory before we eat. You know—introduce you to a few of the leading slaves—all that sort of thing. Then when you show up for work tomorrow you'll be an old hand."

At precisely ten minutes before twelve Ham stepped into

the elevator at 120 Broadway that would take him to the offices of Martin and Kuhn on the eighteenth floor. It was his first visit. Uncle Charlie did not approve of his relatives or his impecunious friends drifting in and out of his private office as if it were a public rest room.

The elevator doors slid apart with a hiss and Ham stepped out uncertainly. He had expected to find himself in a corridor, flanked by lettered doors. Instead he stood in a large pine-paneled area lit by the subdued rays of table lamps. Facing the elevators, at a distance calculated to cause unwanted intruders to lose their bravura as they shuffled toward it through yards of high-pile carpet, stood an enormous desk; behind this barricade sat the ever-vigilant Miss Manners.

Miss Manners; not too young, not too old, not too handsome, not too homely; Miss Manners, keeper of the gates, capable of being a denying dragon or a welcoming angel as circumstances indicated and who always read the indications correctly.

Before a visitor emerged from the elevator Miss Manners knew which lever to pull. "Oh, Mr. Woodbridge, good morning. You're looking so well. You must have been on a vacation. Please take a seat. I know Mr. Blankenthorp wants to see you. Just let me make sure there's no one with him. Would you like to see a copy of the *Wall Street Journal* while you're waiting?"

Or "Mr. Perkins, did you say? You have an appointment with Mr. Andover? [a note of incredulity in the voice] Please take a seat and I'll see if he is in."

Or "What did you say your name was? Battenkopf? May I ask what you want to see Mr. Appleton about? I don't think he's in. Just a minute till I find out."

And for the dregs, "No, Mr. Hoxie's out. No, I've no idea when he'll be back."

Miss Manners had an attachment on her phone which made it impossible for even the most alert caller to hear what she said. Mr. Blankenthorp's secretary would appear promptly to lead the Class A visitor to the inner sanctum. Miss Manners advised Mr. Perkins, Class B, that Mr. Andover was in a meeting. He had been advised of Mr. Perkins' presence, however, and Miss Manners was sure that he would be able to break away for a moment and come out to see Mr. Perkins in the reception area.

Mr. Battenkopf, Class C, was advised that Mr. Appleton was out, but Mr. Gruber, who was thoroughly familiar with the situation, would be glad to talk to him if he cared to wait. This Mr. Battenkopf did—for forty-five minutes.

The gentleman who had failed to batter down Mr. Hoxie's gates had left immediately.

Ham knew nothing of these internal matters, but he was nonetheless surprised when the woman behind the big desk arose quickly and came forward to greet him.

"Mr. Martin! [How in the world had she known who he was?] I am Miss Manners, the receptionist. Your uncle is expecting you. Do have a seat while I telephone his secretary and tell her that you are here. Perhaps you would like to look at the *Wall Street Journal* while you are waiting." She handed him the paper, made little fluttering motions with her fingers and returned to her desk. There she spoke a few words into her soundless telephone. "Miss Truesdale will be right out," she beamed, her tone managing to combine motherliness with a trace of seduction. "We have heard so much—excuse me please. No, he is not in. No, I have no idea when he will return." She hung up the phone crossly and resumed her beam. "—about you. We understand—excuse me please." She picked up the phone as a comely woman with fading blonde hair entered the area.

The newcomer approached Ham with quick, businesslike steps. "Oh, Mr. Martin. I'm sorry to have kept you waiting. I am Miss Truesdale, your uncle's secretary. I'll lead the way, if you don't mind."

Ham didn't mind and followed her down a series of corridors, their walls lined with colored prints of old New York.

Ham would never forget his first sight of Uncle Charlie's office. It was an enormous corner room paneled in walnut with bookcases on two sides. Uncle Charlie, on the phone, raised a hand of greeting. Ham walked over to one of the broad windows and looked out over the roof of the Sub-Treasury. Across Wall Street he could catch a glimpse of the J. P. Morgan offices. He was standing in almost the exact center of the financial complex which furnished the United States with so much of its economic blood.

"Don't look so scared," Uncle Charlie said finally, placing the receiver back on its cradle. "You won't have to run the Sub-Treasury or Morgan's for some time to come. And all this stuff you see around you—" he waved his hand at the bookcases and the paneling. "Just eyewash for the paying customers. Come on. I'll give you a quick peek at the setup.

"First I want you to meet Hoodby. He writes the folder we send out three times a month to all customers and prospects, making common stock recommendations. You're going to be his assistant, but don't get too puffed up about that till you see the sort of thing he'll ask you to do."

Had Mr. Hoodby been born in the Middle Ages he would surely have been a monk. His tonsure was simulated by a bald spot on the top of his head and his long, bony face and sunken eyes belonged to a religious fanatic rather than to a statistician.

Uncle Charlie introduced them, then waited impatiently while the formalities were exchanged. "Come, come. You two will have plenty of chance to talk tomorrow. I want to introduce you to Brunner. You're going to be his slavey too."

Brunner, he explained as they moved down the corridor, was the firm economist who prepared a letter once a month on what Uncle Charlie referred to as "the general economic mess."

Unlike Mr. Hoodby, Mr. Brunner might have played the part of Mr. Pickwick without recourse to makeup. "Don't let that jolly old belly-shaker fool you," warned Uncle Charlie as they left Mr. Brunner's cluttered office after a hasty handshake. "He's keen as a blade. Best economist in town, which is faint praise in my opinion. And if he asks you to get some information for him be sure you get it right or he'll never trust you again. This is the board room. You know—the place where they post stock prices."

Rows and rows of chairs, partly occupied by dull-eyed men, staring moodily at two lanky youths on a platform who were busily posting numbers on a green board which covered one entire wall.

Uncle Charlie shuddered as he closed the door. "That place gives me the jimmies. Those fellas sitting there every day watching the market go up a quarter or go down a quarter. Now I'll show you Statistics where you'll have your desk. Then we'll go out and have some lunch. I'm beginning to rumble."

He opened a glass-paneled swing door, disclosing an enormous room filled with rows of little desks occupied by young men who were poring over manuals and charts. No one looked up. Uncle Charlie allowed the door to swing shut.

"Looks like a robot convention. Come back to my office while I pick up my hat, then we'll go over to the Down Town Association."

As they entered the reception area on the way to the

elevator Miss Manners shot from her desk like a clay pigeon released from its trap. "Oh, Mr. Martin," she cooed as no clay pigeon could, "it's such a pleasure to have met you and we are all so delighted that you are going to join this wonderful firm."

"Listen, boy," said Uncle Charlie as they came out on the narrow sidewalks of Pine Street, "they've been giving you the Treatment today, but let me warn you. Tomorrow you'll be just an employee. Don't let your feelings get hurt. You'll be just an ordinary wage earner and a damn poorly paid one at that."

On his first morning Ham arrived early. To his surprise Miss Manners, cool and collected, was already at her desk opening mail.

"Good morning," she said briskly. "Early bird, eh? Well, at this time of day not a worm is stirring." Her manner had changed from that of a receptionist to that of an old-timer talking to a green associate. "There are lockers in the men's room behind Statistics. Pick out an empty one. The key will be hanging on the hook inside." She returned to the mail.

Ham had bought a *Wall Street Journal* on the way downtown. Having found a locker and disposed of his hat (young men wore hats in those days), he sat down on a chair beside Mr. Hoodby's empty desk and tried to read but found his mind more inclined to go woolgathering. The first eighteen years of his life had been spent among unchanging and familiar surroundings. Then, beginning with 1912, he had been catapulted from one new experience to another; Harvard, training camps, France, the Guaranty, marriage, and now here he was, about to beat a path through another unknown country. Would his life ever stabilize or was incessant change normal procedure in the big world outside Messina?

People began to occupy the desks around him. Some merely stared at him curiously. A few came up and introduced themselves. Mr. Hoodby bustled in. "Glad to see you're the kind that gets in early," he said, nodding unsmilingly. "Your desk is going to be in Statistics. Let's see, you've been working in Statistics at the Guaranty so you must know *something*. Not much perhaps, but *something*. Good. We're just starting on the new folder. We're going to write up Dodson Chemical, Sunny Service Stores, and Kenso-Macklin Drugs. You take Dodson. Make up the usual statistics, then talk to me. Maybe I'll arrange an interview with the treasurer. Here's some of our old folders. Look them over for style. You should be able to get the Dodson figures together before the end of the day. Anything else?"

There was so much else that it was hopeless to go into any of it. Better to play by ear. He took the folders. "No, sir. Not at the moment." Mr. Hoodby looked pleased. No one had called him sir in a long while.

It wasn't difficult work. The statistical data was assembled from manuals and annual reports. The material for the company's history and prospects was also obtained from annual reports to the stockholders, typed interviews with treasurers and commercial bankers, and an occasional report of a trip to the plant itself. All of these were in the files but he was puzzled as to why certain companies were chosen for recommendation. They did not strike him as among the country's most desirable investments. As the days passed, however, and more and more work fell on his shoulders, he had less time to think of such matters.

In fact the pressure increased to a point where he was taking work home almost every night. Barbara groaned as she saw him enter the apartment clutching a briefcase. "Good God, dear, do you realize this is the third night in a row you've come staggering in with that thing? You're developing a distinct list to starboard."

"Well, that's a loving greeting I must say for someone who's been working his head off all day."

"But do you have to work it off all night too? Aren't we ever going to have any more *fun* out of life? Is it just going to be work, work, work, business, business, business, the way it was with Dad? This isn't what we planned, Ham. I have money enough right now, thanks to Dad, to let you do what you've always wanted to do."

"I don't want your money or your father's money," he said. "Let's get that straight. I'm going to roll my own."

"Of course you are, Ham. No one is trying to make a dependent out of you. But isn't there some compromise? You're going to be in your twenties only once. Do you have to spend them in the salt mines? Don't *I* count for anything?"

"Of course you do. More than you know. But you don't win races by taking it easy. You either go all out or you get stuck in the middle, or possibly bring up the rear. It's what you *do* that counts, not how much money somebody left you. More than that. It's what I do in the *beginning* that counts most. Right now, while they're sizing me up."

To his surprise she began to cry, then she quickly wiped her eyes and stiffened. "All right," she said. "I might have known it would be this way. Oh, Ham, why can't we chuck it all before it's too late and *live?*"

"On your father?" he asked. "No, I can't do that."

She rose, walked to their bedroom and slammed the door behind her. Miserable, he set out the card table, opened his briefcase and went to work.

All day Ham had been preparing a memorandum on the National Sanitary Fixture Corporation. It was to be included among next week's recommended stocks. The N.S.F.C. was a new company composed of a dozen or more manufacturers of bathroom fixtures. They had been put together into one basket on the apparent assumption that, although none of them had been able to do particularly well alone, amalgamation would congeal all their separate virtues into an invincible whole and their separate weaknesses would evaporate.

Uncle Charlie's firm had been one of the underwriters that had put this jigsaw puzzle together a year before. The results to date gave no indication that the weaknesses had yet evaporated, but the company's new treasurer was filled with optimism. There had been extraordinary, nonrecurring costs involved in connection with the merger, he had written cheerily in the annual report. Unexpected problems had arisen and there had been unforeseeable labor difficulties. As a result the stock had declined to a point where, in the opinion of Martin and Kuhn (Mr. Hoodby), it offered an unusual opportunity to the farsighted investor.

Ham had been working up data for Mr. Hoodby long enough to develop some critical judgment of his own. He went over the National Sanitary figures again and again, comparing them with those of the company's more established competitors. This folder was going to a long list of people who had confidence in Martin and Kuhn; people, many of whom had no business buying anything except high-grade securities. Mr. Hoodby was either careless, or in his dotage, to include a name like this in a bulletin purporting to deal with sound investments. His duty was clear.

He walked across the room to Mr. Hoodby's desk and sat down. "Finished?" asked Mr. Hoodby, without looking up from a huge sheet of figures which he was studying with gleaming eyes.

"I want to talk to you about Sanitary Fixtures."

"Stuck on something?"

"No, sir. I just don't think it's the kind of stock that belongs in this bulletin."

Mr. Hoodby looked at him as if he had not noticed his presence until that moment.

"What say?"

"I know it's presumptuous of me, sir, but I don't think we should recommend the stock of Sanitary Fixtures in a bulletin of this kind. This goes out to a wide list of people who have reason to believe that the stocks which we recommend are, in our opinion at least, top-grade equity investments. Certainly we can't put Sanitary Fixtures in that category. It's a speculation not an investment, and I'm not sure how good a speculation it is. The company's been losing ground steadily since the merger. The treasurer is full of good reasons why, but for my money he's whistling in the dark. I suppose that's what he's paid for. Would *you* want to buy Sanitary Fixtures at the present market?"

As Ham talked Mr. Hoodby slowly turned into a medieval monk. His small deep-set eyes blazed with frantic zeal. The muscles of his long, lean face became set in ridges of tension. His brown, somewhat wrinkled suit turned into a cassock and it would not have been surprising if he had drawn a crucifix from its folds and held it out to ward off the evil that was threatening him.

Instead of a cross he drew out a pencil and began to doodle furiously on a pad of paper, obviously fighting to regain his composure.

When he spoke his voice sounded strained and unnatural. "You have chosen," he said, "not only to criticize my judgment but to oppose firm policy. Possibly your relationship to the senior partner gives you this right. I resent the personal criticism, but when it comes to matters of policy I step aside. I suggest that you discuss the situation with your uncle." His eyes gleamed balefully as if he had said, "I suggest that you have a cozy chat about this with the boys over at the Inquisition Office."

Uncle Charlie listened, his hands locked behind his head. The suggestion of a smile occasionally caused the corners of his huge mustache to lift.

"And you really had the nerve to say all that to old Hoodby?"

"Why, yes, sir. What else could I do? I couldn't write a favorable report about a company in which I didn't believe." Uncle Charlie turned in his swivel chair until he could look out over the roof of the Sub-Treasury building. "That Sanitary Fixture Corporation's been a disappointing situation. The boys who conjured it up were so anxious to create a deal that they couldn't see the bunkers. The underwriters have been trying to support the market for the stock hoping the management could eventually get the bugs ironed out. There's no reason why they can't if they get a little tougher and fire some of the old dodos who aren't pulling their weight. I think they will work it out, but that doesn't mean—"

He broke off and was silent for a few moments, seeming to be turning something over in his mind. Ham made no comment.

"How long have you been in Statistics?"

"About two months."

"That's what I thought. I was going to move you into the bond department for a few months, but what you said to old Hoodby has changed my mind." Ham's heart plummeted. So this was the end of a budding career.

"I'm going to jump you right up to the underwriting group. We need fellows around this place who have the courage to say what they think. You'll be under George Brownlee. He's a partner, as you know. If you don't you ought to. That's a fast-stepping bunch of young men. They'll have your tongue hanging out, but I think you can stick. Come along with me and I'll introduce you to Brownlee. You can spend the rest of the day getting settled in your new quarters. If you left any dime novels in your old desk downstairs I suggest you don't try to collect 'em until Hoodby's gone for the day. I have troubles enough with you fellows without adding mayhem. How about you and Barbara having dinner with me tonight?"

For the first time since he had left college, Ham found himself in an atmosphere where he had a sense of belonging. His work still dealt with basic research, but he was now in a position where he could see the end to which it applied. This was not work; it was a game in which imagination and ingenuity played major roles. At the desks all about him there was a never-ending series of discussions about mergers, reorganizations, refinancing, and the other monetary problems that went with a booming and expanding economy.

He liked the men with whom he worked. They were keen, ambitious, high-pressure individuals who carried a briefcase home each night as a normal part of the day's routine. Ham wondered if they all got hell from their wives.

The story of his conversation with Mr. Hoodby had gone around the office and to Ham's surprise had been considered very funny. He was received by his new associates as one to be handled carefully because of his relationship with the Boss. They treated him with the unwilling deference engendered by fear until it gradually became apparent that he was not only one of the hardest workers in the department but that he was also a person who could be trusted. Only then did they accept him.

Their appraisal was confirmed when, after a few weeks with the underwriting group, he walked over to his immediate boss, a stocky square-faced young man by the name of Hobbs with a brain like a calculating machine. "Got a minute?"

"Sure, sit down." Hobbs removed a pile of papers from the chair beside his desk. "Have I been doing something unethical?"

Ham grinned. "I've got an idea. My father-in-law is the head of American Sheet and Tubing."

Hobbs nodded. "I know it."

"Okay. Do you know anything about the Sawyer Laboratories?"

"More or less. Good little company in spite of itself."

"Right. They've always had a good product, but it's run by a bunch of old gaffers. They would fit into American Sheet and Tubing like a piece into a jigsaw puzzle. They'd fill a gap in A.S.&T. and they'd get the management they need if they're going to survive."

Dick Hobbs looked at him suspiciously. "Did you ever speak to your father-in-law about this?"

"Of course not."

"What does your uncle think about it?"

"I haven't asked him. You're the first one I've mentioned it to."

Dick Hobbs half turned and stared through the window for several minutes. "You may have something," he said finally. "That's a horseback opinion of course. Glad you spoke to me first. Let's see if Brownlee is free. We can kick this around with him." He picked up his phone. At least this young fellow was an Organization Man.

Barbara was depressed. She sensed that this husband of hers was moving forward in the business world and that he was happy. She could feel it in the confidence of his voice, in his seemingly tireless buoyancy, even in the eagerness with which he opened his briefcase after dinner and laid out his papers on the card table.

She was glad that he was living fully, but at the same time she was increasingly jealous of this intangible force that was separating him further from her each day. She was sure now that he would never write. Such daydreams had been given up. She was caught; destined to live the kind of life from which she had tried so hard to escape.

In a short while she would have a baby. That at least was something to which she could look forward. They didn't see many people these days. It disturbed Ham if she played the piano. She had fallen into the habit of reading after dinner and going to bed early.

He would push aside his papers then and rise to kiss her good night. The kiss became a peck and one evening he forgot it in his absorption. An instant later he sensed the fact that she had gone and looked up just in time to see her close their bedroom door softly. He rose quickly and followed her.

"You left so quietly I didn't hear you," he said, putting his hands on her shoulders. "Trying to sneak out on me?"

"I didn't want to disturb you." Her voice was dead.

"Going to bed?"

"I thought I'd read for a while."

He kissed her, but her kiss was as lifeless as her voice. "I'm going to knock off myself pretty soon," he offered with feigned cheerfulness.

"Don't wake me up if I'm asleep," she said, moving away from him and starting to take off her dress.

There was a troubled look in his brown eyes as he re-seated himself at the card tale. Whatever he did in the office seemed right and whatever he did at home seemed wrong. It all stemmed from this damn writing business. How could a man write if he had nothing to write about? That seemed so obvious that it shouldn't need explaining, yet Barbara treated him as if he was willfully selfish. He loved Barbara and his inability to lead her into her dream world left him with a sense of guilt, as if he had somehow betrayed her.

Barbara was an incurable romanticist. That was the trouble. Brought up in a home where money was never mentioned because it was so abundant, she had grown to regard it as something rather degrading, something alien to beauty and creativity. Now, through her father's generosity, she had enough of it to continue ignoring it. At that point Prince Charming forgot his role entirely and decided that money instead of being degrading was in fact a most exciting commodity. What a mess.

He pulled an office memorandum toward him impatiently, but corporate adventure had suddenly lost its lure. Jamming his papers back into his briefcase, he pushed away the card table and walked over to the open window. The moon was almost full, mysterious and, as it seemed in those remote days, unapproachable. Beneath it the gray-black city sprawled endlessly. How many of those millions of people who made up this living carpet must have problems and perplexities far greater than his. The siren of a fire engine on Lexington Avenue rose and died away.

In order not to disturb her he undressed in the guest room, so soon to become a nursery. Then he opened the door to their bedroom and slid between the sheets. In the adjoining bed Barbara lay quiet. He could tell by her breathing that she was not asleep, but he accepted her obvious desire to be alone and, turning on his side, tried to clear his mind by thinking of a blonde he had met that summer in Rock Harbor. The blonde refused to come into focus and gradually turned into Millie. He tried making his mind a blank. On the street below a night sanitation crew was crashing empty garbage cans on the sidewalk as a protest against the fat cats above who could sleep while they must work.

He turned over and let his thoughts take charge. Gradually they became incoherent and at some point disappeared altogether.

No young father could have been more anxious and expectant about the coming event than Uncle Charlie. "If I can't be a grandfather," he said, "at least I can be a grand-uncle and what the hell's the difference when you come right down to it?

"I've been thinking what I could give my grandnephew for a coming-out present. He won't be of an age where he'll appreciate a silver porringer. I don't know why he should at any age. All he wants is food and warmth. Those are things that you and his mother will have to supply. So I've decided to make him a very unusual present. I'm going to give him a hundred thousand dollars—"

"But, Uncle Charlie—"

Charlie Martin held up a plump hand. "Don't interrupt me. I was going to give it to him with the stipulation that you invest it for him by putting it into this firm as capital and becoming a partner. So you can watch it and all that sort of thing. Kind of a cute idea, what? You'd be working for your own kid.

"I have an old sourpuss of a lawyer, though, that's allergic to cute ideas. If he could find some legal reason for banning Santa Claus he'd be the happiest man in New York. When I told him what I had in mind he obviously thought I was in my dotage. Just brushed the whole thing under the rug with his foot.

"I never fight with my lawyer. Only when I know I have some chance of winning. I merely go around him like a boat avoiding a rock. In this case I'm going to help my grand-nephew by giving *you* a hundred thousand dollars. You will then be made a partner in the firm and the hundred thousand will be your capital contribution."

Mr. Martin stuck his thumbs into the armholes of his vest and beamed at his nephew, who stared at him in open-mouthed amazement.

"But, Uncle Charlie, I wouldn't accept such a gift. It is entirely too generous. Don't think that I'm unappreciative, but you have already done much more for me than you should. You have given me the most wonderful start in life that a country boy ever had."

Uncle Charlie's beam was replaced by an expression of annoyance. "Isn't it about time you stopped talking like one of the characters in the Rollo books. Godamighty, boy, we don't take partners just 'cause they're relatives. That's why we usually *don't* take 'em in. In spite of being a relative, though, you fit into this business the way a hand fits in a glove. You've got what we want and unless I'm mistaken we've got what you want. The whole thing's made to order."

His tone softened, became more confidential. "We have to

keep filling in at the bottom with young men, Ham. You must see that. The only reason I'm giving you a hundred thousand is because you have to bring in a minimum amount of capital to join a firm like this. I'm a rich man, Ham, with no living relatives except your father and yourself. I might just as well leave you something when I die as hand it all to Harvard, although I'm sure they'd squawk if they heard that. Okay. So all I'm doing is making you a little advance and cheating the government out of a bit of inheritance tax. That's something that really gives me a boost. Now, have I succeeded in penetrating your thick skull?"

Ham was silent, as conflicting emotions battled within him. He was at a crossroads, the most important of his life. All the idealism which had been implanted in him during his early days pointed in one direction. All his present enthusiasms and desires pushed him in the opposite.

"You don't seem to be very happy about it," said Uncle Charlie, selecting a huge cigar from the humidor on the table behind him and removing the end carefully with a small gold clipper which he carried on the end of his heavy watch chain.

"It isn't that, Uncle Charlie. I'm just simply all mixed up. Because of your generosity and because of your belief in me, you are handing me life on a silver platter. I think people have to work and fight for what they get or they take it for granted and go soft. I've never been happier than I have in this office, but— Don't you see what I mean, Uncle Charlie?"

His uncle's face almost disappeared behind a cloud of blue smoke. "God, Ham, you do need a lot of drying behind the ears. Do you think, as a junior partner in this firm, that all you'll have to do is to sit on your ass and coast for the rest of your life? Boy, you don't know what work is. As long as you're an employee you can clean off your desk at the end of the day and go home with nothing on your mind but your hat. At the end of the month you receive a check and you don't have to worry about where the money came from.

"When you become a partner you never close your desk. You carry it around inside you, day and night. It's your brains that put the money in the till to keep the show on the road. It's your ability that brings in the business. You have to cultivate the right people and then you have to feed 'em ideas that will bring a profit to *them*. The profit to the firm will follow automatically. If that sounds too simple, let me tell you that I've seldom seen an idea, good or bad, that didn't have a risk tied to its hind leg. You've got to appraise these risks from a dozen angles. If the odds against you look too great you drop the whole thing. It's always easier to say no. But if the odds look favorable you must have the courage to go ahead in spite of risks and you must have the drive to make the project gel.

"You've got a way with people, Ham. They like you. What's more important, they trust you. You're a little too serious perhaps. It's all right to be earnest, but carry it inside you, not on your sleeve. That doesn't bother me though. You'll learn the light patter as soon as you begin to move around a bit more. What does concern me is that you get started moving. I don't suppose you belong to any clubs?"

"Only the Harvard Club."

Uncle Charlie waved this aside impatiently. "No, no. That's just a bunch of Harvard alumni. Nice chaps and all that, but you need places where you meet all sorts of people—people who bring profitable business to this firm. Places like the Union, for instance, where you can meet and talk, and the Down Town Association where you can take a man for lunch, or the Piping Rock where you can do a little golf entertaining—"

"But, Uncle Charlie, we can't afford such places."

"If you are any good you'll be able to by the time you get by their Admission Committees. Most of my generation will be dead or in wheelchairs before you get in the D.T.A. In the meantime you'll find plenty to do cultivating your own crowd. They're the boys, remember, who are going to be running the show when you are forty-five—the utility companies, the big industries, the banks—all that sort of thing. You've got to grow up with 'em; know 'em so well that when you phone 'em and say who you are their secretaries will sound as if you were the one person they'd been waiting for all day.

"A lot of this is accomplished around tables, Ham; lunch tables, bridge tables, dinner tables, poker tables. You and Barbara have got to do a lot of table work. You're going to need a larger apartment, a nurse to take my grandnephew off Barbara's hands, a waitress—what-do-you-call-'em—and a cook that can turn out a dinner you don't have to apologize for.

"Of *course* you can't pay for these things and there's no reason Barbara should just because she has all the money for the moment. These things are your work tools, just like hammers and shovels and all that sort of stuff. The firm supplies your work tools. When you're made a partner you'll have an expense account. We can fix that up later."

"But, Uncle Charlie—"

"Don't start that Rollo business again, for God's sake. Remember what I just said. We're handing you a lot of expensive tools and we expect you to make some expensive things with 'em. Simple as that." He glanced at his desk clock. "I have to meet a fella for lunch at the Racquet Club. Detroit bloke. Awful bore. I know what he wants and he's not going to get it. Why don't you come along—my assistant? Show

you how to turn a man down and keep him in the paddock.
Free lunch anyway."

Barbara was so preoccupied with pregnancy that her reaction to the news of Ham's impending partnership was that
of a patient in a dentist's chair while being told a funny
story by the dentist. Ham said nothing of what Uncle
Charlie would be expecting of him (or her).

It was only during the restless waiting weeks which followed that she began to sense the full significance of what
had happened. As she had always suspected, Uncle Charlie
had never for one moment intended to allow Ham to wander
off into the Elysian fields and she was convinced that Ham
himself had little wanderlust—in that direction at least.

She felt betrayed, sorry for herself, and there were moments when hate was not far distant. When she tried to
rationalize the situation she was aware of the fact that she
was a one-way dreamer. She knew what she *didn't* want but
she wasn't quite sure what she *did* want. Marriage had given
her enough freedom from her old ties to make her realize
that.

Ham was inducted into partnership a few days before the
birth of Michael Martin. He found the former a much more
casual ceremony than becoming a father; a short meeting
with an attorney in Uncle Charlie's office, a previously prepared certified check signed, presented, endorsed and
handed back, documents signed and witnessed by bored
clerks, a trip down the row of partners' offices with much
handshaking and banter. He remembered what Uncle
Charlie had said about business patter. These fellows
switched it on and off like an electric light; genial, urbane

pleasantries at which everyone laughed with a heartiness scaled to the seniority of the speaker. Once this ritual was over they all ducked back into their offices and resumed telephoning.

At the end of the corridor was his own office. It was the smallest of the lot, but he would never forget the pride with which he entered it. To be surrounded by his own four walls was so different from sitting in the great open spaces to which he had been accustomed. Perhaps this feeling of security was a lurking vestige of primitive man's desire to live in a cave. Whatever the cause he knew that he could work harder and more efficiently here than he had ever worked before.

Outside of his new office sat Miss Kelly, red-cheeked, snub-nosed, pert, and ridiculously young. Little did he realize that forty-four years later "Kelly," gray, worldly-wise and efficient, but still with the twinkle in her eye and the corners of her mouth always poised for laughter, would still be with him, having devoted her life to promoting his. Nor did he suspect that this red-cheeked girl would grow to know and under-stand him better than anyone else in the world, better than his father or mother ever had, certainly better than Barbara, or his children; better perhaps than he knew himself.

The ceremonies ended, he re-entered his office and sat down in his new high-backed desk chair wondering what in the world he was supposed to do next. A few minutes later Miss Kelly stuck her head around the corner of the door. He noticed for the first time that her face had a distinctly gamine quality, a charming gamine to be sure, but one who might stick her tongue out at him unexpectedly. It was a face of such restrained impudence and merriment that he uncon-sciously grinned at it. The grin was immediately returned.

"Feeling lonesome now that they've put you in a cell?"

"Not until they start padding it."

"I brought up your 'things,' as they call them, from your old desk and stowed them away in this one as best I could. You may want to rearrange them."

"Thanks."

"Personally I'd rearrange most of them in the scrap basket. They won't do you much good up here."

"Did you read everything?"

"No. Just glanced over them. Here is something to help pass away the time. These are copies of yesterday's partners' letters."

"What did you do, steal them?"

"Gracious, no. Every partner gets a copy of every other partner's letters. Daily routine."

"Sounds like the secret police."

"Yes. Kind of an open-faced police. Is there anything else you want?"

"I didn't want anything in the first place." Talking to this girl was like a game of verbal ping-pong.

"Good. If you need me just press the buzzer. I'll be right outside reading *This Side of Paradise*. Do you like Fitzgerald?"

"Very much."

"Splendid. That gives us something in common to start with." The head disappeared so suddenly Ham felt that he was at a puppet show. The atmosphere on Partners' Row was certainly different from that in Statistics.

At lunchtime he had a sandwich and a cup of coffee at the Savarin bar in the basement, feeling guilty that he was not "cultivating one of his contemporaries." Afterwards he spent a miserable afternoon reading the copies of yesterday's partners' letters and in frustratedly wondering what was specifically expected of him. Outside his door Miss Kelly read F. Scott Fitzgerald, held inconspicuously on her lap. Doing nothing did not appear to disturb her in the least. He was glad when the office boy placed the evening edition of the *Wall Street Journal* on his desk. He read it from front page to back and went home.

Becoming a partner, however, was a far easier matter, than becoming a father. In the early twenties the ritual of having a baby had changed greatly since the days of Pawnees and Apaches who merely squatted in a mountain stream, produced their new offspring, tied it to a slab of birchbark which they slung over their shoulders and went trotting home to cook supper. It was all so basically simple that the male parent seemed to ignore the proceedings entirely.

Ham became a father in a large building on the southeast corner of Madison Avenue and 62nd Street, housing an establishment known in the élite baby trade as "Miss Lippincott's." In a city of five or six million people there were of course many other places where one might achieve paternity, but in the twenties young women of social distinction would not have dreamed of entering the sacred sorority of maternity except through the expensive portals of Miss Lippincott's.

"Just to be on the safe side" the doctor moved Barbara there a week before the "party," as he lightly called it. Everyone made the most out of childbirth in those uncrowded days. Ham could still remember Barbara vividly as she lay, half propped among the pillows, wearing a new bed jacket and looking radiantly beautiful, as expectant mothers should. A completely unnecessary special nurse puttered in the background. Barbara's time was largely spent receiving flowers, overseeing their arrangement in vases, and listing the donors. Her mother popped in and out twittering like an agitated bird. Her virgin friends called on her, entering timidly and leaving on tiptoes.

At last the labor pains began. Ham found himself suddenly

excluded as one unclean. At the end of the corridor was a small room apparently designed for castoffs. The table was strewn with battered back numbers of the *Saturday Evening Post* and the *National Geographic*. He chose a couple and sat down in a faded chintz-covered chair near a window. Below the traffic of Madison Avenue ebbed stolidly north and south, either unaware of, or indifferent to, the drama that was taking place just a few flights above.

A tall, thin young man entered and seated himself on the edge of the sofa. He was extremely pale and occasionally his prominent Adam's apple worked convulsively. They did not speak. The newcomer continued to stare through the open door like one in a trance. From time to time he crossed and uncrossed his knees, folded his arms, or rested his elbows on his knees and ran his fingers through his hair. Whatever his position his eyes never left the doorway.

From somewhere down the corridor there was the unmistakable sound of a muffled scream. Both men sprang to their feet. Ham's companion ran a trembling finger between his stiff collar and his neck. "Oh, God," he said. "Oh, my God." Beads of perspiration appeared on his forehead. Then, giving his finger a final run through his hair, he disappeared down the hall.

Ham shifted to the sofa where he could also watch the passageway. A door opened. They were wheeling someone out on a stretcher carriage. He recognized the nurse. The still body on the stretcher must be Barbara. A second nurse joined them. He moved to the door and stood there staring after the retreating figures, his hands clasping the doorjambs so tightly that the knuckles stood out like white marbles. Barbara's mother was approaching. He couldn't talk to her now. He couldn't!

She entered dabbing at her face with a tiny handkerchief.

"I must be a sight," she said. "You'd think they'd have a powder room or at least a mirror in a place like this. But, no. I guess you'll just have to shut your eyes and take me as I am."

"Barbara," he gasped. "Is she—I mean is she—all right?"

"Who? Barbara?" asked Mrs. Baker, winding some loose back hair around her finger. "Oh, she's fine. Everything normal and the way it should be. Couldn't ask for anything better."

Ham stared at her incredulously. How could this woman— this mother—sit here and talk like that after the dreadful muffled scream he had heard a few minutes before.

"She'll be her old self after a few weeks of complete rest— complete, mind you." She shook her finger at him. "Rest is the one important thing after childbirth. You must keep the trained nurse for at least three weeks and after that of course you will have a baby's nurse. Barbara looks like a strong girl, Allen, but actually she's rather fragile."

That seemed to exhaust the subject of Barbara as far as Mrs. Baker was concerned. She stared out the window for several minutes, apparently lost in thought.

"You know," she said finally, "I haven't had a chance to really tell you how pleased Mr. Baker and I are about your having been made a partner in your uncle's firm. You're a bright young man, Allen, and we're quite proud of you."

"I am a very lucky one to have been Uncle Charlie's nephew. That's probably more like it."

"Don't talk like that. Mr. Baker was saying just a few evenings ago that Charles Martin would never have taken you in if he wasn't sure you had exceptional ability. Those were his very words. 'Exceptional ability.' "

"I appreciate your confidence, Mrs. Baker. Only time will tell if I deserve it." He could hear Uncle Charlie saying,

"For God sake, stop talking like Rollo." When would he feel secure enough with people like Mrs. Baker to talk like a human being? Probably when he had more money than the Bakers did.

"Of course Mr. Baker and I were in sympathy with your original idea of writing. Self-expression is a splendid thing, if you know what I mean. I hope you will agree with us, however, that writing is not something at which one 'makes one's living,' as the saying is."

"What you really need, Allen, is a bigger apartment where you can have an adequate staff and Barbara can have more of the social life to which she's accustomed and which she loves so dearly. When I was a girl—"

Mrs. Baker rattled on, apparently quite content with the sound of her own voice and demanding nothing from her theoretical listener. Ham took advantage of the opportunity and concentrated on the corridor.

"—Rupert Barrett—you know—my mother's brother— moved to Chicago. Heaven knows why. Chicago of all places! Those awful slaughterhouses and things. Rupert wasn't a practical man at all, if you know what I mean. Thought about nothing but playing the piano. Lost all his money. Just let it run through his fingers. Toward the end I think he was giving lessons or concerts or something when he was hit by a trolley car. In a way it was a blessed relief. His widow, she was one of the Boston Griscoms, very sensibly went home to her family and rather disappeared. Poor thing. The humiliation, if you know what I mean. Her daughter—"

Her voice faded from Ham's consciousness, his thoughts preferring to linger with Uncle Rupert who had brought disgrace to his family through his finger dexterity. At home in Messina he had been brought up to believe that the highest honor that could come to a man was through public recognition in the arts. In this new world money not only was the measuring stick but apparently it must be made in certain stipulated ways if one wanted to be "in."

But who was he to criticize his new world? Wasn't he about to become one of those very people in order ultimately to achieve the positions which they now held? Didn't his realization of this make him a traitor to everything in life that he had been brought up to believe was good? But what could he do? As a family man—a man with dependents— what right did he have to turn his back on the opportunity Uncle Charlie had placed before him? Of one thing he was certain. The only way he could justify his decision to himself was to succeed so unmistakably that the whole world would be forced to acknowledge his achievements.

"—she had a sister," Mrs. Baker was saying, "who moved to Baltimore after her divorce and there she married Charles Gray. He was related—"

"It's a boy." Barbara's nurse was beaming at them. "A splendid little boy. Eight pounds, four and a half ounces. Would you care to see him?"

Feeling like a stranger, uncomfortable and out of place, Ham walked unsteadily down the waxed floor behind his mother-in-law.

Barbara lay limp among the pillows, pale and exhausted, strands of dark hair, damp from perspiration, clinging to her forehead. As her mother and Ham entered the room she smiled at them. It was a wan smile, but, as Ham remembered it years later, she had never looked more loving than at that moment.

He couldn't think of anything to say except "Darling" as he bent over the bed and touched her forehead with his lips. He wanted to ask her forgiveness for his selfishness in getting her into such a mess, but instinct told him not to go overboard. Barbara didn't seem to look at things as he did. In spite of her exhaustion she was obviously happy.

A nurse entered carrying a tiny cocoonlike bundle, wrapped in a white blanket. She laid it carefully on the bed beside Barbara and turned back a corner of the blanket disclosing a wrinkled little face, like that of an ancient brownie. As Ham hung over the bundle he tried desperately to prevent his feeling of shock from finding expression in his eyes.

Roger Baker appeared in the doorway. "Sorry to be late to the party. Hello, Mom. And how's the proud mother?" He kissed Barbara clumsily. "Good heavens, here's the heir apparent. Getting into things early, isn't he?" He examined the tiny bundle more closely and Ham sensed that Roger shared his dismay. "It's a baby," he said. "Yes, sir. That's a *baby.*"

"And you're a pig," murmured Barbara. "He's a beautiful little boy and his name is Michael."

"It's time for you to go," whispered the nurse. "We don't want to tire Mrs. Martin."

"Let's go down to the Harvard Club and open a bottle in honor of Mike Martin. We can go to the Plaza, Mom, if you'll come with us."

"I think I'll wait here. Mr. Baker is calling for me with the car and I'm sure he'll want to see his first grandchild."

"Good. He'll get sick of that sort of emotionalism soon enough. 'By, Mom. 'By, mother superior. Have a good supper, Michael."

"Pig," called Barbara weakly, as they closed the door behind them.

Barbara refused to have a nurse after the trained nurse had left three weeks later. This was her child and she proposed to bring him up herself. Her days were spent bathing and powdering Michael, preparing formulas with the meticulous care of a chemist mixing a lethal compound, or just sitting watching him while he slept.

She had chosen the name. Everyone was calling their son Michael in those days. Ham had hoped she might want to call him Allen, but the thought never seemed to have occurred to her. He said nothing.

Professor Martin had had a slight stroke just before the baby was born. As a result it was several weeks before Fanny dared to leave him with a practical nurse and make the trip to New York to see her grandson. It was not an entirely satisfactory visit. Fanny could not understand the modern techniques of infant care, but she was slightly afraid of Barbara's cool assurance and efficiency, so she made no comments. She was deprived, however, of all the pleasure of teaching a new mother the old familiar tricks, but she swallowed her disappointment.

Barbara's mother kept appearing at odd moments, chirping restlessly about the apartment like an uncaged canary and, unlike Fanny, giving out a steady stream of advice, orders, and opinions to which Barbara paid little attention. The two grandmothers had nothing whatever in common and the one occasion when Mrs. Baker took Fanny to the Colony Club for lunch was an obvious failure.

Each evening after dinner Barbara was so exhausted that she went to bed immediately. Then, for a relaxed hour or two, mother and son talked about the old days and the changes that had taken place in Messina since he left.

She never referred to his career except to congratulate him on the opportunity Uncle Charlie had opened up for him with such unbelievable generosity. Her avoidance of the subject was so obvious that it made Ham uncomfortable and he was on the verge of bringing it up himself. Then he realized that it would distress her and that her silence was not accidental.

The day finally came when Ham and Uncle Charlie put her on the westbound train. As they drove back to Wall Street in Uncle Charlie's long, black car they were both unusually quiet. Ham felt depressed and was grateful to the office for the opportunity it gave him to bury his thoughts in work.

Barbara had taken Michael into their bedroom so that she could hear him better at night. Ham now slept in the guest room. More and more they seemed to be slipping into two different worlds, Barbara's was dominated by Michael, Ham's by the office. As their worlds spun further and further apart the minutiae of their daily lives became less and less important, each to the other.

"May I come in, Uncle Charlie?"

Uncle Charlie was sitting with his back to the desk, chewing an unlit cigar and gazing intently out the window. He seemed able to think better in this position. "Of course, Ham. Come in. I was ruminating. Sit down. What's on your mind?"

"Are you familiar with Sawyer Laboratories?"

"Not specially. Don't think much of the outfit based on what I do know. What do you want to do? Put the stock into widows' margin accounts?"

Ham ignored this. "I think they're shy on capital and management."

"Probably the understatement of the week. Do you want to float a bond issue?" Ham wished that whenever he started to talk business his uncle wouldn't treat him as if he were teasing an eight-year-old boy.

"I think they might be receptive to a merger."

"With whom, for heaven sake?"

"American Sheet and Tubing."

"Your father-in-law's outfit? You must be crazy."

"Not necessarily. Each has something the other one needs."

"Even if I thought that was true—and I don't say that I do—there'll be no merger as long as that mush-brain Donahue Brandon is president of Sawyer Labs."

"He had a stroke three days ago."

Uncle Charlie, in the act of lighting his chewed cigar, dropped the match in the ashtray and leaned forward. "How do you know? Why do *you* know when nobody else does?"

"I met his son, Bobby, at dinner last evening. He got tight as usual. We shared a cab going home and he asked me up to his apartment for a nightcap. There he spilled everything. Said his father couldn't speak very clearly, but he'd managed to get it across to Bobby that no one—not even his associates—was to know the nature of his illness. Bobby thinks he's going to die and he's scared to death about what's going to happen to the company because if the old man goes Bobby inherits control and he couldn't control a loose kiddy car. What's more he doesn't want to try."

Uncle Charlie nodded. "Might be a sound analysis. Got any thoughts on the subject?"

"Yes, sir. Sawyer Laboratories are doing things that A.S.&T. isn't equipped to do. They would fill out a weak place in Mr. Baker's over-all picture."

"How do you know?"

Ham looked surprised. "Because I've made it a point to study my father-in-law's business."

"Have you mentioned this to anyone?"

"Yes, when I was with the underwriting group I suggested the idea to Mr. Hobbs. He took me in to see Mr. Brownlee and we discussed it in a general way."

"What did Brownlee say?"

"He was noncommittal. Felt there might be something in it, but he wanted time to dig up the facts."

"Why didn't you ever mention this to me?"

"Because Brownlee said he'd take it up with you if it seemed worthwhile."

"You handled it perfectly right. Apparently Brownlee didn't think much of it, but what you've just told me changes things a lot. Wait a minute. I'll get Brownlee to come in."

George Brownlee listened to Ham's story and turned to Uncle Charlie. "This is a horse of another color. We've studied this situation pretty carefully since Ham first suggested it but we concluded the timing wasn't right. Now perhaps it is."

This time Uncle Charlie succeeded in relighting his cigar. "George, do you agree with Ham that this would be a desirable merger?"

"I certainly do, particularly in view of what has happened to Brandon. He would never have agreed to any merger if he were in good shape. I'm sure of that."

Uncle Charlie turned to Ham. "How would you go about feeling this out?"

"I'd suggest that you have a preliminary talk with Mr. Baker."

Uncle Charlie shook his head. "No. That's *your* job."

"But I'm his son-in-law. He might think I was trying to make money out of the family connection."

"Not if you were bringing him something that would make money for him. If you didn't, he'd have no part of it even if you were his grandmother; but if you put it to him in the right way and if what you say is really so, he'd know that even if he doesn't go for this particular deal he could count on you to give him a first look at anything you thought might be interesting in the future. Don't you see?"

"In a way, only I'd hate to muff this. It's a big one."

"You won't muff it, if your idea's a sound one, and we think it is. Only don't let's sit around thinking about it. Call him up at his office right away and ask if you can come over and see him. Do you agree, George?"

"Absolutely."

"Good. Now let me ask you, Ham. If Baker is interested and asks what you think the next move should be, what are you going to tell him?"

"I'm going to suggest that you and I talk to Bobby and then to Mr. Brandon's attorneys."

"Bobby! For God's sake. What's that pipsqueak got to do with it?"

"At the moment quite a bit. Unless he was drunker than I thought last night his father realizes he's through as the executive head of Sawyer Laboratories. Bobby is his only child and his sole heir. He told me last night, almost in tears, that his old man has left everything to him in trust with the exception of the company stock. As you know, the stock of Sawyer is closely held. It's listed on the Curb, but the market is thin as paper whereas the stock of American Sheet and Tubing is listed on the big board and has a broad market. Do you see what I'm driving at?"

"Can't say I do. What percentage of the company's stock will this Bobby inherit?"

"He told me it was around ninety percent."

"Why in the world didn't his father put that in the trust too?"

"It would be my guess that he wanted to give his son a chance. According to Bobby, he's always thought responsibility might make a man of him."

"What does Bobby say about that?"

"He couldn't disagree more. He doesn't want to be made a man of. Says the pagans had the right idea. Sit in the sun and play a flute. All he wants is enough income to live up to the highest pagan standards. Give Bobby a chance and he'll be in there cheering for a merger in which his only occupation will be depositing dividend checks."

Uncle Charlie looked enquiringly at George Brownlee. "That's a fine basis for negotiation," Brownlee commented. "The present owner of the stock is half dead and his principal heir is half-witted."

"If that wasn't so we wouldn't be discussing a merger." Uncle Charlie turned his chair around and studied two pigeons making love on the gutter of the Sub-Treasury. "I'm convinced this is an excellent deal for everybody concerned. If it could be put through while Brandon's still alive it might make things simpler. If that can't be done I'm sure his executors and Bobby would heave a mighty sigh of relief if they knew there was a built-in market for the stock."

Uncle Charlie whirled back to face his desk. "Ham, I think you've got something important here and that things are much more propitious than they seem. The main thing is not to lose any time. Other people may be watching this situation too. Now get on the phone and set up a date with old prune-face before *he* has a stroke."

It was the first time that Ham had been to Mr. Baker's office. It was located on the tenth floor of the old National City Bank building and exuded an atmosphere of mustiness which seemed to extend into the corridor and to greet all callers with an invisible embrace as they stepped off the wobbly elevator.

At the end of the corridor were two modern frosted-glass doors with a panel above them announcing that this was the home of the American Sheet and Tubing Company. Mr. Baker did not believe in being too close to his operations. He maintained a separate office on the door of which one read in small lettering the inhospitable legend "Mr. Baker, PRIVATE." Ham opened it with some misgivings and found himself in a large room where several elderly men were working over ledgers. No one looked up. They were separated from stray callers by a heavy mahogany rail on the outside of which a gray-haired woman was typing busily.

No one paid any attention to him. "I beg your pardon," he said finally. "My name is Allen Martin. I have an appointment with Mr. Baker."

The typist waited until she had finished a sentence and then looked up with the anoyed expression of one who has been rudely interrupted in the midst of a fascinating experience. "Who?" she asked.

"Martin. Allen Martin. I have an appointment—"

"Yes, you told me that before." She rose stiffly and passed through a door into an inner office. Ham caught a glimpse of Mr. Baker sitting at a huge desk. Then she returned, closing the door behind her. "He'll see you," she said resentfully. "He's terribly busy, but he'll see you, Go right in." She pressed a button and there was a click in the gate of the mahogany rail.

Mr. Baker looked up brusquely as Ham entered his office. "Well, well. Unexpected pleasure. What brings you here this time of day? Nothing the matter with Barbara—or my grandson?" Mr. Baker was so outraged that Michael had not been named after him that he would always refer to him as his grandson.

"No, sir. They're both fine."

"Quite. Quite. Well, what's on your mind?"

"I want to talk to you about Sawyer Laboratories."

"What do you want to know? You've got an up-to-date statistical department at your shop or you should have if you're any good."

"Did you know, sir that Mr. Donahue Brandon, the president, has had a stroke and is not expected to live?"

The expression of Mr. Baker's face did not change except for his eyes which contracted at the corners as they focused more sharply on Ham.

"Where'd you pick that up?"

"I'm not at liberty to say, but I can assure you that the source of my information is reliable."

"How long has this been going on?"

"Three days, sir."

"You seem to be so well informed perhaps you know what percentage of Sawyer Laboratories stock Donahue Brandon owns?"

"My guess would be around ninety percent."

"Not a bad guess," said Mr. Baker, allowing a faint smile to flicker across his thin lips. "The figure is eighty-eight. Why do you come to me with all this?"

"Because his son is his sole heir. Everything will be left in a trust except the stock of this company."

"Why did he leave that outside the trust?"

"I'm led to believe Mr. Brandon thought that if his son succeeded him as head of the company it might steady him down. He left the stock to him outright because he didn't want to tie his hands in any way."

"What does the boy think about all this? What's his name?"

"Robert."

"Yes, yes, of course. How does he feel about taking over?"

"He most definitely is not going to step in. This stock could easily present a problem to both Robert and the estate. Even if Mr. Brandon lives he will never go back as the active head of the company. If anyone came along with a good merger offer I think he might be able to do business."

"Quite, quite. Yes, yes. My, my." Mr. Baker straightened his fingers and stared at his fingernails for several seconds as if he had never noticed them before.

"Are you suggesting that my company make such an offer?"

"No, sir. I'm only trying to find out if you're interested."

"Why do you come to me? Because I'm your father-in-law and you think it would be easier to make a profitable deal for your firm within the family? Look here, young man, I don't like family deals. They lead to trouble if anything goes wrong. I'm tougher when I'm dealing with a member of my family than I am with a stranger."

Ham felt his back stiffen. "I didn't come to you, sir, because you were my father-in-law. If I may say so I thought I was doing you a favor by telling you of this situation. I certainly did not expect or want any favors from you."

"Why did you think you were doing *me* a favor?"

"Because in my opinion Sawyer Laboratories fits perfectly into your over-all picture. It fills in a gap in your organization—rounds it out. But, sir, it's sheer impertinence for me to be saying these things to you. You know very well whether I am right or wrong. If I am wrong there is no harm done. I will merely ask you to regard this conversation as confidential and Martin and Kuhn will feel free to discuss the matter with the heads of other corporations who we think might be interested." As he spoke the words he wondered who the other corporations were.

Mr. Baker placed his forefingers on either end of a pencil, raised it from his desk and rocked it. Finally he put it down and glanced at his wrist watch. "Don't try to bluff me,

Martin, now or ever. Meet me here at three with your uncle and your lawyer. Bring anyone else from your office that you want. I'll have my lawyers and a few of my financial officers present. Don't bother to bring any figures on Sawyer; we have them all here."

The following weeks were so jammed with work that Ham found it almost impossible to recall them later in any detail. They were like a 400-piece picture puzzle dumped on a card table. Eventually the pieces were fitted together and became a whole, but he could not remember the sequence through which this came about nor did it seem to matter greatly. The important thing was that, after weeks of labor, the last piece finally slid into place. In the paneled board room of American Sheet and Tubing the final signatures were affixed and notarized, the younger lawyers nervously began to pick up the papers which littered the long table, the tensions which had so often threatened to upset the entire project suddenly evaporated. Everyone rose, shook hands with everyone else, and exchanged meaningless compliments. The king was dead. God save the king.

Ham remembered going into a large conference room where a portable bar had been set up. Mr. Baker had produced an ample supply of preprohibition liquor and, when the decibels had risen to a point where he knew he would not be missed, Ham had slipped away to phone Barbara.

"Thank heaven," she had said. "Now you may be able to come home once in a while and see something of your family."

He had waited for a word of praise, a flicker of recognition of his first big accomplishment, but none was forthcoming. "I hope so," he said.

"Michael has an earache. I've called Dr. Bowers. When are you coming home?"

"I'll be up to dress sometime before six."

"To *dress!*" Her voice was almost a scream of incredulous protest.

"Darling, you've forgotten. Uncle Charlie's giving a partners' dinner at the Knickerbocker to celebrate the occasion. I told you about it."

"I'll never understand men. They act like juvenile cave dwellers. First they jettison their family and almost ruin their health trying to do some incomprehensible job and then, having finished it, instead of going back to their families, they ruin what's left of their health by going on a tribal drunk."

"But, Barbara dear, we're not going on a tribal drunk. I'll be home very early."

"And I'm supposed to sit up with a sick child while you whoop things up at the Knickerbocker. Can't you tell your uncle that your son is sick and you can't come?"

"Dearest, I don't want to be immodest, but to some degree this dinner is given for me. I dreamed up this project and I had a lot to do with putting it through. I thought you'd be proud of me."

"I'd be prouder if you'd think of something occasionally besides piling up money."

"I'm sorry about Michael," he said in a voice made flat by control. "I'll be home around six."

He replaced the receiver noiselessly in its cradle. What was the use? She was overwrought and upset. He must try to see things from her point of view. He returned to the group in the conference room. The sun of his triumph had disappeared behind a cloud. Why did Barbara always seem to have the power to transmute happiness and self-confidence into a feeling of guilt?

The conference room was filled with a roar of voices. His father-in-law met him at the door. Against the background of these big booming men Mr. Baker reminded Ham of a wood sprite who has become accidentally mixed up with a herd of elephants.

"Well, well," he said. "Couldn't find you anywhere. Getting worried. Had something to say to you." Ham wondered for an instant if he was in for another scolding.

"Sorry, sir, I went to telephone Barbara."

"Fine, fine. Right thing to do. Hope she's as pleased as we all are. That's what I wanted to say. You did a fine job, my boy. Fine job. Yes. Yes." He stared into his untouched highball as if in search of inspiration. Ham remained silent. "Quite," he said finally. "Fact is it was such a fine job we want you to come on the Board of the merged company. You know. New broom. Making you present of five hundred shares new stock. They'll be on your desk when you get back to the office. It'll be in your name. Just a token of recognition. Small token. Quite."

"But, sir, I don't know what to say. What we did was done as a firm, not by me alone. We will be amply compensated. I am deeply touched by your invitation to join your Board, but that honor should go to my uncle, sir. He was the guiding spirit behind this whole thing as far as the firm is concerned and obviously he is a man of much wider experience."

"I told him we were going to invite you to become a director. Told him about the stock gift. Agreed to both. Okay?"

"You've been both kind and generous, Mr. Baker. Now I'm going to ask you a favor. I would appreciate it if you do not make that gift of stock. I accept the directorship with pleasure, but I would feel better if I buy my own qualifying shares and take no further stock position."

"What's that? What's the matter? We're not doing anything wrong. We have nothing to hide. Don't see what you're driving at."

"Well, to begin with, you're my father-in-law, sir. I am in the investment banking business. We have just been your agent in completing what we hope will be a most successful merger. As you say, we have done nothing wrong. Far from it. But in this business of mine I am determined to lean over backward to avoid the slightest suggestion of a conflict of interests. I think you must see my point and you are too good a businessman not to agree with me."

"Of course. Of course. But I think you're a damned fool. No conflict here. Won't argue. I'm no damned fool. Will tell my lawyer to reverse transaction."

"Thank you, sir, you're very understanding."

Barbara met him at the apartment door. "Where in the world have you been? I thought you were never coming. Dr. Bowers has been here and he's awfully worried about Michael's ear. He may have to open it tomorrow. Do you have to go to that awful dinner?"

He avoided the question. "Let me get you a drink," he said. "You look as if you needed one."

He went out to the pantry, pulled out a gallon jug of bathtub gin from the cabinet under the shelf and made a shaker full of orange blossoms. When he returned she was sitting on the sofa staring at the empty fireplace. The corners of her mouth were drooping; always a bad sign.

He filled two of their best wedding-present glasses. Barbara drank half of hers in one gulp and made a face. "It tastes like medicine," she said. "Oh, Ham, I'm so worried. Dr.

Quincy came to see Michael just after Dr. Bowers left. He gave him some medicine just to ease the pain, but when he wakes and starts crying I just can't bear it. I just can't *bear* it, I tell you." He reached over and took her hand, but it lay in his, limp and unresponsive.

"I've got something else to tell you. I've known it for a week, but you pop in and out so fast I've never had a chance to tell you properly."

He looked at her anxiously. "Good God. Is it something awful?"

"No, it isn't something awful. I'm going to have another baby. Dr. White told me last week there was no doubt about it. I didn't want to mention it until I was sure."

He leaned over and kissed her, then raised his glass. "The proud father salutes you."

"You've been home so little in the last few months that I think the world might well question who the proud father is."

"What are we going to call it?" he asked.

"It isn't an 'it.' It's a 'she.' "

"How do you know?"

"Because I do. That's the way they run in my family; boy, girl, boy, girl, boy—"

"Hold everything. What are you going to call this 'she,' presuming you've already made up your mind?"

"Patricia."

"Holy smoke. What are we starting here? A bit of old Erin? By the way, don't I get in on this at all?"

"I didn't say you weren't going to be consulted. I'm consulting you now. I suppose you want her to be named Fanny or some old-fashioned name like that."

"Sort of a Russian consultation," he said, draining his glass. "I've got to go and dress."

She sat upright and stared at him. "You mean to say you're still going to that dinner and leave me in this mess?"

"You know I wouldn't if I didn't have to. I'll come home as soon as the last speech is made and I'll phone you during dinner. By the way, your father asked me to go on the Board of his company."

She rose and walked toward the passage to their bedroom. She paused in the doorway. "Good," she said. "I suppose you'll be running A.S.&T. before you get through."

A door slammed. He emptied the shaker into his glass, drained it, and went to the guest room to dress.

Business boomed. The Golden Twenties were in full swing. Companies merged. Stocks rose, split, then rose again. Secretaries with good ears made modest paper fortunes, then raised their sights another notch. Headwaiters dreamed of retirement among the green valleys of Europe. Tycoons commuted to Long Island in powerful speedboats that were forever ripping off their propellers on the bobbing flotsam of the East River. New clubs were organized, each more exclusive and luxurious than their predecessors. Seats in the board rooms of the brokerage houses were hard to find.

Companies, *almost* regardless of their products, were expanding. Their stock, *completely* regardless of their products, was soaring. New companies were coming into being like mushrooms after a spring rain. The opportunities for corporate financing were endless and, although the competition was ruthlessly keen, Ham, under the cynical, experienced eyes of Uncle Charlie, quickly learned the paths that led to the center of the maze.

His success wasn't all due to Uncle Charlie. As a born

hunter knows where the big game is to be found and how to stalk it, he instinctively seemed to sense where big business was in the making and what buttons to push to force himself into the inner circles from which all but the knowing were barred. His very attitude was that of a hunter, emotionless —focused on his objective to the exclusion of all outside distractions.

He quickly learned to hide his intensity, however. To the world he was a charming, relaxed young man who could lounge in the Brook or Links Club before dinner, making an occasional quip or comment, but always listening, always putting two and two together. He was universally popular because his quips were to the point, his comments shrewd, and he never argued. More important, he was acquiring a reputation for being a "comer" and that was something these men could understand and admire. Young Martin had reached that nebulous point where he was worth cultivating.

Uncle Charlie did not have to guide him for long. More and more the old man and the young one sat together in the former's office discussing various projects as equals. These talks usually took place in the late afternoon and Uncle Charlie was apt to continue them in his limousine as they were driven uptown.

"Don't let's talk any more business," he said one night as they inched their way through the traffic. "To hell with it. I'm tired. Thank God for you, boy. I don't know what I'd do without you. I saw that old ass of a doctor of mine yesterday and he found about ten things the matter with me. It seemed to give him great pleasure. I'll bet the old goat's full of termites himself. But the point is he says I have to let up. The trouble is he knows all the things I enjoy in life and the old sadist took them away from me. At least he thinks he did.

I'm not folding by a long shot, but it's a great comfort to have you aboard."

"It's good to hear you say that, Uncle Charlie, but you've plenty of partners who have both experience and ability."

"Listen, Rollo, I've got plenty of partners and most of them have more *experience* than you, but they're specialists, Ham, specialists. Davidson, for instance, is one of the best margin men in the Street. He knows every account; just when to turn 'em off, just when to let 'em run. He looks like a benign old gaffer but he's tough as a Western steak. The trouble is that ticker tape's like an umbilical cord to him; once he lets go of it he's lost.

"Then there's Craig. He's a top statistician. He has figures coming out of his ears. But that's that. Once he's unloaded them they're somebody else's business. Harwich is a top-grade government bond man, but he's not happy unless he's jugglin' three decimal places. Bartow is such a good office manager that his idea of recreation would be to sleep in the place and keep an eye on the cleaning squad.

"And so it goes right around the circle. Specialists, all of them. You and I are the only ones in the bunch that see the picture as a whole; the only ones that know how to go out and get business. Let's face it, boy. You know I'm right."

Ham was silent. Uncle Charlie wound down the window of the limousine and tossed out the butt of his cigar. "I don't suppose there is much you *can* say to that kind of talk, but it's the reason I'm glad you're with me. It used to be all on my shoulders. I didn't build up this firm right. Filled in at the bottom and left the top empty. We're havin' a good year, best we ever had, but it's largely due to me and you and Davidson's starry-eyed customers. That end of the business worries me; a lot of customers' men who don't know anything, talking all day to a lot of dreamers who know less. This boom isn't going to last forever and when the party's over a bunch of these people are going to get hurt. They always do, but you can't stop 'em. If they don't speculate here they'll speculate somewhere else."

"Why don't we get out of the margin end of the business?"

"Because we've got a bear by the tail. We've expanded so fast we need those margin account commissions to keep the ball rolling."

"But if you gave up—"

"Oh, to hell with it. Let's talk about ourselves. That's always more interesting. You and I have developed three quarters of the worthwhile underwriting business of this outfit during the last year. As one of the junior partners your cut in the profits is all out of line with the results. As you know, the whole picture gets its annual review in another month and at that time you're in for a much bigger slice of the cake. There's bound to be a squawk, but I don't care. It's the producers who get paid in this shop—and in any other, I guess."

He sank back in the corner and mopped his face with his large colored-silk handkerchief. "That's the end of business. Curtain on Wall Street. I wanted to get that off my chest, but I'm tired, bone tired. What the hell's the matter with me? I used to be able to go home after a day like this and wine and dine half the night. What did that old veterinary do to me? I heard a good one in the Down Town Association today. Sanderson of the Appellate Division told it at lunch. It seems that there were three fairies at a prizefight and one of them said—"

Patricia was born without any real trouble, but with the usual fuss and feathers. She was a wizened little monkey like her brother. Barbara considered her beautiful, however, and would sit for hours watching her in her bassinet. Barbara still refused to have a nurse and her complete absorption in her children worried Ham. The only people she saw from one end of the day to the other were her mother and Delia the cook. Ham's bed had been dismantled and stored in the basement so she could have both children with her. The guest room had become "Ham's room."

He needed to entertain for business reasons, but he couldn't bring anyone home to face this diaper-strewn disorder. Clubs were all right, but there was no place to sit around and talk afterward. Uncle Charlie stepped into the breach and gave small, extravagant dinners in his apartment. He was obviously tired, however, and shortly after the brandy and cigars he would excuse himself and leave the show to Ham.

"Listen, boy, I can't take this sort of life much longer," he said one day as they were walking back after a tense negotiating lunch in a private dining room at the Broad Street Club. "Lunch, yes, but not dinners too. You simply have to have a bigger apartment and more service. It's ridiculous for Barbara to wear herself out taking full care of two young children. She's hiding behind 'em, that's what she's doing, and it isn't fair to you. You need a wife, not a nurse. It's part of your life to entertain socially—to move around with your own crowd—and, in addition, it's part of your life to stuff filet mignon and fresh asparagus into characters such as we've just been arguing with. I've always been against using the home for business entertainment, but things have changed, particularly since we started to work the provinces. You know damned well that if you go to Omaha City or Kalamazoo or Medicine Hat they'd invite *you* to *their* houses and if you don't invite them to yours when they're in New York they'll put you down as a snob—and that's a fighting word with most of them. Have you talked to Barbara about moving into something bigger?"

"I've mentioned it, but she doesn't seem to want to discuss it."

Uncle Charlie made a clicking noise with his tongue and said nothing until they had reached the end of the block and started to wind their way through the crowded sidewalks of Wall Street. "You've got a problem on your hands, boy. What does Barbara's mother think?"

"The only time she discussed the matter with me she felt very much the way you do."

"Oh, well, don't worry. When things are obvious something is bound to happen. By the way, please don't mention this conversation to Barbara. I think that's important."

Ham looked puzzled. "But why? I thought it might influence her if she knew how you felt."

"No, please accept my judgment on this. Don't say a word. Just let things drift."

Ten days later Barbara called him at the office. She sounded as if she was crying. "Oh, Ham, can't you come home? I'm almost crazy."

"What's wrong, dear? Nothing the matter with the kids is there?"

"No, it's Mother. She's been here all morning. We've had a terrible scene. She insists on our moving into a bigger apartment. She's adamant and when Mother gets adamant —oh, Ham, you just can't do anything with her. Do you know what she's done? She's taken an *option* on a great big barn of an apartment in one of those new buildings on Fifth Avenue. She can't run our lives like that, Ham. She wanted me to go and look at it and I said I wouldn't. Then she said the most awful things: she said that I'd always been a rebel and that I was selfish and that I wasn't being a good wife to you by refusing to take my place in the world in which I was brought up. Oh, Ham, you *know* I can't stand up against her when she gets like this. Never could, never will. Won't you go up and see her and tell her we don't *want* a bigger apartment, and that I'm happy right where I am. *You* can do it, Ham. She adores you."

Ham was silent for a moment. "Are you there, Ham? Don't tell me we've been cut off."

"I'm here," he answered, "but I don't know what to say."

"Just tell her we won't do it. There are only two people Mother's afraid of—you and Dad. Success scares her. Just tell her to keep out of our lives."

"I'm in a bad spot, dear. I want you to be happy, but in this case I'm sorry to say I agree with your mother."

He heard a gasp, then there was no question that she was crying. "Barbara dear, pull yourself together. You know as well as I do that we can't go on living as we are. In the first place, I'm damned if I'm going to be exiled permanently in the guest room. Secondly, it's not good for the kids. They should each have their own room. And finally I need you. These are our crucial years. I need a wife to stand beside me, not a baby's nurse."

Her voice was choked, but her tears had stopped. "Oh, how could you talk to me like that? You're hard and cruel like the rest of them. Why did you ever marry me? You knew what I wanted. Why did you pretend we were going to live in a little chintz-covered world? Why did you make me think that your own ambition was to live a creative life when you never had any intention of doing any such thing? Oh, I hate you."

When he replied his voice was even, but coldly firm. "Listen, Barbara, I want you to spend the next few hours calming down and doing some straight thinking. Every man has some field in which he feels at home, some field where he can live with a sense of belonging and face every day with anticipation. Some men never find their field. Those are the ones that Thoreau was referring to, the ones who lead lives of quiet desperation. Many don't find their field until they are middle-aged when, for all practical purposes, it is too late. By a fantastic piece of luck I found mine almost immediately and I don't propose to jump over the fence because I think the grass is greener on the other side. The grass around me is just the kind of grass I like and fortunately I know it."

"What are you doing, scolding me or giving me a philosophical lecture?"

"Neither. I'm telling you some facts for you to think over before three-thirty. I've found my field but I need *you*, not only as the mother of our children, not only as my bedroom wife, but as the wife who stands beside me and does her share in rounding out the picture. I hope you're not too upset to get what I've said. It's terribly important to us both."

"What did you mean by saying I had to think this over before three-thirty?"

"I meant that I'm going to pick you up at three-thirty and we're going over together to look at the apartment your mother has picked out."

"I won't do it. I told Mother I wouldn't and I won't."

"Don't say that. Think it over. You'll see how important it is to you and to me and to the kids. I've got to go now. There are two starving customers sitting outside my office waiting to be fed. See you at half past three."

He had no idea what was going to happen when he entered the apartment, but he wasn't surprised to find her dressed for the street and waiting for him, calm and unsmiling. "Come on," she said. "Let's go and stake out our Fifth Avenue acreage. I must get back to the kids."

It was undeniably a big apartment, its rooms large, high-ceilinged, and the whole place abounding in the waste spaces which the architects of the twenties seemed to consider affluence symbols. Barbara wandered from one bare chamber to another, making no comment other than to remark on the convenience of Central Park which rolled away in a sea of green treetops beneath the living-room and library windows.

"Well," he said, as they finally shook off the real estate agent and hailed a taxi. "How did you like it?"

"That's not the question," she replied. "How did *you* like it?"

"How many servants would it take to run it?" he countered.

"A cook, a butler—I'm thinking in terms of a couple—a waitress-chambermaid, and a nurse. That's minimum, plus a cleaning woman coming in five days a week.

"And then if we're going to live like that," she went on, "you'll want a car and a chauffeur, someone to take you down to Wall Street and back every day and to take us out for dinner and the theater and all that sort of mishmash."

He looked at her in astonishment. She was sitting bolt upright looking straight ahead, her face expressionless. "Do you think you can swing a show like that?" he asked.

"Certainly," she said. "It's nothing new to me." Then turning her head for the first time she looked out at the park and murmured, "Unfortunately."

"But the apartment itself—do you think it's attractively laid out or hideous or what?"

"It's like all big apartments. It will do what you want it to do. You realize of course what it's going to cost to furnish such a place. We have to start from scratch. I can't do that kind of buying. I would want the best decorator in town."

"I'll have to do some figuring," he said. "Will you ask the renting agent to extend the option for a few days?"

"You ask him," she said coldly. "That's your department. My role is to stand at your side and fill out the picture. All right, I will, but tell Mother to keep out of my hair while I'm doing it."

"Listen, boy, you've got to start thinking bigger. Don't forget the old saw, 'You can't make an omelet without breaking eggs.'" Uncle Charlie, obviously pleased at this change of heart on Barbara's part, was in one of his blandest moods.

"I don't think you have any idea how much money you're making, Ham. Your interest seems to be in acquiring it rather than counting it. Last year was our record year and if we keep on the way we're going this year will beat it all hollow. Go ahead. Take the apartment. I've been advising you to do something like this for months."

"Uncle Charlie, you didn't suggest to my mother-in-law that she talk to Barbara, did you?"

"My dear fellow, your ma-in-law may sound a little balmy once in a while but don't be fooled. Underneath the balminess she's got a will of iron. She's felt the same as I did from the start and she's just as pleased as I am."

"How do you know?"

Uncle Charlie fidgeted in his chair. "She called me up," he said, then changed the subject quickly. "By the way, Ham, when did you see your father and mother last?"

"It's been almost a year."

"That's what I thought and it's all wrong. Has Barbara ever been out?"

"No, sir."

"You mean to say she's never met your father except at your wedding?"

"I'm afraid not. She's talked to him on the phone quite a lot and we've planned to go out, but every time something happens. We've had to call off about four trips."

"Well, this is one you're not going to call off."

"What do you mean?"

"I mean you're going to take Barbara under your arm and hightail it out to Messina for a long weekend. That brother of mine isn't going to live forever, you know."

"But, Uncle Charlie, I couldn't go right now. I've got too many irons in the fire."

"I'll pull 'em out for you. Never get the Indispensable Man complex. What do you think we did around here before you showed up, Superman? Well, I'll tell you. We did pretty damned well.

"You go and dictate a memorandum on each of your irons and put each one in a neat little blue folder. Tomorrow I have to go to a funeral. That's my principal pastime these days. You can clean off your desk. The next day you can brief Brownlee and me. We'll give you as much time as you want. And that night you'll take the train for Chicago."

"But Barbara can't leave the kids. She wouldn't dream of it."

"Rubbish. We'll put in a trained baby's nurse and the Bakers can jolly well move in for a few days and see that they don't swallow any buttons. You leave that to me. You work on Barbara. Your doctor can dig up the nurse. No problem."

It turned out as Uncle Charlie had decreed. Things usually did. Four days later they were pulling into the familiar little station at Messina. Barbara was pale and nervous, worried over what lay ahead as well as what she had left behind.

Fanny was waiting for them in the new Ford sedan Ham had given them for Christmas. To Ham's surprise his father was with her. He looked much older and was much more uncertain of himself than he had been the previous year. They slipped into their old grooves so quickly, however, that it was hard to believe so many months had elapsed since their last meeting.

Fanny seemed to sense Barbara's uneasiness and insisted upon sitting with her in the back seat while Ham drove. "Your father's quite deaf," she warned him as he stowed their bags in the trunk of the car, "and he's become very vague. You know. Easily confused. Just go along with him. Don't try to straighten him out. He's merely apt to get the past a little mixed up with the present."

They started up the hill from the station. "Don't know if you'll be able to find your way," said the Professor, peering out anxiously. "Everything's changed so."

"It still looks pretty nice to me."

"Certainly. Certainly," nodded the Professor. "All right except for the pesky automobiles. Is that your wife?"

"Yes, Dad, that's Barbara."

"Of course, of course. You know I'm retired now."

"Mother told me."

"Yes, I'm working on a book. Won't be as popular as yours. Dry. Scholarly. How's *your* book coming along?"

"Your father's very interested in the book you're writing," said Fanny quickly from the back seat. "He hoped you'd want to talk it over with him, but I told him you didn't want to discuss it with anyone until it was finished."

"That's right, Mother. Not till it's finished."

"Too bad, too bad," murmured the Professor, shaking his head regretfully. "I might have been of some help to you. But there's nothing to prevent our talking about *books*. Have you read any Hardy lately?"

"Not for quite a while, Dad. I've been reading a new author though that would interest you. His name is F. Scott Fitzgerald."

"Never heard of him. This fellow Hardy though. He's got style, feeling. I've marked some passages I want you to read. If you could write like that I'd be proud of you.

"*Lord Jim* is another book everyone ought to read if he's writing a book himself. What's his name— Fanny? For heaven sake who wrote *Lord Jim*?"

"Joseph Conrad, dear."

"Of course. Sometimes I think my memory's slipping. Conrad's eternal search for the right word and his success in finding it should be an inspiration to any young author. Do you have the first draft done?"

"Not yet, Dad."

"That's the hard part, particularly with a novel. You don't know quite where you're going and you don't know your characters. Once the draft is out of the way—" He warmed to the subject as they drove through the elm-arched streets. As the car stopped before the old, familiar house he snorted impatiently. "That's the trouble with automobiles. They get you there so fast you never have a chance for a nice quiet talk."

To Ham's relief and delight Barbara and Fanny seemed to have some bond in common that was the source of endless conversation. Barbara accompanied Fanny on her morning trips to the market. In the afternoon Fanny took her for drives through the rolling Indiana countryside.

On the second evening of their visit Ham found his mother alone in the kitchen. "Oh, Allen, I've been waiting for a chance to talk to you. She's a darling, Allen. I just love her.

You're such a lucky boy! I know how busy you are, but don't ever get so busy that you can't find time to let her know you love her. Women are curious creatures. They have to be reassured about things like that every so often."

Fanny and Barbara's absences left Ham in the company of his father much of the day. He sat once more in the big worn chair while the old man, sitting in his accustomed place behind the desk, brushed aside the intervening years and talked once more to his fourteen-year-old son about the treasures that were stored on the shelves around him.

"Take any of them, Horace—any one that appeals to you. Read them. Absorb them. Their ideas and their style will become part of you and will reappear later when you begin to write yourself. Writing has always been based on plagiarism."

He would punctuate his sentences by pausing, as he used to, in order to relight his pipe. After an hour or so he would grow visibly weary. "I think I'll take forty winks now and then get on with my own book. I don't lie down or anything, I just doze in that chair you're sitting in. What are *you* going to do?"

"I think I'll take a walk."

"Fine, fine. Watch out at the crossings. These plaguey automobiles whiz around the corners so."

Ham would wander aimlessly through the once-familiar streets. They had become less familiar each time he visited Messina. His interest now was in what was unchanged. That which had changed was ugly. It depressed and irritated him as if some stranger had meddled clumsily with things that did not belong to him. He saw no one whom he recognized, nor did he look anyone up, not even Millie. What was the use? They had nothing to say to one another after the first two minutes. He fell into the habit of going into Messina's new hotel once a day and telephoning Uncle Charlie to find out how everything was going. It hurt his feelings to learn that everything was going extremely well.

On the next to the last day Barbara insisted on staying out of the picture and letting Ham be alone with his mother. "I know what we'll do," said Fanny. "We'll take a picnic lunch and drive out to Johnson's Falls. I don't think you've ever been there. They were a day's journey when you were a boy. Now you can get there on the new state highway in a little over an hour. I know a picnic sounds crazy in the middle of winter, but there's a lean-to near the falls with a brick cookout sort of thing in front of it. We can build a fire there and be as warm as a bug in a rug."

They drove across the plains into the spruce-covered hills which had been taken over as a State Park. She drove the car to the top of one of the highest. "You don't see much of the falls from here, but you see Indiana. Look. Isn't it beautiful—and big?"

On three sides the great fields lay spread out before them to the horizon, sleeping under a blanket of snow. Clumps of trees huddled around the scattered farmhouses sheltering them from the winter storms.

There was a neat pile of firewood in the rear of the lean-to. Fanny sat on a thick bed of fir branches which had been spread over the dirt floor and watched Ham build a fire. Time was so eccentric, so unpredictable. The hands of a clock moved almost imperceptibly or they flew around its face like the spokes of a moving wheel. Only a few years ago she had been reading aloud to this broad-shouldered man while he ate his supper at a sewing table. Now she was just a mite afraid of him.

They heated the soup and laid out the sandwiches and hard-boiled eggs. Fanny shivered pleasurably as the fire and the soup sent their warmth through her fragile body. "It's worth getting cold," she said, "just to experience the bliss of getting warm again."

She leaned back on her elbows and watched the fire. "Tell me more about your life in New York. It's hard for me to get a real picture from letters, much as I love yours."

He told her as much as he thought she could understand about the work he was doing and the routine of his daily life. He described the series of events which had led to his becoming a director of his father-in-law's company. He gave a long account of her grandchildren, one of whom she had never seen, and ended by scratching a floor plan of their new apartment in the snow outside the lean-to.

She shook her head. "It's all so hard to grasp. Tell me, Allen. Is Barbara happy with all this?"

"Frankly I don't know, Mother. I'm afraid she isn't and it worries me."

She nodded. "I've talked a lot with Barbara in the last few days and I think I'm beginning to understand her. She loves you, Allen, but she thought that you were going to lead her down the paths she was seeking."

"But she wasn't even sure what paths they were."

"She thought you would point them out."

"But, Mother, Barbara has no conception of the economic facts of life. She has no idea that butter and eggs cost money; that they're not things that just appear on the breakfast table. I had no money and I was darned if I was going to live on her family or on Uncle Charlie. Obviously the first thing I had to do was get a job that paid me enough to live on."

"Uncle Charlie saw to that," she said, half to herself, then turning she looked at him intently as if trying to emphasize her words. "And you were too young, too inexperienced, to know that if you were going to be what they call a man of

letters you had to be a man of letters always—from beginning to end, regardless of money. It's a world apart. Perhaps
Wall Street is also. I'm sure you can't jump from one to the
other as the fancy suits you. You've been tremendously successful. I've heard a lot about it from Uncle Charlie. So successful that the world of business has swallowed you. Of
course I'm proud of you, Allen dear, I've always been proud
of you, but where does it leave Barbara? In a way she's worse
off than she was before."

"I don't know, Mother, I really don't know. The whole
thing doesn't make any sense to me sometimes. Am I supposed to resign and get a job as an English instructor in some
college at two hundred dollars a month? Would that make
her happy?"

"I don't know either, Allen. There are so many things that
come up in life that have no easy answers. Sometimes there
are no answers. You have to be true to yourself and at the
same time try to understand Barbara. As I said the other day,
don't let yourself get too busy for such things."

"Have I disappointed you and Father?" he asked abruptly.

"That's one of the questions which perhaps has no answer.
Remember that your father and I came from a long line of
people who made what little money they had in the field
of words. They did all sorts of different things, but words
were always the hard core of their livelihood. As you know,
some were teachers, like your father; others were journalists,
editors, research scholars, lecturers; a few even wrote books,
though I don't think they were very good ones.

"Your father was a born scholar, but he has always envied
the acclaim that is given to the writer of successful books.
He realized that he would never receive it, but when you
were born he hoped that you would be the medium that
would vicariously translate his craving into reality. Don't

think he was alone in this. I was just as enthusiastic about the idea as he was. From the time you were a little boy we tried to develop the dream in you. For a long time I thought we had succeeded. Perhaps we would have under different circumstances. So you ask if you have disappointed me. I suppose the honest answer is yes. In spite of all my pride in you, you have left the field which I had hoped you would love as I do."

"Why do you keep referring to yourself, Mother, and not to Dad?"

"After he had his stroke, Allen, his mind became confused. He talked a great deal about you and kept asking what you were writing. It seemed to worry him so that I finally spoke to Dr. Barnes. On his advice I lied to your father for the first time in my life. I told him that you had a little job with Uncle Charlie, just enough to keep the wolf from edging through the door, and that you were writing a novel. That seemed to satisfy him. He stopped worrying, but he's so excited about it I think he's told half the people in Messina."

Ham groaned. "Don't worry about it, Allen. They are so engrossed in their own affairs that most of them have forgotten about it already. Even if they haven't they're going to be much more interested in the news that you're making oodles of money. I hope you're not cross at me for what I did."

She picked up a stick and poked the embers of the fire. "Now the confessional's over. Let's talk about other things. It's getting cold up here, though. Suppose we gather up the luncheon things and drive home slowly. It feels like snow."

The following night on the way from Chicago to New York he tossed restlessly in the upper berth of Drawing

Room A. The bedclothes had come loose and were wrapped around him like a shroud. Pullman porters never seemed able to make up an upper berth properly. They didn't really make it up. They threw it up.

Barbara's even breathing indicated that she was asleep. He wondered just what she had told his mother. Apparently everything. But what in the world was there to tell? He had been shot with luck, loved his work, labored at it like a salt mine slave, and was making lots of money. His mother had said "you have to be true to yourself," but there was small consolation in that if people thought that the ends were not worth accomplishing. He rearranged the pillows and banged his head into them savagely. To hell with it. He was doing nothing wrong and so plum to hell with it.

The pace of the boom quickened month by month. During the winter of 1924-25 it began to show signs of the frenzy that was yet to come. New issues popped like firecrackers causing the financial sections of the newspapers to insert additional pages and the overworked staffs of the brokerage houses to tear their hair. Underwriters phoned their friends. "Joe, I took the liberty of putting you into a thousand shares of Blackwater Electric. We brought it out this morning as you probably saw in the paper. Don't worry, Joe. Never mind what it is. It's already been sold, at a nice profit. We'll send you a check. Not at all. Pleasure to do it."

Women were coming into the market in increasing numbers, guided by dinner-table rumors. "Last night I sat next to a man—he's so high up I can't mention his name—who told me in the *strictest* confidence that there's a pool operating in Bolling Trucks. He said their objective was 85. Got that? 85! And it closed at 48 last night. Wow! Pick me up

100 shares. I'm going to play this one safe. Put in a GTC order to sell at 80 or better. No use trying to squeeze out the last drop."

Locker-room conversation was devoted almost entirely to financial matters. "I hear Peter Hubblewhite's making money so fast he doesn't know where to keep it. I'm glad for Pete's sake. He could use a little for a change. Sam told me he was buying a Rolls-Royce. He says it isn't extravagant because his old Ford is shot to pieces and Rolls-Royces don't wear out."

Ham never worked harder than he did that winter. He tried to follow his mother's advice and pay more attention to Barbara, but the office pressures made this harder and harder. He had long since moved into a big office next to Uncle Charlie's. Two young assistants, not yet completely recovered from overexposure to the Harvard Business School, shared the office which had formerly been his.

He found it necessary to travel more; in fact he had reached a point where, with the aid of Nembutal, he could sleep fitfully all night in a Pullman, bathe and breakfast at a hotel at seven in the morning, read the *New York Times* and the local paper and enter a strange office at ten o'clock at least simulating the appearance of an alert young business-man.

Uncle Charlie unwillingly added to his burden. "I don't know what's the matter with me, boy. I guess it's just old man's disease, goddamit. Dr. Snow says I got to get out of here every day at three o'clock and go to bed. To *bed*, Ham; in the middle of the afternoon! Did you ever hear anything so degrading? But for once I haven't got the strength to fight the old fool.

"This place is rottenly organized. It's my fault. You and Brownlee and I can hardly keep up with the underwriting end of the show and Brownlee's not really an outside man. Certainly you can't do it alone or you'll be in bed with me, God forbid. We've got to bring a couple of young partners up fast. We can't touch the specialists. They're too valuable where they are. If it's all right with you I'm going to pull young Haley out of Statistics and assign him to you. He's been a partner only a short time, but he's sharp as a tack, he's got excellent connections, and he gets along with men without hitting the night spots all the time. What d'you think?"

"I agree. Fine idea."

"All right. Let's say Haley, then. I'll talk to Bartow about it this morning. But Haley isn't enough. We need more help. Any bright thoughts?"

"Yes. Make junior partners out of those two young fellows that are working in my office. They're good. Need a lot of theory kicked out of them, but my kicking leg is still pretty solid. They're terrific workers. Down here every night till nine o'clock."

"How do you know?"

"Because I'm often down here with them."

"What does Barbara think of that?"

Ham shrugged. "What else *can* I do?"

"I don't know but, goddamit, boy, we're getting so many partners in here the place looks like the Mexican army. Can't any of the present ones help you or are you helping them?"

"They're learning, Uncle Charlie, but each one's going to have his own job to do. We're growing. Who's going to staff the out-of-town offices?"

"What out-of-town offices? Hell's bells, boy, we're not going to have out-of-town offices on top of all this madhouse are we?"

"We have to, Uncle Charlie. It's the trend. We're badly behind the procession now. It isn't just a matter of publicizing our name and raking in a few more shekels. We just can't cover the whole underwriting waterfront from New York. We need offices headed by men who can go out and button things up in their areas after we've broken the ground. We need an office in Chicago and one in San Francisco right now and we need them badly. The Southwest, the Middle West, and New England can come later."

Uncle Charlie seemed to be visibly shrinking. "No wonder I'm tired. All right, we'll make your two little boys juniors and blame you if they don't turn out. I hope they have the initiation fee. Would it be too bold to ask what their names are?"

"John Twining and Baxter Green."

Uncle Charlie made a note on his desk pad. "Okay. Got a lunch date?"

Ham pushed down a lever on Uncle Charlie's intercom. "Miss Kelly, do I have a lunch date?"

"No, sir. Mr. Stevens just called to say he couldn't lunch with you. Said he had to go to Washington, and quick. Said he was sorry, but you'd understand."

"Right. I'm lunching at the D.T.A. with Mr. Martin."

"Don't forget you have a meeting at Bell, Black and Shriver at 2:30. I've put all the papers in your briefcase. I'll bring it in and you can go there from lunch. Brown Brothers building, 58 Wall."

The intercom clicked. "For God's sake hurry up," said Uncle Charlie. "I'm a weak old man and I want a drink."

Barbara had found in Fanny someone to whom she could pour out her heart knowing that her point of view would be understood. She returned to New York resolved to follow Fanny's advice; to try to appreciate Ham's talents and live with the consequences. She had been self-centered and selfish. Fanny had shown her that without ever using those words. Now she was prepared to make amends; to live Ham's life, not as a martyr but as a loyal wife whose desire was to promote his interests and make him happy. Her resolutions encompassed more than Ham. As Fanny had said, it was up to her to create an atmosphere in her home that would enable her children to grow up into normal, uninhibited men and women.

For the first month after their return from Messina she was so busy getting the new apartment settled that she hardly had time to notice the increased tempo at which Ham was working. In fact she was so tired at the end of each day that it was rather a relief to have him call up to tell her that he would not be home for dinner. It gave her a chance to have hers in bed and turn out the light at half past eight. When he came home to pack his suitcase for a three-day trip she looked forward to the interval as an opportunity for three blissful nights of reading and rest.

It was only when the interior decorators had sprayed the last room with beige paint, laid the last rugs and placed the last piece of furniture—when the last towels had been stacked in orderly piles in the huge linen closet—that she began to feel like the sole inmate of a deserted chateau. She couldn't go on having her dinner in bed for the rest of her life. Eating alone at the end of the long dining-room table made her so restless that frequently she had to get up and walk through the strange rooms between courses.

She gave a few small dinners but they did not work out very well as Ham usually called up at the last moment to say that he couldn't get away from the office. As his unpredictable social habits became known, people hesitated to invite the Martins to their houses realizing that they also would probably end up with that hostesses' nightmare—an extra woman.

She plunged headlong into the whirlpool of New York life; charitable committees, lunches, lectures, concerts, bridge. Most of these escape activities involved only women, however, and women usually bored her. She attended cocktail parties which at least were bisexual. She went alone. It was so obvious that Ham couldn't come that she didn't even bother to tell him of the invitations.

At these parties she met a few publishers and authors and an occasional musician or journalist, all of whom she cultivated assiduously. As a result, she began to receive occasional luncheon invitations, and when they learned about her home life, which she didn't make it too difficult for them to do, they began asking her to evening parties of their own. For the first time she found herself among the people she had always wanted to know; an easy, freewheeling group which dared to have its own thoughts and to express them without inhibitions.

In the beginning she only went to these parties when Ham was on some business trip. As time went on, however, she began to accept particularly attractive invitations even when he was in New York. The chances were about even that he would not be home for dinner. It seemed rather stupid to sit alone night after night in anticipation of something that probably wouldn't happen.

As a result Ham occasionally returned home in the evening only to find Barbara dressing to go out. When this happened he left almost immediately for the Knickerbocker Club. He didn't object to what Barbara was doing, but he was damned if he was going to stand beside her in the living room and be introduced to her escort.

He didn't object because he couldn't. Barbara was a young

and vital woman who loved life and the society of intelligent people. He was sure that she would have liked nothing better than to have had him accompany her to these affairs, whatever they were. She was merely going alone down the path that she had expected they would walk together because there was no alternative. He had made that so, not Barbara.

In an odd way he was relieved. It made his own life much more flexible and dispelled his uneasy sense of guilt to know that he was not always causing her to eat dinner alone and go to bed with a book immediately after. This would not last forever. These were the days when he must give everything he had to the firm. Later they could relax together and he would enjoy his children.

As for Barbara, she was moving, experiencing. She had re-entered the stream of life and no longer felt like an old rowboat that had been cast up by the tide on a deserted beach, but it all left her with an empty feeling. She had decided to go Ham's way, to stand beside him, share his problems, be of help to him, but she had failed entirely. He was moving so fast, his problems were so alien that there seemed no way that she could participate in his life. When he called her up one afternoon and asked if she would like to go out for dinner with him that evening she was so happily surprised that it was an effort to keep her voice normal. "I'd love it," she said. "I'll put on my new dress for you."

Later the dim lights of the oak-paneled room, the sound of blended voices all about them, and the warm exhilaration of champagne suddenly swept away all the loneliness and doubts and she felt only tenderness for this handsome man who was fighting so hard for something that he at least desperately wanted.

"You look radiant, darling."

She moved closer to him on the banquette seat. "I'm

happy. That's even better. Oh, Ham, I wish we could do this more often."

"Perhaps we can."

"I hope so. I do hope so. You don't know how I miss you sometimes and something like this brings us together, just as we used to be. Nothing else matters."

"I'm so glad to hear you say that. There have been moments when I've wondered and I didn't blame you. It's been awfully dull for you; alone, night after night, having me upset your parties at the last minute because I couldn't make the grade, rattling around in that big apartment while I go tearing around the country. Don't think I'm unaware of it. I miss you too—dreadfully. But what can I do? I've got that old bear by the tail again."

Her tone changed slightly. "Sometimes I think you have a permanent grip on it. It hasn't always been easy, Ham, but I'm proud of you. You're one of the successful young men in the Street. I hear it on every side. People come up to me and say how wonderful it must be to have a husband that everybody's talking about. Oh, I admit it hasn't always been easy. If it were it would mean I didn't love you. But that apartment's so darn big, Ham. I've tried to fill in the gaps and you've been sweet about it, but it isn't what I want."

"Poor Barb. It's not what I want either. If there were some way—" He lit a cigarette and watched the smoke curl out into the shadows. "I think I have an idea. Let me sleep on it overnight."

The waiter filled their glasses and left. "I've been very much worried about Uncle Charlie," he said. "I haven't talked to you about it because there wasn't much I could put my finger on. His old, wonderful buoyancy seems to be draining away, day by day, like sand in an hourglass. For the last few months he really hasn't been doing anything, to speak of, at the office. I give him a detailed report every morning. He just nods and says 'good boy' or something like that. It's as if he didn't give a damn. He usually has lunch with some old cronies at the Down Town Association. Then he goes home without coming back to the office.

"Today we had a long talk, one that will affect both our futures. That's why I particularly wanted to get you off and talk to you tonight." She hoped her face didn't disclose the hurt those words caused her. So this dinner, which she had thought was a momentary return to the old days, was nothing but another business meeting, probably to warn her of worse things to come.

"What's the matter, dear? Did he fire you?" Keep it light.

"Well, not exactly. He started off by telling me about the capital contributions of the various partners. The long and short of it is that he has more capital in the firm than all the other partners put together. Apparently they could all withdraw and the firm would go on very nicely, but if his capital was pulled out they would have to bring in more money or merge or liquidate.

"He doesn't want that. He built this business and he's proud of it. I don't blame him. He's got a big staff. He's loyal to them. Wants to protect them.

"And now comes the bombshell. He has drawn up a new will in which he leaves all of his firm capital to me with the expressed desire that I leave it in the firm and carry on as senior partner. He wanted me to talk to you about it. If we don't want to carry on, he's considering withdrawing his capital while he is alive and arranging for a merger with some other firm.

"I've seen the will. He has set up a trust for my father and mother, a trust for each of our kids, and he's left you a tidy sum outright. He called it an attempt to compensate you in some small degree for all the loneliness he has caused you. Isn't that like him? He seems in a great hurry to put all this through, for some reason or other. He wanted to know our answer by tomorrow if possible."

Barbara's eyes never left his face while he talked. Her own was as expressionless as a croupier's. Ham was obviously excited, but trying his best to be neutral as if he feared to influence her judgment.

So this was the crossroads and he was asking *her* to decide. How utterly ridiculous. Without committing himself Ham had already reached the only decision he could possibly make. Let him be the one to put it into words.

"What do *you* think?"

"I don't know what to say, Barb. I want you to be happy and I know the kind of life you hoped we might lead when you married me. We might have worked it out if it hadn't been for Uncle Charlie's generosity—if he hadn't introduced me to this other life when the timing was perfect. I love it, Barb. You know that. It's real. It's exciting. Every day is a swim-or-drown challenge and I'm afraid I like challenges. The life we dreamed of would look awfully small and inconsequential now."

"But you're so young, Ham, and this is such a terrific responsibility your uncle is thrusting on you."

"It's a terrific challenge and, as I just said, I like challenges."

"I have every confidence in you, Ham, I know you are going to meet it. But it is going to cost you a high price."

"How do you mean?"

"Oh, I don't know. It was a stupid thing to say. But you're a killer, Ham. Once you get your teeth into something you never let go until you've brought it to earth. I suppose it's the hunting instinct that's in every man more or less, but it's stronger in you than in most. I guess I'm just scared. I'm scared of the fierce intensity with which you approach life. I'm scared that eventually it might change you—make you into somebody else."

"Not as far as you're concerned. You ought to know that by this time."

"Let's get back to earth, Ham. You know what my hopes were. I never tried to hide them, so don't let's waste time on them. We are dealing with realities now. Every man has his own dish of tea. Some never find it. You're lucky. You've said that yourself. You found your dish of tea almost overnight and it wasn't all Uncle Charlie's doing either. You had what he wanted or you wouldn't be where you are. Now you're being handed an unbelievable opportunity; something that most men strive for all their lives and fail to achieve. Take it. Take it. I realize that is what you've already decided, though perhaps you don't know it. But don't forget, once a month or so, that you have a family."

He half turned, threw his arms around her, and kissed her. The diners at the neighboring tables smiled indulgently. Youth and champagne. A heady mixture. "God bless you, darling."

Her eyes smiled at him through her tears.

The pace of the market became faster and faster, the ticker tapes lagged further and further behind, stock prices skyrocketed, margins were pushed to the limit as the amateurs climbed aboard the gravy train. People found themselves rich (on paper) beyond their most extravagant hopes. Tycoons on their way to Europe paused on gangplanks to make statements to the press predicting five more years of prosperity. Call money rates rose steadily—8 percent, 10 percent, 12 percent, 16 percent, and, for a brief moment, 20 percent, but no one paid any attention to red lights. This was a one-way thoroughfare on which the only light was green. No one would have paid any attention if Elijah had stuck his head through the ceiling of the Stock Exchange board room and taken up preaching again. He would have been called an old scrooge.

Each morning at 8:30 Davidson met with Ham in the latter's office and went over the margin situation. Uncle Charlie seldom came in now until just before lunch and then after a brief talk with Ham he left for the Down Town Association. Without a word being said the office was recognizing Ham as the crown prince. Underneath the surface there were heartbreaks, jealousies, even hatreds. The usual derogatory rumors started to seep through. A few chose not to cooperate, but they only tried it once. Ham was confident that if he worked harder than anyone else and had a greater knowledge of what was going on he could afford to be tough.

The margin department was one of his biggest worries. By Ham's orders margin requirements on specific stocks were raised, reappraised, and raised again. The small, weak accounts were being gradually eliminated. Customers' men were instructed to reduce stock holdings whenever possible, thereby causing much anguish in the rows of little desks and a few resignations. Ham no longer fought for a place in many of the underwritings that were emerging like sausages from a machine and as a result the firm was frequently squeezed out of the more desirable issues. Rumors went around the Street that since Uncle Charlie's illness Martin and Kuhn had lost its drive and was headed for dodoism.

H. Allen Martin, Jr., was born July 20, 1927. His father was in Dallas at the time, struggling with a public utility merger. Barbara broke the news to him over the phone in a voice so weak that he could scarcely hear her.

"Don't tell me that you can't drop whatever it is you're doing for a couple of days and come back to see your new son?"

"I want to of course, but if you knew—"

"He's going to be called H. Allen Martin, Jr."

"I'll catch the first train up. Don't tell him. I want to surprise him."

He phoned Haley to come down immediately and take over, had a meeting with his Dallas attorneys, and the next day he was in New York.

In the fall of 1928 Ham sold all of his personal securities and bought short-term governments. After an argument he browbeat Barbara's trustees into selling all her common stocks. Uncle Charlie was a harder nut to crack. "Goddamit, boy, you've got your wind up too early. The time will come. Sure. But it's not here yet."

When Ham returned to his own office he sat at his desk, hands folded, motionless. Miss Kelly entered with a sheaf of letters which she laid beside him. "You look like a dog that's mislaid his favorite bone. What's the matter?"

"Oh, I don't know. Timing I guess. I can't be the only one that's right. I'm beginning to think that maybe I'm the only one that's wrong. We're shaking out the margin accounts like ripe apples. Davidson's ready to resign. Now I've sold everything I own personally and Barbara's common stocks have been sold. Uncle Charlie thinks I'm nuts and that's that."

Miss Kelly placed the palms of her hands on his desk and leaned slightly toward him. "Look here, boss. You've made a lot of money. It's wicked the way you pull it in while I slave without a raise for six months, but let's talk about that later. The point is you've decided not to lose it, which is more than all these muttonheads around you have done. Of course your timing is wrong. It *has* to be. If you'd waited you never would have sold. When things started to slip you'd have kept on waiting until the market came back a little which would have automatically made you a member of the board room boys' chorus 'As soon as this market recovers I'm going to sell—and *quick*.' What they don't know, and you seem to know, is that when this daydream topples it ain't goin' to come back no mo'—for a long, long time anyway."

She paused for breath, her face flushed. "That's quite a speech," he said.

"Well, what I was trying to say was 'stick to your guns.' You're beginning to have a following. When you sold I let everything go—all five shares. You're carrying more responsibility than you thought, Mr. Martin."

He had just returned from the Coast. It was too late to go to the office and for once he was glad. All he wanted was to go to bed and sleep for two days. He called the office. Miss Kelly was still there.

No, nothing had happened, but there was a discouraging lot of paper work on his desk.

"I can't handle it tonight no matter how important it is. I'm pooped."

"I can tell it in your voice," she said. "Don't give it another thought. Take a couple of drinks and go to bed."

He arrived home in time to see the children, Michael now

eight, with soft curly, blond hair framing an angel's face, and Patricia, six, dark with an instinctive flair for the dramatic which was a forerunner of things to come. H. Allen Martin, Jr., was, quite properly, asleep in his bassinet.

Nannie, the English nurse, brought the two older children into the living room as soon as she heard Ham come in. All traces of the day's rough-and-tumble had been scrubbed away. Their clothes were immaculate. The butler brought in cocktails with two pieces of cinnamon toast for Michael and Pat, who sat side by side on the fire-bench, staring curiously at Ham as if he were a casual stranger who might be expected to say something funny or to produce something interesting from his pockets.

They made Ham uncomfortable. He didn't seem to have anything to say to them, funny or not, and obviously they had nothing to say to him.

At the end of half an hour Nannie entered like a well-starched warden and took them away. "They're so adorable," said Barbara. "But they don't know you. They don't see you enough. They're scared of you and for some reason you're a little bit scared of them."

"I suppose so," he said. "I must try to work out something better. By the way, I met a friend of yours in Chicago who wanted to be remembered—" Anything to avoid another argument about his work habits. He was too tired to face that.

Conversation lagged and it was a relief when dinner was announced. They ate their soup in silence and as the soup cups were being removed Barbara put her elbows on the table and clasped her hands in a characteristic gesture. "Ham, do you remember the night a long, long time ago when we had a special dinner together to talk over Uncle Charlie's offer and I was complaining about your never coming home any more until everyone was asleep?"

"I'll never forget the dinner, but you've talked about my overtime so often that I've forgotten that part of it."

"No, you haven't. You said you had an idea and then we began talking about something else and you never told me what it was."

"Oh, I do remember. I'd been worried about Miss Kelly and I still am. We never get a chance to start dictating until about half past five. Then we go at it hammer and tongs until God knows how late and all the poor girl has for dinner is some miserable sent-in sandwiches and a paper cup of coffee. Nobody can stand that indefinitely. Now, my idea was to combine work and pleasure. Miss Kelly and I will leave the office say around six. She will have dinner with us. That will ensure her a good meal and give me a chance to see you and the kids. Then after dinner she and I can go into the library and work. How does it strike you? I don't know why I didn't follow up the idea before this."

She looked at him incredulously. He couldn't really mean it. She felt anger rising, but he was filled with such boyish enthusiasm that she choked it back.

"Why don't you have your files sent up?" she said, trying to make her voice sound playful and failing badly. "We could put them in the dining room so that Miss Kelly could refer to them during dinner."

He was so absorbed in his idea that he missed the sarcasm completely. "The file problem has bothered us, but Miss Kelly says she can bring up whatever papers are necessary. That girl is a wonder."

"It must be fun for her working for you, dear. What are you going to do tonight? Burrow around in a brief-case?"

"I'm going to bed. Three nights on the road leave me as

limp as an old feather boa. I have to be up early. We're
having a special partners' meeting at 8:30. Are you going to
sit up?"

"I think I'll read awhile."

To Ham's surprise the first dinner with Miss Kelly was
not nearly as easy and informal as he had hoped. Neither
she nor Ham had a cocktail in view of the work that lay
ahead of them. Miss Kelly was ill at ease and badly needed
one. In deference to Barbara, Ham kept off the subject of
business. The fact that Miss Kelly knew as much about the
Martin family as Ham himself caused her to choose her
words carefully and Barbara seemed particularly morose
about something. It was a relief to everyone when Ham
found himself sitting at the library desk, a neat pile of papers
in front of him and Miss Kelly installed in her accustomed
place at the end of the desk, looking like an eager retriever
waiting for the ball to be thrown.

On the second night tension was relaxed largely due to
the fact that no one tried very hard to be interesting. Ham
discussed a few minor matters of business, merely to fill in
the frequent conversational gaps.

"By the way," said Barbara casually while they were finishing their dessert, "I've asked Tom Janicki for dinner tomorrow night. You know. He's the new young novelist that
everyone is talking about." She turned her sweetest smile on
Miss Kelly. "The one who wrote *Shadows on White.*"

Ham looked up in surprise. "Janicki!" he said. "Didn't
know you knew him."

"Oh, sure. He's a fascinating character. He's asked me to
go with him to the opening of Steinmark's *Broken Barriers.*

There's going to be a party for the cast afterward. It ought to be fun."

"Well, surely you won't want me for dinner," said Miss Kelly quickly. "I really ought to go and see my mother. I've been neglecting her dreadfully."

"Oh, but, my dear, we *do* want you. I'm counting on you to make a fourth. There's no more horrible combination than a man and wife and a bachelor friend."

Tom Janicki was a tall man with receding hair and a long, straight nose, a combination which would have given him a slight resemblance to a head on a Greek coin had it not been for a shoestring mustache. To make up for his frontal hair deficiencies he wore it long in back where it seemed to grow more easily. Its wavy strands, threaded with gray, swept past his ears and ended in a series of tiny curls at the nape of his neck. He was fifteen minutes late.

"Ah, my dear," he cried, crossing the room to Barbara with the effortless grace of a swimming swan. "Forgive me and it's an early curtain too. Shall we blame it on the traffic or on my failure to pick up a cab promptly?"

Barbara allowed him to kiss her hand, then turned quickly to introduce him to Miss Kelly.

"Charmed," he said, kissing her hand also. "You must be the sister of Linda Kelly, my favorite actress."

Miss Kelly assured him that she was not.

"Strange," he said, giving his mustache a thoughtful tweak, "you look so much like her I would have spoken to you on the street."

"I'll bet you would," thought Miss Kelly, remaining silent.

"And this is Mr. Martin." Mr. Janicki rushed toward Ham his hand outstretched eagerly. "I am *so* pleased to meet you at long last. I have heard so much about you from your lovely wife."

"I hope she was merciful. What would you like to drink?"

"A martini, if I may. Just a drop of vermouth and a twist of lemon peel."

"That sounds splendid," said Miss Kelly unexpectedly. "May I have one also?" She was speaking with an overcultured voice that Ham scarcely recognized.

"Let's all have the same and make it simpler," said Barbara.

Mr. Janicki sat down on the small sofa beside Barbara and crossed his long legs. Ham wished he could cross his like that. When he tried the top leg always stuck out slightly instead of hanging straight down, relaxed and easy, like Mr. Janicki's.

"Well, well, this *is* cozy," exclaimed Mr. Janicki. "I always admire this room. You certainly have a touch, Barbara." Ham avoided Miss Kelly's quick glance. "Did any of you go to Lottie Brophy's party last night?" They all shook their heads in the manner of those who regretted their inability to accept. Miss Kelly was the only one to speak.

"No, darn it all," she said.

"I couldn't go either, but I hear it was quite a brawl. That little squirt André Benito had his face slapped. You know him. He's that obnoxious little halfpint that's never been the same since Dunwright published his book of poems, figuring they must be good because nobody in his office could understand them. Sometime during the evening he asked Minerva McKenna to dance with him. You know Minnie, six feet two, all woman and a yard wide. She looked down to see who was making the noise and said, 'I don't dance with a child,' and Andy said, 'Sorry, I didn't notice.' Minnie slapped him so hard he tripped over something, hit his head on the piano bench, and was carried out triumphantly on the shoulders of his ill wishers."

At this point Mr. Janicki burst into such wild laughter

that he almost lost control of his martini. "Have another one," said Barbara. "I hate to rush you but I forgot it was an early curtain. I would have set dinner ahead if I'd had my wits about me."

"I think I'll have another also" said Miss Kelly.

"You all know Jock Koestler?" said Mr. Janicki through a mouthful of shrimp cocktail. Miss Kelly nodded vigorously. "I'm sure you have heard about his conversation with Sam Goldwyn."

This time nobody admitted anything.

"Do tell us," said Barbara nervously. Mr. Janicki did. In the middle of the story Barbara rang the little silver table bell beside her plate. "I'm sorry to interrupt," she said, "but we must push this dinner along if we're going to get to the theater." Mr. Janicki lapsed into a sulky silence, lit his second cigarette since coming to the table, and stared at a portrait on the opposite wall. In the confusion of changing plates and serving a new course everyone forgot that the story was unfinished and it remained so.

There was a moment's silence during which nothing could be heard but the clink of knives and forks against china. "I know how authors hate to talk about books that they are writing," said Barbara in the forced tones of desperation, "but we would all so love to hear about your new book—or perhaps it's a secret?"

Mr. Janicki became immediately animated. He glanced at his wrist watch. "I don't mind talking about it in the least. In fact I find it's rather helpful. You may think it—what shall we say?—rather frank in spots. You see it is my theory that every human being consists of two people. One is the outward person, the one that everyone sees and we think we know—civilized, if you get what I mean—sophisticated, controlled, dancing to whatever tune custom happens to be playing at the moment. The other is the inner person who is living in the primitive jungle—a being whose emotions and instincts are about on a level with those of an anthropoid ape—an uncontrolled jumble of lust, savagery, brutality, and animal selfishness."

He looked about to see what impression he was making. "That applies to everyone at this table. To you, Miss Kelly, for example—"

Miss Kelly put her napkin to her mouth. "Good God!" she exclaimed. "How did you guess?"

"That was a Freudian gesture you just made, but we won't go into it now. And of course it applies to you also, Mr. Martin, and to you, Barbara."

"And *you*, Mr. Janicki?" asked Miss Kelly anxiously.

"Of course," he said impatiently. "Naturally. Now, the novelist who doesn't deal with the two sides of a man's character isn't dealing with people at all. He's dealing with puppets the way the nineteenth century writers did: Thackeray, Brontë, Hardy, George Eliot—the whole pack of them until at the end of the century they degenerated into slop like *The Rise of Silas Lapham* and *The Trail of the Lonesome Pine* and *The Light That Failed*."

Barbara looked at his untouched plate. "Please eat something, Tom." Mr. Janicki, however, was becoming visibly excited.

"I'd rather talk," he said. "You shouldn't have started me. Now my novel deals with a young artist in Greenwich Village who falls in love with a beautiful Italian girl whose father runs a delicatessen—the buxom, primitive type—the girl, of course, not the father. They have absolutely nothing in common—the artist and the girl, I mean—but they are mad for one another." Heedless of the food before him Mr. Janicki developed the story of ripening love, most of which appeared to have ripened in a Greenwich Village bed. "Eventually they were as one," he said, "until—"

The maid came in and leaned over Barbara. "Do you want me to serve coffee and brandy at the table, ma'am?"

Mr. Janicki refused to recognize another interruption. He merely raised his voice to a half shout. "They were absolutely mad for one another until she heard that he was a homosexual—"

The maid looked at Mr. Janicki with a bewildered expression and began to make little fluttering motions with her hands. "I don't believe we'll have time for coffee and brandy, Mary. Just put the tray on the sideboard and let anyone help themselves if they wish. We're awfully late now. Tom, you haven't eaten a thing."

"She was a simple country girl who had never heard of bi-sexualism," shouted Mr. Janicki. The maid fled. "Freud, as you know, goes into this fascinating subject very deeply, but Carmolita read nothing but detective stories and the comics—it all went right over her pretty head."

"Who is Carmolita?" interrupted Miss Kelly.

"The delicatessen girl," said Mr. Janicki impatiently. "Well, in the meantime a handsome Italian lad—a complete monosexual type gets into—"

Barbara glanced nervously at her wrist watch. "Tom, we simply must go. We're hopelessly late now. I'll get my things. You ring for the elevator. These two have no engagement. They can have coffee and brandy in the library—if they want it."

"Who was the homosexual?" asked Miss Kelly. "The father or the artist?"

Mr. Janicki looked at her to make sure she was not pulling his leg.

"Hopeless," he cried. "Hopeless. No one can concentrate in this confusion. The pace of modern life quickens in direct ratio to the speed of transportation. Books are no longer written for reading but for condensation—just so we can talk about them—and then we don't even have time for that. I'm going to get out an annual book containing condensations of the year's best condensations. We must leave you now and I envy you both the quiet tempo of your lives. Good night, Miss Murphy." He kissed her hand. "And good night, Mr. Martin, I envy you particularly."

And then after a farewell leer from Mr. Janicki they were gone. "I'll bring the coffee tray into the library," said Ham.

They sat on either side of a small table. "Coffee or Sanka?"

"Coffee please. Two lumps and strong. How about lacing it with a dash of brandy?"

He gave her a brimming dash and handed her the cup. "Skoal," she said.

"Skoal, yourself."

"I'm sorry I made such a fool of myself at dinner."

"You didn't. You made a fool out of Janicki. But that wasn't difficult."

"Well, I won't apologize any more. Perhaps it was all to the good. It helped me to understand things a little better."

"You've always understood things. That's why I like you."

She shifted quickly to safer ground. "Once you told me a little about your early life in Messina. Tell me about your father and mother. What were they like?"

They finished their coffee slowly while he talked. "Gosh," he said finally, rising and walking over to the desk. "I don't feel very much like starting in on that pile of letters."

"I have no intention of it," she replied. "Let's have a

Scotch and soda and then I'll go home. It will do you good to relax for one evening."

He went to the portable bar in the corner and returned with two drinks. "Now tell me about college and what became of your literary life. I'm particularly interested in that part."

"I hope you're not going to start giving me hell about my writing."

"Why should I? If you turned into a writer I'd lose my job."

Time flew by unnoted. "Good heavens," she said, glancing at the little ormolu clock on the mantel. "It's after ten and I have to go all the way to Brooklyn."

She rose quickly and they stood, facing each other, in the middle of the library. "That was a great story," she said. Unsecretarial eyes were looking straight into his. An invisible magnet was pulling them slowly together. As his arms started to rise she backed away. "Please," she said. "Please. I'd rather be your secretary. Help me find my coat."

When she had gone he went back to the library. Its emptiness was almost tangible. He poured himself another drink and sat down to review this extraordinary evening. After a while he became conscious of the fact that his mind was not working at all. He was merely sipping whiskey and staring blankly at nothing, going through the traditional routine of the lead man in an English drawing-room comedy. Disgusted he set the half-filled glass on the table and went to bed.

On October 12, 1928, Uncle Charlie died. The end came just as he would have wished it. The previous afternoon he had called Ham at the office. "I'm in the dumps," he said. "Come up and have dinner with me."

"I'd like to, Uncle Charlie, but we have a closing tomorrow morning. That Northwestern Electric show."

"To hell with it," came the old booming voice. "Let your slaves take care of the make-ready. If they can't set up a closing by this time they ought to be fired. What lawyer is covering this?"

"Farnsworth, sir."

"Good man. Call him up. Tell him who's doing the preparation and to stand by with a life preserver this evening. Tell him you're dining with me. If all hell breaks loose they can always reach you here, but warn him not to keep calling with a lot of silly questions. Six-thirty. See you then."

It was a mellow evening. Uncle Charlie did not mention business. It was as if the firm of Martin and Kuhn had never existed. Instead he talked about himself. It was the first time Ham could remember him discussing his own past. They sat over their martinis for a long time. Good gin was worth lingering over in 1928. At dinner Uncle Charlie broke out a bottle of his best Bordeaux and they ended the meal with a half bottle of champagne.

Ham watched him with affectionate admiration. Here was one of the few survivors of a dying breed, keen-witted, shrewd, with a thorough knowledge of how to reach his financial goals. More important, however, he was basically and above all a gentleman-sportsman. Had he lived in England a hundred years earlier he would have been a country squire, riding to hounds, passing the port round and round the table in anticipation of early gout, mindful, in a bluff noisy way, of the welfare of those who lived on his land, blasphemous except when the vicar was at his table, ruddy of cheek, autocratic and beloved.

His basic type had been kept alive in the United States by a diminishing group of Anglophiles on the Eastern seaboard. There, a quarter century before the population explosion had clogged the open country with monotonous developments, they had donned their pink coats and ridden, hell for leather, after fleeing foxes. At their clubs they drank and puffed and swore at all automobiles which they didn't own personally, but their favorite gripe revolved around the steadily increasing taxes which were slowly reducing the boundaries of their age-old worlds. Custer was not the only one to have had a Last Stand.

By today's standards they were selfish, perhaps, sometimes arrogant, and not always civic-minded, but they lived by the code of a gentleman as that code had been developed through the generations in England and ultimately had been exported to Virginia and Maryland, Boston and Philadelphia, coming to a lingering death in the twentieth century as the masses slowly took over.

Uncle Charlie's reticence about his past had disappeared with his second martini. Memories were pouring from him like water through a broken dam. He could remember the Civil War, the parades and the news of Lincoln's assassination. He had loved, desperately. It was difficult for Ham to adjust to the idea of Uncle Charlie as a lover. His suit was successful, but two years after the wedding his young bride died of some obscure disease. Uncle Charlie had never been sure just what it was. He doubted if the doctors had been either. "Most of those fellows weren't fit to be horse doctors."

Faced with the problem of readjustment he refused a Grand Tour of Europe ("Cheaper to get drunk in New York") and plunged into Wall Street.

"For five years I never stuck my head out of the goddam place except to go home and sleep. I just wanted to anesthetize myself with hard work. I wasn't trying to be a success—just to forget. I worked so hard at it that at the end of five years I had arrived in spite of myself. The woods were full of girls kickin' around waitin' to be dragged to the altar but none of 'em were for me so I decided to marry business instead. Never regretted it."

He continued to talk ceaselessly during dinner. It was as if he was trying to condense his life story into the span of a single evening.

"Let's go in the other room and have a brandy," he said finally, rising from the table.

Seated once more in his favorite chair with the little table beside it, he poured a great slug into a balloon glass and continued to talk, but after a while his words came out more slowly. Eventually he began to nod and finally fell asleep. Not knowing quite what to do, Ham picked up a book and read.

The phone rang. Ham answered it quickly, trying not to waken the old man. It was Farnsworth, reporting that everything seemed in order and reminding him that the closing would be at eleven o'clock.

Uncle Charlie stirred and opened his eyes. "I'll bet it was that goddam overconscientious lawyer." Ham told him what Farnsworth had said.

"What'd he want to call about that for? Doesn't he think we can *assume* anything?" He yawned. "Sorry to conk out on you, boy. I just get so damned tired these days that I'd go to sleep in front of a firing squad.

"Ring the bell for Fibbins, will you, like a good boy. Tell him to make a couple of Scotch and sodas. After that I think I will go to bed and finish my nap."

They sat, quiet. Ham was waiting for Uncle Charlie to continue. He felt that he had something else that he wanted to say. Eventually his uncle placed the highball glass on the table and took a deep pull at his cigar. "I'm glad you're on board, Ham. You and I are of different generations and things have changed a lot since I was your age. But basically I feel that we think alike. You're going to be running this show soon. There are a couple of points that might be helpful for you to remember.

"First of all, don't try to make money too fast. Don't get excited and push for the last nickel. There will always be plenty of other opportunities in the future. When you are dealing with money look at everything in the light of cold reason. Stamp out wishful thinking as if it were a bedbug. And for God's sake do your own thinking. Don't pay any attention to what others tell you or advise you.

"The second thing—and this is tremendously important— whatever it costs you, run your business in the best interests of your customers. Most of 'em don't do their own thinking. The nearest they can get to it is wish-thinking. They look to you. If you advise 'em wrong and they lose money they'll hate you and leave you. If you're lucky enough to advise 'em right, you'll probably kill their wish-thoughts and they'll hate you for that. But right or wrong, tell 'em what you believe an' to hell with the torpedoes. There'll be times when it looks as if you couldn't win, but if you always conduct your business in the best interests of your customers, as you see it, you'll eventually come out on top.

"Now I'm beginning to talk like Rollo, and when I get that way it's time to hit the hay. Ring for Fibbins again, will you? I hope I didn't spoil your evening, Ham. If you knew how much good it's done me you wouldn't mind the waste—Oh, Fibbins, won't you give me a hand? I think I'll turn in. Good night, Ham. You're a great fellow. Don't thank me for anything you may think I've done for you. I'm the one that's thanking you—right here and now."

As he walked unsteadily out of the room leaning on Fibbins' arm he walked out of Ham's life. During the night he left the world which he had enjoyed so thoroughly. The doctor called it "heart failure." To Ham it seemed relatively unimportant. What really mattered was that he had slipped out quietly from a changing environment which he would never have understood, and that his last act had been to enjoy a nightcap and a cigar.

Ham was named as sole executor of Uncle Charlie's estate. It was a relatively new will and followed the plan his Uncle had discussed with him a few months before. He must have known then that he was approaching the end of his road. To Ham he left the amount of his investment in the firm with the provision that no part of it be withdrawn as long as Ham was a partner. He also left Ham a special bequest of $250,000 and whatever books, pictures, and furniture he might want from the apartment. To his brother and sister-in-law he left a trust fund of half a million dollars. On their deaths it would go to Harvard University. To each of Ham's children he left a trust fund of a quarter of a million and to Barbara a quarter of a million outright.

A sum of half a million dollars was placed in an escrow account with his bank, the proceeds to be used for establishing similar trusts should there be more children. If there were none at the end of a specified period the money would go to Ham. The remainder of his estate after taxes and expenses was left in the form of a scholarship fund to Harvard University.

At this point one could almost hear Uncle Charlie breathe a sigh of relief. He had thought of every detail and he hated details.

Fanny had come on for the funeral. Ham had asked her to remain at his uncle's apartment until she heard from him. When he telephoned to her she sounded panicky. "Allen," she cried. "Your lawyers have just been talking to me about Charlie's will. This is incredible. I never heard of so much money. We wouldn't know what to do with it."

"You don't have to do anything with it. It's in trust. The bank and I are cotrustees. We'll do all the work. You and Dad can just sit back and receive the income."

"But we wouldn't know what to do with so much income."

"Cheer up, Mother, perhaps it won't be as much as you think after you've paid your taxes."

"Oh, I hope not. We're simple people, Allen. We've always lived simply. It would worry us both to death if we had to spend a lot of money every year."

"You can *give* it away, Mother, if it really worries you."

"We *can*? Oh, Allen, why didn't you say so? You mean we can give it to the college and the hospital and the Red Cross and people like poor Mrs. Norcross who's so crippled with arthritis she can scarcely get out of the house, and we can help with the new parish house the church is building and—"

"Whoa, Mother. You're talking like Andrew Carnegie. The first thing I want you to do before you build parish houses is to put your own house in shape, inside and out. Nothing's been done to it for years and it's falling apart."

"It is *not*, Allen. It's as sound as it ever was except for the porch railing. I'll have you know we've taken care of that house. And if you think we're going to toss out all our lovely old furniture and put in a lot of horrors from Grand Rapids you're just mistaken that's all."

"Mother, please don't go to pieces. We don't have to decide all these things today and you don't have to throw anything out. As soon as I get straightened up here I'm coming out to Messina to explain everything. That will be soon enough to talk about details. Besides it will be two years at least before the estate will be settled so you won't need to worry for quite a while."

"Oh, good," she said in a relieved voice. "I promise not to worry until I hear from you. But here I am burdening you with my troubles when your own burdens are so much heavier. I didn't quite understand all that part about Uncle Charlie's capital in the firm. What does it mean?"

Ham tried to explain to her as simply as possible. "Gracious, Allen, I'm glad I'm not in business. I still don't understand, but, as I see it in my fuzzy way, Uncle Charlie left you his interest in the firm which was so big that he was top partner, or whatever you call it, and if you stay on you'll be top partner in his place."

"You're not so fuzzy as you think, Mother. That's exactly the situation. If I stay on I'll be top partner."

"But are you going to stay, Allen? Are you going to make this awful business your life's work? You don't have to think of earning your living any more. If writing doesn't appeal you could devote yourself to scholarship and make a contribution to human knowledge and understanding. Oh, Allen—"

"I'm afraid I have to stay. There are too many people depending on me and there are also a lot of other reasons."

"Heavens. I just can't grasp it. To me you're still a little boy delivering papers to make circus money. But let's not go into that now. I can see you've made your decision."

"There was no alternative, Mother. I couldn't let Uncle Charlie down and the truth is I'm happy in this business. It fits me."

"I know. You told me you liked it when you were in Messina. But I'm holding you up, Allen dear, and we shouldn't be talking about all these business things with dear Uncle Charlie just dead. You must have a thousand things to do."

"I have, Mother. I'll call for you and take you to the church."

"I'll be ready," she said.

The following day he called up Farnsworth, the firm's lawyer, who was also his personal attorney.

"I want to sell every security in Uncle Charlie's estate except short-term bonds. Have I the right?"

"As soon as you've qualified as executor. But aren't you acting rather precipitately, Ham? In the first place, your uncle didn't agree with your theory that stocks should be sold at this time. Up to date he's been right and he profited considerably by keeping his position. In the second place, his estate is a substantial one as you know. Some of his holdings represented special situations. They have a thin market and you might depress their price considerably by suddenly dumping them."

"Harry, we understand markets pretty well in this shop. It's our *business*. We don't *dump* securities. What I'm asking you is, do I have the right to sell?"

The answer came back cold and formal. "As sole executor you have the right to sell everything in the estate as soon as you qualify." There was a moment of silence. "But I have to advise you that your right to speculate with the proceeds would be challenged."

"What nonsense. I'm going to put everything into short-term governments. Don't be so touchy, Harry. I just wanted a legal opinion and I *didn't* want my investment judgment warped by a nonlegal argument. Now I want a nonlegal opinion. The whole Street knows that most of the capital in the firm belonged to Uncle Charlie. What it doesn't know is whether money is going to be pulled out or left in the firm.

They should know quickly. What I'm proposing to do is to call a partners' meeting right away and give them the whole story. Any bright ideas?"

"No, I agree. The quicker the better. Let them pass the news along to the money brokers and the bankers. Cover the money brokers first. They're always itching for something to talk about as they make their rounds."

"Right. Call me up if anything occurs to you."

The partners, hastily summoned, entered Ham's office and seated themselves on the folding chairs that Mike, the floorman, had set out for the occasion. After murmuring words of sympathy they sat with silent frozen faces like prisoners awaiting the decision of a jury.

Ham looked about the room and burst out laughing. "For heaven's sake, cheer up. This firm is not about to be liquidated or merged. Now let me tell you the whole story." One could almost see the tense bodies relax. Cigarettes appeared and the tiny flames of lighters seemed to burn away the gloom. Ham told the story, slowly and without reservations. "And there you have it. The only change will be that circumstances have made me the senior partner. This is the best firm in the Street, but I want to make it better. With your help this can be done. I need every one of you behind me. I can smell a storm up ahead. We may be coming to some rough going. That's when I'll need your help and your advice the most."

The room was silent as each of the partners of Martin and Kuhn evaluated Ham's words by the light of his own self-interest. Ham toyed with a paper cutter, waiting, his eyes on the desk blotter.

Bartow was the first to speak. "Ham," he said, rising and grasping Ham's hand, "you're a lucky fellow and we're lucky because of it. I don't know anyone I'd rather work with or in whom I have more confidence, now that my dear friend Charlie is out of the picture. I'm with you—all the way."

The other partners rose, shook his hand, and gave him their allegiance. Some were forthright and enthusiastic. Some merely mumbled. He made a mental note of the latter. "Just a minute," he said. The group stopped and a new cloud of anxiety crossed their faces. What was coming now?

"What I have just told you is far from being a secret. Divide up the money brokers and the Wall Street banks among you. Advise them by phone immediately so the Street will know where we stand."

As the last man left, Miss Kelly entered and placed a pile of mail on his desk. "Nice going, boss," she said.

"How do you know?"

"I was standing outside waiting to get at you. There are some important letters there."

"Nuts, I'll bet you don't know which ones they are."

She sidestepped the barb. "It sounded like a group of knights giving the oath of fealty to their new king."

"Which are the important letters?"

"It might be a good idea to clean up the whole mess quickly. Now that the knights are through the peasants will soon be crowding in to pull their forelocks."

Spring, 1929. Rumors continued to fly, the market continued toward the stars, call money rates hovered around 16 percent, brokers' loans increased weekly. Ham's responsibilities did not actually increase. He had been running the show for months, but without Uncle Charlie to nod approval he felt like Atlas with the world on his shoulders. He was aware that appraising, cynical eyes were watching, waiting for the false moves that he must not make.

As the securities in Uncle Charlie's estate were liquidated in a rising market he had agonizing moments when he questioned his own judgment. Was it possible that shrewd old Uncle Charlie had been right and that he was mistaken? He had been wrong on the sale of his and Barbara's securities for six months. No, it was a matter of timing and he was sure that he was nearer right than he had been six months ago.

He turned the office over to Brownlee and young Haley and made a tour of the out-of-town offices: Chicago, San Francisco, New Orleans, Detroit, Atlanta, and Dallas. They were all making money and in no mood for caution; certainly not for retrenchment.

"But, sir, we're in the biggest bull market in history. Our customers are making money and they want to keep right on doing so. If we begin to preach gloom and disaster to them and tighten up on margin requirements, they'll just transfer their accounts to some other house and we'll look like monkeys."

"Don't be scared, Pete. Do as I tell you. You won't lose your job—unless you *don't* do as I tell you." He had developed a most disarming grin, a useful thing when you had to get tough with people.

In New Orleans there was a message to call the New York office immediately. This he did as a matter of routine at noon each day. Something must be fouled up. They put Brownlee on the phone at once.

"Sorry, Ham, we've got bad news for you."

"You wouldn't have called me up about good news, you old vulture."

"It's not business, Ham. It's family."

"Not Father?"

"I'm sorry to say you've guessed right. He had another stroke two days ago and passed away last night."

"Phone Mother that I'm taking the first train north to

Chicago or Indianapolis, whichever is quicker. I'll phone her as soon as I know my arrival time. Explain to her why I'm not stopping to phone her until I get things lined up. Tell her I'll call before noon. Phone Barbara. Does she know? Well, she's probably out somewhere, but keep at it. Tell her what my plans are and to meet me in Messina as soon as possible. I'll try to get in touch with her also. Got it, George? Good boy."

On the following evening he walked into the little house on Maple Street. There were voices in the living room. "Mother," he called, "it's me, Allen."

She came running out and threw her arms around his neck. "Oh, Allen. Thank God you're here. I've been very brave and self-contained. Now I can cry." She put her face against his coat and let two days of dammed-up tears come pouring forth. Eventually they stopped. She pulled out his handkerchief and dabbed her eyes and his coat.

"Oh, Allen, I'm sorry. I've ruined your clean handkerchief but I've wanted to cry so very much. Now I have and I feel better."

"Is Barbara here?"

"Not yet. She's on her way to Chicago. She'll be here before noon tomorrow."

"Poor Mother. You've had to handle everything all alone."

"It gave me something to do, Allen. That was the one thing I wanted more than anything—something to do."

"Who are those people in the living room?"

"Just neighbors. I don't think you know any of them. Things have changed a lot. I know they want to meet you, but I want you to myself for a while. Why don't you go up by the back stairs and freshen up. I'll explain it to them and when you hear them go you can come down."

His room was unchanged. The old dance cards still hung on either side of the mirror above his bureau. The Messina High School banner still occupied a good part of the wall opposite his bed. Between the windows was a photograph of Millie. He sat on his bed trying to recapture the feeling of belonging but was unable to do so. He heard the voices below move into the hall, the compounded chatter of good-bys, then the door shut and there was silence. Fanny was waiting for him at the foot of the stairs.

"Let's go in the kitchen and talk," she said. "It's the only place that isn't haunted for me at the moment. I want to tell you all about it."

It was a simple story. The gradual decline of a man whose time clock was running down. The story of a mind clear as to the past but becoming increasingly confused about the present.

"Toward the end your father used to ask why you didn't come home for dinner. I had to explain to him every night that you were in New York. It was pathetic to see him struggling to understand. 'Of course, of course,' he would say. 'New York, yes, indeed, I know what he's doing. He's a good lad, a bright boy.'"

"Did he still believe I was writing that book?"

"To the very end. I encouraged it. This was a case where I'm sure it wasn't wrong to lie. It seemed to make him happy; gave him something to think about. One of the last things he asked me was how your book was coming on. I told him it was almost finished. He smiled that lovely, quiet smile of his and said, 'Good, good. Wish I could see the manuscript.' He always said that."

Ham put his hand over his eyes. His lips were compressed

with pain. "Oh, Allen, I shouldn't have told you. It's upset you and hurt you. It shouldn't, Allen. I mean it. I know what's going through your mind. Remember your father wasn't quite rational toward the end. Had he been he would have been as proud of what you've done as I am."

"I'm glad you told me, Mother."

"I just want you to know that I believe in you, Allen, my strong and clever son."

Barbara returned to New York immediately after the funeral. Ham stayed on for a day or two trying to persuade Fanny to take a trip, go to Europe, go on a cruise, anything to get away from Messina until her mind became adjusted to her new life.

"Someday, Allen, but not now. You don't adjust to a change by running away from it. You have to face it—look it straight in the eye."

1929. Spring came and went almost unnoticed. In August the market showed signs of flattening out. "Everyone is away on vacation," people explained to one another. "Wait until they get back after Labor Day. Then the market will begin to zoom again."

One evening in late August Ham sat at his desk writing and rewriting a memorandum. The floor around his swivel chair was littered with crumpled balls of paper. The following morning when the partners met in the board room for their usual conference he looked around the table at the familiar faces with a quizzical smile.

"I would like to open the meeting," he said, "by reading a memorandum which I wrote last night. This would go out in the form of a telegram to every New York customer who holds securities. It would also go to all out-of-town offices with instructions to send it immediately to individual customers. After I read it I want your comments. No punches pulled."

He picked up a paper from the table and read slowly. "There are various indications which lead us to believe that security markets may suffer a setback in the immediate future. The New York stock market has moved upward so fast during the last three years that this could easily develop into more than a temporary recession or readjustment.

"We have three recommendations.

"The first is that all margin indebtedness be eliminated by the sale of common stocks.

"The second, in the order of conservatism, is that *all* common stocks be sold.

"The third is that *all* securities be sold, both stocks and bonds.

"We further recommend that cash resulting from such sales be invested in short-term government obligations."

He laid the memorandum on the table and looked at them calmly. "What are your reactions?"

No one spoke. A few showed shocked surprise. Most of them doodled on the fresh pads which were laid at each place prior to the morning meetings.

"What's the matter? You fellows usually have pretty strong convictions."

Davidson was the first to break the silence. "This is a pretty personal question, but have you sold all your own securities?"

"Six months ago. Cleaned out everything. I even browbeat the trustees of my wife's trust to do the same."

"Nothing more dangerous than a sold-out bull," said Craig, without taking his eyes from his doodling.

Everyone laughed nervously. Again there was silence, finally broken by young Haley at the other end of the table. "I know I'm one of the juniors in this outfit and that all you fellows have had more experience than I have. On the other hand, I have strong feelings about that memorandum and I judge you want us to say what we think. We all have capital in this firm and I don't see why we shouldn't speak out."

Young Haley was one of the brightest of the new partners as well as the most aggressive. That was why Ham had chosen him as his assistant. He had a square, determined face and fearless brown eyes which seemed to bore straight through his opponent in an argument. They were turned now on Ham, serious and unflinching.

"It takes the commissions from the purchase or sale of approximately 30,000 shares of stock each day to pay our overhead. Is that right, sir?"

Ham nodded. "Approximately."

"Okay. If you send out that message and if everybody should sell out immediately and if the next day the market went to hell they will all think you are Jehovah, but—and this is a big but—after they have bought their short-term governments they'll be so proud of their astuteness they'll sit on them like brooding hens and spend the rest of their days clucking superciliously at their stupid friends who went broke in the big crash. That part is all right, perhaps. The trouble is that they gradually turn into chronic bears. The day when they should get off the nest and reinvest is always just around the corner. They'll keep rolling over their short-term governments and if the income from them isn't big enough they'll eat into the principal; anything, rather than go back into the market. And in the meantime *who's going to pay our overhead?*"

He paused. Several heads nodded agreement. Noticing someone opening his mouth to speak Haley hurried on.

"Now let's suppose again that everybody followed your advice and liquidated. And let's suppose this time that instead of the market falling out of bed the next day your guess was off by 90 days. Let's say that during this period the market continued to rise; volume increased; everything went wild the way it is apt to at the end of a big bull market. *Now* what are your sold-out customers going to do? Sit on their governments and cluck contentedly? Not on your life. They're going to another brokerage house. They're going to say that this firm has gone loopy. And some of them may even ask their lawyers if they can't sue us for the profit they would have made in Tin Cans Consolidated if they had bought a thousand shares instead of following our cockeyed advice. Silly, of course, but they won't come back, no matter how right you eventually prove to be. And in the meanwhile *who's going to pay the overhead*?

"You've left out one recommendation that would have at least made your memorandum consistent. If they want to continue speculating let them go short. Oh, I know what you're going to say. There's nothing constructive in a short position. Well, there's nothing constructive in their long position either. The margin accounts are gambling just as much as if they were putting their chips on the green cloth. The only reason for not advising them to go short is because it is a waste of words. They've been brought up to think a short position is somehow wicked. I suppose they think that running an account on a 20 percent margin is investing. Well, that's off my chest. Sorry to be so wordy, and more than sorry to have to disagree with *you*, sir."

There was a silence, then everyone began to talk at once. Ham rapped on the table. "What you say, Haley, interests me a lot. The gist of it is, if I understand you, a stockbroker can't do anything but advise his customers to buy—if he wants to eat."

Harwich spoke up. "Oh, come on, Ham. You're jumping at a conclusion that just isn't so. I've been advising my customers to reduce the percentage of common stocks in their accounts for several months."

"You mean that where they had 85 percent of everything they own in commons you persuaded them to cut back to 75 or 80 percent?"

"Sometimes even more than that, Ham."

"Why did you do it? Because you're a bond specialist?"

"That's hitting below the belt. I did it because I think this market is getting out of hand."

"Did you advise anyone to get out of common stocks entirely?"

"No. My timing might be wrong or my whole appraisal of the situation might be wrong."

"Did it ever occur to you that you could be even more wrong holding equities than selling them?"

No one spoke. It was obvious that the boss was on the warpath.

"This telegram goes." There was a murmur of protest which rapidly rose to full-throated consternation.

"We're going to lose half our customers." "It's the end of this firm." "Why should we be our brothers' keepers?"

Ham let them howl. Meeting no opposition, they finally subsided. "I've thought of all those things," he said. "If we go into the red because of this wire, then we're in the wrong business. The majority of our customers expect sound professional advice from us based on sound thinking and not a lot of hand-me-down conventions. I want the complete cooperation of every partner. If any one of you feels that he cannot give it—then he should resign from the firm immediately. Will anyone who is at complete variance with what I am about to do please speak up now?"

They were silent, their eyes intent on the doodles which were rapidly covering their scratch pads.

"Okay, gentlemen. Let's get into our hurricane cellars and wait for the blast from the out-of-town offices. George, can you and Haley wait for a few minutes and go over the wording of this wire with me? If we're going broke we might as well do it in unambiguous Oxford English."

Ham braced himself for the deluge, but to his surprise it turned out to be a mere trickle. The majority of the firm's customers paid no attention whatever to the telegram. A considerable number came to the office and talked anxiously to the partner they knew best. A few reduced their indebtedness. Some compromised by eliminating their more speculative items. Three people sold all their common stocks. A large segment agreed entirely with the telegram and congratulated the firm on its courage in sending it out, but decided "not to do anything at the moment."

What particularly interested Ham were the written comments that began to reach him. "It gives me confidence to deal with a firm that has the courage to say what it thinks." "Congratulations, Ham. If you're going to commit suicide it's refreshing to see it done in a nice, clean way." "We naturally don't agree with you, but it's heartening, in this cockeyed world, to have somebody say what he thinks."

If they wouldn't pay any attention to him at least they knew where he stood. "Raise the margin requirements again and keep them up," he told Davidson. "Don't get sentimental about it. If they don't like it they can take their accounts somewhere else."

That was what shook the apples off the tree. "We lost twenty-four accounts yesterday as a result of the last raise," said Davidson despondently.

"Probably because they didn't have any more securities to put up. What are you whimpering about? Wouldn't you rather have them leave us now while they have something left than sell them out later and leave them dead broke and the firm in the red?"

"But when is this doomsday of yours coming, Ham? It's always around a corner that we never reach. What have you got—a private line to God?"

The winds began to blow right after Labor Day. Instead of going up as anticipated, the market turned downward. "A technical reaction," "a healthy shakeout," said the economists rushing in with drums beating. From Babson came the solemn (and lonely) warning of breakers ahead. The only heed the market gave was to cease declining and begin to rise. A derisive laugh arose from Wall Street. Tycoons made stronger gangplank predictions of prosperity. The sun shone once more on the land of milk and honey.

During October the rise stopped. It became evident that something was wrong. "Get them to sell. Get them out now" was Ham's plea from morning until night. But the margin customers who had glimpsed a vision of financial independence largely chose to wait. When their half-fulfilled dreams of financial independence began to evaporate they seemed willing to perish rather than to relinquish them. If prices came back of course they would sell. This was only a temporary upset. A few couldn't take the firm's pessimistic advice and went to more farseeing (which meant more optimistic) houses.

On October 24 the bottom fell out in a frenzy of selling, much of it forced by impaired margins. The floor of the Stock Exchange looked like an ant colony that has suddenly been trod upon by an elephant.

A group of bankers announced the formation of a money pool for the purpose of supporting the market. The avalanche hesitated for an instant like a suspicious dog being offered a rubber bone, then resumed its downward plunge.

At last the bottom was reached. Not a clean-cut bottom, but a turgid, muddied swirl of confusion. The market seemed to have been converted into a bargain counter, but there were few cash customers left to step up and buy. Ham was one of the few. He bought and succeeded in bullying Barbara's jittery trustees into making a few cautious purchases. Slowly, like a patient recovering from a dangerous illness, the market gained strength and the United States gave a sigh of relief. It had been a terrific ordeal in which fortunes had been lost and dreams shattered, but the danger was over. Once more the country could move forward with confidence. Never sell America short.

"We're losing money, boss, look at these figures for the last week."

Ham nodded, scarcely glancing at the sheet Davidson had placed in front of him. "I know them better than you do." He reached into his desk drawer and pulled out a black loose-leaf book. "And look at these new accounts that have come to us in the last month. These are the ones I'm watching. These are investment accounts; the accounts of rich individuals, estates, trusts, foreign accounts—"

"I know. I know, Ham, but there's no activity in them. Brokers' commissions pay the rent. Accounts like those you're showing me don't generate commissions."

Ham looked at him silently for several seconds, his troubled eyes belying the faint smile that played around the corners of his mouth.

"What I'm going to say will probably hurt you. I haven't talked it over with anybody yet so I'm going to put the 'Confidential' stamp on it. This firm is not going to accept any more margin accounts. We're going to start an investment advisory service on a fixed fee basis and accounts like the ones in this book are the only ones we're going after. Underwriting and investment counsel will be our principal business."

Davidson stared at him in astonishment. "Are you crazy, Ham? We have—or used to have till you and the market ruined it—the best margin business in town. This market is coming back. I *tell* you it is. The recent mess will be forgotten in a year. Don't lose your nerve now, Ham, for God's sake."

"I'm not losing my nerve and I'm not crazy, but I'm not going to stay in a business that is dependent on commissions for its overhead to such a degree that it doesn't dare to tell customers when to get out of the market and stay out. There are plenty of other ways—far sounder ways—of making money in the financial world. The way I've outlined is one of them. It sure isn't foolproof but it's the way we're going to operate."

Davidson struck the desk with his open palm. "Then you'll do it without me."

"It doesn't surprise me to have you say that. You are always free to resign and I think you'll find your partnership hasn't been unprofitable."

A week later he returned from the office early. Barbara was out. She was always out these days. He went into

Michael's room. All three children were there and the place was a shambles. They paid little attention to him and he was too tired to be anything but a damper. After a few minutes he returned to his room and threw himself on the bed. Christ, those kids might just as well have no father or mother. He hardly knew them and he was sure they felt the same way about him, if they felt anything. But it was the old question. What else could he do? Someone had to provide the money to keep the show going and he was that someone. Barbara was the one who should be watching, giving them some feeling of belonging. Where was she anyway? Where was she every time he came into the apartment? He was half asleep when he heard the bedroom door open. "Good heavens," she exclaimed. "What are you doing home at this hour—and lying on my beautiful spread with your shoes on? You told me you weren't going to be home for dinner. I'm going out. Nannie's going to feed the children. I told the couple they could have the evening off."

"I'll go to the club," he said.

"Nothing the matter is there? You're feeling all right?"

"Of course I'm all right. Can't a man come home from work at half past five without his family sending for the doctor? I was tired, that was all. We had a rough meeting this afternoon at the office. I tried to put something over and my partners beat me down."

"Oh," she said. She was looking in the mirror while she removed her dress. "I have to hurry. I'm going to an opening tonight. Eight-fifteen curtain. That means quarter to seven dinner."

He watched her as she hung up her dress in the walk-in closet, stepped out of her slip and tossed it across the arm of a chair. Beautiful, slender Barbara; more desirable today than she had been as a bride.

"Don't you ever kiss a guy when you come home?"

She crossed the room and brushed his mouth with her lips. He tried to put his arms around her bare shoulders but she evaded him. "No funny business," she said. "I'm really tearing. They're calling for me in less than half an hour."

"Who are 'they'?"

"Jack Torrence. You know. He's senior editor of Arch and Company, the publishers. He's bringing Peter Balowitz, the one who wrote that extraordinary book last year about Poland in the war."

"A Pole?"

"Of course. He's one of the most gifted young writers in New York."

"Don't you want to hear what happened at the partners' meeting?"

"Naturally, but I'm about to jump into the tub. Could you capsule it?"

"Forget it," he said.

"Is it about money?"

He nodded.

"Then I'd forget it anyway. Are we bankrupt?"

"No, dear. Not bankrupt."

"How tedious," she said, "just to go on getting richer and richer while ordinary people are jumping out of windows."

He watched her getting ready for the bath. "I sometimes think that people like you should see a psychiatrist," he said. "You live in the lap of luxury. You curl up in it like a cat, but you resent anyone who makes enough money to pay your bills."

"Let's go and see one together," she said.

"See who?"

"A psychiatrist." She closed the bathroom door behind her.

He remained lying on the bed, pretending to be asleep,

until she had gone, then went to the library, poured himself a slug of Scotch and sank into a chair.

On an impulse he called up his lawyer. "Harry, what are you doing for dinner?"

"I was just getting into my soup and fish, I'm going to the Century monthly shindig."

"Can't you chuck it and have dinner with me at the Knickerbocker?"

"What's the matter? Internal Revenue caught up with you?"

"No crisis, Harry. I just wanted to talk something out."

"Can't it wait till tomorrow?"

"Of course it can, but I don't want to go to bed with my thinking all jumbled up the way it is now."

A deep sigh came over the line. "Okay, if you don't mind my being in a dinner jacket. Meet you in half an hour. Knickerbocker bar."

He wasted no time on preliminaries, but poured out to Harry Farnsworth his growing dissatisfaction with the margin department and his decision to eliminate it and concentrate on investment counsel service and the under-writing of new issues.

He told of his preliminary talk with Davidson and how the latter had threatened to resign. He finally disclosed the fact that there had been a partners' meeting that afternoon at which they had unanimously disapproved of eliminating the firm's margin business. "They all seemed to think it was their bread-and-butter activity. They were lukewarm about the investment counsel business. Said the overhead would eat up the profits. The meeting broke up in a fearful wrangle.

Nothing decided. Several partners threatened to resign.

"It doesn't make any sense, Harry. There isn't a partner in our shop that wouldn't stand on the steps of the Sub-Treasury and declare that our firm was the most conservative in Wall Street and that he proposed to keep it that way. Our customers, with the exception of a few traders, would raise their right hands and swear by everything holy that the last thing they wanted to do was speculate. Dyed-in-the-wool conservatives, all of them.

"It's all hog-wash, Harry. It's *all* speculation. Speculation is the basis of the whole thing. But everyone has been so conditioned by antiquated ideas of financial respectability that they insist on speculating in a one-way street. It's like a roulette game where the players are required to bet always on 'even' and it is a sacrilege to bet on 'odd.'"

Harry nodded. "After you begin to swear a little better you'll sound like Charlie. You seem to have the situation pretty well pulled apart. What do you want me to do?"

"Help me to put it together again."

"That's what I thought you were going to say. It's a hard nut to crack though, because it depends on the correct answer to one question. Let's forget the market for a moment. What do you see ahead for business in 1930?"

"I've got all the brains around the shop working on that one, and it's hard to come up with anything convincing. The old indicators are mixed up. About all I can say is the outlook is smoky."

"Exactly. At the moment everything is on the up-and-up security-wise, but markets are not apt to drop into their boots the way this one did in October unless there are breakers ahead. If there are they must be big ones. So the question is whether the rising market we're seeing now is only a temporary readjustment.

"Okay. As you say, no one can tell. But you have to assume something. Let's assume, for the sake of argument, that the biggest breakers are still ahead. Have you any margin accounts left?"

"A few."

"Are they solvent?"

"A few are in good shape because they kept pouring in additional securities during the crash, a few are still under-margined and a very few are underwater, but this rise in the market is helping them."

"Good. Well, you know your business. I don't. But you seem anxious to get my advice on things about which I am totally ignorant, so here goes. I urge you to get rid of all margin accounts on this rise. Then, instead of cutting out your margin department, refuse to take any new accounts *for the time being*.

"Second, don't go into the investment counsel business right now, I beg of you. People are not going to pay to be told to do nothing.

"Third, don't be too eager-beaver about going after these straight, out-and-out investment accounts. If they want to come to you that's their risk. If you drag them in they're going to expect you to make money for them and if you don't they'll tell their friends you're a stupid ass.

"As for the underwriting business, you're already in it— been in it for years. I don't think you need to worry about it because I don't think there'll be enough to put in your hat in the foreseeable future.

"Now, having ruined my evening, I'm going to cost you another Scotch and soda, tell you one dirty story and go home to bed."

"Thanks, pal. If we run the firm the way you suggest, we can all go home and go to bed—and stay there."

During March, 1930, Ham's aunt in Chicago telephoned that his Mother had pneumonia and was dangerously ill. Once again Ham hurried out to Messina with foreboding in his heart. Barbara and Michael had the grippe and the nurse seemed to be coming down with it. Barbara would have accompanied Ham in spite of everything if the doctor hadn't forbidden it. In a way Ham was relieved to be going out by himself. If his fears should materialize he preferred to be alone.

Fanny was at home with nurses around the clock, having refused to go to the hospital. Old Dr. Barnes met him in the downstairs hallway. "Let's go in here," he said, pointing to the Professor's study, "so I can brief you a bit."

Ham motioned toward his father's worn high-backed chair behind the desk. Dr. Barnes smiled and shook his head. "That's yours now, Allen, but no matter who sits in it I will always see your father with those all-seeing eyes peering out above his beard, like a wise old owl looking over the top of a bush."

Dr. Barnes seemed to be avoiding the one subject of vital importance. He talked about the changes which had taken place in Messina, all of which he resented; he told about the fortunes and misfortunes of the families with whom Ham had grown up and he tried to get Ham's idea on the future of the stock market.

Ham gave him only half his attention as his eyes wandered about the room and among the familiar objects on the desk. Nothing had been changed. The lead ruler with the knob in the middle, the paperweight from the bank, the fading picture of Fanny and the Professor on their honeymoon, the worn, leather-bound dictionary presented to him by some graduating class, all lay in their accustomed places. On the table beside the chair the round pipe rack was filled with still faintly malodorous pipes. "Tell me about Mother," he interrupted.

Dr. Barnes pulled himself back into the present with a visible effort. "She's very sick, Allen, very sick indeed. Double pneumonia."

"Is she going to die?"

"We hope not, but she is fragile—very fragile. She has never been her old self since your father's death. Seeing you is going to be the best medicine in the world for her. She talks about you all the time, the way your father did."

"Didn't Father have some kind of hallucination about me before he died?"

Dr. Barnes glanced up sharply from under his heavy white eyebrows. "Fanny told me she'd talked to you about that."

"She did, but quite a while before he became so confused; he was very upset when I went into banking after the war. Do you think Mother was equally disappointed?"

"Listen, Allen, I'm a doctor, not a psychiatrist." There was a trace of irritation in Dr. Barnes's voice. "Your Mother's a saint. She has one of the most beautiful characters I have ever known. Of *course* she was disappointed. I don't have to tell you that. You know it. But her love for you is completely unselfish. She dislikes money because of what it does to people, but when she heard of your success in New York she said to me, 'Allen is doing what makes him happy. That's the important thing.' "

He pulled out a huge handkerchief and blew his nose as if it were a trumpet blaring defiance at the young man on the other side of the desk. "A wonderful woman. Now I'll go upstairs and tell her you're here. You stand at the foot of the stairs till I beckon you to come up. Try not to look shocked when you see her. She's lost a lot of weight and her color's bad."

In spite of the doctor's warning Ham found it hard to control his expression as he walked into his mother's familiar room. She was so pale that the outline of her face tended to merge with the pillows and she seemed lost in the huge double bed she had shared with the Professor for so many years.

When she smiled, however, her face regained its old familiar expression. "Allen," she said, stretching her arms toward him, "darling Allen. You came."

He knelt by the bed so that she could lock her fingers behind his neck as she used to do. "Of course I came. I came to find out what you mean by being sick. You used to boast that you were never sick."

She said nothing, just lay on her side with her arms around his neck, her eyes gazing into his. She seemed to be probing for something, seeking an answer to a question that lay deep and unspoken within her.

To break the silence he told her about Barbara and the children, all the tidbits of his life that he thought would interest her. She listened with apparent attention, but she was listening to his voice rather than to his words.

Suddenly she turned her back to him and was seized with a paroxysm of coughing. Dr. Barnes and a nurse, both of whom must have been standing in the hall outside, immediately opened the door and entered the room.

"Time for you to go now, Allen," the doctor said in a low voice. "She tires easily. Wait for me in your father's study."

For four days Fanny fought for life, but it was a losing battle. Ham was with her as much as Dr. Barnes would allow him to be. She seldom spoke and he said little, merely sitting beside her bed holding her hot, dry hand. Sometimes she seemed scarcely aware of his presence and lay quite still, staring at the ceiling, sometimes she dozed and occasionally she turned her head toward him and smiled.

She died in the middle of the night as gently as she had lived. Ham was asleep in his old room. Dr. Barnes had gone home to get a few hours' rest. Only the nurse was with her.

Three or four jumbled days after the funeral Ham found himself, late one afternoon, on the train to Chicago. In Messina his parents, reduced to two copper urns of ashes, lay buried beside one another in the little graveyard behind the Brick Presbyterian Church. Judge Baxter, Ham's godfather, had agreed to handle all the legal work in connection with the estate and to dispose of the house and its contents. As the train pulled out of the familiar old station Ham peered into the dusk feeling that this might well be his last glimpse of what he had always thought of as his home, but as the town dropped behind and the train began to climb the easy grade toward the hills, he realized that Messina no longer meant for him a place, but rather two faces, one handsome, severe, ascetic, the other radiating gentle affection. For him there was no longer a Messina to which he might return had he wished to do so.

These two people, to whom he owed everything, were the ones he had disappointed. He shook himself physically like a dog coming out of water. This was ridiculous; mawkish. He had nothing to be ashamed of nor any reason for feeling guilty. He went out onto the swaying platform and lit a cigarette. After a few puffs he snapped it away and returned to his seat.

April, 1930. At the offices of Martin and Kuhn there was a muted atmosphere. All margin accounts had been closed out except for a few which were still underwater and threatened to remain in that condition as permanent marine exhibits. The optimistic lips of the customers' men having been sealed, most of them had already drifted into fields where they could express themselves more freely. The only busy spot was Statistics where ambitious young men, finding themselves for the first time in direct contact with the boss, slaved over economic reports, evaluated them, and took them personally to Ham's office. He studied them until his eyes could scarcely see the typed pages. He interviewed the men who had prepared them. Gradually he became convinced that his first flash hunch had been right. Trouble lay ahead; deep economic distress, deeper possibly than anything this country had ever witnessed before.

He was convinced, but he must be doubly convinced. If he made a mistake at this point it might do irreparable harm to the firm. He would make one more checking.

Having done so, he wrote the attorneys who were handling Barbara's trust. Several days later Miss Kelly announced that Mr. Galter was on the phone. "He sounds as if he needed defrosting."

Ham sighed and picked up the receiver.

"Mr. Martin, around September first you insisted on our selling all of your wife's equity stock. We believed that you were correct and acquiesced in your request. Time has indicated that we were right in so doing. Now the market has started to go up again and we feel that she should resume a normal investment position. We understand from your recent letter that you do not agree with us."

"I do *not*," said Ham. "In fact, I have just about concluded a study which indicates not only that the stocks which she sold should not be repurchased or replaced but that every long-term bond that she owns should now be sold. She should hold nothing for the time being but short-term governments."

"We are used to acting in the capacity of trustees, Mr. Martin. We are investors not traders."

"Mr. Galter—are you there, Mr. Galter?"

"Of course, Mr. Martin, I am waiting for you to proceed."

"Sorry, I thought you might have stepped out for a cup of coffee. First of all, Mrs. Martin's trust is worth far more today than it would have been had I not called you up around the first of September and put pressure on you to make the sales which you did."

"I object to that language, Mr. Martin. You made certain suggestions. We followed them because we ourselves believed that was the proper procedure to take. We do not recognize 'pressure' as you express it. We now wish to reinvest Mrs. Martin's funds so that she will again have a balanced portfolio. We believe—"

Ham interrupted him. "I know, I know. But let me tell you, sir, that after the most careful consideration of the facts I am convinced that this country is on the verge of a major depression; one which will make the prices at which stocks are selling today look fabulously high within the next few years."

"Mr. Martin, as I said before, we are trustees, not gazers into the crystal ball, and we refuse to let you force us into a speculative position, even though it is a negative one."

Ham's jaw tightened. "Okay, when I hang up I will make a transcript of this conversation which I will give to my wife and to my lawyer. I promise you that you will be held accountable for any failure to take prudent action or for any action that you may take which results in material loss to Mrs. Martin."

Mr. Galter's voice was vibrating with tension. "We are lawyers, Mr. Martin. We know the laws regulating trusts, possibly a little better than you do. There is no occasion for you to threaten or bluster. We are not easily intimidated."

Ham inhaled deeply and let his breath out slowly. "Mr. Galter, we are both grown men. I suggest we stop this childish bickering and that you permit me to tell you how I have reached my conclusions. I thought I could spare you a lot of technical detail, but I see that I cannot."

For the next fifteen minutes he discussed the various factors which had caused him to reach his conclusions. Mr. Galter listened, grunting occasionally with impatience. His grunts finally ceased, and he was obviously listening with close attention. Eventually Ham stopped.

"Well, that's about the story in a nutshell—a big nutshell I'm afraid."

"Mr. Martin—" the voice at the other end of the phone now was dry, contained, and even— "may I say first of all that your desire to accumulate money might occasionally outrun your prudence and influence your judgment."

Holy cow, here was a new character playing the same tune in a different key.

"In this case, Mr. Martin, you have marshaled your facts convincingly. We deal in facts here, rather than in mirages. I want to talk to my associates about this. We may wish to meet with you so that all of us can hear at first hand your reasons for anticipating what we call an economic recession. And let me say this, Mr. Martin, should we decide to sell Mrs. Martin's long-term bonds and hold only short-term United States obligations until the general situation becomes—er— uh—what we might call more stabilized, it would be a great help to us if you would permit us to run the trust unaided by speculative suggestions for at least a period of time."

"That depends on how foolishly you run it," replied Ham and replaced the receiver with sufficient force to make sure that Mr. Galter realized that the conversation had been terminated.

The following weeks were exhausting ones for Ham. Night after night he remained at the office reading, thinking. The idea that was taking shape was so drastic, so opposed to the general thinking of the Street, that he was determined not to leave any unexplored corners while arriving at a final conclusion.

One evening, almost staggering with weariness, he arrived home just as Barbara was sitting down to dinner.

"This is a great honor," she said coldly. "We might have had something special if we had known that we were going to be favored with your company."

"Oh, Barb, for heaven's sake lay off the Katharine Cornell line. You know I'd get home if I could and that I don't enjoy eating dinner alone in Wall Street restaurants. I never was more busy in my life. I'm tired—dog tired—and when I do get home at a decent hour it would be nice to be greeted with a little understanding instead of a lot of flapdoodle."

"Busy doing what?" she asked in a controlled voice. "My friends tell me Wall Street is dead."

"Well, I suppose it sounds stupid, but I've been researching."

"About what?"

"I've been looking into the crystal ball and I'm frank to say that I don't like what I see, which brings up subject number two. I'm leaving tomorrow afternoon for a swing around the country. I want to talk to the boys who make things and find out what *they* think about the future. I'll be away about two weeks."

"What are you going to do with all this hot information when you get it?"

"It's just as easy to make money in a depression as it is in a boom—as long as you don't get confused about which is which."

"Money!" Her voice was sharp and edgy now. "Don't you ever think of anything else? Don't you ever think about beauty or creativity or intelligence—or your children? I haven't the presumption to include myself. Money, money, money! That's all I hear about. I'm sick of it. You can spend the rest of your life panning for gold in the Sierras but leave me out of it."

"Leave you out of it! When have I dragged you into it?" He was angry now. "You're one of those damned pseudo-intellectual snobs who sneer at money and avoid those who haven't any. You hate the stuff—filthy, vulgar, contaminating—but you wouldn't know what to do without it and you sure are an expert at disposing of it. What do you think your father did all his life—sit cross-legged on a cushion, holding a daisy and contemplating beauty?"

"I'd trouble you not to bring my family into it."

"Well, they're in it. How can you keep them out of it? Your mother brought him a tidy sum which he quadrupled. How? By thinking about art? No, by working himself to death so that you and your mother could have all the comforts and frills demanded by a phony money-based thing you call Society."

"That's a cowardly, cheap thing to say. You know I didn't want those things. I was running away from them on the unfortunate day when I first met you."

"Well, you accepted everything that was within reach quite gracefully while you ran. The trouble with you is that you don't know the meaning of reality. You don't know what it is to be even modestly poor as my parents were. In a little town like Messina—"

She leaned forward, her clenched fists on the table, glaring at him. "Don't tell me you're going to pose as the boy who worked up from the bottom. The little lad from Messina who made good! How can you have the nerve? If it hadn't been for your Uncle Charlie you'd probably be working in some Messina shoe store today. The little boy who made good! The little boy who had a wonderful father and mother who devoted a large part of their lives to a futile attempt to make him into a perceptive, creative man only to have him throw it all in their faces and become the biggest moneygrubber in the world's grub pile. I'm fed up with it. From now on you live your life and I'll live mine. I hate you."

She covered her face with her hands, burst into tears, and left the room.

"Mrs. Martin isn't feeling well," he said to the white-coated serving man. "She's gone to her room. I'll have my dinner in the library."

When he returned from his trip the former conclusions he had reached from statistical data were largely confirmed by his observations in the field. He had sent daily reports to Miss Kelly and had dictated his summarization over the telephone from Duluth. As a result each partner had received a copy of the complete report and had had time to absorb Ham's point of view before the latter returned to New York.

His first move was to call a meeting of the partners. They filed into his office, shook hands, and took their seats with such uniform solemnity that Ham immediately concluded they had already discussed the report and reached a conclusion—and that it was one he wouldn't like.

He reviewed the highlights of his trip. "I have come back more convinced than ever that we are on the brink of a serious depression. I have no opinion as to how long it might last or how deep it may be, but, on the basis of the old saying 'the higher they go the harder they fall,' I would think it might last a long time and be extremely severe. That is the assumption we should make in preparing ourselves for the storm that is most certainly coming."

He paused, inviting comment. No one spoke for a moment, then young Platt who was now working in Administration held up his hand as if this was a class in school. "Sir" (young Platt had never been able to call Ham by his first name even though he was a partner), "how does one go about preparing a firm like this for a storm?"

"Good question." Ham grinned. "And a tough one. Still working on the assumption that I'm right, let's see where we stand income-wise. First, no more margin accounts. That's easy. We haven't been accepting any since the break. Second, during a period such as I visualize there'll be little or no underwriting business of the kind that we want to be in. Third, as for the investment accounts that we hold for customers, the greatest favor we could do for the owners would be to get them out of equities and long corporate bonds and into one- to five-year governments for the duration."

"Which most of them wouldn't do," interrupted Davidson.

"Which most of them wouldn't do," Ham agreed, "and they'd hate us so, because they hadn't taken our advice, that they'd probably transfer their accounts to another house."

They stared at him gloomily. Tom Reese spoke. "Having completely eliminated all sources of income, Ham, who is going to pay the rent?"

"That's what we're here to discuss." Ham tried hard to keep his tone relaxed. The only answer was almost too brutal to contemplate.

Davidson stood up, a formality that was never tolerated at a partners' meeting. "Ham, what I'm going to say is very difficult. If I don't express myself well, please forgive me. I'm going to be quite frank with you. We have always been frank and we're not going to change now. When we received your report we knew that this firm was about to be put on ice and that having reduced the income to almost zero, our expenses had to be reduced to as near that figure as possible.

"Again to be quite frank, Ham, we've sensed this dilemma for weeks in view of your attitude toward the future and we've been sounding out a few outside firms with large capital and a thin organization. Deming and Company have made a very interesting offer. They will merge under the title Deming and Martin, to preserve your uncle's name." Ham's face was expressionless. "They will take almost all the partners. The younger partners in Deming and Company have ambitious plans for expansion. Most of the older ones—and they're a majority—are ready for retirement. They will also take all our present employees who care to work for them."

He paused, licked his lips, obviously dreading what came next and hoping for an interruption. Ham did not move a muscle or take his eyes from the speaker's face.

"You see," Davidson continued more hesitantly, "we don't quite agree with your conclusions, Ham. We think you're much too pessimistic. This is a strong, virile country and, in our opinion, it's going to pull out of any recession very quickly and continue to go forward." He paused, groping for words. "Well, that's what we believe and also what Deming and Company believes.

"We also think you're much too conservative, Ham. As has been said in this room before, we are not our brothers' keepers, but you seem to feel that we are. The only purpose in a firm like this—the only reason that this big staff struggles in from the suburbs each morning and struggles out again each evening—is to make money with which to support its families. You're rich, Ham. You don't care about money. As a result you turn off income sources as casually as you would turn off a faucet.

"To sum it all up, we like you and we admire your principles, but we feel that we must approach business in a less idealistic way. Deming and Company feel as we do, in addition to which they have plenty of capital. I guess that what I mean by all that is they are not including you in their merger proposal. What *we* are proposing is that those partners who wish to join Deming and Company resign (and I think that will include almost all of us). As for the staff— you select whomever you want. If they care to stay with you we certainly want them to.

"I guess that's all." He turned to the other partners. "Have I covered the ground?" The assent was unanimous, almost noisy, expressing general relief that the ordeal was over.

Ham moved for the first time, leaning forward on the desk. Only two thin lines at the corners of his mouth betrayed his tension. He looked at each face around the room. Some met his eyes. The majority avoided them.

Finally he spoke. "This meeting has proved to me as nothing else could have done that I have surrounded myself with men capable of making up their own minds and of acting on their conclusions. Only a few minutes ago I presented you with one of the most difficult problems I have ever faced. Assuming certain conditions, how were we going to cut our cloth to meet them? I find that you have not only decided, but you have actually cut the cloth.

"You have arrived at a splendid solution. I hope sincerely

that I am wrong and that you are right. I hope that you will be happy and rich, and incidentally I want to thank you for believing that I am indifferent to money. I won't go into the reason why this pleases me so much, but at the moment it just happens to.

"From here in it's more or less a lawyers' party. I'll get Harry to come over. Eventually each one of you will have to get into the act, but right now I suggest that you let George Brownlee represent you in the preliminary talks: it's quicker."

"You seem to be in a hurry to get rid of us." Craig's laugh was forced.

"I am. I want to get you settled in your new nest before the storm breaks and Deming and Company changes its mind."

Harry whistled softly when Ham told him the news. "Boy, oh, boy! Won't Wall Street gobble that one? Have you any loans outstanding?"

"None."

"No brokers' loans? No commitments of any kind?"

"None."

"I can hardly believe it. I'll be over as soon as I shovel my desk clean and cancel a few minor appointments. By the way, after we get through at your office could you have dinner with me? I think it's important."

"Of course. We'll be waiting for you here at your convenience."

They went to the Union Club that evening. In the great high-ceilinged dining room, with ample space between the tables, Harry felt there was more privacy. He plunged into the subject.

"What are *you* going to do?"

"Three hours ago I would have been obliged to tell you I didn't know, but while you fellows were mumbling over details this afternoon I did a lot of thinking. I'm going to liquidate the firm. That's obvious being as how I'll be the only partner left."

"Shades of Uncle Charlie!" murmured Harry. "When I think of how many dinners he and I used to have in this very room while he was building up the firm. But that's beside the point. He was right and you are right. The tune has changed and you are dancing to new rhythms. I'm particularly pleased at your decision for a reason that's worrying me."

"What's that?"

"A blowup like this usually means that there is something rotten in Denmark. If all your partners desert you like rats leaving a doomed ship, and you remain aboard, the finger of suspicion is bound to point to you. You are doing the only sensible thing under the circumstances, much as I hate to see it done."

"I'm glad to hear you say so, but I'm not getting out of Wall Street."

"What are you going to do?"

Ham reflected for a moment before replying. "I'm always careful when I'm talking to my lawyer. During the last few weeks I have been told, on the one hand, that I am a money-mad lunatic, devoid of all finer feelings and, on the other hand, I have been called an aesthetic conservative—such a crazy conservative, in fact, that nobody could work with me who had any hope of making a living. I think it might be interesting to find out who's right."

Harry raised a finger. "Let me interrupt you just a moment while I order a bottle of wine." He beckoned to the headwaiter.

"Do you have—"

"Number 27, sir? Of course. Right away."

Harry settled himself back in his chair. "Sorry. Now go ahead with your confessions."

"During the past year I've been impressed by the fact that the majority of common stock buyers are speculators rather than investors, no matter how much they disclaim it. Not only that, but they are one-way speculators. Their speculation is always for a rise in the price of stocks; never for a decline."

"I suppose you mean they should go short as well as long?"

"If they are interested in making money on the changes in stock prices, of course they should, but only under certain conditions, only when the country is obviously reaching the end of a speculative binge such as we are seeing now. Over the long pull the trend is upward. I'm perfectly aware of that. Ever since the days of the Renaissance the civilized world has been in the midst of a quiet inflation. Every once in a while, though, men dream of getting rich without working and build up a children's tower of cards which eventually gets so high it can only topple. I'm going to follow the topple down."

"Okay, Ham. It may be all right for you, but you know perfectly well that most people would lose their shirts if they started to go short. The American people are not temperamentally fitted for that sort of thing. It makes them nervous. They'll hold a long position while the market is declining day after day, confident that eventually it will go up again and all will be rosy. And it will, Ham, you know that as well as I do. A tragically large number of people may go more or less broke by hanging on to stocks right now, but eventually the tide will turn. New money will come into the picture from God knows where, and this country will go forward again. It's ridiculous to think otherwise. Positive aggressiveness is in our blood. That's the reason why the great majority of people couldn't possibly go short. They can only think positively, and thank heaven for that even if a lot of them are about to get mashed up doing so."

"That's a good speech, Harry. I like it because it doesn't make me into a rascal."

"Of course not. It's not a moral question, but while we're on that let me remind you that to most people the short position has a slight odor of tainted meat."

"I suppose you're right, but I propose to deal with facts and not prejudice. If I do anything harmful I count on you to set me right."

"Well, while we're on that, just exactly what *are* you going to do after Martin and Kuhn is liquidated?"

"I'm going to set up my own office where I can follow my own convictions and be myself. All my life people have wanted me to be what I wasn't. Whatever I've done seems to have been wrong in their eyes. In spite of the fact that I've done pretty well, I've left a trail of disappointed people behind me.

"I like what I'm doing, Harry. It seems to fit me. It's an atmosphere in which I feel at home. On the other hand, my mind doesn't seem to run in conventional grooves like so many of these fellows down in the Street. Perhaps it's because I didn't cut my teeth on the *Wall Street Journal* and the financial section of the *Times*. I didn't come to New York with a lot of stereotyped notions. I was just a small-town product with no preconceived ideas. That fact alone made me able to look at things objectively. I guess I'm a loner, Harry. I want to get completely on my own while I can still do my own thinking—free to follow my own conclusions without hurting anyone but myself when I'm wrong."

"You still haven't made it quite clear what you want to do,

but I think I know. You're either going to be a very rich man, Ham, or you're going broke. You want freedom. Go and wallow in it for a while. You're not going to be happy. Man isn't built for freedom. It's just something he craves when he hasn't got it and that he can't live with when he has.— And just one more point, Ham, before I stop moralizing—if you're successful be prepared to have some people call you a common gambler."

Springtime, 1931. Ham sat in a corner office on the twenty-third floor of a building on lower Broadway watching a great ocean liner being coaxed into its stall by three diminutive tugs. Across the Hudson River lay Hoboken looking sordid in spite of the sunlight and beyond it the industry-poisoned flats of the Hackensack Meadows, crisscrossed by roads, railroad tracks, and dredged inlets where ore ships, looking like nesting hens, lay between the mudbanks waiting to unload.

A traveler, returning to this scene after an absence, would have been puzzled. A change had come into the picture which he might have found difficult to identify at first. After he looked long enough, however, he would have noticed that it had occurred, not on the ground, but in the atmosphere above it. The spring sunshine fairly sparkled over the black-brown meadows where, two years before, it had struggled to penetrate a blanket of sulphurous smog. Now the chimneys which had produced the smog stood black and stark against the clear sky.

The office from which Ham stared so thoughtfully was impressive, paneled in teak by its former occupant and with carpets so thick that they gave the impression of walking through light snow. His old desk, standing at right angles to the window overlooking the river, was littered with reports and papers. He pushed a button. Miss Kelly's cheery face appeared in the doorway.

"You look bored," she said.

"I am," he replied without turning his head from the window.

"So am I. Oh, God, I'm bored. Can't I even have a record player to liven this place up?"

"No," he snapped. "This is an office, not an ice-cream parlor."

"It's a morgue," she said. "A nice, orderly morgue and I am going to be one of its first customers if we don't do something about it. You look terrible. You have a hangover."

"Just a little one," he said.

"You didn't sleep, did you?"

He turned to her crossly. "For heaven's sake what is this, a physical examination? Do you want me to take my shirt off so you can listen to my heart?"

"No, no. I am much more concerned with having you keep it on at this particular time. Tell me, if you care to. Is she still going out every night?"

He nodded.

"With that same old crowd, I suppose. Who comes for her? That horrible man who writes the disgusting plays?"

He nodded again. "Yes, presuming you mean Ackerson."

"You seem to use the apartment principally for bathing and sleeping. You could do that more cheaply in a good Turkish bath."

"I know," he said, "but I'm damned if I am going to stay home and say good night to my wife when she goes off with some literary playboy leaving me to eat alone."

"I'd be glad to eat with you," she said. "I could be your dinner sitter. That might cause some excitement."

"Too much," he said.

"You know, boss, you're in a tough spot. First of all, you've got a wife who doesn't know what she really wants. The only thing she seems to be sure of is that she doesn't want a husband who's making money and she has some sort of an immature idea that her escape lies through a lot of pseudo-intellectuals.

"You might be able to stand it if you had something interesting to do during the day. The trouble is you pressed the right button when most people were jumping out of windows. The money machine went into action for you. Now there's nothing to do but sit here and watch it go round and round until the time comes for you to push the button that turns it off. I hope you know when that time comes."

He turned to face her. "Listen, Miss Primrose," he said, "I know perfectly well what I am doing and why I am doing it. And now I'll tell you why I rang for you. Make a careful note of this, I don't want any mistakes. Double my short position in GM, GE, U.S. Steel, and Chrysler—at the market. Spread the sales over five of our special brokers. You know the ones and how to do it."

Miss Kelly whistled as she made hasty notes in her dictation book. It was a low, respectful whistle which managed to convey surprise, disapproval, and a certain amount of admiration.

"You think I'm crazy?" he asked, turning back to the window. He had learned to interpret Miss Kelly's whistles, grunts, and silences.

"No, but—well, this thing has been running your way now for over a year and you've been increasing your position steadily. You've made so much money it makes me slightly sick, but someday the party has to end—and here you are digging in deeper than ever."

He turned for the first time and grinned at her. "Every man needs a warning light and I couldn't imagine a better one than you, but I regret to tell you, dear Kelly, that this depression is not over by a damn sight. A situation like this sets up a kind of chain reaction which goes faster and faster with time. Sure there'll be a bottom, but you'll know when it comes. It's much easier to tell a bottom than a top. When the end comes the whole economy will be exhausted; supine. It will just lie there for a while, gathering its breath and its strength for what the writers call 'the long climb back.'"

"Like a little boy that's rolled downstairs." She closed her notebook. "I'm glad to hear you talk about the climb back though. It sometimes seems as if we had gone too far down to ever be the same country again."

"Of course we will. Just as Harry once said. Well, maybe not the *same* exactly, but we'll be just as rich, or richer, than we were before the crash. A lot of things will be different, though. We are seeing the next to last great opportunity to make money, unhampered by regulations. What we've been going through is like the open ranges of the West before barbed wire was invented. When the present show is over the boys in Washington will be stringing so much barbed wire around that we'll be up to our necks in the damn stuff for the rest of our lives."

"But people like you will be able to get through it. That's the extraordinary thing," she said.

He shook his head. "If you're talking about making money in the stock market, the answer is no. In the short period of a decade we're being given three chances to make money so easily that it's almost disgusting. The boom of the twenties. The terrible aftermath we're going through now. The third will be when the bottom has been reached and stocks are selling for prices that will look incredible ten years later. After that it's finished."

She leaned forward and tapped her pencil on the desk for emphasis. "But why is it, boss, that so many men who were highly successful in the first phase failed to see the second and went flat broke?"

"I don't know. Naturally I've thought a lot about it. Most of the men that you're speaking of had far more brains than I have. Why couldn't they have seen the end coming just as well as I did? All those men and women who made fortunes of varying sizes before the crash, and then just stood by like rabbits hypnotized by a snake and watched their paper profits melt away until their loans were called and they had nothing left. Put in those sale orders and let me know when they're executed."

When she returned he was again staring across the river, chewing reflectively on the bow of his glasses. "I think the principal reason they overstayed in 'twenty-nine," he said, before she had a chance to report on the sales, "was because they were one-way speculators. To me it always seems to come back to that. As I said a few minutes ago, most of them had built up paper fortunes bigger than they had ever anticipated. For the first time in their lives they saw financial independence right around the corner. They couldn't bring themselves to sell because they had frozen themselves into the idea that, once they sold, their dream was over, and they always needed just a little bit more to make it come wholly true. That's what I mean by speculation being a one-way street. It never occurred to them that when the interest on call money rose to 16 percent and over something must be screwball somewhere and that it might be wise to sell out and sit on their hands until they saw what was going on. It certainly never occurred to them that, if this was the end of the upswing, they could reach the promised land just as easily, and even more quickly, by following the market down on the short side."

"Why are people so scared of selling stocks short?"

"For various reasons; principally I think because they don't understand the first thing about it. They don't understand how anyone can sell something he doesn't own. It sounds a little like the old shell game to them; a little tricky; not quite kosher. The result is they don't want to have anything to do with it."

"Boss, I've been giving orders to sell short to your brokers for over a year and I still can't understand it. Look here, let's take a case. You sell a hundred shares of General Motors short. Right? You haven't got a share of General Motors to your name, but in a couple of days you have to make a delivery of a hundred shares to the fellow who bought it. All right, where does it come from?"

"My broker borrows a hundred shares and delivers them."

"Who does he borrow them from?"

"From another broker. There are a number of brokers in the Street who are lending specialists. In this case one of them goes to a customer, or whoever, borrows the hundred shares and lends it to our broker who delivers it to the man I sold it to. Simple?"

"Childishly simple," she said, "but I guess I'm too old to understand it. Who gets anything but trouble out of this merry-go-round?"

"The man who originally lends the stock gets a fee. So does the loaning broker."

"And you get the money for the stock from the fellow you sold it to?"

"No. That goes to the loaning broker as security for the borrowed stock. Don't you see? This borrowing business goes on until one of three things happens: I either have to buy in the open market because there is no stock to be borrowed, or until the stock drops enough to give me the profit I want, or until the stock starts to go up and I buy in the open market and take my loss.

"Don't look so dazed. Can't you see? It's just the reverse of an ordinary purchase of stock. I thought you were bright."

"I am," she said. "I just don't understand very well."

"It's so simple. The only difference between buying long and selling short is the way in which you tip the hourglass. In both cases all that counts is the relationship between the purchase price and the selling price. Don't you see what I mean?"

She frowned slightly. "I think so. You have a genius for making simple things sound complicated. Let's go back to what you said about the feeling people have that there's something immoral—something unconstructive—or whatever you want to call it—about selling short. Don't they have some reason to think that, when the market is going down and little people with margin accounts are being sold out, it's not quite cricket for someone to sell stocks that he hasn't got, and to force the market even lower?"

"That's just fuzzy thinking. Remember there are two sides to every transaction. There's always a buyer as well as a seller. When I sell a hundred shares short I have to find a buyer and I sell to him at the price he thinks is right. As a matter of fact the buyer is the one that's pressing the market down. He naturally wants to buy at the lowest possible price. It's the short seller who is holding the market up. It's to his interest to *sell* at the highest possible price. What's immoral about that? And then don't forget that when things really get black it's the short interest covering its position that furnishes the buying without which—oh, without which . . . Just leave it at that. What is this anyway? A business school?"

He reached over and seized the ticker tape. "This market looks sloppy. I assume you got those sales off."

"Of course I did. You're hopeless. Everytime we're having a nice cozy chat you stop to think about making money."

All during the long year which followed, while men sold apples on street corners and gangs of men, working on charity-sponsored projects, leaned on their shovels with listless hopelessness; while banks closed and factories lapsed into silence, Ham sat at his desk and sold.

In spite of all that he could do to conceal his identity his name became known through the Street as one of the biggest operators of his time. The financial columnists picked up the story and estimates of the amounts he was making were part of the daily gossip of the Street. How could this madman be blocked—this man who presumed to make money while respectable people were losing theirs or had already lost it? They beat their brains in vain. He only sold the stock of the largest companies, avoiding special situations where he might have difficulty borrowing the stock to make deliveries.

He learned what it meant to be hated and despised because he had the temerity to succeed while others failed. When he approached a group at any of his clubs it was apt to become silent and he passed on, picking up a paper or a magazine from the long table and retiring to a corner. He and Barbara were seldom invited out for dinner now except by those who hoped to profit from the contact. When he went to his downtown lunch club he instinctively kept away from the common table and ate by himself in the most inconspicuous place in the room. After a while he did not go to the lunch club at all, but ferreted out little places on the West Side above Battery Park where he seldom knew anyone. Even on the street he could feel the difference in the greetings. They still spoke to him, but no longer with the old heartiness; just a word of recognition as they hurried past.

What was this money curse which seemed to follow him everywhere in half a dozen different guises? Other people made money and were held in esteem by their fellow citizens, their friends, and their families. From the moment he had begun to acquire it, however, he had become a disappointment to his father and mother, alienated his wife, and now, just because he had done what seemed to him the obvious and sensible thing to do and his judgment had proved to be correct, his friends and acquaintances treated him as if he were a leper.

The only time he had been criticized for *not* making money was when he tried to save the margin customers in his old firm. Then his partners had turned on him and branded him as a radical conservative; thrown him out of his own firm, to all intents and purposes. How he missed Uncle Charlie and longed for an opportunity to talk with him amid the comfortable shadows of his uncle's library. He was sure that Uncle Charlie would have had an answer.

Gradually bitterness began to seep into his thinking. If the world was going to disown him because he did what he thought he should and in spite of the fact that what he was doing could hurt no one but himself, then he would go it alone and to hell with them. He would go his own way, follow the dictates of his own judgment, and if he was wrong he would bear the consequences—alone.

His resentment did not include his father and mother. In their eyes he had betrayed them and therefore in his eyes it was so. In so far as they were concerned the old feeling of guilt remained and always would.

April, 1932. He sat in the same place only this time he was not gazing out over the river. He was studying a series of charts on a table beside his desk, his hair rumpled by nervous fingers. There were furrows between his eyebrows and his jaw was tense and set.

Suddenly he reached down and pushed a button on the side of the desk. Miss Kelly stuck her head in almost immediately. "What were you doing? Looking at me through the keyhole?"

"Boss, I know you so well I don't have to. I've known for the last hour that you were trying to decide something and that it was something big—and I think I know what it is."

"You were right," he said. "And it is important—at least for you and me. I've decided to begin covering."

"Hallelujah!" she cried. "I've been so scared for the last two months I couldn't sleep."

He handed her a slip of paper. "Thanks for not telling me. Here's a list of brokers and the particular man in each shop that I want to speak to. Get them for me in that order. And when you get them I want you to listen in (not that you wouldn't anyway) and take stenographic notes. Don't let them know you're there. If you don't understand, keep quiet and do the best you can. It's going to take a bit of doing to close out without letting everyone in the Street know. There are three others with big short positions and they're smart like foxes. I've decided to be the first out. They'll spot it fast enough and between us we'll run this market up to where it was in 'twenty-nine if we're not careful."

He phoned the brokers and then sat back to watch the ticker, bored and strangely listless. The party was over, or at least it was on its way to being over. The tension generated by a dangerous adventure had been suddenly released. Once again he had come through white water, where other men had drowned, and found it ridiculously easy. Miss Kelly had asked why this was. A good question. What quality did he have that other men lacked? It didn't take brains to do what he had done. The moves were as obvious as those of a child's game.

As he had often said, it was probably because he had been raised in a small town where thinking was simple and direct; where one could see things clearly, unblurred by previous conceptions, and be sure that what was seen was really there.

He suddenly realized that he had no idea where he stood financially. Old Joe Brennan, who had come with him from Martin and Kuhn, kept the books. Beachum and Beachum, Certified Public Accountants, hovered watchfully over Joe from their aerie on the twenty-fifth floor of 40 Wall Street. Ham completed the security chain by keeping a watchful eye on Beachum and Beachum.

When he had sold his first shares short he had issued strict orders that he was not to be informed of cumulative book profits. He was only to be advised if the operation was running at a serious loss. It hampered one's judgment to concentrate too hard on figures. Markets tolerated no wish-thinking. Markets tolerated no romanticism. They must be entered and abandoned when the signs were right and without reference to one's personal gains.

He pressed the button for Miss Kelly. "Now that we've made up our mind to go ashore I guess there is no harm in having Beachum and Beachum get in touch with Joe Brennan. I want a report on my total net worth—the whole ball of wax. By the time they get around to it I should be out of the market."

Miss Kelly grinned. "If you're not interested in what you're worth, Joe Brennan and I are. He's been figuring your position every night from the start. At the close of the market last night—"

"Don't tell me," he said. "I only want to know when we have made the turn-around and I want Beachum and Beachum's figures, not yours and Joe's. You're prejudiced in favor of a raise."

"You're psychic," she said and closed the door gently behind her.

He felt suddenly tired. Every ounce of vitality seemed to have flowed from him, as if from a bottle, uncorked by his decision. He rang again for Miss Kelly. "Phone James and tell him to bring the car down right away. I'm going home early. And don't tell me you're glad. I know that in advance."

"The party wasn't over a day too soon," she said. "James will be down in a jiffy. Make yourself a drink."

"Damn it, can't I do anything in this office without you telling me when and why? I was just going to and now you make it *your* idea. Call James and go home."

"After you, sir," she said with a faint suggestion of a curtsy.

An antique corner cupboard stood at one end of the big room. He walked over to it slowly and opened the double doors which screened a small icebox and shelves of glasses and bottles. Mixing himself a double Scotch he returned to his chair, put his feet on the radiator cover, and looked out on the familiar scene. He was suddenly seeing it with different eyes. For over two years it had been made ugly and sinister by its association with strain and uncertainty. Now, in the rays of the slanting sun, it became suddenly beautiful, a modernistic painting made up of great splashes of browns and grays, seen through the amber light of a fading day. As the whiskey took hold he felt less weary and filled with an unfamiliar calm—the sudden calmness of a runner who has staked everything on a single race and won.

He was almost asleep when James stopped before the apartment house entrance.

"Here we are, sir."

Ham straightened up, angry with himself for this display of weakness. The doorman would think he was tight. "Good evening, Henry."

"Good evening, sir. Home early."

"Yes, taking a bit of a vacation." He walked briskly across the foyer to the elevator, conscious of the doorman's eyes following him, hoping that he was walking a straight line.

At the sound of footsteps old Dennis stuck his head out of the elevator door in order to discover who his prospective customer might be. This advance knowledge would give him a few seconds to consider the most suitable topic of conversation. He had one unbreakable rule; never to disagree with a tenant. This made it essential not only to present two sides to any subject under discussion so that he could move quickly from one to the other as circumstances dictated, but also to avoid subjects on which a particular tenant had strong convictions.

"Good evening, Mr. Martin."

"Evening, Dennis."

"Looks a little like rain."

"Does it? I haven't paid much attention." (Tenant not in a good mood. Be careful.)

"It may hold off, sir. The rain I mean."

"Yes. By the way, is Mrs. Martin at home, do you know?" (Danger. Dennis pulled his ear lobe to symbolize thought.)

"I couldn't say, sir. I just came on. Tom would be more apt to know but he's just gone home."

The elevator stopped and Ham crossed the small foyer. In this section of the building there was only one apartment to a landing, so his door was never locked. He opened it quietly and entered. Dennis watched him with something like compassion on his gnarled features. Then he closed the elevator door softly and returned to safer ground in the lobby.

As Ham removed his overcoat he became conscious of a low murmur of voices from the library, so low that he couldn't recognize the speakers. A man's black homburg and topcoat were thrown carelessly on a chair. He recognized Barbara's voice when she laughed. It was a laugh he had not heard in many years; not a laugh brought forth in response to humor, but the happy, almost childlike, laugh of one who has cast off all restraint, all conventions, and become for the moment solely and completely a woman.

He picked up the black hat and looked at the inside band. "N.A." It was Ackerson as he had already suspected.

He walked noiselessly to the door of the library. Barbara and Ackerson lay stretched out on the long sofa so absorbed in each other that he might have entered and stood before them without their noticing. On the coffee table, in front of the sofa, was a whiskey decanter, a bowl of ice, and two half-finished highballs. He didn't wait. He didn't want to hear their mumbled conversation. Striding into the room he stopped before the coffee table, seized one of the highball glasses and threw the contents over Ackerson's head from which it ran down over Barbara's face. "Get out," he said. His voice was pitched lower than usual and he spoke very slowly. (He suddenly saw himself acting the part in a movie.) "Get out, you low-grade mongrel. Get out of here, you son of a bitch." (That was better.)

Ackerson had disentangled himself and risen unsteadily to his feet. His hair, which he wore quite long and ordinarily brushed back behind his ears, fell across his forehead like that of a sheepdog. "Why you—you—" he began, reaching for the neck of the whiskey decanter.

Ham put it quickly beyond his reach. "No dramatics, you louse. Just do as I tell you. Get out while you're alive."

Ackerson staggered to the door, brushing his hair back with his hand as he went. Ham followed him. As he passed through the door Ham kicked him—kicked him so hard that Ackerson lost his balance and almost fell. "I seldom do that even to dogs," he said. "Get out." (That was a good scene. Don't spoil it. Just stand there.)

The front door of the apartment slammed. Ham remained half-dazed in the front hallway and a few moments later he heard the elevator door open and shut. Dennis would now have something real to talk about. Barbara had not moved from the sofa. She sat on the edge, nervously arranging her hair and her dress. Finally she rose and walked quickly past him without a word. He heard her footsteps go down the corridor and then her bedroom door closing. He went over to the coffee table, found a clean glass and poured himself a drink. He held it in his hand for a few moments, staring at it blankly. Finally he replaced it on the coffee table untouched and hurried out of the room. Snatching up his hat and coat from the chair where he had laid them, he left the apartment.

When he returned that night, slightly drunk, he found an unaddressed envelope on the hall table. He knew it contained a note from Barbara before he opened it and he knew that she had gone. At the moment he didn't really care. His heart, or wherever the seat of his battered emotions might lie, was anesthetized. Ripping open the envelope he glanced at the hasty scrawl. "I am leaving. Ever since I married you you have been one of the most brutally selfish men I have ever met. Now that we have reached the parting of the ways I feel nothing but relief. I wonder why I didn't do it long ago." He tore the letter into small bits and tossed them into the copper urn under the hall table which served as a scrap basket. Before going to bed he took two of the sleeping pills the doctor had once given him and which he had never used except on a train. The dramatic thing would have been to gobble up the entire bottle, but he was tired of watching himself as an actor. He was too tired to think. Even the matter of his living or dying had become immaterial. Barbara was gone. Okay. He was pulling out of his short position, which would leave him without any job or goal whatsoever. Okay. He had three children. This was the first time he had thought about the children. Good heavens, what was he going to do with them? He would most certainly fight to keep them out of Barbara's hands and he thought that, in view of the scene which had just taken place, he might win his fight. But then what? How did a busy man raise three children? But he was not a busy man. He was a man without any job whatsoever. He might devote the rest of his life to taking them all to Europe and fishing with the boys. He hated fishing. Oh, hell. These things would work themselves out somehow. He went back to the library, poured himself another drink and having consumed it hastily went to bed.

Miss Kelly could not keep the startled expression out of her face the next morning when he appeared at his usual hour. "Boss," she said, after she had reported on the progress of his covering operation, "something is all fouled up. Is there anything I can do to help?"

"Nothing," he said. "Nothing whatsoever. I don't even want to talk about it."

"If you don't want to talk about it it must be a whopper."

She gathered up her notebook and pencils and silently rose to leave the room.

"Sit down. Don't go rushing off when I'm right in the middle of a sentence." He told her everything. She listened without comment. She didn't even try to lighten things up with a quip and for that he was grateful. They merely sat for a long time in silence.

"So now what?" he asked finally.

"If you want my advice, keep moving today and get some rest tonight. Move *now*. Clean up your desk. Make sure that everything is going the way you want it to go as far as the covering operation is concerned. Have lunch with a couple of your less conservative cronies over at the Down Town Association. Go up to the Biltmore afterward and have a Turkish bath. In the meantime I'll make a date for you with a couple of your more dissolute friends at the Knickerbocker who I am sure will be delighted to dine with you in the hope that you'll give them a few tips on the market. Go home from the Turkish bath, have a drink, change your clothes, go to the club, and be in bed by ten o'clock. I said ten o'clock. And don't get down here tomorrow morning until you are so sick of staying in bed that you start itching and twitching. That's my advice and it won't cost you a nickel."

He smiled for the first time that day. "I'll take it," he said. "Where do we start?"

"You've been shoveling things into that right-hand drawer for months. Let's get after it and either give the stuff the heave-ho or take care of it in some other less sensible way."

They went to work.

It was almost five o'clock when he entered the apartment that evening. He almost gave his usual shout of "Hi" to put

Barbara on notice that he was home. Well, he didn't have to do that any more. His feet almost left the floor when he heard her familiar voice calling "Hi" from the living room. Without taking off his hat or coat he rushed in. She was sitting in her accustomed chair reading a magazine.

"For God's sake," he said. It wasn't exactly an appropriate remark, but it was the only thing he could think of at the moment.

"I know," she said, laying the magazine on her lap. "I couldn't take it. I couldn't leave the children. I've been through hell today and my pride is all bent and twisted, but if you care to have me back as the mother of your children, I'm here. I'll be a good wife in so far as I can. I know the rules. I expect nothing—nor should you. The old dreams were buried today with due ceremony."

He remained standing in the middle of the room staring at her.

"Well, aren't you going to take your hat off?" she asked.

He removed his hat and coat, threw them on the sofa, and sat down beside them, his head buried in his hands. "I'm all mixed up," he said. "I can't follow these superemotional changes."

"You don't need to," she replied. "Just be yourself, that shouldn't be any effort. It's all you've ever been."

"Oh, God," he groaned. "Are we going to start that all over again?"

"No," she said. "You're quite right. I only brought it up from force of habit and I promised myself not to. Where are you going for dinner tonight?"

"I'm having dinner with two Swiss bankers at the club."

"Good," she said. "I was afraid you might be dining at home. I don't think I could have stood it. The kids will be back in a little while. They have each gone to some kind of a party. I think I will go and lie down for a bit before they get here."

Miss Kelly thrust her head through the door of Ham's office. She had a new hair-do which accentuated her gamine look. Ham, tired and irritable from lack of sleep, looked up prepared to be cross, but found it difficult.

"Did you buzz?" she asked.

"You know perfectly well I didn't buzz. You merely want to stick that little nose into my affairs and find out what's been going on. All right. You know the story; come in and I'll give you something new to occupy your time besides reading novels."

"Lucky if anyone gets a chance even to eat in this office," she said.

He brought her up to date. When he finished she sat silent, looking out the window. "Well, what am I supposed to do now?"

"It's a toughie, boss," she said. "A real toughie. But it would have been tougher the other way."

"I can't go on eating at the club every night while she eats alone at home."

"That's the truth," she said. "You might just as well face up to it. You have to go home, act as natural as you can, have cocktails, eat dinner together, and see what happens."

"It's impossible," he said. "I can't do it. After all that's gone on I can't do it."

"Under the circumstances you *have* to do it. Just be your-self and see what happens."

"You're a helpful little thing," he said. "Now go back to work and wait until I really buzz."

She grinned. "I'm sorry," she said, rising. "Truly sorry."

He was as nervous as a bridegroom when he entered the apartment that night. To his surprise he heard the sound of laughter from the living room. The three children were there with Barbara, playing some game which demanded that the loser try to stand on his or her head. Barbara looked up as he entered the room. Her face clouded. The children caught the change in the atmosphere and became silent.

"Go on," he said. "Go on. For goodness' sake don't let me stop you. I'm going out to make a drink. What will you have, Barbara? The usual?" She nodded. "And all of you? What about a Coke?" They raised their hands in noisy approval.

"It will ruin their supper," said Barbara, "but to heck with it."

When he returned with the drinks and took his usual place on the sofa behind the big coffee table, the game went on, but he could feel that the spontaneity had oozed out. What amazingly intuitive creatures children were. He realized that this was the first time the five of them had been together for many weeks. How smart of Barbara to interpose them during this bad period before dinner.

He delayed them as long as he could, after they had been summoned to supper by the nurse. Finally he could procrastinate no longer. He was alone with Barbara. What in the world did you say to a person whom you had once loved and who was now in your house merely to take care of the children—a kind of legalized governess.

She picked up a magazine, seemingly quite at ease. "It suddenly occurred to me," she said, thumbing the pages aimlessly, "that the children seldom see us together." It struck Ham that this was not the most auspicious time for discussing family closeness, but he said nothing.

"They're getting older, you know," continued Barbara in an even voice. "It may be quite a shock to you to learn that

Michael is ten, Pat will be eight in two months, and Allen was four last month. They're no longer something to be dismissed by sticking your head into the nursery two or three times a day and receiving reports from Nannie as to how they are eating and what darling little things they are. I thought I would try to make this period before dinner into a kind of play hour. It shouldn't interfere with your evening cocktails. I don't believe in doing things behind the children's backs anyway. If it bores you you can go to the club, or take to the library. I think they should be in here though, rather than for me to go to the nursery. It may give them a greater feeling that this is their home and that they belong to the whole of it and not just to a few rooms."

She tossed the magazine back on the table and picked up the evening paper. "How sorry I feel for all these millions of people who are without jobs. Selling apples on street corners. Poor helpless, confused people. Citizens of one of the richest nations in the world. It is so grim I don't like to think about it."

He hoped she was not going to allude to the fortune which he had made while the rest of the world was falling apart. She didn't follow it up, however. The thought occurred to him that she might not even realize what he had been doing during the past two and a half years.

She yawned. "Do you want to mix me another?" He made one for himself also. He must remember that after a few martinis he was apt to get a bit quarrelsome. Nothing must shake him out of his coolness tonight.

They talked intermittently, impersonally, as two people might who had just met each other in a summer hotel. He became so carried away by this illusion that at one point he almost asked her how long she was staying. It might have bothered him more were it not for the fact that on the few occasions when they had dined together recently their conversation had not been what might be called animated. Dinner over, she rose. "I'll skip coffee," she said, "I'm in the middle of an interesting book. I think I'll go to bed and read myself to sleep. You look a bit tired yourself." It was the first personal word she had spoken all evening.

"Mr. Beachum of Beachum and Beachum is on the wire," said Miss Kelly.

"I don't suppose it would do any good if I told you that this is going to be a confidential conversation—that you are not expected to listen in."

"No, sir."

"No, sir, what?" but Miss Kelly had closed the door and gone back to her desk. Ham picked up the receiver. "Is this Jim?"

"It certainly is. We've finished a preliminary audit of your books and I want to be the first to congratulate you. At the close of the market on Friday afternoon your total net worth was eleven million, eight hundred thousand and seventy-two dollars and forty-seven cents."

"Holy cow," interrupted a small female voice.

"Is that you, Miss Kelly?"

"No, sir. Excuse it please," said the voice, followed by an almost inaudible click.

"This includes everything of course; the amount you received on the liquidation of the firm and the bequest from your uncle, as well as the net profits from your—er—recent operations. You are to be congratulated. It isn't everyone who can do so well in such—shall we say unsettled times."

"That would be a very appropriate thing to say, Jim, and

thank you for your kind words. Praise from you is something to be proud of."

"Thanks, Ham. You'll receive the full report by hand to-morrow. Let me know if everything is not clear. I won't hold you up. I know how busy you are. I just thought you'd be interested."

"I am slightly, Jim. Much obliged. See you soon."

During April, May, and the first part of June the market continued to edge lower. By the end of May Ham owned nothing but short-term governments and was working hard over a list of securities for immediate purchase. It might be a bit premature, but the amount involved was so large that he decided to complete his buying as far as possible in a declin-ing market. Prices couldn't go down much further without disappearing entirely.

Before he began to buy for himself he called up Barbara's trustees. "You asked me not to bother you for a year or two," he said. "I agreed not to and I've kept my word. Now I want to tell you that I'm about to buy for my own account and I thought you might like to know it. You've handled the trust investments so beautifully to date that I hesitate to inject myself into the picture."

"Not at all, Mr. Martin. You are very kind. We are quite proud of the way we have handled Mrs. Martin's trust. When you think what has happened to other fiduciary funds during the last two years I think we are warranted in in-dulging in a bit of self-congratulation. We have heard rumors that you yourself have been quite successful. I don't know that we quite agree with you that this is the turning point, but I will tell my partners that you are buying."

"That's very good of you," said Ham. "By the way, I wonder if it would be helpful if I sent you a list of the securities in which I am particularly interested?"

"By all means, Mr. Martin. We will be glad to have your list on file. When we buy we shall, of course, prepare our own list, but it will be interesting to have yours for purposes of comparison."

Ham had made the turn-about. His new investment portfolio was complete. Overnight he had become the boy wonder of Wall Street. There were those who still sneered and said, just as Harry Farnsworth had predicted, that he was nothing but a speculator and a small-time gambler, but those were terms that stuck only if one failed. Money was the yardstick and a man who had accumulated a fortune while everyone else was losing theirs ultimately commanded respect.

Magazines and newspapers sought interviews which he refused to grant, after which they wrote inaccurate articles about him. Friends and strangers bombarded him with requests for advice on their personal, and usually shrunken, holdings. A large university asked him to give a series of lectures on the subject of common stocks as an investment. A publisher hounded him to write a book to be titled "It's a Cinch to Make a Million." Business leaders with whom he had only a nodding acquaintance now cultivated him at the club and sought his views on the economic outlook. Charities begged him to join their boards. An advertising firm offered him a tidy sum to pose for a whiskey ad. He kept in the background, refused publicity, and did a lot of thinking.

The big show was over. There probably would never be another like it during his lifetime. F.D.R.'s bright boys were already devising ways to prevent that and to make America depressionproof. He had bought stocks and bonds at such ridiculously low levels that there would be no need to make changes for a long time. Many of the items he would probably hold for the rest of his life. What was he to do now? He certainly wasn't going to continue staring across the Hudson.

There was nothing wrong about making money, but there had to be some excitement connected with it, some end in view other than the mere accumulation of dollars. He had amassed a fortune greater than he had ever dreamed possible; amassed it while he was a relatively young man. Money meant little, however, if it was represented by a lot of stocks and bonds lying in a safe-deposit box. It was only meaningful when one was personally responsible for making it work. Then it came to life; a beautiful piece of machinery capable of producing power from otherwise inert material. The Rothschilds, the Morgans, the Lehmans had not been content to sit on their fortunes cutting coupons and collecting dividends while they watched the world go by. They used their money to produce power. Power! Power that was felt in all parts of the world. They were shrewd, but honorable men, these great ones, and they seldom abused their power, with the result that they brought to their doors the world's leaders, doers, and men of vision.

His own door opened. "Go away," he said.

"What's the matter, boss? You've been sitting here for half an hour without making a sound. I just looked in to see if you'd had a stroke or something."

"Damn it all, can't a man be given a chance to think?"

"Not for more than half an hour. It's bad for your brain." She laid the morning mail on his desk and remained, looking down at him with a worried expression.

He riffled through the pile of letters. "When I answer these

—or throw them away—I won't have anything else to do all day except to have lunch with that damn fool O'Connor and let him grind some nuggets out of my hide for his favorite charity."

She sat down beside the desk. "The party's over, isn't it? I've been thinking about that myself for the last two weeks. We can't go on like this. That's for sure. We'd both be gibbering before the end of the month. I've got an idea. Want to hear it?"

"I'll bet it's cockeyed," he said gloomily. "I have one an hour and they're all cockeyed."

"I don't think this one is."

"Shoot."

"Why don't you form a new underwriting house? Call it Martin and Company. You'll be doing something for your uncle and something for yourself at the same time—and hopefully something for the business world and me."

He looked up incredulously. "You mean build up an organization from scratch? I couldn't do it. Anyway, under the terms of the merger I'm not allowed to start a business under the name of Martin as long as Deming and Martin continues to exist. I had to agree to that or the merger wouldn't have gone through."

"I know all that, of course," she said impatiently. "But here is a piece of news I'm pretty sure *you* don't know. Promise to keep it to yourself?"

He nodded.

"I have a brother-in-law in Deming and Martin. That's why you have to keep this quiet or he'll be in the back of the doghouse. The point is they've had a bad time over there. Lost most of their business. I guess their customers all committed harakiri. At any rate, my brother-in-law thinks it would be a cinch to make a deal which would let the old fellows out with enough money to continue paying their club dues. There are still a number of your partners left among the younger group. I hardly need to tell you how they'd feel about coming back to work with you."

"Why? They practically threw me out of my own firm three years ago because they thought I was too conservative."

"There's no need to comment on that, boss. The thing is that if you want to get back in business—and if you don't we're both going nuts—here's an organization all set up for you and a lot of the top men you've already worked with."

He looked at her admiringly. Why didn't men marry women like this? "Have you made them an offer yet?"

"Don't fool about this, boss. It's for real. But of course it's up to you."

"Thank you," he said. "That's very gracious of you. Now you go out for lunch, or drink a gallon of coffee, or do whatever occurs to you. I want to do some telephoning—some private telephoning."

She picked up her book and went to the door, where she paused for a moment. "When this gels don't forget I'm still your secretary and on top of that I get a handsome raise."

"I've made a note of it," he said, his hand reaching for the phone.

"Can't I listen in?"

"*No.* Oh, operator. I want RE 4-1742. Get lost, won't you please, like a good girl? No, operator, I was speaking to my secretary."

V

May, 1934. THE LOBBY OF 40 WALL Street was so jammed with people hurrying in all directions that they reminded Ham of the little bugs that skate so crazily along the surface of meadow ponds without ever colliding.

He pushed his way into an already overcrowded elevator. "Morning, Mr. Martin."

"Morning, Jim."

They still had operators running elevators during the thirties. It was much pleasanter to be greeted by a human being than to have to reach over someone's arm to push a button. Eventually the car came to a cushioned stop at the thirty-second floor. The doors opened soundlessly and Ham emerged into the glaring white marble area between the elevator banks.

There were only two offices on the landing. Ham turned to the left toward a wall of glass over which a bronze strip carried the name "Martin and Company."

Through the glass he could look into the big lobby of the office whose upholstered interior was filled with geometric shadows and light cones produced by expensive-looking table lamps. On one side a hidden light in the ceiling covered the receptionist's desk so precisely that one had the impression its beams had been trimmed off at the edges by a pair of shears. Seated at the desk in the semi-shadow, the golden-haired, soft-spoken Miss Bennett presided over the entrance like a benign dragon whose hidden fires were kindled and ready to emit sparks at the first sign of danger.

"Good morning, Mr. Martin."

He paused for a moment before the desk. "Good morning, Miss Bennett. I had to go to a meeting this morning. That's why I'm so late." (Never let the staff think you're easing up or they'll do likewise.) "Anything special going on?"

"Nothing, Mr. Martin. We've been busy as usual" (never let the boss think that you aren't overworked), "but it's been largely routine."

He nodded and proceeded down the corridor to his office, glancing in at his partners in their smaller offices. They were all so engrossed in their work that they did not hear his noiseless passage.

Miss Kelly's paneled anteroom was bigger than many of the junior partners' offices. On the left was a smaller, unpaneled room in which a stenographer and a man surrounded by account books were working silently. They raised their eyes without moving their heads as Ham entered the anteroom, then lowered them quickly.

"Good morning, Mr. Martin," said Miss Kelly in a tone unusually formal for her. "Your mail is on your desk. I have some messages I had better give you before your phone goes into operation."

She followed him into his corner office which absorbed the huge desk without crowding half a dozen upholstered chairs, a long sofa, and a round table. Miss Kelly sat down beside his desk.

"Listen, boss, can't you put those two harpies in that room off mine somewhere else? They watch me and listen to everything I say until I'm almost crazy. I can't even have any fun on the phone with you any more. It has to be 'Yes, Mr. Martin. No, Mr. Martin.' I wish I'd never dreamed up this idea of a new firm in the first place. The trouble is I give you a nice, simple idea and you're not satisfied until you have it gold-plated."

"Do you have any messages or was that just another idea?"

"Yes, Mr. Martin. Messrs. Tonler and Bates are coming in at 2:45 with their accountant to discuss that Arkansas-Oklahoma matter. I've asked Mr. Healy to sit in. He's right up to date on the details."

Ham nodded approval. "Those three men from the First National of Louisville are coming at four. Then that man Higgenswait from the State Department is coming at five and you're driving him up to the Knickerbocker for a pow-wow. You've never told me what that's all about, so don't ask me."

"I won't," he said, "my mistake. Awfully sorry."

"You're testy this morning. You ought to try to get a little shut-eye before your dinner party."

"What dinner party, for heaven's sake?"

"You're giving a dinner at eight for that big-shot Dutch banker whose name I can't pronounce and don't even seem to be able to remember. There's a list of your guests on the side of your desk, though. I've typed the Dutchie's name in caps."

"Barbara knows all about this of course. I'd completely forgotten it."

"*Knows* about it! I've been talking to her on the phone about it every day for the last week. I've sent her another list of the guests with a suggestion of how they should be seated and what they do for a living to help her conversationally. I've left a list of the phone calls that came in this morning on your blotter. You're supposed to call them all back the minute you come in."

"Good Lord. Is that all?"

Miss Kelly glanced quickly at her book. "Well, of course you know you're having lunch with Roger at 12:30."

"Roger who?"

"Your brain sure is gummy this morning. Roger Baker. Your brother-in-law. Don't drink at lunch. You've got a hard day ahead of you. Stick to clam juice."

"Thanks. What can I eat for lunch—shredded wheat?"

She rose. "You don't appreciate loving care. I'll go now if you don't mind."

"I don't mind at all," he said, already absorbed in his mail.

Roger was waiting for him in the lobby of the Down Town Association. Here, in the midst of a city rapidly gearing itself for a change so great that it would hardly be recognizable in a few decades, the Down Town Association stood like a rock on which the increasingly heavy seas of a new world left no mark. No House Committee would ever paint its varnished woodwork, change the location of the long coatroom or modernize its spacious washroom. Its architects had planned well and the aging building met the requirements of the passing generations with an easy grace while time added a patina which was recognized and valued by its younger as well as its older members. One might well wonder, if men set such value on the old, what the forces were that struggled so ceaselessly to demolish it and replace it with a brash, garish, and unfriendly new.

Roger rose when he saw Ham enter. He had grown fat and somehow unkempt, although his clothes were obviously made by an expensive tailor. The image of the old handsome Roger of college days was still recognizable but it was becoming blurred.

They found a window table upstairs. Roger ordered a double martini. Ham, under the shadow of Miss Kelly, stuck to clam juice. They brought each other up to date on their personal affairs. Ham did not see much of Roger these days. Their paths, like their interests, were becoming more divergent with the years.

Roger had married a peach-skinned blonde from Louisville whose goal was obvious to everyone but the groom before they left on their honeymoon. After the happy couple had spent two years patterned on the lives of the F. Scott Fitzgeralds, old Mr. Baker bought Peaches off and after her divorce she disappeared in search of other game.

For three miserable years Roger had worked in his father's company, after which Mr. Baker, to the great relief of all concerned, established a trust fund for him, the income from which was enough to keep him in clothes, rent, food, and drink. It was too late for him to take up music seriously. He knew all the Cole Porter songs and played his way up and down the Park Avenue circuit on an amateur basis, the darling of uncertain hostesses.

"I feel like a piano player in a whorehouse," he said, draining the last few drops of his martini. "I could use another of those. Just a single this time. I don't want to get it up my nose. I have a big brawl coming up tonight, but it's a musical crowd and I might be able to work in a bit of real music once in a while in the unlikely event I stay sober."

"It's a hell of a life you're leading, Rog. Isn't there anything in the musical field you could do other than being a second Paderewski—a music critic, for instance, teaching, lecturing—I don't know much about those things but there must be something."

Roger shook his head. "I wanted to be a great pianist. You know that, Ham. Then when the Old Man sat on me and made that impossible, I seemed to lose all interest. I didn't care whether I accomplished anything or not. In fact—although I didn't spell it out at the time—I guess I felt that the only way I could get even with the Old Man was *not* to accomplish anything. But let's not talk about me any more. It's a bore."

"How is your father?"

"For heaven's sake, Ham, if you don't know who does? You're on his Board and his Executive Committee."

"I realize that, but about the only time I see him is at the meetings and since Fitzhugh McDonald became president and he went up to chairman of the Board he seems to be moving further and further back among the shadows."

"How do you mean?"

"He turns everything over to McDonald. He officiates as chairman. He has an agenda in front of him. He reads the next item to be considered and then says, 'Mr. McDonald will you carry on please.'"

Roger shook his head. "Poor Dad. He used to be such an uncompromising old autocrat. We were all scared to hell of him. Now he's like a broken-winded race horse. Let's not quibble and pussyfoot, Ham. The Old Man's going gaga. He won't quit until the grim reaper mows him down, but he's going to be a problem in the meantime. Well, I guess there's nothing you can do about it. How are Barbara and the kids?"

"Well, you know the over-all situation, Rog, but I admire that girl more than I can tell you. I have to do a lot of entertaining these days as you can imagine. I'm putting on a big show tonight. Barbara hates it, but she never whimpers and she puts on the best dinners of anyone I know in New York."

"Still an arm's-length relationship, I suppose."

"Oh, sure. More so than ever as the mold sets. As for the kids, they're just what you'd expect kids to be. Michael has the charm of the devil, but he's a hell-raiser, Pat's promising, but she looks to me as if she might be a handful when she moves up in her teens."

"How about Allen?"

"He's a queer little kid, Rog. I can't seem to figure him out. A cute little tyke and all that, but he doesn't seem to get into things at school. He always has his nose in a book. Anything that has to do with words is his dish. For instance, at his school the junior tads have their own little paper and, believe it or not, he's the editor—works as hard over it as if it were the *New York Times.* Not bad, some of it. You know. Kid stuff. It's abnormal though for a boy only seven years old. Sort of worries me."

"I wouldn't get upset. He'll get over it."

"Oh, I suppose so. He gets wonderful reports."

The talk became desultory.

Ham returned to the apartment shortly after six, hoping to be able to stretch out for a few minutes before he had to dress for dinner. Barbara met him in the hall and silently handed him a letter.

"You'd better read it sitting down," she said.

He went into the library and sank into his favorite red leather armchair which had once belonged to Uncle Charlie. He unfolded the letter. It was from St. Matthew's School.

Dear Mr. and Mrs. Martin,

It is with deep regret and sincere sympathy for you both that I write to inform you that we have been obliged to expel Michael from St. Matthew's.

Briefly, the facts are these. Yesterday afternoon Michael and two other St. Matthew's boys broke into the summer home of Mr. Elliott Tate on Pleasant Hill about a mile from the School. They got in through a cellar window and found their way to the billiard room. According to their story they decided to play a game of billiards.

The Tates' caretaker, whose cottage is directly behind the main house, heard a noise and came over to investigate. He took the boys by surprise. As we have the story up to date, he seized a billiard cue from the rack and started to go for them when he was stricken with a heart attack and died instantly. In falling he hit his head on the edge of the billiard table, leaving an ugly bruise.

The boys were terrified of course, ran back to the School, and reported the tragic accident to me. The police were called, the three boys placed under arrest and an investigation started immediately. The School furnished the necessary bail. I have moved the three boys to my house and notified them of their expulsion. They must remain here for the time being for questioning. We have employed the services of a local attorney.

Although this is an ugly affair and will hurt the School's community relations, counsel does not believe that the boys will be held directly responsible for the Superintendent's death as it was not brought on by any act of violence on their part.

You may telephone Michael and we suggest that you do, but I strongly urge you not to visit the School until you hear from me further which will, of course, be soon.

Again my deepest sympathy to you both. Don't hesitate to phone me.

Sincerely yours,
Alpheus H. Hood
Headmaster

Barbara was standing in the doorway watching him. "Oh, Ham, what are we going to *do?*"

"I don't know until I telephone Harry."

Harry Farnsworth was not in his office nor his apartment. His wife didn't know where he could be located. She would have him call as soon as he came in.

"No. Don't do that. Thanks just the same. I'm having an important dinner tonight. Tell Harry I'll call him as soon as our guests go, no matter what time it is. I may have to talk to him at some length."

Barbara rose and walked to the door. "I hope you enjoy your dinner and squeeze out another million on the side."

He turned with an angry reply on the tip of his tongue, but she had disappeared down the hall in the direction of her room. After all, it was the first time she had erupted since she returned home after leaving him in 1932.

1940. Ham and Michael sat facing each other in the library of the big stone-fronted house on 72nd Street, which Ham had bought the previous year. Two of the room's sides were lined with books from floor to lofty ceiling. The other two walls were paneled with fumed oak and between the windows hung the portrait of an ancestor. Ham was not clear whose ancestor it was. The space called for an ancestral portrait and this was a Gainsborough. Who was going to quibble with a Gainsborough? asked the interior decorator.

Inside the massive wrought-iron front door which opened and closed with the slow dignity of the entrance to a safe-deposit vault, the ground floor was largely occupied by an enormous marble hall which led from a small reception room at one end to a huge dining room at the other. Should the vistor be tempted to explore further, he had the choice of an elevator on the right and a curving marble staircase on the left down which an infantry battalion might have marched four abreast.

On the second floor were the library and the living room where the hypothetical infantry battalion might have assembled preparatory to the descent. The bedrooms (if any) were discreetly hidden on the floors above.

There was no doubt that Michael was a good-looking and charming young man. His blond hair was cropped close. It was the beginning of the "crew-cut" vogue. Michael's startlingly blue eyes had a mocking expression that would have melted the heart of the most icy debutante. It was only when one came to the mouth that a close observer might have hesitated. It dropped at the corners just enough to indicate that under certain conditions it might give to his otherwise handsome face an expression of stubborn defiance.

At the present moment this is just what had happened. As Michael sat glaring at his father, his face expressed sullen resentment.

"It's so hard to talk to a person, Michael, who doesn't seem to give a damn about anything. Doesn't it occur to you that it's a serious thing to be dropped from Harvard at the end of your sophomore year just because you refuse to do any work?"

"No."

"But what are you going to do now?"

"I don't know."

"Well, you're not coming into Martin and Company. I can assure you of that."

"That's the last thing I'd want to do."

"Well, another thing, you're not going to come stumbling into this house after midnight every night. That's another certainty."

"I wouldn't live in this mausoleum if you paid me."

Ham lit a cigarette. His hand was shaking slightly with frustration and restrained anger, a fact which irritated him even more.

"Listen, Michael, you and I are not good for each other. We seem to live on opposite sides of the fence. I have to go to a dinner tonight. Why don't you have dinner with your mother? She understands you better than I do. She'll appreciate company."

"I can't. Got a date."

Ham pushed himself out of the red leather armchair. "Go your way," he said, "but if it's the way I suspect you don't go under my house flag."

He walked out of the room.

When he returned home that night Barbara was waiting for him in the library. "We have to talk about Michael," she said without preamble. "Whether you like it or not we have to. You and Michael cannot live under the same roof. You don't understand one another. You each bring out the worst qualities in the other. He knows that and wants to get out. He wants to live in that mews or whatever you call it in Greenwich Village. They're tiny houses. I told him I would rent one for him if there were any available."

Ham sat down on the sofa and buried his face in his hands. "My God, that's about the worst spot that you could have picked. I know that place. It's filled with just the type of people he shouldn't be going around with—not at this point."

"That's where he wants to go. He's entitled to choose his own life."

"I'm not going to pay for it."

"Nobody expected *you* to. I'm paying for it with my own money."

"I'm tired," he said, after a pause. "Terribly tired. Too tired to quarrel. Do whatever you want."

"Thank you" she said. "That's just what I plan to do."

Ham put Michael out of his mind. Unconsciously he had handed him to Barbara. He did not miss him inasmuch as he had seen little of him during the past six years. Michael had been away at school and college, in addition to which Martin and Company was growing so fast that it required his full attention. He gave it without reserve, for there he was happy. As he passed through its double plate-glass doors each morning, he felt suddenly excited and fulfilled. Martin and Company opened its arms to him in welcome. It needed him, approved him, and applauded his successes. Subconsciously he thought of it in feminine rather than masculine terms; an entity to which he could turn with the assurance of being understood, for whose welfare he could work unselfishly as one works for the welfare and protection of a person who is loved.

He lunched with Pat in the front dining room of the Down Town Association where properly escorted ladies were now admitted. There was no question about it, Pat had fulfilled her early promise and become a beautiful girl. Girl? She was a woman. Her face lacked the naïveté, the over-eagerness of an eighteen-year-old. It was the face of one who, knowing life, has accepted it as a sailor accepts the weather, ready to take advantage of it when the winds are fair and knowing how to protect himself against them when they are adverse.

She sat now, erect and yet at ease, sipping a glass of sherry and watching her father's face. "I just can't understand your generation," Ham was saying, "you never want to finish *anything*. Michael drops out of Harvard for no reason at all, as far as I can see. Your case is a little different, perhaps. Michael is lazy. He hasn't enough intellectual curiosity to fill an eyedropper. But that's not true of you. You're interested in everything; everything past, present, and future. Brandon Hall can give you more of what you want than any other school in the country. But suddenly you decide to drop it. Is this a disease that you and Michael have contracted? And what are you going to do in one year at a Swiss school? You don't *know* anybody. You hardly know French. What purpose is served? What are you after? What—"

"Dad, please . . . Is it all right if I say something? You're getting red in the face. I don't know *what* I'm after in the sense that you mean. I couldn't set it down in a neat office memorandum, that's true. Yet in another sense I know very well what I'm after and, equally important, what I'm *not* after. Brandon Hall is everything you say, but its prim efficiency smothers me. It's a robot factory. I want to be myself, not a robot. I—"

"But why Switzerland?" he cut in. "Why in the world Switzerland?"

"Because I love mountains, Dad, if you really want to

know. I want to be near them. You don't know anything about me, I'm afraid, but I always have wanted them near me. Mountains—big, climbing mountains are the world's greatest individualists. Man can never make them conform. Just when he thinks he has, they turn on him and kill him. The schools in Switzerland are not only near the mountains, they are notoriously good, but not with the smug, stuffy goodness that they are in this country. Oh, Dad, don't let me stay here and suffocate. *You* didn't stay out in that town in Indiana and suffocate. Mom has told me all about it. You did what *you* wanted to do no matter what people said or thought. In one way or another that's just what *I'm* going to do. It isn't my fault, Dad, if I happen to be made like you."

He knew he was defeated, but he held out until the meal was over and then surrendered.

"Thank you, Dad," she said as they parted eventually in front of 40 Wall. "I think you'll always be glad that you opened what you once called the escape hatch, even though you may not always approve of the things I do once I get through it. When you don't, remember we're just alike only I belong to a bolder generation."

"If she's bolder than I was," he thought as he entered his office, "she's going to be a handful." He was apprehensive and at the same time rather proud of his only daughter.

Ham sat up late that night giving shape to an idea that he had been tossing about in his mind for a week. On the following morning he attended a board meeting of the American Sheet and Tubing Company. Mr. Baker still insisted on presiding, but it was a painful experience for everyone present.

Fitzhugh McDonald, the new president, took tactful charge. He had just completed an analysis of the company's position and his report was far from encouraging. A.S.&T. earnings had dropped off sharply in 1939 and were continuing to decline. The company's competitors had spent millions on modern plants which utilized labor-saving machinery that American Sheet and Tubing lacked. These companies had also spent additional millions in research and in the development of new products, a field which A.S.&T. had completely neglected. The cost of bringing Mr. Baker's company up to a level where it could compete successfully was almost prohibitive.

The report was received in gloomy silence. No one appeared to have any ideas, or if they had they didn't care to stick their necks out at this point by expressing them. Finally they fell back on the standard practice in such dilemmas and instructed the president to appoint a committee to look into the matter and report back to the Board. Mr. Baker glared silently around the table like a trapped animal. The meeting was adjourned and the Board members glanced nervously at their watches and scurried away.

Ham returned to his office. "There are a lot of telephone calls for you," said Miss Kelly.

"I don't want them. Phone the important ones. Say I'm tied up in a meeting. Usual apologies. Try to get messages if you can."

"Oh, oh," said Miss Kelly softly.

"Never mind 'oh, oh.' Just do a dragon and guard the gates for a while. Get me Farnsworth."

"He's in a meeting," she reported in a few minutes, "but I told him it was important and he's coming out."

"Who told you it was important?"

"I knew. Osmosis."

"Well, don't try to be so darn psychic. Hello, Harry. Sorry to get you out of your meeting. I'll be brief. Do you know Arthur Bradford of International Steel and Wire? Good. Well, do a little chore for me. Call him up. Ask him if he would care to have lunch with me, very privately, at his early convenience. He'll know what it's all about and it will give him a chance to sidestep if he wishes."

"Of course I'll be glad to do as you say, Ham, but has it come to this?"

"Has what come to what? Don't jump at conclusions, Harry. Let me know what Bradford says after your meeting is over. Much obliged."

He heard the phone give an extra click after Harry replaced the receiver. "And don't you jump at conclusions either," he said, but there was no response.

Six months later, during October, 1941, the merger of American Sheet and Tubing Company with International Steel and Wire was publicly announced. The latter had clearly been the merging company, but, in order to save face for Mr. Baker, the merged company was given a new name: The American Steel and Wire. Ham was elected chairman of the Board. Mr. Baker had been persuaded to retire, fighting every inch of the way out.

It had not been a successful merger from the point of view of the Baker family. American Sheet had always been a closely held corporation. When its operations were placed under a magnifying glass and appraised by two large accounting firms, the worth of its stock turned out to be startlingly low, so low indeed that for a while International Steel and Wire considered dropping further negotiations. If it had not been for Ham they probably would have done so. The amount which International finally agreed on was low, but Ham realized that if the stock of A.S.&T. had lain

in the Baker vaults for another decade its worth would probably have been far less.

Following the closing Ham returned to his office, his face
pale and drawn. "You look awful," commented Miss Kelly.
"How about a short snort?"

Ham shook his head. "Not until yardarm time, if it's all
right with you."

"Was the curtain scene tough going?"

"Worse than I had thought it ever could be. Poor old
Baker broke down and cried. I had to take him out. Then
he told me that he'd lost a lot of money in the crash. That
was something I hadn't known. He's going to have to sell
the house in New York and the place in Rock Harbor."

"But where is he going to live? Not with you, I hope."

"Good God, no. He has it all worked out. He's going to
buy a small house in Vermont and another in Florida. Then
he can bypass New York and he never wants to see Rock
Harbor again."

She shook her head. "Poor old fellow. Well, boss, you
finally won."

Ham stared at her, unbelieving. "Don't tell me you're
going to join that chorus! After all these years? You're the
one person I can't and won't take it from."

"I'm sorry. It just slipped out. You know that I've believed
in you ever since the day I first met you. I just can't seem
to stop words from rolling out before I have a good look at
them to see what they mean. Please forgive. That was a
stupid thing to say."

She picked up a sheaf of opened letters from her desk and
riffled through them. "You have quite a bit of mail. Here's
one about young Allen from Dr. Wilson of Whiting."

"Good Lord. Don't tell me Allen has been fired from
Whiting. I couldn't cope with it today."

"Heavens, no. Quite the opposite. He's been made editor of the school magazine and Dr. Wilson says he is writing some really remarkable things—way beyond his age. He's sending you a collection of them."

"I suppose I'll have to read them all and write Wilson a long letter."

"But aren't you proud of him? Don't you want to read them?"

"Of course, of course. He's awfully young though to get swallowed up in a sea of words. He ought to be outdoors exercising; doing things with other boys."

She glanced at him doubtfully. Something in his expression made her change the subject. "Who in the world is going to buy that hotel of a house in Rock Harbor?"

"I am—I have."

Horace Allen Martin shifted uneasily in his Pullman seat on the five-o'clock out of Boston, and adjusted the chair back. They didn't make these parlor car chairs as comfortable as they used to. Nothing was as comfortable as it used to be. The dull pain around his heart was better, but he was still conscious of it. Perhaps a drink would help. He rang for the porter and ordered a Scotch and soda.

It was odd how everything that had happened during the first four decades of his life was crystal clear, but then, beginning in the 1940's, the sequence of events became increasingly jumbled and his memory of them decreasingly sharp. There were exceptions. Certain happenings stood out like bare branches against the silver of a twilight sky. Perhaps other things became confused because, although they had seemed vitally important when they occurred, they were too much alike when viewed in retrospect to retain their identities; just so many telephone poles converging toward the horizon behind a speeding train. So much alike. Meetings, conferences, the incessant ringing of telephones, business lunches and dinners (why did so much business have to be conducted while you were chewing something?), speeches, the overorderly confusion of underwriting closings, planes, the frustration of strange foreign cities. All important at the moment of happening, but they had merely been the stones that formed the wall and now the wall was all that he could see.

The memories which were really vivid seemed to have little or nothing to do with business, or money, or success. They concerned the arrows which pierced his armor and entered his naked flesh.

His son, Sergeant Michael Martin, lying face down among the trees of a French forest, his rifle still clutched in his extended hand. No one had been there to record his final moments. Alone in a strange wood, crouching, numb with fear. Crack! Twenty-four years of life ended. One arrow which could never be removed.

Pat had begun to fade slowly into the European picture, drifting from one ski resort to another during the winter season and climbing her beloved mountains when the snow had left their lower slopes.

Tongues wagged, eager to magnify any infringement of the taboos, particularly if their close friends were involved. "Just a little ski bum, my dear. I was told . . ." "They say she jumps into bed with almost anyone. Please don't repeat that. It might get back to her mother and father and I am so fond of them both . . ." ". . . an Italian Count, my dear, and you know what they're like. Her poor sweet mother! My heart aches for her." "Just a common little tart . . ."

"That's what money will do. Thank heaven I'm not cursed with it."

They received postcards from her occasionally bearing illegible messages. They replied faithfully, but their letters were meaningless because there was nothing to say. Once, after hearing a particularly ugly rumor, Ham had written her a long letter begging her to come home and expend her excess energies in more constructive ways. Her reply was light-hearted and gay. Obviously she was not going to become involved in a gloomy debate on her way of life.

Remember, Dad, what I once told you when we were having lunch together at one of your Wall Street clubs. You and I are alike. You're a man. You can find all kinds of more or less respectable ways to use up what you call "excess energies." You happened to find them in Wall Street, but you would have found them no matter when or where you were born. Four or five hundred years ago you would have been one of those licensed pirates who traveled around with characters like Drake and Balboa under the title of "gentlemen adventurers." It's different with a girl. Females like me find it difficult to obtain congenial employment of a kind which leaves us with any identity of our own. So don't forget, dear Papa, that, had you, by some misfortune, been born a girl you would have acted just as I'm acting—only probably worse.

Your devoted mimic

Pat

He put the letter in his pocket so that it would not fall into Miss Kelly's eager hands and never brought up the subject again. Another arrow.

In the fall of 1950 he returned home one night somewhat earlier than usual. A free evening was a bonus which his age was causing him to appreciate. Somehow or other such bonuses seemed to become scarcer each year in spite of his efforts to delegate work to the younger partners.

As he let himself in through the ponderous entrance door, Udding emerged from the shadows to take his hat and coat. Udding had been acquired almost simultaneously with the 72nd Street house and was rapidly taking on the patina so necessary to an old family retainer.

"Good evening, Udding. How in the world did you know that I would come in that door at that particular minute?"

"I was waiting to let you know that Mrs. Martin has gone out, sir."

"What's so unusual about Mrs. Martin going out?"

"Yes, sir. She left a note for you on the hall table. She said it was important, sir, and would I be sure that you got it as soon as you came in." Udding stepped to the hall table and pointed to the letter as if to prove what he had said. Then he picked it up, handed it to Ham and disappeared. Ham tore it open with fingers which shook unaccountably.

Dear Ham,

For the second time I am leaving you, but this exit is not made in a state of high emotion. I returned to you before because of the children. You are aware of all that. During the intervening years I have done everything I told you I would try to do. Now the children have gone; my darling Michael forever. As for Pat—well, all I can say about Pat is that she will never return to the nest permanently, and Allen is teaching at Harvard. He will never return either. He will be the famous one. They have all left. My job is done.

I am going to Reno to get a divorce. There is no third party in the picture. I merely want to be free. I am sure you will not oppose it. I am enclosing a card giving my lawyer's name and address. I have told him that I do not want any money from you in any form. My father's wedding gift and your uncle's generous bequest have increased beyond belief due to your skillful handling of my affairs. For this I am appreciative in spite of the fact that your skills along these lines were what tore us apart. But why go into all that now—or ever?

I don't leave you in anger. On the contrary, I am sorry for you. As I see it you are impelled by forces over which you have little or no control. They may ultimately bring you unhappiness rather than peace. I hope that is not so.

As soon as I am settled in or around Reno, I will send you my address. Write me when and if you care to. I am determined that this is going to be a civilized separation.

Barbara

He sat in the unlit library, his head in his hands. He was alone. The final arrow.

Half an hour later he rang the bell for Udding.

"I will not be home for dinner tonight. I'll be at the club."

"Yes, sir." Udding hesitated. "I'm sorry, sir, if I may be so bold."

"Thank you, Udding." What had Barbara said to him?

After a few minutes he snapped on the lights and called Miss Kelly at her apartment. "Oh, boss." she exclaimed when he had broken the news. "I'm sorry—so very, very sorry." That was what Udding had said. Perhaps there was nothing else to say. The phone was silent.

"Are you there?" he asked.

"Yes," she said in a muffled voice. "Forgive me. This is a bit sudden. It slowed down my reactions. They're back to normal now. Listen. You're going out for dinner I hope?"

"Yes, the club."

"Good. Just use that tomb of yours for sleeping. Have a few drinks, but don't get tight. That's just dramatics and this is no place for dramatics."

"Thank you, doctor. I have that all written down."

"And get down early. We're going to work harder than

we've ever worked before. It's the only out."

"Thank you again, doctor. It all sounds like great fun. I feel better already." (And the curious thing was that he did.)

"God bless," said a small voice followed by a faint click.

He drew a deep breath, walked down the marble stairs, and into the night. He was not entirely alone.

1951. Miss Kelly was as good as her word. Ham's only recollection of the following weeks was being driven like a galley slave. Miss Kelly permitted no detail to go untended. The reputation of the firm was growing and Ham found himself spending more and more time on planes. Chicago, San Francisco, Washington, Dallas were in his back yard. He no longer needed to inquire his way through the streets of Rome, Paris, Buenos Aires, or Rio de Janeiro.

He lost weight and was constantly tired. Then one night he was awakened by a severe chest pain. When Dr. Partridge eventually arrived, full of gusto and bravado, he listened to Ham's chest for a long time, shifting his stethoscope to and fro like a geologist searching for oil. Finally he straightened up.

"You're going to the hospital," he said.

"Hospital? What for? A miserable little pain in my chest?"

"If it was so little why did you make me come over here in the middle of the night? You're going to the hospital for observation."

"Observation of what?"

"Don't play stupid, Ham. Heart. What's more you're going in an ambulance."

"Oh, doc, not now. I'm up to my neck in a dozen things. Give me a week."

"Nuts. All you fellows are alike. Don't show off. Where's the phone?"

He was in bed in a large corner room with green-tinted walls. Dr. Partridge was standing beside the bed. That was one scene whose edges would always remain sharp. "Now you're going to do as I tell you for the first time in your life. You're to see no one except your immediate family." Ham suppressed a smile and said nothing. "No telephoning till I say so. Who do you want me to talk to at your office?"

"Miss Kelly."

"Who's she?"

"My secretary."

"Can she turn over your affairs to the right person or persons?"

"She can turn over anything including you if you don't watch out."

He didn't remember much about the hospital except a succession of nurses and doctors. Pat flew back from Europe to see him. He asked them not to bother Barbara. She was taking a vacation in the West. Allen came down from Boston.

"I've got some exciting news for you, Dad. The Book-of-the-Month is going to take my new novel. I'm leaving a typescript for you to read when they let you sit up." He sat beside the bed and outlined the plot. Ham tried to be enthusiastic but for some reason he found it difficult.

When Allen had left he lay staring at the ceiling, trying to analyze his emotions. He should be happy; proud of his successful young son. How delighted his father and mother would have been. Instead of being happy, however, he was in the middle of a black depression. Instead of being proud he was irritated and gradually his irritation built up into resentment. What did Allen care if his father was lying helpless in a hospital bed? He had not even inquired about

Martin and Company. He was so full of his own accomplishments that he had no room for sympathy, no room for appreciation of the accomplishments of others. He rolled over angrily in the bed so that he could look out at the East River. Allen was the only one left. When he should have felt nothing but affection for him he found only a growing alienation for his youngest child seeping into his being like slow poison.

Eventually he was released from the hospital and permitted to go back to his office for two hours every morning. At the end of ten days he was to make an appointment with Dr. Partridge. What good were two hours, for God's sake? You might just as well tell an overseas flight pilot to fly for only twenty minutes at a time. And why did doctors always want to see you after a certain period? He had seldom gone to Dr. Partridge with some minor ailment without being asked to come back at the end of a week or something of that sort. He never did, of course, but what a cheap way to drum up business.

He spent a miserable ten days on his two-hour schedule. Instead of finding a great pile of papers waiting for him he found his desk swept clean. The vultures! He'd show them who was the boss. But when he started to check up on the channels that fomerly converged at his desk Miss Kelly quietly intervened and he found himself ignominiously defeated.

Complaining bitterly he went to see Dr. Partridge at the end of the tenth day. It was what he had anticipated only worse. No reason why he shouldn't live a long and happy life if he slowed down. Don't come down to the office until ten o'clock, go home at four, an hour's rest after lunch, no night work, four ounces of whiskey a day. He restrained himself with an effort and made no comment. When Dr. Partridge had finished he rose and extended his hand. "Good-by, doc.

Thank you for all the trouble you've taken with my carcass."

Dr. Partridge looked at him with narrowed almost angry eyes. "Have you heard a word that I've been saying?"

"Each one is carved on my brain."

"And do you have any intention of doing what I'm telling you to do?"

"What am I paying for?" It was a good question in view of the fact that he had no intention of following any of the doctor's orders.

Miss Kelly was waiting for him, sitting beside his desk in the inside office.

"What's the verdict?"

"Not guilty. I'm released to live life just as I want to. No restrictions."

"Thank God," she said. "I was afraid they'd tie you down like that Gulliver fellow. Let's go."

At home Ham was obliged to create an entirely new technique of living. When Barbara had returned to him after that Ackerson fiasco twenty years before, his life had been stiff and formal. She had said that she was returning not as his wife but because of the children. For a long time she had lived up to the spirit of that statement. She gave wonderful dinners when called upon to do so, she was a perfect hostess, but he dreaded eating alone with her and invented opportunities for avoiding it.

The strain had obviously been as great for her as for him and gradually she had begun to thaw. An outsider might have considered it a rather inconclusive thaw, but at least they talked as two mutually attracted strangers.

On the occasions when he was home for dinner, and they were alone, he began to look forward to the cocktail hour.

Even if personal topics were forbidden, Barbara was intelligent and they could at least talk about the strife-torn world, about books and the theater, and even about amusing things that had happened to each of them during the day—always providing they didn't touch on topic A.

It was a more bearable pattern, but still incomplete and frustrating. Lying beneath every word and gesture the old tension remained. They had merely learned to live with it more comfortably.

Now that she was gone, however, her going had created an emptiness he would not have dreamed possible. It did not make much difference what they had said or what they had not said. It was the fact that there was no one there; no voice to answer him when he spoke. The aloneness of his life was unbearable.

Nothing disturbed the internal stillness of the house. There were no sounds of footsteps on the marble staircase, no heels clicking on the bit of bare flooring at the living-room entrance. Only Udding moved about, but Udding seemed to have been born without footsteps. He did not walk but rather slid through the shadows. On the few nights when Ham was home it was startling to have his confidential, almost conspiratorial voice announce dinner from a few feet away after he had entered the room silently and unnoticed.

Giving dinner at home became a practical impossibility. Udding and the cook (he realized that he didn't even know her name and had seen her only once) were knowledgeable and skillful buyers, but they couldn't know what kind of dinner was called for on special occasions, and Barbara's absence was more conspicuous than her presence had been.

He gave the whole thing up after one or two attempts. His male dinners were given in one of the private dining rooms at the Knickerbocker and his mixed parties either at "21" or Passy, depending on the nature of his guests. Miss

Kelly helped when opportunity offered, but basically he was alone.

They had finished with the morning mail and Miss Kelly had risen to go back to her desk.

"Sit down a minute," he said, almost sharply.

"When anyone talks like that it's apt to mean I'm going to get fired."

"Okay. Can you have dinner with me tomorrow night?"

"Oh, boss, I'm too old for that night and day work. We tried it for a while."

"Who said anything about work? I'm asking you to have dinner with me. We'll go to '21.'"

Her astonished eyes were round and in them he saw dismay.

"I couldn't. I'd love to. You know that, but I wouldn't—I couldn't—oh, hell, you know what I mean."

He laughed; his old free laugh which she hadn't heard in weeks. "You really are a primitive. I'm not planning to attack you in a taxicab or otherwise molest you." To his surprise she was blushing. "I just want to talk over something with you."

"But why do we have to go to '21' to do it?"

"Listen, Miss Primrose. Let's go back to where we came in. Will you or will you not have dinner with me tomorrow night?"

"I will," she said, "with pleasure."

They sat on a banquette at the north end of the long oak-beamed room. Philip had placed the traditional white carnation in Ham's buttonhole, they had drunk the traditional martinis out of the chilled, tall, stemmed glasses and now, having disposed of their filet mignon and fresh asparagus, they sipped the remains of a bottle of Lafitte and watched the red-jacketed waiters in their ceaseless movement among the tables.

"You wanted to talk about something."

"That's right. I almost forgot it. Will you marry me?"

She covered his hand with hers. "You're not drunk? Tell me truly, you're not drunk?"

"I never was more sober in my life. You and I have belonged to each other for almost a quarter of a century. I've always adored you and you know it. Now I love you. I'm free—and—well, I want you to be my wife."

She released his hand and began drawing railroad tracks on the tablecloth with a fork. "Ham dear," she said without raising her eyes, "I've never been happier in my life than I am at this moment. But the answer is no. I was afraid that this might be what was on your mind and I dreaded it because it could shatter something very fragile and very precious, something that is much more important to me than marriage.

"Of course I've loved you since I was first introduced to you outside your new office. Unfortunately, however, my darling Ham—I'm not going to call you that again—unfortunately, boss, you're two men. One of them is Mr. Martin, the sensationally successful financier. The other is Ham Martin, a charming romanticist, who has tried to raise a family and create a home for them and who has been, if I may say so, sensationally unsuccessful.

"I am lucky enough to have Mr. Martin, and to share with him all the things that really mean something to him. I have trouble enough holding him in line. If I married you I'd have

Ham Martin to cope with as well as The Boss. If I have trouble handling the latter I *know* I couldn't handle the other one."

"You might find them easier to handle if you drove them as a team."

She shook her head while the ever-alert table captain lighted Ham's cigarette.

"No," she said. "I don't have to be possessive with Mr. Martin. We're both doing what we love to do and we're doing it together and, I might add, having a lot of fun in the doing. The only thing we're possessive about is time. But if I became Mrs. Martin things would be very different.

"I'd want you home—want you for myself just the way Barbara did. I'd be jealous of your business trips, your business successes—just as she was. Now they are part of our common life. I understand them and am sometimes more anxious than you are about the results. Now the entertainment and the rest of the evening boohoo never bothers me because they belong to another world in which I have no part. As Mrs. Ham Martin I'd make your life miserable and when I start making someone's life miserable I'm an expert.

"You're lonely, boss. I know that. I'm a woman as well as a secretary. But don't ruin something good in order to cure something bad. You're not as lonely as you think; you have all the money in the world, an absorbing business and half the old gals in New York are making passes at you, even though you're too busy to notice them. Mr. Martin isn't lonely and as his secretary I'll stick with him like a leech, but as Mrs. Martin, no. Can't you see why? Don't make it any harder for me."

He was silent. "You mean, I gather," he said finally, "that you won't marry me."

"The one thing I like about you, boss, is your quick grasp of situations. Did you hear my reasons or were you thinking of your trip to London on Thursday?"

"I heard them," he said. "Let's have a brandy."

"Okay. And now you know that I'm the girl who loved a man too much to marry him."

He nodded. "You should have worked for Byron or Shelley or one of those fellows. They were made for that sort of thing. —Waiter, will you bring two brandies, please."

He left her eventually in front of her apartment house. With one hand on the taxi door she threw her arm around his neck, pulled him toward her, and kissed him. "That's for Ham," she said in a choked voice, "with so much love and appreciation. Just make it love—oh, so very much love." She was out of the cab, closing the door quickly behind her. "Good night, boss. And thank you for a magic evening."

He watched her as, with head held high, she crossed the white lobby of the apartment house and entered the elevator. "Knickerbocker Club," he said. A moment before she had been in his arms. He knew she would never be again.

Spring put on a particularly sparkling show in the year 1966. April was like a wood sprite, capricious and gay as if trying to dance away the memories of an icebound smog-blanketed winter city.

Striding down Fifth Avenue in what had become his customary prebreakfast walk, Ham had never felt better in spite of the fact that he had passed his seventy-first mile-stone on January 22. He didn't feel like a man in his seventies. He felt the way Ham Martin had always felt, strong and eager to meet the challenges of the coming day, the coming week, the coming months. It was one of those rare moments when he was in complete harmony with his private world. He had beaten Dr. Partridge. If he had listened to that old raven he would have been a semi-invalid by this time instead of young Ham Martin, zooming down Fifth Avenue in the early morning, leaning slightly into the April gusts. He had beaten life itself. He was indestructible, tough as an old oak, prepared to stand against whatever winds might strike.

He suddenly recalled that he had asked Harry Farnsworth to have breakfast with him in order to discuss some sagging negotiation. His euphoric mood evaporated as he turned and hurried back to the house. Bad business to keep people waiting, even an old friend like Harry. They might think you were slowing down—getting fuzzy around the edges.

Two hours later he walked into his office. "Congratulations!" cried Miss Kelly. "I'm proud of you both. I suppose *you* get into the act indirectly."

"Congratulations about what? What are you talking about?"

"Gee, boss, don't you read the morning paper any more?"

"I haven't had a chance. Had breakfast with Farnsworth and rode downtown with him."

She leaned down and picked a *New York Times* out of her wastebasket. "The next thing I know you'll be having conferences in your shower." She opened the paper. "There he is. Isn't that a terrible picture of him? 'Harvard professor-novelist wins Pulitzer Prize. Allen Martin's *House on the Dunes* receives fiction award.' Aren't you proud?"

He stared blankly at the printed page and his son's face stared back at him. Allen was smiling slightly and as Ham continued to stare the smile seemed to become almost derisive. "Don't look so damned astonished," it seemed to say. "Somebody had to do the trick and I knew you were too busy making money."

"Can I have your paper? I left mine at the house."

"Of course. I've ordered a dozen extra copies for you."

"What am I supposed to do with them? Clip one for me—and—oh, yes—send one to Barbara, just in case she hasn't seen it. Oh, yes—and Pat."

"Barbara's already wired you. I took it over the phone a few minutes ago." She handed him a typed memo.

"Has that fellow Brigham of Coatesworth and Barnes phoned this morning?"

"Not yet."

He turned without another word and entered his office, the newspaper and the memo clutched in his hand. She watched him with troubled eyes. Never during all the years she had known him had she felt sorrier for him, understood him better, loved him more.

It was as if Allen had struck her boss in the face; a blow as unexpected as it was unprovoked. She knew that he would be sitting at his desk, his feet on the window sill, smoking furiously while bitterness and frustration built up within him and she had denied herself the power to help. The phone rang. "Oh, yes, Mr. Brigham. He's expecting to hear from you. Hold on a moment please and I'll put him right on." God bless Mr. Brigham. No call had ever been more welcome.

VI

He roused himself into conscious-
ness as the train left 125th Street and entered the tunnel.
The whiskey had made him feel groggy and even more
tired than he had been when he boarded the train in Boston,
but the discomfort in the chest had more or less disappeared.
He followed a porter along the dimly lit ramp. No wonder
the railroads were losing out to the airlines. They didn't
even have enough imagination to light their platforms
decently.

As he emerged into the station Patrick spotted him and
came forward to take his bags from the porter. "Sorry, Mr.
Martin, but I had to park on Lexington. It's getting harder

337

and harder to find a place to leave a car around this station."

He followed Patrick onto the darkened sidewalk. "Stay right here, sir, and I'll bring the car down." When he eventually drew up in front of Ham people waiting for taxis glanced at the elderly man getting into the shiny black limousine, assisted by a chauffeur. Their eyes were unfriendly not only because of this display of pampered wealth but also because the long black car made it momentarily impossible to signal passing cabs.

It all happened the way he had pictured it on the train. As he entered the vestibule of the 72nd Street house, the heavy grilled door swung slowly open disclosing Udding in his black morning coat and sharply creased striped trousers.

"Welcome home, sir. I hope you had an enjoyable time."

"Thank you, Udding. It was quite an occasion. A bit strenuous for a lot of old men. Any special news?"

"Not a thing, sir. We didn't know whether or not you would have dinner on the train, but the cook has prepared one for you. It will be ready whenever you wish."

Ham hesitated. "I'm very tired, Udding. I think I will go to my room, take a hot bath, and go to bed. You might bring up a shaker of martinis. Put the ice in a bowl and I'll shake them myself. I'll ring when I get to bed and you can bring me a light supper. I really don't want dinner. Just a cup of hot soup, scrambled eggs, tea and toast."

"Very good, sir. I'll advise the cook and then come up to unpack your bag."

"Splendid. Bring the martinis with you when you come."

The hot bath felt good as did the fresh sheets on his familiar bed. It hardly seemed necessary to telephone Dr. Partridge, but he did so just as a precaution. Dr. Partridge told him to take two sleeping pills and stay in bed the next morning. He would drop in on his way to his office.

Ham was annoyed. Pretty casual way to treat a heart patient. Probably the old quack was entertaining friends and half in the bag. He poured himself a martini and pushed the bell angrily for his supper.

Once Udding had brought it he had no desire to eat. He felt exhausted and depressed. He always became depressed when he was tired. Nothing new about that. There was a knock at the door which immediately opened and Allen entered. He was so young, so strong, so self-assured that he irritated Ham even as he hesitated in the doorway. (Don't be an idiot. This boy is all you have left.)

"Hi, Dad."

"For God's sake, where did you pop up from?"

"I've been in New York on business for a few days. I knew you were in Cambridge, but when I phoned and Udding told me you were coming down on the five-o'clock I decided to stay over a night and check up on you."

"Why aren't you staying here?"

"Oh, I had a lot of things to attend to around the midtown area so I took a room at the Harvard Club. It's much more convenient. I'm pulling out early in the morning so I'll sleep there again tonight."

"Have a drink?"

"I'd like one if you have some Scotch."

"I'll have Udding bring up a bottle and some ice."

"I appreciated your letter about my book and the prize, Dad."

"It wasn't a very good letter. I'm glad you stayed over. It gives me a chance to tell you again how proud I am of you." (Why did those simple words come so hard?) "Thank God the Martins have finally discovered that the pen is mightier than the dollar and gone back to their last." (What a stupid, insincere thing to say.)

"That's not entirely true, Dad. What did you really think of *House on the Dunes?*"

"Well, I hate to admit it, Allen, but I've been so frantically busy that I haven't had time to do more than skim through it hastily. The copy you sent me is still right here on my bed-table. Give me a rundown. From what the reviews said I figured that parts of it might be autobiographical."

"There's a lot of autobiography in it, Dad. Maybe that's why the book has succeeded. If you want I'll give you the general idea of the story."

Udding brought the Scotch and made two highballs. Ham drank half of his in a series of gulps and felt better. Allen finished his synopsis and picked up his drink. "What do you think of it?" he asked.

"Sounds good." In spite of all his efforts his voice sounded grudging.

"Dad, you've got a guilt complex."

"What do you mean by that?" Ham asked, half angrily.

Allen was silent for several minutes. Finally he rose, crossed the room, and sat down in a chair near Ham's bed. "Dad, something's worrying me and it's been worrying me for a long time. I'm a pretty perceptive guy and I've become increasingly aware that you're beginning to hate me, either because of my writing or because it has been successful. I can't make out which. Now, there's some underlying reason for this. There must be. You're a broad-gauged, generous, and certainly a logical person. Whatever the cause, it must be a deep and powerful one. I didn't want to bring this up but I'm convinced now that if I don't we're going to drift apart. That I am going to fight against because I happen to love and admire you. You've been a hero of mine ever since I was a little boy and heroes in my life are not a dime a dozen."

"Thanks for the kind words, Sonny." (He hadn't called him Sonny in thirty years.) "I think you exaggerate my feeling about your writing. By the way, why did you say a few minutes ago that I had a guilt complex?"

"Mother told me something years back about your early life. She didn't go into it very deeply. I remember that it seemed to upset her. I didn't think much about it at the time and it was so long ago that I've forgotten most of the details. Didn't your father and mother want you to write or something of that sort?"

"I'm afraid they did. My father, as you know, was the head of the English Department at Messina College. He was a bookman from head to foot and in her way my mother also was a lover of books. Father was a scholar and he wrote a number of books during his life. The trouble was that they were so full of scholarship that there wasn't any room left for the humanities. He knew it and it frustrated him. He would have given his eyeteeth to have written *The House on the Dunes,* but he never could have done it—not possibly.

"I suppose he figured that the next best thing was to make a popular writer out of me. He started to work on me when I was about eight. Mother, of course, thought it was a grand idea and to be truthful so did I, knowing very little about it. It was all quite logical. Mother used to say that, as a family, there was ink in our blood. I never heard of a forebear who hadn't had his finger in an inkpot at one time or another."

"Didn't you write quite a bit at one time?"

"Oh, sure. Kid stuff. School and college papers. That sort of thing."

"You wrote a story once that was published in the *Atlantic.*"

"How did you know that?"

"Mother showed it to me. She let me read it. I thought it was terrific. Why didn't you keep on?"

Ham groaned. "Lord, do we have to go into all that again?"

"But you've never gone into it. Not with me certainly. This whole part of your life has always been a mystery area to me. Sort of a locked room that no one was supposed to enter."

Ham held out his empty glass. "Want to get me a refill?"

He sipped the new drink thoughtfully for several minutes before setting it on the bedside table. The only sound in the room was the faint ticking of an alarm clock.

"It's too bad," he said finally, "that you never had a chance to know my Uncle Charlie. He died the year after you were born."

Slowly and deliberately he unlocked the door to the room that contained his life; opened it and led his son in. One hour and two highballs later he closed and locked the door again and glanced about the bedroom like a surfacing aqualung diver trying to re-establish his bearings. "That's about it," he said.

Allen leaned forward in his chair. "What you've been doing this evening," he said, "is to plead guilty on all counts: guilty of breaking your parents' hearts, guilty of ruining my mother's life, guilty of making an assortment of minor characters unhappy by your stubborn refusal to become a writer or to stop making money."

"How would you have felt under similar circumstances?"

"I don't know, Dad. It's hard to put oneself in someone else's place, but I'm going to tell you something your usually astute mind seems to have failed to understand. Probably you never were a writer and you never would have been one. If you were, you would have written. The gates were wide open for you.

"You have a fine mind and you practically ate the English

language for breakfast from the time you were able to toddle.
You could have written well if you had wanted to, I'm sure
of that. But the urge to do so just wasn't there. True enough,
you wrote at college. That was because you were ambitious
and you hadn't yet learned where your real interests lay. As
for the story about the Belgian girl, that was a knockout, but
I suspect that it was true and that the heartbroken hero may
have been H. Allen Martin."

"Let's not go into that."

"Sorry, Dad. I had no intention of it. What I want to point
out is that you were *trained* to be a writer, but your *genius*
lay in the field of finance. Finance is just as much of an art
as playing the piano or cooking a soufflé. People say to their
sons, 'Why don't you get out and make money?' as if it were
a thing that anyone could do if they set their mind to it. The
handling of money is a talent like any other art. You had it
to an amazing degree. Had your genius lain in the field of
writing no amount of exposure to Wall Street could have
made you into the great investment banker that you are
today.

"Instead of feeling guilty you should be grateful for the
opportunities that came your way and equally grateful because, deep within you, you had the instinct to seize them
and make something of them; something that is your creation
just as much as *The House on the Dunes* is mine.

"I think you're a great person, Dad. If I could only make
you see yourself from where I stand. You've lived a life of
creative accomplishment and you have done it in such a
way that you have won the respect and admiration of everyone who knows you. My hope is that someday I may also be
able to look back on a life of creative accomplishment, but
I could never achieve it in your field any more than you could
have achieved it in mine.

"And just one more thing. Except at the start you never

really worked for money, Dad. Once you got under way, money was just a by-product of your financial genius. That I am sure of."

Ham reached for his glass. "I see your point. In a way I'm inclined to agree with you. I'm so used to being clobbered because I can't seem to help making money that it's refreshing to hear someone talk about the other side of the coin. I'm glad you did, Allen. You've done something for me. Now let's stop discussing me, and you tell me about your plans."

It was almost midnight when Allen left. His father had dropped off to sleep in the middle of a sentence. Making him as comfortable as he could without waking him, Allen stood for a moment looking down on this man who had lived so fully and been so unappreciated by those who loved him most. Now, relaxed in sleep, the fatigue lines had already begun to disappear. He seemed at peace.

Udding, seated in an antique armchair near the door, was also asleep. He wakened with a start as Allen came down the stairs.

"Dad's going to stay in bed tomorrow. I'd suggest you bring up his breakfast about nine."

"Yes, Mr. Allen. I'm glad you came, I think it did him good."

"Perhaps it did. I hope so. Good night, Udding."

"Good night, sir."

But when Udding brought up the breakfast tray the next morning there was no answer to his knock.